THE LEGEND OF QUITO ROAD

THE LEGEND OF QUITO ROAD

DWIGHT FRYER

Dr. Frankle,

I hope Quito Rd.
speaks to you.

sepia™

THE LEGEND OF QUITO ROAD

ISBN 1-58314-706-3

www.kimanipress.com

Printed in U.S.A.

This book is dedicated to my youngest daughter,
Adrienne Michelle Fryer (June 7, 1984–January 28, 2001).

Adri, Pops loves you and, before I see you again,
I will tell many to protect themselves and their loved
ones against the bacteria and viruses that cause meningitis.

Disclaimer

Many places mentioned in this book actually exist. Examples include Lucy, Tennessee and Quito Road, along with Beale Street, the home of the blues, in Memphis, Woodstock, Millington, Hope on the Bluff Missionary Baptist Church and Peckerwood Point. I fell in love with this geography and its people when I lived near Meeman-Shelby Forest State Park, just north of Memphis, Tennessee. Any similarities, however, between the fictional events and fictional characters portrayed in this novel and actual persons or events are coincidental.

Acknowledgments

God, I praise you for preserving me and steadfastly calling until I listened and told this story. My wife Linda, my daughter Amanda, my parents James and Mary Fryer, and my brothers and sisters, your love, support, and example have lifted me all the days of my life. Linda Gill, at Kimani Press, thank you for looking into a crowd of ambitious writers and listening to what I had to say and believing in this book. To the Kimani Press team, I appreciate all your insight, guidance, and input that have improved this work and made this project so rewarding. I am eternally grateful to the many wonderful people that shared support, feedback, and wisdom. These include Rosa Hamer, my high school English teacher and a positive force in my life for over thirty years, Ferdinand Holmes, Henry Maier, Bridgett Rawls, Carl Poplar, Michael Mosbey, Tom Heroux, James E. Fryer (Big Brother, I would be nothing without you), Marion Lisa Fryer, Carol Fryer, Melverta Scott, Richard Williams, Sybille Noble, and Claire Ruddy. The folks at the Iowa Summer Writing Festival and The Hurston Wright Foundation and my classmates from both of these writing venues, thanks for creating such wonderful environs for aspiring writers to learn, grow, and meet literary professionals. Dr. Jeffery Allen, Mat Johnson, Hubert and Jeffery Hamer, and Dr. Randall Harrison, your encouragement meant the world to me. Rosalyn McMillan, I can never thank you enough for sharing your kernels of writing experience and publishing savvy—this book would still be on my shelf without your insight. General Secretary Tyrone Davis and Rev. Keith McGee, you shepherded me through troubled waters; the grace I received under your care healed many wounds. Marcless Bill Sneed, Sollie Sneed, Jr., Joe Sneed, Levi Williams, Robert S. Strong, Lemmie Vanpelt, Roscoe and Delilah McVay, Frank Gibson, Herbert and Lillian Harrison, Harold Brock, Joe Scott, Dennis H. Jones, Dudley Woodey, Allen Prewitt, Chester L. Berryhill Sr., W. Otis Higgs, Henry Fason, and R. C. Smith, it has been my honor learning to be a man by watching your tracks. Carl Poplar, Don Lockhart, Jesse Broom, Jr., Clifton Monix, Larry Taylor, Kevin McVay, and McKesson Haynes, Jr., my brothers in spirit, your love and especially your wisdom made this possible. I am eternally grateful for the impact on my life by the fine folks at the best transportation company in the world—a small snapshot include Laurie Tucker, Brian Phillips, Carl Asmus, Dottie Berry, Steve Miles, Glenn Sessoms, Herbert Mhoon, Fred Martin, Jr., Rob Carter, Edith Kelly-Green, Mike Glenn, Mark Dickens, Glenn Chambers, Lamont Sneed, Lori Dilonardo, Kye Beverly, Barbara W. Smith, Susan Russell, Cathy Ross, Graham Smith, Mike Redmond, Roy Golightly, Donald Comer, and Nik Puri. My Omega Psi Phi Fraternity, Inc. brothers, especially the Epsilon Phi Chapter in Memphis and Gamma Upsilon Chapter in Wichita, Kansas, I love you for listening to my dreams. Thanks to the teams at Porter-Leath Children's Center and the Leadership Institute of Memphis, especially the Class of 2004, for the chance to serve others. Education and preparation has been my ticket from poverty—thank you to my alma maters, the University of Memphis and Christian Brothers University for planting and nurturing your seeds in me. I speak many blessings, like you have upon my family and me, to the people at St. Mark Missionary Baptist Church, Wilkinsville, Tennessee, St. Mark United Methodist Church, Wichita, Kansas, Mississippi Boulevard Christian Church, Christ Baptist Church, Featherstone Temple CME Church, and Pilgrim Rest Baptist Church, in Memphis, Tennessee, Pettis Memorial in West Helena, Arkansas and Moore's Chapel in Colt, Arkansas, Bishop William H. Graves and the Christian Methodist Episcopal Church, and worship centers all over this globe.

Be not deceived; God is not mocked:
for whatsoever a man soweth, that shall he also reap.

—*Galatians* 6:7

1—THE SEED WAS SOWN

October 1860

Gillam Hale, a master distiller, a brewer of intoxicating spirits, lived his early life as a rare issue-free black man—one born to parents who were free. He now stumbled in the rain along a Mississippi River bluff trail between two white men on horses who had sought him for two years.

The band traveled slowly, just north of Memphis. Their course lay hidden to them, except during the frequent flashes of lightning. The horses acted as true guides. After the group rounded a bend, lightning spooked both horses and the rope around Gillam's neck jerked him forward. He tripped and fell hard to the muddy ground on his back.

"Wait, boss! Wait, bos…!" The lynch-man's noose muffled his cries.

"Stop, Raford! You killing him!" Allen Sawyer, this venture's chief investor, shouted from the rear horse.

"Whoa, whoa boy." His red-haired business partner pulled the lead horse to a stop and looked back.

Sawyer jumped to the ground and tried to loosen the rope's hold on Gillam's neck. It was attached to the saddle horn of the surgically impaired male horse his partner chose to ride because of its large size and complete willingness to comply with his every command. "Damn you, Raford! He ain't worth a penny to us dead."

Raford Coleman spat out his reply: "He made just one damn batch since we bought him, so he ain't worth much to me!"

Gillam lay on his back in the cold mud. He thought, I'm valuable to Sawyer 'til he gets his money I took.

Sawyer eased the knot and, in an instant spark of lightning, looked in Gillam's face. Gillam feigned terror. The slaveholder's mistaken judgment at that moment equaled his error in Memphis's Auction Square two years earlier when he'd shouted the highest bid for the enslaved whiskey maker.

"Get up, Gillam!" Sawyer commanded.

Gillam tried to get on his feet but his hands were bound behind his back and he gripped something by which he could regain far more than his balance. As he fell back down, he remembered the words of his father, "Boy, be sure what you plant. Whiskey's the devil's seed. You reap what you sow."

Sawyer lifted Gillam to his feet, as Gillam laughed inside but put on an air of gloom. Sawyer removed his soaked hat, ran his hands through his blond hair and returned to his saddle. He wondered how his love for strong drink and gaiety had brought him to this miserable task.

Red-headed Raford jerked the rope again and kicked his big gelding forward.

Gillam felt the rope around his neck tighten again. The cord cut his wrists, but he smiled, hidden by darkness. Gillam Hale held no fear in his heart.

Three blasts from a distant riverboat's horn signaled another difficult journey on this cold October night. The rain slowed to a drizzle and the noise of the storm lessened. In his dominant left hand, the whiskey-making slave held a narrow shard of glass. He had fallen on it earlier when he slipped in the mud on a high bluff. He began to cut the rope the second Raford Coleman jerked him forward.

Gillam struggled to keep up with Coleman's horse. His muscles ached, but hope fueled him. "Raford Coleman," he mumbled out of earshot of the white men, "when we get to the edge of the river, I'll fix it to where you never hunt a colored man again." The piece of glass sawed through the wet cord and Gillam waited.

The backwoods trail wound through dense woods until the narrow path overlooked the Mississippi River. Gillam freed his hands and maintained pressure on the rope as he removed it from his neck. "I's falling, boss! Boss, help me!" he screamed. He tumbled down the bank and pulled Raford and his horse with him.

"Nigger bastard!" Raford shouted.

Sawyer jumped from the saddle and strained to see.

Gillam, Raford and his horse hit the muddy waters with a gigantic splash. The river swallowed all three. There was no sign of life.

The solitary blond slave owner stood alone with his skittish horse.

"Raford! Raford! Raford!" Sawyer screamed. "Raford Coleman! Rafe!" His horse attempted to pull away, but the wiry Sawyer held him fast. "Raford!" Sawyer shouted again. If that Nigra's alive, he thought, the current'll take him downstream. He forgot his partner as he remembered the reason he had set out on this frightening night, his money. Sawyer swung back into his saddle and turned the mount downriver and southward toward Memphis.

His horse's hooves produced sucking noises that seemed loud in the sudden calm that followed the violent weather. Sawyer pulled his animal to a halt a short distance away and continued to scan the dark waters. He never heard a sound of anything alive. Only the noise of the river answered his silent prayers. The riverboat horn sounded repeatedly over the loud splashing from the paddle wheels of the nearby steamship. Another long, hard blast sounded just before a single human scream pierced the night. The tortured cry ceased and silence settled as the boat's wheel stopped churning.

Against the wind, Allen Sawyer shouted, "I wish I never got involved in this damn whiskey business."

From his hidden place at the river's edge, a shivering Gillam Hale agreed.

2—THE GHOST OF QUITO ROAD

December 1932

Gillam Hale's son, Gill Erby, sat in the front wagon seat during the family's weekly ride to town.

Gill reflected on his age of sixty years and turned to look down at his thirty-four-year-old wife. He surveyed her small features and freckled nose, the only blemishes on her light-skinned body. She was, by blood, barely a Negro, but, in the world Gill Erby knew, you were either a Negro or you were not. Sarah Erby was a Negro and he was glad she was. Her straight black hair was tied into a neat ball under her simple bonnet. Everything about her was delicate, from the tips of her toes and fingers to her fine eyelashes. As he watched, a single sturdy leg, covered by a thick cotton stocking, slid from beneath her flowing skirt. The thickness of her calves reminded him of her inner strength.

For Gill, she was a beautiful sight to see, easy on the eyes, some would say, even after years of looking at her. Gill suppressed a smile that he could call such a beautiful woman his own.

Sarah Erby had looked like a baby when he first brought her home in a wagon pulled by his young mules, Dick and Dan. She turned eighteen just before Gill married her after his first wife died in childbirth and left him with a houseful of kids. Sarah still called him Mr. Erby; he simply referred to her as Baby.

He visualized the faces of each of his twelve children. His previous marriage produced six of his offspring and his current marriage to Sarah brought the other six to the world. Four of those children, all boys, had died. Gill Erby clearly remembered their faces. A boy's death meant one less male child to carry on the family name. The loss of a son stole a pair of strong hands that would never guide a plow through the soil. The pain only the death of a child brings troubled this man.

Everything about him spoke strength, his muscled arms and thick fingers. All who knew him witnessed that he was a good man, a steward at the local Pleasant Grove Colored Methodist Episcopal Church. Gill Erby, however, possessed skills church folks ought not to use.

"Haw, get up there!" he yelled and slapped the reins. The team turned onto Quito Road toward Lucy, Tennessee. Gill looked down on the animals' backs as they pulled the family wagon. "Whoa, Dan!"

The mules appeared identical, but Dan was as mean as Dick was gentle. Nothing Gill tried changed Ole Dan. It cost too much to replace a mule, so this beast occupied a major part of his daily struggle to feed his large family and survive in a world not friendly to sharecroppers, especially one with black skin.

Sarah and three of Gill's daughters sat in the back of the

wagon. "Son," as Raymond Simon Erby's mother Sarah called him, was the only living male offspring. The family crossed the wooden Big Creek Bridge and Gill noticed Son looked into the woods at a brightly colored redbird. The male bird flitted back and forth from limb to limb before he stopped to offer his trademark song. The man's mouth turned upward into a smile fueled by his only son and boyhood memories. His boy reminded him of his own father, Gillam Hale. "You sure is Papa's seed," he mumbled softly, but Son couldn't hear him over the clatter of the wagon wheels on the rickety bridge and rushing waters of Big Creek. The sounds transported Gill to one particular tale Gillam had told over and over. Gill remembered the night Papa killed Rafe Coleman Sr., as if he'd been there instead of not yet born. It was a feat no colored man in Shelby County, Tennessee, before or since, performed and lived to tell.

"Redbird, redbird in my sight, see my boyfriend tomorrow night," Sarah brought her husband back from his Mississippi River dream. "Mr. Erby, where you today?"

"Right here, Baby." Gill Erby half turned and looked down at Sarah. "I remember when Papa and I used to walk Quito Road into Lucy. Oh, he told some kind of stories about the Ghost of Quito Road."

"Why you bring up that wives' tale?" She looked into his light brown, catlike eyes and flashed Gill a smile. "Ain't no such thing as a Ghost of Quito Road."

"Now, Baby," Mr. Erby spoke over his shoulder to Sarah. "My Papa said *it was so a Ghost of Quito Road.*" He turned for a moment to enjoy a look at her smooth skin and dimpled cheeks. She pouted her tiny lips and he wished he could smooth her furrowed brow.

"Papa, was it a real ghost?"

"Naw, Son, the Ghost was a slave the white folks couldn't catch. That Negro hid along Big Creek and over on the Mississippi River bluffs to the west of here."

"Why'd the white folks want to catch the Ghost?"

"He was a runaway," Gill Erby relayed. "Some folks said he stole a lot of money from the Sawyers—they owned him."

"Did he take the money?"

"He did. Papa said the Ghost believed the Sawyers *owed* the slave the money for taking his family." The old man paused while it all soaked in. "But they wanted him back 'cause the Ghost was a distiller."

Sarah rolled her blue-green eyes in disapproval.

"What's a distiller, Papa?" Son chirped.

Gill Erby smiled wider than he normally would and looked over his shoulder at Sarah. "Son, I'd better wait 'til you a bit older to tell you why he was so valuable. For now, just know folks called him the Ghost of Quito Road. Every now and then, people'd see him, but no one caught him before slavery ended. The colored folks would see the Ghost and they'd keep it a secret. They'd say, 'I see you, but I ain't see'd you.'" He released a hearty laugh.

"Mr. Erby—" Sarah changed the subject "—what you gone say to Mr. Conrad?"

"Don't know." He added, "By my figures, we ain't clear on this year's crop. The Coleman brothers might not carry us to next season."

"Don't fret, it'll work out," Sarah said.

"I know, Baby, but it's so close to Christmas. I don't know where we'd move to this time of year."

Silence fell on the wagon. The pungent smell of smoke from a coal-fueled fire filled the air as the family came to the edge of town. Ole Dan acted up and Gill Erby yanked on the cutting bridle that always had to be kept in the mule's mouth. Ole Dan is mean as the man who sold me these mules, he mused. You'd almost think that man and this mule is pappy and son 'cause their disposition is the same.

A breeze picked up and chilled the warmer than normal December weather. Gill looked toward the southern horizon and noticed that a thin layer of clouds blocked out the afternoon sun. In the distance, a mother shouted for her children to come inside and a colored man wielded an ax in his struggle to split wood for someone else's evening fire.

"Gee, mule, gee!" Gill Erby shouted the command for the team to turn right into the alley in the middle of the small town.

Thirteen-year-old Tom Coleman ran out the front door of the store owned by his father, Conrad, and his uncle Rafe. Tom hollered to Gill Erby's boy, "Son, you want to come out back of the store to play?"

Gill said softly, "Ask your momma."

Son bounced on the wagon seat. "Momma, can I go play with Tom?"

"Son, we won't be here long."

Son's eyes, inherited from his father and grandfather, begged her, and Sarah couldn't resist.

"Go play," she relented, "but come in the store after a while and I'll let you buy a treat with the dime you earned at the Sawyer house this week."

Son's feet hit the ground before Sarah spoke her last words. "Yes, ma'am!" he shouted over his shoulder while the boys headed for the back of the store.

Ruth Coleman, Tom's mother, greeted the Erby family. "Hello, Gill. Sarah, how're you today?"

Gill Erby tipped his hat. "Miss Ruth, we mighty fine. I trust you all right?"

"Gill, I've been so busy with my Christmas plans that I can't tell if I'm coming or going. But everything's just fine."

"Miss Ruth, I'm here to settle up with Mr. Conrad."

"He's in the office, meeting with Jim Falls. Go on back there and have a seat until he's ready."

Gill Erby eased his hat from his head and said, "Thank you, Miss Ruth." He turned to look at Sarah and walked to the back without another word.

"Sarah," Miss Ruth said, "I know you want to see that material your mother ordered for your daughters' dresses."

The girls giggled in chorus, but stopped when they heard Sarah's reply.

"Yes, ma'am, but with the way our account looks with y'all, we need to let the cloth go back."

Miss Ruth, a slender lady with tiny hands, marched around the counter. "Leave the details to Mr. Conrad and Gill, they can work something out. Let's get your girls outfitted for Christmas and the school term after New Year's."

The two women made eye contact and Miss Ruth pulled cloth bolts from a shelf unit against the wall.

Out back the two boys explored the rear of the old plank building. Tom and Son were best friends, from families on opposite sides of the racial dividing line. Tom was Raford Coleman Sr.'s great-grandson. They met when Sarah's boy accompanied her to Conrad and Ruth Coleman's household to do some housecleaning.

The Coleman's icehouse stood across the narrow alley in back of the Coleman store. The big metal sign across the top of the icehouse building framed Coleman and Sons with Drink Coca-Cola on each side.

Tom climbed to the top rail of the old slaughter-pen fence. A solitary red-and-white bull stood in one pen. A large Hampshire hog, black with a white band across his shoulders and middle, grunted, raised his head and flared his nostrils to sniff the boys. The pig sought a meal, but he'd not eat again before his turn on the slaughter-room floor.

A dormant yellow-jacket nest, the size of a man's fist, hung from the metal lean-to roof just above Tom's head. Descendants of the wasps that built the nest the prior spring warmed their bodies in the sunshine. When the sun dropped lower in the winter sky, they would crawl back to safety in a crevice in the weathered lumber under the roof. Had it been June instead of December, these next-generation sentinels would have taught the boys a lesson about territory and caution. Animal blood, black mud and fermented animal waste produced a pungent odor only a slaughterhouse can offer. The two country boys didn't notice a thing; they were at home.

"Son, my papa will kill our bull."

Son squinted through the weathered fence rails at the animal. "Tom, that ain't y'all bull."

"Son, there's no such word as *ain't*. Daddy told me today he's gonna kill that bull and sell it in the store to people for a lot of money."

"Mr. Conrad ain't gonna kill nothing. That bull belong to Jim Falls."

"How many times I got to tell you that my momma says *ain't* isn't a real word? Uncle Rafe says Jim can't pay his rent, so Papa and Uncle Rafe took that bull. Jim Falls and his family got to move."

"They got to move this close to Christmas?"

Tom jumped to the ground. "Yeah, Uncle Rafe and Daddy fussed. They hadn't paid rent. Uncle Rafe said some niggers over there haven't paid and need to move, too."

"Tom Coleman, I told you to never use that word. My papa won't let that be said in his house."

"Your pappy may not like it, but my uncle Rafe says it all the time. What's it to you if I say *nigger?*"

With no warning, Son's left fist connected with the side of Tom's red head. The two boys grabbed each other and fell hard to the ground in an evenly matched wrestling contest.

3—SWEET TREASURE ON ICE

On that same December day inside the icehouse across the alley behind the Coleman store, Bennie Gorlan finished unloading five hundred pounds of new ice in the cooler room. Without pause, he started to unload the heavy bags and other supplies from the back of an old truck.

"What Mr. Conrad and Mr. Rafe need with this stuff?" Bennie muttered to himself.

He took his cap off and surveyed the large bags and the five-gallon jugs. The young man scratched his head. "White folks business." The eighteen-year-old colored boy could not read, so the labels on the stuffed burlap bags did not reveal their contents to him. His muscles rippled beneath his golden-brown skin while he emptied the truck's cargo. That's when he looked out the window and received the scare of his life. Son Erby and Tom Coleman, locked in a tussle, rolled over and over on the ground next to the slaughter pen!

Bennie dropped the fifty-pound bag. Granulated white sugar burst onto the floor. He jumped over the mess and exited the icehouse front door in a run. The youth hoped for Son Erby's sake that he got to the boys before anyone else found out or that white boy got hurt. He raced across the courtyard and yanked the two youngsters apart.

"Son Erby, you crazy? Why would you fight Mr. Tom?"

"He called some colored folks niggers!"

"You act like some kind 'a fool! I don't care what Mr. Tom said." He pounded his palm. "You-can't-fight-him."

Son Erby deflated. Even a thirteen-year-old colored boy knew this situation could turn sour.

"Bennie, me and Son're friends. We were just tussling."

"Mr. Tom, let me learn you one thing today…this here col-ored boy'll get killed if he fights you. You wants your friend dead, keep fighting with him."

Tom Coleman dropped his head.

"Tom—" Son's defiance returned "—if you called the col-ored folks in the bottom that, you called me that. Besides, my daddy can't pay his rent, so Mr. Conrad and Mr. Rafe will make us move, too!" Son Erby stormed toward the front of the store.

After a few seconds, Tom shouted, "Son, wait a minute!" He ran to his friend. "I'm sorry. I promise I won't say it. Momma and Daddy don't say it, it's just Uncle Rafe. I won't say it again as long as I live. Cross my heart and hope to die if I ever do."

Son eyed him for sincerity. "Tom, you promised."

"I heard Daddy tell Momma he'd work something out with Gill. You won't move. You'll stay here in Lucy and we'll always be best friends."

The power in his thirteen-year-old friend's speech mystified Son. Tom was confident. His voice held no fear. Son wanted that same power. He wanted never to worry about paying rent. Grandma Birdie Mae often said, "Keep some money in your rear pocket!"

Son said, "My momma's gonna give me a dime!" With that, the happy youngsters raced toward the storefront, and Son shouted, "Tom, someday, I'll own a house and land. Nobody'll make me pay rent. You hear!"

When Bennie walked back to the icehouse, he looked for a broom to sweep up all that sugar. His inexperience provided no insight on why the Coleman brothers needed four hundred pounds of sugar.

4—A RAW DEAL

Gill Erby waited while Mr. Conrad finished his talk with Jim Falls.

"Mr. Conrad, I ain't got nowhere to go this time of year. You and Mr. Rafe done took my bull. Can't you hold off 'til next spring for me to move?" Jim Falls's voice resounded with anger, "It's Christmastime."

Mr. Conrad offered no reply for a short while. "Jim, we talked through this time and again already. Mr. Rafe wants you gone because you still owe us over five hundred dollars even after you traded the bull on your debt. Our rule stands for no one to stay with that much on the book. Sorry, Jim. Move by the end of the week or Rafe will get more involved. I can't do nothing else."

Jim Falls begged in a more humble voice. "Mr. Conrad, can't you let me cook some this season?"

With that, Gill Erby heard the scorekeeper scoot his chair

back from the office desk. Gill knew Mr. Conrad stood when he made his next comment.

"Jim, maybe it'll work out better for y'all at your next stop. Leave the house empty and put all the equipment out back by the barn. Rafe'll go out to check on the place Saturday morning."

With that, Mr. Conrad swung the door open and stepped through the narrow passage. He was taken aback to see Gill Erby.

Jim Falls held his hat in one hand and said not a word when he walked past Mr. Conrad and Gill. Normally, Gill Erby spoke to everyone; but he stood silent. He felt the anger and hurt of the evicted sharecropper.

"Gill, close the door and have a seat." Mr. Conrad waved him into the office. When the slightly built Mr. Conrad sat down, he ran his hand through his thinning brown hair.

Gill Erby spoke first. "Mr. Conrad, I ain't cleared nothing in two years. I figure I owe you and Mr. Rafe near two hundred fifty dollars."

"Sorry you heard my talk with Jim. Gill, you always got a place with me and Mr. Rafe."

"But, Mr. Conrad, I ain't got no way to pay you but to trade the mules I bought from Mr. Rafe back to you."

"Hell, Gill, your folks came from Daddy's farm before the Great War of the Rebellion. You always got a place to stay long as Rafe and I got something. Now, Rafe and I done talked about what you owe. Two hundred fifty dollars is 'bout right. Let's carry that to next year."

Gill held his head up but he made no eye contact. "Thank you, suh."

Mr. Conrad raised his left eyebrow. "Here's how we're working this deal." He squinted both eyes at Gill. "Mr. Rafe and I want you to do some work for us since you finished with your crop. We need help in the slaughterhouse and we need some other work out at the farm." He paused to gaze intently at Gill over the top of his wire-rimmed glasses.

Gill Erby relaxed. No move at Christmas was good news, but he did not like the sound of the other work. He knew it involved cooking. "Mr. Conrad, what kind of work you and Mr. Rafe need at the farm this time of the year?"

Mr. Conrad leaned back in his chair; he put his hands behind his head. "Gill, you know what we want."

"Mr. Conrad, I don't like to speak about it or do that no more. My Sarah'd have a fit." He rocked back and forth in the chair.

"Why would you tell her? Miss Ruth don't want to know about these matters."

Gill wanted to point out how Mr. Conrad would be home in his warm bed while he worked out in the cold and wet, but thought better of it.

"Mr. Conrad, that fine for you, but I don't keep nothing from my wife. And this'll take the best part of three or four days away, off and on. Whether I want to or not, I got to tell her."

"I know how you feel, but this is the deal Mr. Rafe wants me to offer you." Mr. Conrad smiled and added, "Besides, no one can get as much out of a setup as you can. Old Gillam Hale taught you good! And, when you make it for us, we never hear any complaints. Mr. Rafe got an Italian down in Memphis that wants something ready for Christmas. He's real connected, so we won't have no trouble. He needs a hundred and twenty-five gallons."

Silence engulfed the tight space.

Mr. Conrad's impatience showed. He reared back in his chair and exhaled. "We used Jim Falls for a spell, but that idiot is as bad at this as he is at farming. So, you gone do it?"

"Let me ask you something. How much'll I clear?"

"Ten cents a gallon, you can use that to get your Christmas out in a few weeks. We'll advance you groceries on credit until you settle up your account after harvest season next year."

"Mr. Conrad, it'll take a lot of water to get that much. You got me any help?"

The thin white man furrowed his brow. "No, Gill, we don't want anybody outside me, Mr. Rafe and your family to know. This stuff's getting tighter and tighter. Take your boy with you."

Gill Erby wanted to point out that young Tom Coleman would never do this type of work, but decided against it. He rubbed his smooth-shaved chin. "One last question. When I got to finish the hundred and twenty-five gallons?"

"You need to get started tomorrow to finish in time. That Italian fellow wants it by Friday."

"Lordy mercy," the bound man whispered, "I got to start on Sunday morning!"

"Well, Gill, I'll tell Mr. Rafe the Ghost of Quito Road will cook again!" The white man stood up and slapped Gill on the back. "Can you get here before eight? I teach Sunday school tomorrow and need to get to church on time."

"Yessuh, I'll be here by 7:00 a.m. to load up."

When the boys entered the storefront, they heard Miss Ruth and Sarah talking.

"Sarah, let me know if that's not enough for the dresses. If you want, you can get some groceries on the book."

With that revelation, Sarah gave Miss Ruth a list of staples. She turned to her boy. "Son, pick out the treat you gone get with your dime."

The boy already knew what he wanted. His eyes latched onto a huge jar of thick, soft peppermint candy sitting on the counter next to the cash register. Sarah handed Son his dime.

He turned and said, "Miss Ruth, how much is the stick candy?"

"They're two for a penny."

The colored boy studied the matter and said a most surprising thing for a poor boy with a shiny new dime in his hand. "One penny's worth."

"Is that all you want?" The white woman frowned as she handed him the two sticks of candy and took his dime. "That's hardly worth opening the jar or the register."

"Just gimme my nine cents change."

"Little niggah, who the hell you talking to like that?" a booming voice rang out from the front door.

The words and their tone startled everyone, even Son, but the boy turned around defiantly. The evening sun partially blinded Son as he looked up at the six-foot-three-inch two-hundred-fifty-pound white man who stood in the doorway. He lost the face in the glare, but tousled red hair covered the top of his head, and Son made out the star-shaped badge on his left shirt pocket. The letters on it read Town Constable Lucy.

Lucy's only lawman reached into his back left pocket and pulled out the police slapper he always carried. The device measured about six inches long and held a piece of lead inside the round spoon-shaped end. Tan leather encased this weapon many peace officers used to subdue criminals.

Sarah stepped in front of Son. The big man froze in his tracks. Her presence unnerved him.

"Sarah girl, that your boy?" Rafe paused to regain his composure. "He growed so I didn't recognize him."

Sarah offered no reply. She glowered at him with rage present and past.

"Rafe! I need to see you." Mr. Conrad interrupted.

The lawman returned the slapper to its usual home. Seeing her made him need a drink. He moved past her and looked down into Son's eyes boldly staring at him.

"Don't cross me no more, boy. You hear?"

Son methodically nodded his head.

Rafe repeated, "Boy, you hear me?"

"Yessuh," Son whispered.

Neither Rafe nor Gill acknowledged each other as Gill turned sideways to allow Mr. Rafe to brush past.

At the back of the store, the bookish younger brother ushered the older one into the office and closed the door.

Miss Ruth placed the change in the boy's hand. This small courtesy—not putting the money on the counter—and the kind look on her face, offered a silent apology for her brother-in-law's behavior. She handed the packages to Sarah and Gill.

Sarah prodded the boy with two gentle nudges.

"Thank you, Miss Ruth," Son said.

The Erbys moved quickly from the store, leaving the grocery list and the items they needed behind.

"See you next time, Son," Tom called after his friend, embarrassed and ashamed.

No one spoke as the family moved single file down the steps to the wagon. Son climbed up front alone. Gill helped Sarah and the girls into the back of the wagon. As the burdened man untied the mules, Ole Dan tried to bite him. Gill struck the devilish mule a vicious blow on the side of the head. Dan immediately settled down and Gill climbed aboard.

"Hack, mule! Hack!" he shouted. Both animals understood the signal to back up. Next, he called "Haw!" while sharply pulling the reins leftward. The team turned sharply to his verbal and physical commands. The mules and everyone felt the edge in his voice. They turned left to head west onto Quito Road toward safety and home.

As the family crossed the train tracks and left the town of Lucy behind, Mr. Erby turned and looked at Sarah. "Baby, stay clear of Rafe Coleman. Son, mind yourself with white folks."

Son whispered, "Yessuh."

They rode along in silence for a while.

"Baby, we ain't got to move. Mr. Rafe and Mr. Conrad gone let us stay through next season and carry our balance to next year at settle-up time."

Son interrupted, "Papa, I know, too! Tom said—"

"Boy, I done told you to keep quiet when grown folks talking. Now hush or I'll follow my first mind to take my strap to you when we get to the house!"

"Mr. Erby, I knew the Lord would fix it. Told you it'd be mighty fine," Sarah interrupted to save Son.

"Well, hear the rest before you put the Lord in it. The Coleman brothers want me start some other work tomorrow morning."

"Mr. Erby, I thought you'd stopped that."

"Baby, show me another way out—Christmas two weeks off."

She paused at first, but delivered her concession as a question. "How long you away this time?"

"Go Sunday and back Monday evening, leave again Wednesday evening and come back Friday night late."

"Lord, Sunday."

The wagon creaked, its wheels bounced over the bumpy road. The mules occasionally snorted and their feet clopped in the damp red sand.

Son waited for a moment when his mother wouldn't hear and whispered, "Papa, can I go?"

His father offered a stern look in reply. Son opened his mouth again, but a wave of Gill's hand silenced him.

A man walked the road just ahead. He dreaded their conversation but pulled the mules to a halt next to Jim Falls.

"Howdy, you want a ride to your fork?"

"Hell, naw! I don't need help from the likes of you," Jim Falls replied.

"You ain't got reason to get crossways with me."

"Crossways, you ain't see'd crossways. Onliest reason you got a place to stay is you cook for the Colemans!"

Gill Erby shouted at the two mules. He popped the reins over their backs and never looked back after the animals bolted past the angry sharecropper.

"I ain't gone forget today!" Jim Falls screamed. "You hear me, Erby! I'll remember today!"

"Mr. Erby, he acts like it's your fault. White folks favor who they want...he know that," Sarah said.

"Baby, he got to take it out on somebody, he ain't gone rear up to Mr. Conrad or Mr. Rafe."

Dick and Dan slowed to their normal pace and walked without guidance; they knew the way home. It took an hour to ride the four miles from Lucy to their house. In the distance, a whip-poor-will's call echoed in the cool prenight air. "Whippoorwill, whippoorwill, whippoorwill." Rhythmically, in a quick cadence, unusual for winter, the bird continued, "Whippoorwill, whippoorwill, whippoorwill."

Son wanted to ask questions, but he kept quiet when he saw his father drift into deep thought and fell fast asleep on his father's shoulder.

In the back of the wagon, Sarah and the girls talked about the Christmas play at church.

The Ghost of Quito Road gonna roam again, the old farmer thought.

He looked down at his only son and whispered, "You gonna be just like me and Papa."

5—A BITTER SEED

"Rafe, why you act so ornery?" Conrad Coleman said to his brother behind the closed door of their little store office.

"Conrad, I'll leave if you gone lecture me."

"Rafe, don't bring that mess around my wife and boy!"

"I don't want to hear no damn lecture!"

The redheaded elder brother pulled a half pint of clear whiskey from his pants pocket. He opened the bottle and took a short swallow before he offered the bottle to Conrad.

Conrad ignored the invite to drink. "He agreed to do that deal for us this week. You can't whip his wife and boy and expect him to cook for us out in the cold all week."

Rafe pushed the stopper back in his bottle.

"Conrad," Rafe said slowly, "what choice he got? Your Virginia-bred wife done made you forget how to handle niggers."

"I handled my part, Rafe. Gill agreed to pick the stuff up in the morning. You talk to Mr. Capezio?"

"Don't-you-worry-about-a-thing," he spoke in cadence. "We connected all the way to downtown Memphis."

"Even the feds?"

"Hell yeah, them boys like cash, too! Ain't gone be no trouble."

On the South end of Lucy toward Memphis, a brand-new 1932 Ford V-8 Coupe cruised into town. Its new tires still shone and the engine purred like only a new car could. Inside, Chess Gordon smiled. The old man slowed the car while he spoke aloud to himself, "Better drive the speed limit so I won't have any trouble out of that resident idiot called a town constable. It'd be a shame if I had to whip his tail today in my new clothes. Besides, if I go slow enough, he might see it's me behind the wheel of this new automobile. Won't that make him feel good?"

Chess put his hand on the new seat. The old trader had loved every minute he watched the salesman's shocked expression when he paid in cash. Chess had smiled then, and smiled now. When he bought anything big, he used all twenty-dollar bills.

Several townsfolk stopped. The attention added to Chess's joy. He blew the horn as he rolled past them. Lucy Savings Bank's best customer slowed down and pulled the Ford into a parking spot in front.

The lone teller behind the bank cage jumped to attention when the tall man stepped quickly inside.

"Mr. Chess, I wish you wouldn't come through that door so fast. That-scares-the-fire-out-a-me!"

"You ain't scared of bank robbers, are you?" The old man smiled and raised his glasses. The right lens was darkened to cover a blind eye. That discolored eye was not a pretty sight.

After the teller recoiled sufficiently, Chess asked, "Where's Mr. Allen?"

"He's been in his office working on something all day, but he'll want to see you. His daughter's in there. Just knock on the door."

"What time is it?" the young woman whined.

Allen Sawyer Jr. pulled his watch from the small trouser pocket, but offered no reply.

"Father, is it closing time yet?"

Sawyer Jr., the gray-haired banker who made area farmers quake in their boots, melted in his daughter's hands. He softly answered the loveliest young woman in Lucy. "How can I finish if you keep asking about quitting time?"

"You should hire me to help you. Pops, if I didn't stop by here sometimes, I'd never see you at all."

"Young lady, what did you just call me?"

"Pops."

"When did you demote me to that lowbrow term?"

"Where on earth did you get your seriousness?" Amanda looked up at the portrait of Allen Sawyer Sr. "He couldn't have been too serious with those blue eyes and all that blond hair."

Allen studied his daughter from behind. Her thick mop of dark brown hair flowed around and beneath her shoulders whenever she did not have it plaited in one thick pigtail like today. She had a few freckles and olive-toned skin. Her petite features blended well. She was a tall and pretty girl. Amanda, at five foot eight inches, stood one inch taller than her father.

"No, my dear, your grandfather was anything but stern. Papa was a free spirit. He spent most of his time having fun, and he never worked a whole day in his life."

"The blame for your frumpy attitude must rest with Grandmother Sawyer. By the way, did I ever tell you that you look just like Grandfather Sawyer?"

"Only every time you look at that portrait. And, yes, Mother was formal. She doesn't approve of how I spoil you. She *was* shrewd at business. You know she ran the bank after Father started it. He never stayed around long enough to keep up with anything here."

The young college student rolled her chair like a race car toward his big desk. "Father, when are you going to see Grandmother again?"

"I don't know. Mother can't speak or move her hands anymore since her strokes. It pains me to see her like that."

"Why does Grandmother get so upset when you take me to see her?"

Allen Sawyer Jr. rose from his big chair and hugged her. "Daughter, who knows what is going on in your Grandmother's head? The poor lady had two major strokes. She's eighty-five years old."

"So much has changed since Mother died last year. Now I am in school in Memphis and Grandmother is lying helpless from a stroke. I miss them both so very much. When I come home for a weekend, it's just Sarah and me until you leave the bank on Saturday."

"Sarah Erby's been good. I don't know what we'd do without her since Abigail died."

"Can we give her some money for Christmas and pay her more? She never says anything, but I can tell they're having a hard time with money."

"Let me study that."

"But, Father, she's practically part of our family."

"Young lady, don't you ever forget she's not a part of our family!" His face reddened.

"Mother said she's worked for us since I was a baby."

Allen Sawyer Jr. looked directly at her. "Only because your mother insisted."

"But Grandmother and you never liked it."

"How did you know that?"

Amanda shrugged in reply and returned to her seat.

"It's a delicate matter when you set the pay for Nigras," he snapped. "Now, get your pretty self out of here and let me finish my work."

She looked away for a few seconds and then asked playfully, "What are you doing with all these papers about Coca-Cola?"

"These are Coca-Cola financial statements," he replied. "I've studied them thoroughly. They're a strong outfit. And I don't have to tell you anything about their product. In fact, I bet you'd like to stop at the drugstore on the way home to get a Coca-Cola."

Amanda smiled.

"Did you know a druggist invented Coca-Cola?"

"Why would a pharmacist invent a soda-fountain drink?"

"It probably had something to do with the drugs from the coca plant and the cola nut that used to be in the drink's formula."

"In Coca-Cola?"

"Yes, in good ole Coca-Cola."

"Are they still in there?"

"No, the company replaced those narcotic substances with something else after 1905 or 1906. Now, please, just go help with something out in the teller cage."

A firm knock sounded at the office door. Allen Sawyer Jr. longingly surveyed his papers and said, "Come in."

Chess Gordon opened the door partway. "Mr. Allen, can an old man interrupt your family meeting?"

"Chess, you're just the person I want to see. Please come in."

Chess Gordon removed his hat to reveal a comb-over hairstyle when he stepped inside the office. He looked at Amanda. "Mr. Allen, Walter is confused. He told me you were in here with your daughter, but this young lady couldn't be your little girl."

Allen Sawyer Jr. smiled and Amanda blushed.

"Hello, Mr. Chess. How are you?"

"Missy, I'm doing tolerably well for an old man. Drove down to Memphis this morning, went shopping for a new suit of clothes and bought myself that new Ford outside."

Amanda walked to the window and peeked through the blinds at the shiny blue car just outside her father's window. "Mr. Chess, can I go look at it?"

"You sure can missy…take a good look. Get inside and sit down if you like."

"Father, is it all right?"

"Yes, daughter, that's fine."

As she left, Amanda heard her father say, "Chess, I want to talk to you about what I believe to be a great stock deal."

"Is that the new deal your new president-elect been talking about?" Chess replied.

The two shared a chuckle.

"My deal is not as important or complex as his New Deal," said the staunch democrat and FDR supporter. Allen Sawyer looked into the eighty-plus-year-old man's only slightly wrinkled face. "You didn't vote for FDR?"

"I vote Republican all the way. I ain't voting for a Dixie-crat."

"But Franklin Roosevelt is the former governor of New York."

"Yeah, but he still in with Boss Crump and all his ole boys from 'round here. Now, what kind a deal you got?"

"Chess, you got almost thirty thousand dollars with us in a low-interest passbook account. If you invested a portion of that money in a company such as Coca-Cola, that money could more than double in a few years."

"Mr. Allen, you probably right, but that's a little complicated for old folks."

"How old are you, Chess?"

"Don't know. My momma couldn't even tell me. Got to be somewhere between eighty and eighty-five years old. For sure, some time soon, none of this is gone matter to me."

"Chess, what about your heirs?"

"Mr. Allen, that brood of vipers don't concern me. I can't depend on one. Each one of the twelve left soon as they was old enough. When I'm dead, they can do what they want with the land and cash I leave, but I'll take care of Chess Gordon until then."

Allen Sawyer Jr. rocked back in his tall chair. He remembered how well his father provided for him in his will. "Well—" he exhaled a deep breath "—I'd hoped you would join me in this." He pulled his watch from his vest pocket. "If it wasn't for you, I wouldn't even be alive. I just wanted to help you any way I could."

"Mr. Allen, you and your momma done helped me more than I ever expected. I been paid by y'all twentyfold and I never helped you or your momma for no pay. I helped you because your daddy, Mr. Al Sr., was the best man I ever met."

"Thank you, Chess."

"I got more riches than I deserve. Remember, my momma named me Chess 'cause I got real good sense. Mr. Allen, you got a lot on you right now. That little girl of yours will grow the rest of the way without a mother. Your momma don't know she in the world. Then, you got to run this bank with no help."

"Let's walk out together," the banker said as he put his papers back into his briefcase. Sawyer locked the office door, and Chess Gordon said, "There's your help over there."

Behind the counter, Amanda watched the teller perform the bank's end-of-day routine. Chess and Allen laughed.

"Mr. Al, is the government gone repeal the dry law?"

"They might as well. Do you have any trouble getting whiskey?"

"There's more liquor now than before Prohibition."

"All that law did was stop tax revenue from whiskey sales and cause us to spend a lot of money to keep whiskey and people apart."

The two men shared a hearty laugh and shook hands.

"I think I'll stop by the Coleman brothers store and buy the only thing I want from Coca-Cola."

Conrad looked at Rafe and just shook his head. "Rafe, I hope you're right. We need that money to cash flow the cotton gin. There's much to lose here."

"I done told you, this family ain't losing nothing else. I don't care what we got to do."

"Brother, it's after five o'clock. I'm going out front to check with Ruth. Then we're going to head to the house for supper. What're you doing tonight?"

"Conrad," he smirked, "a good Methodist like you might not

want to know that. I'm going down to Joy Street on Nigger Hill to make sure everything's all right."

"Rafe, stop fooling around with colored women."

Tom Coleman stood nearby at the soda box. As Conrad and his son made eye contact, he wondered how much the boy heard.

"Are you and Rafe about ready to leave?" Ruth Coleman was at the cash register.

"Yeah, we're through. I need to come by in the morning to check on the icehouse."

"Conrad, can't you let Bennie do it? You'll be late for church in the morning."

Before her husband could answer her question, Ruth saw a set of headlights pull up to the store. The driver killed the headlights. When the store's front door swung open, Chess Gordon stepped inside.

"How do, everybody? I got here just in time to see the whole clan."

Sixty-two-year-old Rafe stepped forward to reply. "Uncle Chess, what you want today?"

Chess and Rafe stood at eye level, two powerfully built men.

"Rafe," Chess said through clenched teeth, "just call me mister or don't address me. Tom, go back there to that cooler and get me a dope."

Tom frowned and said, "What's a dope?"

"Conrad, you ain't told your son that's what they used to call Coca-Cola when it was feel-good medicine?"

"He didn't have any need for that information," said Miss Ruth.

"Ruth, a boy needs to know these things." He walked over to place his hand on the lad's shoulder, but he looked at Rafe.

"Tom, get me a dope. That's what some called Co-colas when they could cure a headache and anything that pained you." The laughter that hissed past Chess's lips sounded like Rafe's.

The boy walked away toward the back of the store.

Rafe Coleman laughed, eyed Chess like a nervous cat. He stopped and methodically spoke his next statements in a quiet, baiting voice. "Uncle Chess, everybody in these parts of Tennessee knows you and my daddy was half brothers. That makes you our uncle. You ought to feel privileged that white folks like us would call a nigger like you uncle."

Chess Gordon edged toward Rafe and Tom Coleman returned with an unopened soda pop.

"Chess, here's your dope," the boy said.

Chess kept his gaze fixed on his redheaded nephew while he pulled out his pocket watch and used the brightly colored fob attached to his watch chain as an opener.

"I purchased this from that Hindu man that sells Watkins products years ago. He called it a swastika symbol and he told me it's used in Christian and Hindu religion. It's a sign of prosperity and good fortune. He told me it brings good luck and keeps evil away."

Miss Ruth stepped forward. "That shape sure is pretty. I'll ask about these the next time our Coca-Cola deliveryman stops in here. 'Drink Coca-Cola in Bottles—5 cents,'" she read the fob slogan aloud.

Chess replaced the watch but let the red and brass swastika hang from his vest pocket. "They don't make these no more."

"Chess," Conrad said, "it's late. We were just about to get supper. Where you headed this evening?"

"Conrad, I'm going to get my wife and drive down to Beale

Street in my new Ford. See it out there. Paid six hundred eighty-five dollars for the whole rig today."

Conrad replied, "That's a grade-A automobile."

Rafe, Conrad and Tom Coleman stood there and watched him drive away in the new Ford.

6—GIMME CRACK CORN

Gill Erby rose the next day at his usual 5:00 a.m., in his share-cropper's shack on the Coleman farm. He fed his livestock before he and Son left for the Coleman brothers' store. He knew Sarah wouldn't like it. His mother didn't when Papa took him out on his first setup.

"It's a good day to kick one off," he remembered Gillam Hale saying. On his walk to the barn, he broke into a song his daddy used to sing.

When I was young, I used to wait
at Master's side and hand his plate.
And pass the bottle when he got dry
and brush away the blue-tail fly.
Gimme crack corn and I don't care;
Gimme crack corn and I don't care;
Gimme crack corn and I don't care,
old Master's gone away.

The Erby's kitchen stood apart from the little main house to keep the heat away during the summer and to reduce the danger of fire. It was an even smaller house with a lean-to bedroom attached to one side, added for Mama Birdie Mae, as all called Sarah's mother. The old lady had moved in with the Erbys just after Son was born.

Sarah left the bed just after her husband and as she walked toward the kitchen heard him singing. "That man ain't never gone get whisky making out of his blood."

Smoke poured from the kitchen chimney and hung low in the cool morning air. Bacon cooking on the woodstove greeted her nostrils. "Mama Birdie, good morning. How you today?"

Mama Birdie raised up from the oven. She pulled a huge pan of biscuits from the little cavity in the woodstove. Golden brown, full and high, they resembled artwork. "Girl, I thought you was gonna sleep away. It's near to five-thirty and you know we got to get ready for church today."

Sarah put her hands on her hips and mocked a swooning look around the little kitchen. "Good morning, daughter!" Sarah said. "How you today?" The younger woman continued, "I'm doing just fine for an old lady!"

Mama Birdie laughed. "Sarah Erby, you silly as when you was ten!"

Gill Erby entered before Sarah replied, and she decided to speak her mind.

"Mr. Erby," Sarah said, "it's bad enough you going. Don't you take Son!"

"How you know I'm taking him?"

"I ought to say you talked in your sleep again. But I ain't. I heard Son ask you yesterday in the wagon."

"You heard that?"

"Yes, I did. I heard and I know Gillam Hale took you when you were about his age."

"That boy got to learn how to make a living. He can't stay here at the house with you and these girls every day."

She rolled her eyes in silent defiance.

"Besides, it'll toughen him up for spring planting. He gone help more with the crop this time."

"Mr. Erby, this ain't right." Her soft reply contradicted her strong instincts. "God don't like ugly business. I wish you wouldn't…don't teach Son." She paused and then voiced her other concern. "And why start today?"

"We need that money I could make this week! I got to start today because that white man wants me to."

"But, Mr. Erby, what should I tell the elder when he asks where is Steward Erby?"

"Sarah, just whisper to the reverend I'm working for Mr. Conrad Coleman. He won't have nothing to say when I put some money in the collection plate next week."

As the debate continued, Mama Birdie went into her bedroom. The old lady sat down to her old Singer sewing machine and started working on the dress for Louise, Sarah's oldest daughter. Mama Birdie loved thirteen-year-old Son more than anyone else on earth. These events were, to her, like a dry leaf falling from a tall tree.

Several times during the conversation, Sarah looked in at Mama Birdie for support. Mama Birdie never looked up or uttered a word. She continued her work. Her right foot moved the pedal of the old sewing machine rhythmically as she pushed the dress parts under the needle. Mama Birdie Mae only voiced her thoughts on this matter privately, to God.

Lawd have mercy. An old man fixin' to teach a young man something he ought not know. Forgive him, Lawd, and don't take it out on the boy. "Why is it?" she whispered. "Why is it, Lawd God, that the worst things wrong with most us were planted by those who love us the best?"

7—A SECRET SCIENCE

Gill Erby kept the reins in his hands and Dick and Dan pulled the wagon along Cuba Road, west of Lucy, Tennessee. He'd take no chances with his valuable cargo. The wagon carried eight fifty-pound bags of sugar and twenty-five five-gallon jugs. An old waterproof cloth covered the items. Two five-pound bags of baker's yeast hid under the wagon seat. Without yeast, he'd have no whiskey, and Gill Erby was definitely going to have whiskey.

The wagon sank under its load deep into the sandy road.

"Papa," Son interrupted the whiskey-maker's thoughts, "it'd be faster to go back up Quito Road. Why we going to the Coleman farm this way?"

"Son, you remember when I talked to you before about important things?"

"Yessuh, I remember."

"Well, this our most serious talk ever. I want you to understand you got to do what I tell you. You wit' me?"

"Yessuh."

"Never talk this. Don't tell your friends or your momma, grandmama or your sisters. You hear?"

"Yessuh."

"This week we gone do some work for the Coleman brothers. It ain't nothing like you ever see'd before. It's real important you keep this between you and me. If you tell a soul, we might get in trouble and your papa would go to jail."

"Papa, what type work is it?" Son's voice trembled.

"You promise me you ain't gone talk this to nobody before I go further. It's real important you and me get that understanding. Let me hear you promise me!"

"Papa, I promise."

"Now, Son, this is serious business, awful serious for a boy. Remember when we talked about the Ghost of Quito Road yesterday?"

"Yessuh, he was a runaway slave."

"Son, I said that and plenty of folks 'round here know it. But they don't talk it in public. I waited five years after we married befo' I spoke with Sarah on this. Now, I'm telling you that the Ghost wasn't just any man. He was my daddy, Gillam Hale."

"Gillam Hale…" The boy paused while he processed it. "Papa, why's your daddy's name different than ours?"

"Well, I'll tell you that long story after we get things set up. But, for now, I need to get a few things straight. Understand?"

"Yessuh, I do."

"Son, remember, you promised. You know Sarah gone ask, but don't you tell yo' momma one a thing. You hear me?"

"Yessuh."

"This week, we doing the same thing that made Gillam Hale a valuable slave to the white folks." Papa Gill looked around as if someone else was there. One of the mules snorted. He whispered, "Me and you gone make whiskey this week on the Coleman place."

"Whiskey?" the youth said, twisting his face.

"Yeah, that's what we gone do. We'll fill every five-gallon jug in the back of this wagon with white-lightning whiskey."

"Papa, we got twenty-five jugs! What's Mr. Rafe and Mr. Conrad gone do with all that whiskey?"

"Sell it!" Papa Gill spat out. "They'll probably get as much as six dollars a gallon off the whiskey we fixin' to make."

Papa Gill placed his left hand inside his overalls and a strained silence surrounded them from the naked roadside underbrush. Only the noises of the mule team's hooves and the slicing sound from the steel-lined wagon wheels echoed along sandy Quito Road.

Son's breath trails thickened in the winter air as he did the math in his head and pondered the economic possibilities.

On that farm, Mr. Conrad and Mr. Rafe Coleman raised cotton, sorghum and corn—corn so sweet that Son liked to eat it straight off the cob in the field during the summer months. You could use corn for feed or you could grind it into meal. But during this third week of December in 1932, thirteen-year-old Son Erby learned you could use corn for something else.

That week, Papa Gill taught his son to make white lightning like Gillam Hale had showed him. Making illegal corn liquor changed everything for that colored boy. Son was never the same. He learned a secret science and he learned it well.

8—THE FAMILY RECIPE

As the wagon moved along Cuba Road, father and son saw a car coming toward them.

The vehicle slowed as it approached. Its driver signaled Gill Erby to stop.

Gill Erby pulled his pocket watch from his overalls bib.

"Huh, 8:30 a.m.," he said aloud. "I came this way 'cause usually ain't nobody on Cuba Road on Sunday."

"Papa, that's Cousin Chess Gordon. Look at that new automobile!"

Old man Chess smiled wide and looked at Erby the senior and younger sitting up high on the wagon seat. He squinted into the morning sun. His smirk showed he knew more than Gill liked.

"Gentlemen, y'all headed the wrong way to get to Pleasant Grove Church."

"Cousin Chess, we got some work that can't wait."

The men knew there was no reason to say more.

"Gill, come see me after you finished with this."

"Yeah, ah, ah, I'll do that," Gill replied.

Chess asked, "How's my boy?"

"Fine," Son replied with dimples glaring. "When you get that automobile?"

Chess Gordon never saw an opportunity to brag that he did not like. "Son, I bought this car yesterday. Paid cash for it down in Memphis! When you get a little older, I'll teach you to drive."

Son looked to his father, who nodded his approval. "Cousin Chess, that sounds fine!"

The old man laughed and flashed a smile. He put the Ford in gear and snorted the engine just for Son. Before he pulled away, he looked at the covered wagon then glanced up at the Erbys. "Gill, I see you, but I didn't see you." He stopped smiling. "You hear?"

Gill Erby nodded and the Ford engine spinned the car's whitewall tires while it sped away.

"Get that tablet down there so I can teach you how much these white folks fixin' to get off the whiskey."

Son reached down to the wagon floor and retrieved the pad. Papa Gill squeezed one of his hands into the bib of his blue overalls. He extracted a short pencil with no eraser and handed it to the boy.

"Can you do some numbers?"

"Momma wouldn't let me play outside until I learned my times tables. So I just learned them all in one day."

Gill Erby smiled at the pride in the boy's voice. "Well, let's put that learning to good use. How many jugs we got?"

"Twenty-five."

"Write that down."

"Yessuh."

"Now, how much can each jug hold?"

"The writing on them says five gallons."

"That's right. If we put five gallons of whiskey in each, how much whiskey will we make?"

The boy paused before he excitedly blurted out his conclusion. "Papa, that'd be five time twenty-five."

"Work out on your paper five time twenty-five."

The boy wrote the numbers down and did the calculations. Gill Erby smiled when his boy quickly got the correct answer.

"Papa, that's a hundred twenty-five gallons."

"Well, Mr. Conrad is about to teach Sunday school at Lucy Methodist Episcopal Church South whiles you and me out here to make his whiskey. We gone leave the whiskey in the barn at the farm when we through this week. Somebody else'll drive the liquor to Memphis. It'll probably get sold down on Beale Street at some of the colored joints. Now, how much is one hundred twenty-five times six dollars a gallon."

The boy worked at the numbers on his pad again. Son couldn't believe his answer so he checked his calculations. "Papa, is seven hundred fifty dollars right?"

Gill Erby smiled and nodded his head.

"Seven hundred fifty dollars, Papa?"

"Seven hundred fifty dollars is it. Son, remind me to have your momma send your teacher over to Woodstock School some canned goods. She doing a great work in you."

The boy laughed.

"The Colemans got one hundred dollars' worth of sugar and another twenty-five dollars tied up in jugs. The yeast costs less than five dollars and they'll pay me ten cents for every gallon we make. We just might get twelve to fifteen dollars." He thumped his boy in the chest with the index finger on his right hand. "The Coleman brothers'll spend one hundred forty on the ingredients and getting it made, but they gone take in seven hundred fifty."

For the next few minutes, the two rode along in silence. The sun warmed their backs as it rose higher and shone over the wagonload the mules struggled to pull.

"Papa, how do you make whiskey?"

"Son, thought you'd never ask. Many ways. It's been done in many ways. I don't know who'd tell you how many. More ways to do it than man can track. Each stream branch ditch and every nook under a hill in these woods from Memphis to Virginia has a different type of whiskey operation." He paused to smile at the boy. "So, it was and is done in many ways."

"But how we gone make it?"

"First of all, we need a container to set up the ingredients and a cooker to boil the whiskey off. It's better to use copper since you might poison folks with other types of metal. We need water to dissolve the sugar before we make the whiskey."

"How much water you need?"

"We'll haul three hundred gallons of water to make one hundred and fifty gallons of whiskey."

"But I thought we was making one hundred twenty-five gallons."

"We are making that for the Colemans." Gill Erby shifted his neck in a little dip and looked around. "But we making twenty-five more for us," he whispered.

Father and son laughed in a solemn pact.

"After the water, you put in the ingredients and stir it to

make sure the sugar dissolves. Some folks dissolve the sugar real good before they put it with the other ingredients. You wouldn't leave sugar in the bottom of a coffee cup, would you?"

Son shook his head.

"Same thing with whiskey. Your sugar got to dissolve for it to work off." Papa looked at Son. "And it takes at least two days to get ready to cook. If the weather's cold, it could take up to a week depending on the temperature and the stuff you use."

Gill Erby watched Son drink in every word. Each step in his tutor's recipe stripped a layer of the boy's innocence, like water dissolves sugar.

"That's why you need something to make it turn fast."

"What'd you mean by 'turn fast'?" His round cheeks showed their dimples; his light brown eyes blazed in the morning sun.

"The sugars in the mix get ate up. That's called fermentation. Most use yeast to kick it off and eat the sugar. You can just let your plant material work if you got time." Papa laughed. "We ain't got time. That yeast gone get our turn started."

"What does the mix do when it turns?"

"Remember how the water boiled in the black cook pot last month when we cooked the hog lard?"

"Yessuh."

"Our mix'll boil just like that without fire. That's what you call working off or turning over."

"Papa, how do you know when it's ready to cook?"

"Experience shows it's cooking time by three things—look, smell and taste. It's cooking time after the setup works the sugar out. The mix turns by the end of the first day and keeps that up 'til it works all the sugar out."

"Papa, how much yeast do you use?"

"Not much, maybe a pound per hundred gallons. The most important thing is not to let the mix get too cold."

Son perfectly understood what it took to make whiskey. He was the indisputable heir to the legacy.

"Papa," the boy started and then paused, "what happens if the setup gets cold?"

Gill Erby laughed and slapped his boy on the back while he gently tugged on ole Dan's rein to let him know who was in charge. "Son, you gone make a grade-A bootlegger someday! If the setup ingredients get cold, the mash, that's what you call the mix, will stop making alcohol. Now, we ain't out here for our health. What we doing, Son?"

"Making whiskey," the boy flatly replied.

"So, in the cold season, you got to make sure the setup stays kind of warm. The setup container at the Coleman farm stands in a side room in Mr. Rafe's barn. If it turns cold, we'll make a fire to keep it warm. We can't let the turn slow down if we gone finish by Friday."

"What's a bootlegger? Is that a good thing?"

"Son, bootlegger is the name for folks that make or sell un-lawful whiskey. They call them bootleggers 'cause they used to hide bottles of whiskey in their boots."

Son chuckled; his dimples showed.

"Boy, your other question requires a deeper answer. Is boot-legging a good thing? The answer depends on whose camp you believe. The government passed a law back in 1919 that made whiskey or anything with alcohol illegal in the United States. It's called Prohibition. If you caught with whiskey, beer or wine, period, you go to jail if you ain't got friends in the right places or enough money to make you some friends."

"That's a stupid law."

Gill Erby laughed. "You and a lot of other folks think it's stupid. But some church folks say whiskey and anything with alcohol is the devil's water. Your momma says you ought never drink whiskey and she's got her reasons. Sarah don't want me to make it. But I'm just a man trying to take care of a woman and a houseful of young ones. I can make four times as much as I could make doing anything else. That's if the white folks would hire me—most won't 'cause it ain't enough jobs for them either. But I'm gone make some whiskey this week."

Son Erby was absorbed. He now knew whiskey was his future. The new bootlegger burst into laughter, with his father.

"Son, making white lightning just gets in your bones. It's a mighty fine day to kick one off!"

9—THE WAY OF ALL MEN

"Why children always underfoot? Raymond Simon Erby, quit worrying me to death!" Miss Birdie Mae grumbled to her grandson. "You know it's Christmas Day and I got to cook. Get outside and bring in some wood for the cook stove."

"Yes, ma'am." The boy put on his old coat and cap, but stopped and faced his grandmother.

Miss Birdie Mae peered over her spectacles. "Boy, what you got to say?"

"Mama Birdie, why Momma always at the Sawyer's? Today's Christmas and she's there."

"Why you would whine 'bout that? Sarah got to work."

"But, Mama Birdie, it's Christmas."

"Come here, boy. She got to help make ends meet. Allen Sawyer Jr. pays her to make a home for his daughter. She's worked for them since Miss Amanda was born. I reckon she gone keep on, especially since his wife died. Why does this bother you now?"

The boy shrugged his shoulders and lowered his head. Mama Birdie Mae beckoned him to come closer and crushed the lad into her breasts. She patted his back and stroked his forehead. "Don't worry. Gill's gone to get Sarah. Mama Birdie here and I'm gone be here every day." She hugged him even tighter. "Tell you what, fill that wood box, but go to the house first and tell them girls to come help with the dinner."

"Yes, ma'am," the boy pouted as he headed for the door again.

When he opened the wooden door, the old woman stopped him in his tracks. "Son, don't pout like a little gal. You almost a man."

"Yes, ma'am," he said and looked into her eyes before he stepped over the threshold with his head held high.

"Come on in, Gill."

"Chess, how you doing today?"

"Mighty fine. I thought you forgot I wanted to see you."

"Naw, I ain't forgot, just been tied up."

"Today's as good a time as any. Ain't nobody here but us. Pour yourself a brandy and come sit over here near the fire." Chess Gordon waved Gill Erby toward a bottle and glasses on a nearby table.

"Chess, where's your young wife today?" Gill asked while the brandy bottle chinked against the fancy glass.

"My son Johnlee drove Zoar to Memphis to see her momma."

"You trust Johnlee to drive your car?" Gill asked, approaching a rocking chair near Chess.

"Gill, sit down, sit down. Whenever something happens to me, Johnlee gone have a lot of what I got. So I might as well trust that fool some now."

"It just surprised me with the way Johnlee handles himself that you let him drive your vehicle. But I'm glad to see it. If you and your sons coulda got together, you'da done even more."

"That's part of what I want to talk about. You know I been blessed when we consider what we come from. I was born a slave on this place. Me and my momma lived through hell in this house. Now this place's mine, free and clear. Who'd ever thought that?"

"Chess, you a smart man and you work hard. But God been good to you."

"Gill, I don't work too hard. Most of what I always did was like the folks with money do. I hire my work out and see it gets done. And as far as me being smart, you and me both know where I got most of my sense. If your daddy, Gillam Hale, hadn't come along when he did, I'd be like most niggers around here."

"Well, Chess, Momma always said Papa woulda died if you hadn't helped him."

"Mr. Gillam was different than any nigger I encountered. Seem like he knew everything. He could blacksmith, he knew farming. He could read and write and saw to it that many of the colored folks 'round here learned how to read."

"That ain't all he knew. Was it?" Gill Erby asked. Both he and Chess laughed.

"Naw, that wasn't all," Chess said. "Gillam Hale showed me everything I know from wooing a woman to whipping a man and how to set up a whiskey still, too!" Their hearty laughter added warmth to the chilly room.

Cousin Chess drawled, "Gill, when your daddy showed up in these parts, a colored man couldn't stand up to white folks. With Gillam Hale, it was different. He was an issue-free Negro." Chess pulled a pipe out of his pocket and filled it with tobacco.

Gill watched in silence for a time. He knew the story already but never tired of hearing it.

"He hadn't been a slave. Your daddy was a free nigger from up in Maryland."

"Well, how he get all the way down here?" he goaded Chess to continue.

"John Sneed, a friend of Raford Coleman Sr., my bastard-father, kidnapped Mr. Gillam and his whole family. They brought Mr. Gillam down here and sold the wife and five young ones into South Carolina. Your momma never told you?"

"Momma didn't talk about Papa much after he left."

"Gill, you know why he went away, don't you?"

Gill Erby's eyes found the rough wood floor. He shook his head no.

"Mr. Gillam left to look for his wife after his son Joseph came through here as a hobo on the Illinois-Central railroad."

"All I know is that after Papa left, Momma just dried up and died a little at a time."

Chess pulled a piece of straw from a broom that lay next to the stove. He opened the stove door, lit the straw, and used the flame to quickly start his pipe. Smoke billowed from his puffs and the room filled with the smell of cherries and tobacco.

"Chess, that tobacco smells mighty fine and I don't even smoke."

"Got cherry in it. Zoar got it for my Christmas."

They both rocked back and forth in silence for a time.

"Chess—" Gill Erby paused before completing a difficult thing to say "—I sure hate I never heard from Papa again after he went away."

Chess took several long puffs on his pipe first. He blew out the smoke and paused for a few seconds. "Gillam Hale did what he had to do. He left here to find his wife and other children." Chess looked directly into Gill's eyes. "He cared about you and he wanted you to be all right."

The room fell silent, only a low whine from the sap-filled wood in the fire could be heard.

"Gill, did you know Bustie Smith maiding for Rafe Coleman?"

Gill nodded and an even more somber look came to his face.

Chess said, "That damn Jude Smith ain't shit! He won't half work and now he got his woman working for the worse peckerwood 'round here."

Gill just shrugged his shoulders.

"Ain't no wife of mine could be by herself with a man like that."

Gill looked at Chess, thought of Zoar out with Johnlee, and shrugged again.

Chess said, "Hell, you stay on his place and I don't see you letting Sarah maid for him."

Gill remained silent and thought, Johnlee ain't gone drive my Sarah to Memphis either.

Chess pulled on his pipe again. "I got a business proposition for you."

Gill Erby smiled, glad the subject had changed. "I don't know if a bumpkin like me can afford to do business with a fox like you."

Chess coughed as the pipe smoke flew from his mouth and nose. "Hell, you got me choking," he replied. Both men laughed.

Rafe Coleman awoke from a sleepy stupor in the front room of his house. His head throbbed something awful. Scent from the ham in the cook stove filled the house. His skilled nose tested the air and picked up baked ham, corn bread and turnip greens.

"Where on earth did she get turnip greens in this cold weather?"

For a brief moment, Rafe imagined he was back in his papa's house. The tiny bit of little boy in him remembered the last Christmas he spent there with Pa, Maw, Media and Conrad.

"Damn, that a long, long time ago," Rafe said aloud.

"Mr. Rafe, you say something?" a female voice called from the kitchen. It was his new maid, Thelma Louise Smith, but most folks called her Bustie.

Rafe shook his head to clear the remnants of his latest drinking binge. He looked around his living room; his house was further east of his father's farm on Quito Road. He hadn't been to Daddy's place since the month before Homecoming. A frown came to Rafe's forehead when he remembered he had had to ask Chess Gordon for permission to visit Papa's and Maw's graves.

Bustie Smith entered the living room from her perch against the door to the kitchen. "Mr. Rafe, you all right?"

Rafe looked up at the woman. Her dark black skin contrasted with her simple cotton dress. A mop of thick curls covered her head. She walked closer; true concern showed in doe-like eyes set equally apart on her face. Bustie leaned over Mr. Rafe and placed her hand on his left arm.

"Mr. Rafe, you all right?"

Fully awake now. Rafe looked up from his sprawling position on the sofa. Instinct drew his eyes down the front of the colored woman's dress. He immediately saw how she got her nickname.

"Something sure do smell good. What you got on?"

"It's that rose perfume you left in the kitchen for my Christmas present," she stammered. "I got so excited when I saw it this morning that I opened it before I put your dinner on the stove." She raised an arm to Rafe's nose for his assessment of her only Christmas gift.

His question had been about the kitchen odors, but he coyly replied about the cheap gift. "Hmm, hmm, hmm. Now, that smells nice. You like it?"

"Yes, sir. You know I do." Bustie stepped back out of arm's reach and lowered the lids on her big, clear eyes. "And I got baked ham, turnip greens, brown pinto beans and hot-water corn bread on the stove!"

"Thelma Louise," Mr. Rafe called Bustie by her given name, "where on earth did you get turnip greens? Didn't that heavy frost kill all of 'em this weekend?"

"Well, it got most. Last week, I covered some on the back side of the barn with an old cotton tarp. That's how I saved these for you. Guess what else? I just pulled two sweet-potato pies out the oven!"

"Thelma Louise, girl, you just a miracle worker. How'd I make it without you?"

His words touched a place long unexplored by her husband, her heart. She smiled wide, showing perfect white teeth behind full symmetrical lips. Their sudden intimacy unnerved her. She retreated a step.

"Can I get you anything before I walk to Lucy to pick up Christmas for my children?"

Rafe surveyed her. He was now completely awake and every male sense was aroused. "My head hurts something powerful...get me a headache powder and some cold water."

Rafe looked at her from head to toe as she swayed toward the kitchen. The lower half of her body showed she walked several miles every day.

"Thelma Louise."

She stopped in the doorway and turned to face him. "Yessuh?" Thelma Louise could feel his eyes make a complete head-to-toe examination.

"Why, why, uh," he groped for something to say, "why don't you bring me a piece, uh, uh, of that sweet-potato pie when you come back."

"Mr. Rafe, you gone ruin your dinner with dessert before the meal!"

Rafe smiled like an eight-year-old boy. "Girl, go on and get me my water, the medicine and that sweet-potato pie."

She grinned wide. "Yessuh, you the boss!"

His inventory continued as she moved away, and he thought, she ain't walking to Lucy or back home today. He put his stocking feet on the sofa table and waited expectantly. His head no longer ached and warmth covered him. The entire scene brought forward pleasant memories of years past on Daddy's farm in the Quito bottom. "I don't remember feeling this good since then." But thoughts of that bastard Chess Gordon living on Daddy's three hundred and fifty acres crept in. "Hell, that nigger even slept in the very house Grand-daddy built!"

Before he realized it, Thelma Louise stood right next to him with a tray. He gulped the medicine he no longer needed and washed it down. "That's bitter stuff!"

"Here's something to take that bad taste out yo' mouth." As she leaned over and placed a piping-hot piece of sweet-potato pie on the table, Rafe's eyes moved to the bodice of her maid's dress. Steam rose from the pie. It smelled of nutmeg and cinnamon. Rafe looked into her eyes and she returned his stare.

"Thelma Louise, we gone let this pie cool down just a little bit."

The big redheaded man reached up and touched her for the first time. She settled comfortably into his arms, like she belonged there.

"Amanda Sawyer, somewhere along the way, you blossomed into quite the young lady," said Allen Sawyer Jr.

Redness welled up in Amanda's cheeks. "Thank you, Father." The eighteen-year-old whirled around like she used to as a child. The cherry-red formal gown opened like an umbrella as she turned. A white lace collar and jacket formed a lovely combination against Amanda's olive complexion.

"I knew it would be stunning on you."

"Where'd you find it?"

"Lowenstein's Department Store in downtown Memphis. Sarah, how on earth did you get it taken in without Amanda here to try it on?"

Sarah Erby smiled wide from her place in the background. "Mr. Al, I been dressing Miss Amanda so long, I know her exact size. The hem length's easy since she stopped growing years ago. And she thin as a rail at the waist, so you most always got to take a dress in for her."

"Sarah, what would we do without you?"

Sarah's cheeks turned red. She beamed, as proud as a mother. "You better be careful, Mr. Allen. She only thin at the waist. I let that dress out a little up top and below. Boys gone flock to her when they see her in that dress."

"Sarah," Amanda said, "boys are the last thing on my mind."

"Trust me, sugar, with the way you look, any boy that see you gone do all he can to get you to think about him!"

They shared a hearty laugh, and an automobile horn sounded.

"I'll see who that is, Mr. Al," Sarah said as she walked from the parlor to the formal entry hall.

"Father, what time are we leaving for Memphis?"

Mr. Sawyer admired his new Christmas gift, a watch chain, as he pulled out his pocket watch.

"It's almost two-thirty. For us to stay on schedule, we need to leave soon. We're going to stop in briefly to see Mother and from there we'll eat an afternoon Christmas dinner in Memphis."

Sarah peeped through the curtained window then opened the front door and stepped out. "Mr. Erby, what on earth you doing in Cousin Chess's truck?"

Gill Erby slowly approached the front porch of the house and stopped at the bottom of the steps. He smiled wide. "Chess made me a deal this morning. If you ask me, he really gave us a Christmas present."

"How much he charge for it and how we gone pay him?"

He touched her forehead to smooth a wrinkled brow. "I'll tell you on the way home. You finished up yet?"

"Yeah, come on inside. You got to see Miss Amanda in her Christmas frock."

The colored couple walked around the side of the house to the rear so Gill Erby could enter.

"Father," Amanda said, "open your last present."

"Young lady, where'd you get all the money you spent on me? You've already given me a new watch chain and a sweater."

"I saved some of my allowance and the money you paid me for working at the bank."

He pulled the wrapping paper back to reveal *A Farewell To Arms,* by Ernest Hemingway. "I heard about this book. Is it any good?"

"Father," Amanda took the opportunity to appear sophisticated, "I couldn't help but preview it for you to make sure it was appropriate. It's really autobiographical about Hemingway's life, but it has a good love story in it. My only complaint is the book's terse language."

"The folks down at West Tennessee State Teachers College are doing their job," Allen Sawyer Jr. said, smiling.

"Mr. Allen, Mr. Erby's here to pick me up. You need anything else?"

"Where is Gill?" replied Sawyer.

"In the kitchen," Sarah said.

"Gill Erby, it's Christmas. Let me greet you."

Gill eased the kitchen door open and edged into the great dining room.

"Come on in here," Allen encouraged.

Gill admired the fine furniture and wallpaper hunting murals as he inched forward. He approached the threesome in the foyer with his hat in his hands.

"Merry Christmas, Gill," Mr. Allen said. "How are you?"

"Mr. Allen, I'm mighty fine. Merry Christmas."

"Gill, you drive up in an automobile?"

Gill couldn't suppress a broad smile. "Yessuh, I made that racket. Chess Gordon sold me his old Model A truck."

"Congratulations. That's going to be a big help come spring. Getting back and forth faster will improve your farming results. You'll spend less time traveling and more time doing the things that make money."

"I ain't quite thought it out that way, but that makes a good point."

Turning to Sarah, Mr. Allen continued, "Your help made it possible for us to travel a difficult road this year. We don't know what we'd do without you since Abigail died. Open this after you and Gill get to yourself."

"Thank you, thank you! I was just glad to be here for y'all. Nothing could 'a kept me from Miss Amanda this year. Mr. Erby, ain't she pretty?"

Without thinking, Gill blurted out, "As pretty as her momma."

That comment dampened Allen's festive spirit. He recovered, "Sarah, how's your ornery mother?"

Sarah laughed. "Full of fire as ever."

"Give her this envelope and tell her Allen Sawyer Jr. said Merry Christmas."

Jim Falls's eyes were too far apart. He was a small man with a grubby appearance. His oily hair needed a comb and scissors. The wiry gray strands stood all over his head. He needed a shave and his blue bib overalls showed the wear of the clothes of the other down-on-their luck patrons in the illegal bar.

Jim would have blended into the crowd in most hole-in-the-wall establishments. But, here in a colored section of downtown Memphis's Beale Street, the down-on-his-luck sharecropper stood out like a sore thumb.

"Why that peckerwood in here?"

The proprietor of the small illegal bar looked at the group of angry customers from which that shout had erupted.

"Fellas, don't start no trouble in my place."

A nervous Jim looked around and realized the question referred to him.

A stocky colored man stood up, his face scowling. "Look here, Roscoe, ain't gone be no trouble. But I still want to know why that peckerwood's in here."

"Buck, this man enjoying a drink, just like you. Why you got to start some mess?"

"That white trash got places to go. Boss Crump won't let niggers go nowhere but Beale Street. He down here in our way at one of the few spots we can get a drank in public."

Few whites entered Beale Street's separate colored world.

Jim Falls raised his head from his small table. He clenched the quarter-shot glass in his fist. Jerking his head back, he swallowed the last bit of the murky corn whiskey from his second half pint. The white man wobbled to his feet.

"Roscoe, see you next time," Jim mumbled.

He struggled toward the exit. The same angry colored patron fired a final parting shot.

"I better not see your white ass in here next time!"

The colored crowd burst into laughter. Jim Falls closed the joint's front door and stepped into another lonely Memphis evening. Drizzling rain fell as he walked east on Beale, considering where to go. He turned north. An idea formed in his impaired brain. Jim reviewed on unsteady legs his hellish day. His wife had put him out that morning after she told him she had taken up with another man. Before that, Jim could not find work or a place to stay.

"Hell, Memphis ain't for me." Jim turned up the collar of his tattered coat, "I been here just three weeks and niggers talk to me like I'm a damn dog. In Lucy I'm still better than Nigras."

10—AFTER WINTER
COMES SPRING

During March 1933, Gill Erby and Son talked before they put their plows to the land Gill rented on Chess Gordon's Quito Road farm near Lucy. "Son, remind me to take some Polk salad to your grandma this evening. It tastes better than spinach when she cooks it down with bacon."

"Papa, I won't let you forget that!" the boy said about the springtime delicacy.

Gill Erby surveyed the land. "Watch me. Plowing's tricky at first, but you'll get it."

"Yessuh."

"We got this field to plow and the Coleman place. This year I'm handling near to seventy-five acres." He looked into Son's eyes. "This the first year you helping with the plowing. I expect mo'. You ready?"

"Yessuh, Papa."

"See that big chestnut tree 'cross the field there? Mama Birdie calls it Old Jabbok. Son, chestnut wood burns clean, it don't give much smoke."

The two paused to look from Jabbok's full base to its tip top two hundred feet above. The possibilities were clear to the young moonshiner.

"Use chestnut if you cook by day."

The apprentice whispered, "No smoke."

Gill smiled. "Remember, I'm going straight at Old Jabbok with this first row. This turning plow throws the dirt to the left. To make a row, you plow through the field one way. Then you turn around to your left and come back on the other way. Follow right along behind me to my right on this first pass. Stay the same distance from me where I got you lined up so your row'll be straight."

"Yessuh," Son answered, his voice laced with uncertainty.

"You got Ole Dick, he easy to handle." The aging farmer broke into a wide grin and laughed. His pint-size boy stood behind the mule with his small hands on the plow and the bridle behind his neck.

"Papa, why you laughing?"

"Never thought I'd see the day a boy of mine'd stand behind a mule and plow. This is a good day!"

A smile of pride crept to the boy's lips.

"Son, let's see what we can do with this bottomland. I still can't believe Chess rented it to me. Start Dick after I get about seventy-five feet out." Dan moved forward and the turning plow sliced into the black-gumbo soil. Together, the man and the mule moved straight as an arrow toward Old Jabbok.

Blue jays sounded an alarm when Gill Erby and Ole Dan neared the seventy-five-foot mark. Son inhaled. "Get up, Dick!

Get up!" His grin broadened when the mule moved forward, and Son Erby guided a turning plow for the first time.

"Conrad, I don't care what you say! I'll find a way to get Papa's homestead back. That nigger ain't got no business staying on Papa's land!"

"Rafe, this thing between you and Chess got to end. He bought the place fifty years ago. Let it go."

"I still don't know how that old Sawyer witch got herself named executor over Daddy's affairs."

"Politics, but considering the circumstances and the reasons she hated Papa, it's a wonder we got a penny."

"Conrad, you right. Why didn't she just beat us out of the whole thing?" He cradled the Coca-Cola in his large hands before raising the bottle to nurse again.

Conrad shrugged. "This I do know—you need to settle down. Chess is in with some powerful folks."

"I ain't thought of how to work it, but I'm close." Rafe boomed his maniacal cackle of a laugh, "Heh, heh, heh, heh! Baby brother, that nigger don't even know what he got."

"How much you think them double eagles worth today?"

"Whew, five hundred twenty-dollar gold pieces, almost a hundred years old. And there's the other stuff under the ground. I can't imagine."

Conrad stared at the older man. He couldn't imagine the value of the Coleman place treasure either.

Jim Falls rose up from the partially completed headstone. His job included outlining the letters and shapes on the stone face from a stencil with a carpenter's pencil. One of the five colored workers would later carve the letters out by hand. Jim couldn't see how they cut that stone perfectly every time with just a chisel and hammer.

Sweating, he squatted down to the stone once again. He surveyed the marble yard. "John-daddit!" he said aloud, then, for fear of causing a ruckus, silently complained, this work ain't fit for a white man!

Jim noticed Jude Smith glower at him. The huge colored man moved a several-hundred-pound stone as if it weighed fifty. He resumed his task. Something got to change.

The marble-yard steam whistle blew three blasts, signaling the noon dinner hour. Jim walked toward the shelves in the back of the shop to retrieve his lunch bucket. When he returned, the Negroes sat under a big oak next to the railroad tracks that ran past the business, the only shade on the yard.

With his back turned on Jim, Gee Gurley twisted his face into a wicked grin. "Watch this," he said to his comrades. "That trash think he too good to eat with y'all." Gee turned toward Jim Falls. "Come on over here in the shade with us."

Ignoring the invitation, he sat on the north side of a big stone, partially shaded from the noonday sun.

Gee Gurley and Johnlee Gordon doubled over laughing. Jude's bass chuckles and their crowlike cackles echoed amongst the stones.

One hundred feet away, Jim Falls listened; his fury equaled their joy.

Banker Sawyer surveyed a noontime bounty on the platter in front of him: piping-hot roast beef, fresh turnip greens, new Irish potatoes and fresh-baked corn-bread muffins. Water beads on the bottle signaled the coolness of a Coca-Cola next to his empty plate.

"Mr. Al, I'll be in the kitchen if you need anything."

"Sarah, how's Gill proceeding with the ground he rented from Chess Gordon?"

"Him and Son started breaking it this morning. I can't wait to hear how much they got done. Son never plowed befo'."

"That boy grew up fast."

"Too fast I think sometime. We can't keep him in clothes and we never own hand-me-downs for him since he's our only boy."

"Sarah, look at my old clothes for any your boy could wear. I bet you and your mother could do a great job altering them."

"Mr. Al, thank you. I'll look this evening." Sarah walked toward the kitchen door.

"Sarah," he mumbled between chewing and swallowing, "sometimes it's best to let sleeping dogs lie on the porch. You and I know there are folks around here that would not want Lucy Savings Bank loaning money to colored folks. That's why I turned down Gill's loan request."

Sarah never turned to face him. She closed the kitchen door. "That's all right, Mr. Erby found another way to get the money to farm the bottom." Walking toward the kitchen sink, she spat out, "You ought to thank the Lord I didn't poison your lunch."

11—WHERE I COME FROM

The town of Lucy existed on traditions and cycles. Spring brought the hope of planting. Summer involved the rigors from crop maintenance and the eventual rest of lay-by time. With fall, the harvest arrived and that season always included two important events. The annual cemetery clearing happened on the fourth Saturday in September. That tradition spruced the cemetery up for visitors coming to the Homecoming on the fourth Saturday in October. Lucy's townsfolk did it that way every year and had since even the old-timers could remember. September 1933 would be no different.

These happenings created significant barriers that kept Tom Coleman and Son Erby apart. Son worked a lot. His labor provided an important resource for Gill Erby. Conrad and Rafe Coleman never counted on Tom in their enterprises and the Coleman family denied Tom's request to work so Tom's life included only minor responsibilities like the annual cemetery maintenance.

"Tom, how's the work going at y'all's cemetery?" Son asked.

"Nearly finished," Tom replied. "You can smell that stew all the way over to our cemetery. Is it done yet?"

"Miss Samella Smith says it's just about ready," Son said. "I made the fire this morning."

The boys sat atop posts at opposite ends of a wooden crosspiece. That structure braced the wire fence that separated the Lucy white and colored cemeteries. This fence line through a wooded area might as well have been a mountain range. Only a few hundred feet, a thick grove of trees, and this four-foot-high span of pig wire separated the two plots of land, but the two cemeteries and the two Lucy-worlds that used them seemed thousands of miles apart. Those burial grounds and the five churches in Lucy that used them equaled the most segregated places anywhere, especially on Sunday morning.

They alternated whittling sticks with Tom's knife.

"Tom," Son said when he jumped from the four-foot fence, "let's get some stew." Son walked toward the Negro cemetery. The boy stopped fifteen feet away and looked back. Tom froze.

"Ain't you hungry?" Son asked.

"I keep telling you there's no such word as *ain't*."

"I hope you happy when I get in a fuss for talking proper."

"What's wrong with saying it correctly? That's what my momma says to me when I talk bad."

"Quit stalling! You coming or not?"

"Son, can I really go over there to eat?"

"Tom, sure, you can get something to eat." He laughed and gestured in the spotlight of sunshine. "Some of the folks won't

like it, but they scared to say so. You Conrad Coleman's boy!"
Son walked away a few more steps. "So, you coming or not?"

Tom Coleman jumped to the ground and they walked toward the crowd. A very large white marble headstone directly behind the cedar tree caught Tom's eye. It read, Jane Gordon, 1840—1920, Mother of Birdie Mae Lilliard. "Son, whose grave is that right there?"

Son leaned out. "That's Mama Birdie Mae's momma's grave. My momma said she died in 1920, the year after I was born."

Tom shrugged his shoulders as he looked around the graveyard. "That stone must be expensive, as pretty and as big as it is."

Son laughed. "It is pretty, but it can't be expensive. Mama Birdie Mae paid for it and she poor like the rest of my family."

"I don't know, Son. Your grandma may be poor but that's an expensive stone. She got some money from somewhere."

Chess Gordon stood on the back porch of his house. He always stayed close to home on the fourth Saturday in September. He pulled out his pipe and inserted the latest tobacco blend Zoar bought in Memphis. The old man surveyed the back of the house where the bulk of his three hundred and fifty acres lay. A match and his persistent puffs brought his black-and-tan pipe to life.

Brother, as Mama Liza used to call him, swept the chair to the porch's edge with one large hand and sat down. He rocked slowly and looked at the one place out back protected from the afternoon sun. A wide smile crossed his thin lips as the object of his joy crawled some three hundred feet away.

There, among a large grove of white, post, and red oak trees, stood the source of Chess's delight—a white stone burial monument. Providence had provided the beginnings of it for Chess when he was a little boy. Brother puffed his pipe and thought back to his childhood days as a slave on this farm. He remembered his mother, a slave woman named Mama Liza, looking for him on that 1858 summer day…

"Brother! Brother! Chess boy! You hear me calling you!"

"Yessum."

"Get yo' narrow red tail out to that henhouse and bring them eggs in like I tol' you! You forgot to get 'em in yesterday, but you gone do it right now. You hear me?"

"Yessum." Chess grabbed the egg basket and as he turned the corner to the back porch, encountered thirteen-year-old Raford Smith Coleman Jr. Wanting no trouble, Chess dropped his head and stepped off the porch. His feet tangled in something and he fell face-first onto the hard, dusty area behind the back porch.

"What's wrong with you, little nigger? Can't you walk without falling off the steps?"

Chess glowered but didn't dare part his lips for fear of speaking what he really wanted to say. The white boy stood over him. "Get that frown off yo' face or 'um gone whup you like Daddy gone beat that runaway nigger when he catch him!"

"Raford Jr., what that you gone do?" Mama Liza intervened. She descended the steps with a broom in her right hand and a screaming baby in her left arm. "Who you gone whip?"

"Nobody, M-m-mama Liza," Raford Jr. stammered. "I ain't meant no harm. I's just funning with Chess here a little bit."

"You get your narrow white ass 'way from this house and get somewhere to do some work. I got this here boy busy. You get busy or 'um gone take this broom to you."

"Yes, Mama Liza. Um going." He left in a big hurry.

Chess stood up. His mother helped him clean the dust off his clothes and face. While the baby screamed, she took the end of her apron and wiped the tears that formed in his eyes before they could fall.

"Chess, don't you let that fool worry you none. Look over stupid folks. You understand me now?"

The boy nodded his head. "What wrong with Baby Sister?" he asked, gently touching the baby, who looked totally white.

"She be fine after I give her the tit." Mama Liza added, "This baby greedier than any I birthed. She eats more than you." She smiled to hide the sadness that her three older children had been sold away. She picked up the egg basket from the ground and gently handed it to Chess. "Gone do what I said."

Rage pushed him to run the rest of the way to the henhouse. He unfastened the gate and stepped through the crowd of chickens that gathered to beg for feed. Chess fastened the gate behind him, walked the short distance to the chicken coop, opened the door and stepped inside.

Powerful hands grabbed young Chess from behind and slammed the door shut. Chess opened his mouth to cry out, but a hand completely silenced his lips.

"Steady, steady, boy. You all right," his captor whispered.

The assailant guided the boy to look backward into his face. Chess recognized the runaway slave Gillam Hale.

"Now boy, I'm gone take my hand from yo' mouth. Don't say a word. Understand?"

Chess nodded and Gillam removed his hand from the boy's mouth. He held Chess in the iron grip of his left hand and turned the boy to him.

Gillam whispered, "Where the white men?"

"They been gone two days since you run away."

"Where the colored folks?"

"Chopping cotton over in the bottom."

"Chess, I saw what that bastard did. You want to pay him back?"

Tears filled his eyes and he nodded.

"Well, boy, we got a lot of work to do. I can teach you things that most colored folks don't even know exist. How that sound to you?"

Chess flashed a grateful smile as one tear fell from his left eye. "That sound fine."

"If you tell anyone you saw me, I might die. If I die, your learning stops. You want to learn how to do what white folks do?"

"What kind of things?"

"Reading and writing and making money, owning land."

"Gillam, I ain't never met a nigger that could read and write. You read and write?"

"Why, sure I can read and write. Look here." Gillam stooped down again. He picked up a piece of corncob and wrote C-H-E-S-S in the dirt.

The boy looked blankly at the letters and at Gillam.

"That's your name, Chess." Pointing at each letter as he sounded them out, "C-H-E-S-S. That's how to spell your first name."

"Gillam, Negroes ain't s'posed to read and write. How you learn?"

"My daddy showed me."

"How yo' daddy know?"

Gillam laughed. He put his arm around the boy. "Chess

Boy…" He paused. "I like the sound of that. Can I call you Chess Boy sometimes?"

Chess smiled like any boy does when he gains the positive attention of an older male. "That sound fine!"

"My daddy worked as a Methodist circuit preacher. He rode around and preached to the slaves."

"You gone show me some of those things like you said?"

"Every time I see you, I'll teach you something new. But a dead nigger can't teach. Can he?"

Chess shook his head. "What you want me to do?"

"I been in this henhouse for almost two days now. I need something to eat besides raw eggs. Can you get me some food?"

"Uh-huh."

"And, when Rena come back, bring her to me. Don't tell her why. Just get her to come. Can you handle that?"

"Uh-huh," Chess replied. He knew the young slave girl Rena was sweet on Gillam. She would help in any way she could.

"The next thing is the most difficult. Don't tell Mama Liza and nobody else. You see me, but you didn't see me. Understand?"

"I ain't telling a soul!"

"Chess! Chess! Where you, boy? Get on back to this house!"

Gillam looked through the small roost-hole door toward the house. "Mama Liza looking for you. Let's get these eggs out the nest and you back to the house. Remember, don't tell Mama Liza. Figure out a way to bring me some food and think of something to get Rena over here when she come back from the field."

★ ★ ★

On the fourth Saturday of September 1933, eighty-year-old Chess Gordon sat on the same porch where Raford Smith Coleman Jr. tripped him in 1858. On slow and peaceful days like this, he liked thinking about those times with Mr. Gillam and Mama Liza. He loved to look around the old place, think about what had changed, and how much remained the same.

"Of all the deals I ever made, helping Gillam Hale provided my best return."

Chess laughed and he looked at Raford Smith Coleman III on his knees, paying respects in the Coleman family cemetery. Mr. Rafe had to request his permission to enter the property. Chess took a deep draw on his pipe. He let the smoke roll around inside his mouth and then inhaled it. Exhaling slowly as he rocked the willow chair, Chess looked over at Rafe's old pickup truck. He noted the Confederate flag plate stuck in the rear window. "One of these days, that trash gone understand what Stars and Bars mean to a colored person."

On his knees in the family burial plot, Rafe Coleman fought back his tears. He remembered Papa's and Maw's deaths. He recalled the auction of his family farm like it happened yesterday instead of more than fifty years ago. Rafe reviewed the train ride to Morristown, Virginia, where Media reared him and Conrad. But none of those difficult memories brought the tears to his eyes. His tears fell when he read the name Liza Mae Gordon, Mother of Chess Gordon on the monument. "Papa, he buried that nigger woman here with you and Maw!"

★ ★ ★

Amanda Sawyer pored over the old records of Lucy Savings Bank. Her father had assigned her the task of organizing them by category. Her work would help her father prepare for an important meeting with the federal bank examiner.

Amanda was fascinated by the papers in the dusty back part of the bank vault. She reviewed land transactions dating back to 1844 when Grandpa, Allen Sr., bought his first homestead on Quito Road. The past bank financial statements, affidavits on bankruptcies and loan records held her interest.

Next, she examined the Sawyer Lucy College Trust. Her grandfather's will established the trust to start a school in the Lucy area. A document titled "Articles of Incorporation" named her grandmother Alice Sawyer trustee. That college eventually became Lucy High School.

Amanda felt the irony of reading the records that established the trust. When she graduated from Lucy High, she won the scholarship the trust provided to West Tennessee State Teachers College. In one bound secretarial record of the annual meetings, she read a motion from the minutes in 1899; Board unanimously approved adding a new bylaw to the Trust's Articles of Incorporation. No one of Negro descent could ever receive the Sawyer Lucy Trust scholarship.

"No surprise there with Grandmother at the helm."

A stack of old newspaper articles from the *Memphis Press Scimitar* and the *Gazette,* from nearby Millington, Tennessee caught her eye. A short 1877 newspaper headline read: Raford Coleman Jr. Cleared of All Charges. "This must be Mr. Rafe and Mr. Conrad's father."

Yesterday, a jury of his peers found Raford Coleman Jr. not guilty of murder. Coleman, of Lucy, Tennessee, was on trial in the shooting death of Allen Sawyer. Sawyer and Coleman had had a dispute that dated back to the War Between the States. The trouble included several legal disputes between Sawyer and the defendant's late father.

"That explains why Grandmother Sawyer hates the Coleman brothers. Their daddy killed my grandfather!"

In another pile, Amanda found an 1860 Shelby County property tax return of Allen Sawyer Sr. The document contained an inventory of slaves by age. Her grandfather had owned more than one hundred slaves. The listing went on for four hand-written pages. On a separate page, Amanda found more.

The dim vault lighting and the yellowed paper forced her to squint, but this document accounted for a group of slaves by age and name. One named Gillam, age thirty-two, former overseer, distiller and blacksmith, began the list. A note next to his name said: Missing and presumed dead. She started to place the document in a folder of her grandfather's other records when she noticed and read the title again, "Negroes Valued Above Market." This made her examine that page a little closer. Her eyes widened and her mouth dropped open when she saw a line two-thirds down the page, "Jane, age twenty, and her female child, Birdie Mae, offspring of proprietor."

"Amanda, how's it coming?" Her father, with a broad smile on his face, stood in the doorway.

She shrugged her shoulders. She dared not tell him grandfather had sired children by his slaves and that Birdie Mae Lilliard, Sarah's mother, was one of them.

12—SURPRISE INTRODUCTION

The fourth Saturday in September 1933 delivered other traditions of the South and the Coleman family.

"Bustie, this labor took longer than any of the first three I birthed for you," Miss Birdie Mae said in the bedroom of Jude Smith's sharecropper shack on Rafe Coleman III's Quito Road farm.

"Yessum," Bustie panted back to Miss Birdie Mae. "This baby bigger than my first three. That's probably why my labor been so hard."

"Well, girl, I think it almost over now." The old lady paused; a puzzled look covered her face. Finally, she said, "I can see the head poking out and the baby's coming fast. Push for me one more time."

Bustie lifted her hips from the bed and pushed with all her strength. The baby gushed from Bustie's exhausted body into Miss Birdie Mae's waiting hands. The experienced midwife tied two pieces of white string around the umbilical cord and cut between the two knots.

Miss Birdie cleared the mucus from the baby's mouth and nose, wiped most of the afterbirth away and the child began to cry.

Bustie sat up in bed. "Miss Birdie, what is it? Is it a girl or a boy?"

Miss Birdie did not answer. The old lady continued her work for quite a while.

"Miss Birdie, is the baby all right? What is it?"

She wrapped the baby in a clean sheet, walked around to the bedside and laid the child in Bustie's arms.

"Bustie, here's yo' son."

Bustie looked at the newborn and began to cry.

"Don't worry, honey. It's gone be all right. Jude know 'bout this?"

"No, ma'am."

"Fix in your head how you gone tell him. I heard the talk and I hoped it wasn't true." The old lady paused to think. "I think I better stay here a few days while y'all gets used to this little fellow."

Bustie only nodded. Her tears continued to flow.

Mama Birdie Mae smiled. "He's a pretty little thing. And he strong too. Look! He already holding my finger."

Bustie looked down at the infant again. The baby was beautiful, but the way her new son's fair skin contrasted with her jet-black complexion captured her attention. Bustie smiled as she touched the boy's face. She pulled back the sheet to look at his head. She realized the gravity of her situation when she saw that red hair completely covered the boy's head.

13—HANDS THAT ROCKED THE CRADLE

On an early morning in June 1934, fifteen-year-old Son walked around the corner of the house. "Mama Birdie, I finished filling the cook stove wood box."

"You split the wood up small so I can control the fire easy?"

"Yessum."

"Did you split it all like I told you?"

"Yessum, and I stacked it next to the kitchen-house front door like you wanted."

She waved her hand for Son to approach her. "Come here, boy." Reaching into her apron pocket, she pulled out a large piece of sweet horehound candy. "Take this and sit down to talk to yo' granny." She waved the boy into the chair on the front porch.

"Thank you, Mama Birdie. You haven't been to town in over a month. Where you get this candy?"

Laughing, the old woman showed a toothless grin. She

stopped to turn her head and spat a straight stream of tobacco juice across the yard.

"I done told you. I keep that I use. You better learn to keep the things you use, too."

"Mama Birdie, you always say that. What you mean?"

"Most folks don't hang on to what they need. Everybody needs food, clothes and a place to stay. And it takes money to get that. When, I say 'I keep that I use,' I mean it takes money to have what you need and like. Work hard for yo' money and don't spend every dime you make." She spat again. "Most folks make a little piece of change and the first thing you know, they spend every cent."

"But, Mama, if you poor, how you save something when you don't have nothing?"

"Hear me now. I ain't never had much, but you ever know me to not have a little change. You just got to be firm with yo'self. I heard an old man one time say it like this. He shook his hand and pointed in my face. Then he said, 'Girl, you better keep some money in yo' ass pocket!'"

Son laughed while his grandmother spat again. "Mama Birdie, is that how you paid for Great-Grandma Jane's headstone?"

The old woman ignored his question.

"Mama Birdie, is that how you—"

"How far you and yo' daddy get yesterday with the crops over at Cousin Chess's place?" Miss Birdie interrupted.

"We finished the first cotton chopping. I think we'll have to do it one more time right before the Fourth of July week. Then it'll be almost time to go back to school during crop lay-by time."

Son's dog, Shebie, sprinted from underneath the porch. A low growl escaped his throat and the hair stood up on his back.

"What wrong with that mutt?" Miss Birdie spat at the animal. The long stream of tobacco juice struck Shebie in the middle of his back. That quieted the animal instantly.

Son scanned the road in both directions. He saw someone walking west from Lucy on Quito Road. "Somebody coming, Mama. That's why he acting up." The person was still a few hundred yards away, but the boy could see him well through the roadside bushes.

Shebie moved toward the road and out of spitting range. His growls grew more fierce. He barked and even kicked up dust with his back feet.

"Can you make out who it is?"

"Yessum, it's Cousin Johnlee Gordon. That's what's wrong with Shebie. Cousin Johnlee kicked him when he was a puppy and he goes nuts anytime he smells him or hears his voice!"

"Hush that dog."

"Shebie," Son said, "hush! Get under the porch."

The dog stopped his barking but did not retreat to the porch as ordered.

"Shebie, porch!"

Shebie crawled to his hiding spot with a little whine.

"Now I see him." Miss Birdie said. "Look at him! He walks all lanky like he a big ole man. Look at that niggah! That niggah ain't shit! Old man Chess shoulda been sleep when he got Johnlee, shoulda let his first wife, Miss Dora, get her rest instead making that fool!" The old lady held two fingers to her lips. She sent a huge long stream of tobacco juice across the yard farther than any she'd spat earlier.

Son laughed. "Mama, why you don't like Cousin Johnlee?"

"It's simple, real simple. He ain't shit!" she hissed. "That why I don't like him. The niggah just ain't shit!"

The young boy laughed and made a mental note to aim higher in life than Johnlee.

"Mother, I just don't want to go."

"Thomas Raford Coleman, you are going and that's that!"

"But, Mother, if I go, I won't even get to be home for my birthday."

"Tom, do you realize that Aunt Media does not have any family now that Uncle Ethan died. Besides, you'll have a great time. Aunt Media plans to take you to Washington, D.C., to visit the capital. It'll be a wonderful experience."

"But I don't want to go!"

"Tom, if you say that one more time I'll get your father to use his razor strap on you tonight. Is that clear?"

"Yes, ma'am." Tom pouted, knowing when to concede.

"Look at it this way. It could be quite an adventure. It'll be your first train ride alone. The train will take you all the way to Morristown."

"Where is Morristown?"

"It's just seventy-five miles south of the capital."

"Mother, how is Aunt Media related to us?"

"Aunt Media is what you call 'double kin' to us."

Tom corkscrewed his face.

Miss Ruth smiled and then continued, "It's a little confusing. She's your father's sister and she married my father's brother, Uncle Ethan Sneed. So, she's my sister-in-law and my aunt by marriage."

"How did she get all the way to Morristown if she's from here?"

"Young man, I've told you this story over and over. Aunt Media probably saved your Uncle Rafe's and your daddy's lives.

She slipped them out of this area in the yellow fever epidemic of 1878. If she hadn't, they all may have died. Both your father's father and mother and some of his siblings were killed by yellow fever."

"Why Morristown?"

"The Colemans moved here from Morristown before the Civil War. So, Aunt Media said it seemed natural to return there since her father still had connections to people up there.

"Tom, go out to feed your horse. I'll be out soon so we can head to the store to help with the evening customers."

"Rafe, Thelma Louise Smith came by the store the other day. She wanted to charge condensed milk and a few other things," Conrad said.

"Why you telling me?"

"I thought you might want to know."

Rafe sipped his Coca-Cola.

"I let her have the items."

Rafe showed no interest.

"What you want me to do if she comes back again?"

"Hell, do the same thing you do with the other niggers. Don't let her have shit unless she makes arrangements to pay."

"But, Rafe."

"Conrad, don't bother me with that. Let me tell you what I really want to talk about. Why you and Ruth letting Tom go see that ole witch?"

"What you got against her? Where would you and I be if not for what she did?"

"Probably better off! That's where we'd be. Don't think she did us no favors."

"Rafe. She is the only parent I remember. The only parental love I know is Aunt Media."

"One thing you can do is stop calling her Aunt Media. She's our sister, she ain't no auntie of mine! She's just a mean ole spinster that never birthed her own babies!"

Conrad shook his head. "Rafe, why you hate her so?"

"She ain't never treated me like she did you, Conrad. She always doted over you, but the woman acts like she hates me. You don't remember what it was like when she first took us to Virginia, but I'll never forget it."

"There's no way for me to remember. I was less than two years old."

"I was eight. Hell, I'll never forget it. It looks like all that death and sickness did something to Media. Before all that, she treated me fine, but after she got over the fever, she was like a devil woman to me."

"What was different?"

"Media got sick herself, but she lived through the fever. She just lost a lot of weight and looked different, acted different too."

"Rafe, what was all that like?"

Rafe drew silent.

Conrad persisted. "What was the epidemic like?"

"You died, had close kin that died, or you wasn't here." Rafe paused to take a big swallow from his soda bottle. "Folks died all over Memphis and Shelby County. The first one happened when I was a baby. I don't remember that one. But the second one came along in 1878. I remember it like it was yesterday."

"What happened?"

Rafe paused and took a big swallow of his soda. He then pulled a half pint of whiskey from his rear pants pocket.

"You remember when that damn cow got out during calving time about ten years ago?"

"Whew, do I ever remember. That thing smelled awful when we found it dead. The buzzards were eating it like candy when we rode up on the horses."

"Well, how'd you like to smell that and it be a human body?"

They stared at each other; Conrad shook his head in disbelief.

"That's what the summer of my eighth year was like, death and stench."

"But, Rafe, why didn't someone bury the dead instead of letting them stay around until they started stinking?"

Rafe took another big drink from the half pint. He sat silent and seemed a million miles away.

"Why didn't they just bury them?" Conrad tried to pull an answer from his older brother.

"Maw kept saying he wasn't dead. Even after he lay there in the front room for weeks, she said over and over, 'He ain't dead, he just getting some rest 'cause he ain't been feeling good.' If she said it once, she said it a hundred times."

Conrad shook his head. "Rafe, who did she say wasn't dead?"

Rafe paused for a few moments. "Papa. It was Papa. He died and we didn't bury him for a month." He paused while he and Conrad exchanged blank stares. "I looked at my daddy lay dead as a doorknob in our house for a whole month! And my Maw just sat there beside him and said he wasn't dead. He stunk so bad it took your breath, and the flies! Huh, they filled the air like dry dust in the wind."

He drank some more from the half pint and silence returned to the office. Conrad could not find Rafe's eyes; the office walls drew tight around them.

"Why didn't you tell me this before?"

Rafe just shrugged his shoulders in a confused and boyish reply. He took another drink.

"Why you tell me now?"

Rafe's reply exploded from within. "You always ask me why I do this and why I do that! Hell, think on what that was like at eight years old!" Rafe cried, something Conrad had never seen him do before.

Conrad took the half-pint bottle from Rafe's limp hand and raised it to his lips. Two brothers, finally on equal footing, looked into each other's eyes and dared not speak a word. Conrad broke their trances after another swallow from the bottle.

"That's awful. Where'd you get this stuff?"

Rafe wiped his eyes and welcomed the opportunity to grin. "It's from the last batch them two boys cooked us a few weeks ago."

"We made money on this?"

"Baby brother, we make money on whiskey every time."

Conrad paused before he returned to their shared secret. "Rafe, who finally buried Papa?"

Rafe finished off the bottle's contents and whispered his answer, "Chess Gordon buried all the folks 'round here that died. That's how the bastard got all his land. He'd take care of the sick and dying. That nigger ended up with the place when whole families died." He walked to the trash can and flung the empty half-pint bottle into the container. It made a loud clanging noise.

"He buried Papa and Maw and he didn't even read words over 'em. That's how he got our place." Turning to face Conrad, Rafe spat out, "That old Sawyer bitch helped him steal every piece of land he took. I remember it just like it was yesterday. But I'm gone get ours back."

In June 1934 an old woman moaned on a bed in the special first-class wing of the Shelby County Nursing Home in Memphis. Unintelligible sounds escaped her lips. She seemed to be conversing with someone.

"Me me na na mmmemme nana. Me na me na na na." Slurred and barely audible gibberish escaped the woman's mouth.

Allen Sawyer Jr. reached out to wipe the saliva from his mother's mouth.

"Allie, her pulse is so weak. I think the end is near."

"Dr. Turnipseed, you think she understands us?"

"Allie, I don't know, there's just no way to know. She's not responded to anything since the first stroke two years ago."

"Yes, I know, Doctor. She seems like she has wanted to say something for quite a while now. She gets so agitated sometimes."

"Yes, I noticed that also."

"I can't understand what triggers it."

"Allen, sorry I forgot and called you Allie earlier. You're not her little Allie anymore."

Allen Sawyer Jr. smiled. "That's sure true. But she always treated me that way. Until this last stroke crippled Mother, I was always her little boy."

"Yes, and she would do anything to protect you and her interests. Anyone who ever saw her in action knew Alice Sawyer was a major force in northwest Shelby County."

"Yeah, and that is what has made these last two years so difficult. It is so hard to see her end up like this."

"Allen, don't dwell on these recent events. Alice lived a life ahead of her time. She was a powerbroker in a man's world. The businesses you now run bear her stamp, and there's the endowment at Lucy High. That is going to operate in perpetuity. Don't let this end rob you of the joy and legacy your mother leaves."

"Doctor, I know you're right. It has just been so hard to accept that her mind is gone."

The remnants of the once-brilliant mind of Alice Sneed Sawyer lay trapped in the shell of her body. The functioning memory of this matriarch told her she sat at her desk in Sawyer Manor. Alice's last few thoughts attempted to solve the problems most important to her. This dying woman shouted over and over at her only remaining adversary. She thought her words could be heard, but only moans escaped her lips. Her mind floated back to a memory of long ago that continued to haunt her....

It was the summer of 1878; they were in the grand dining room of Sawyer Manor on Quito Road. Chess Gordon said slowly, "Now, just calm down, Miss Alice. Everything's gone be all right."

"Chess, I must save Allie! Why won't you help me? If we could just give him something that will break his fever, I know he will live. We got to get his fever down!"

"All you got to do is sign the Coleman place over to me. You got control of the entire estate since Raford Jr. already dead. Just sign this deed over to me. I guarantee your boy'll be playing by next week."

"How do I know it will work?"

"Miss Alice, ain't but one person in my family died of yellow fever. That was Baby Sister and she always been kind of puny. We been taking these herbs that Gillam Hale showed us."

"Don't ever speak that name in my presence again! He is the reason Allen Sr. is dead."

"Now, Miss Alice, Mr. Allen dead 'cause that white trash Raford Jr. walked up behind Mr. Al at Court Square in downtown Memphis, put a Colt .45 up to his head and pulled the trigger." Chess rotated the hat he held in his hands. Boldly, he looked into the white woman's eyes. "Miss Alice, why you taking care of the young ones of the peckerwood that killed your husband?"

Silence fell on the house. The big grandfather clock continued to fill the room with its tick, tick after tick. It witnessed the birth of an unholy alliance.

"That girl and the two boys are orphans. I won't have it on my conscience!"

"You sick yourself and ought to be in bed. I tell you what, Miss Alice. I'll pay for the three hundred and fifty acres. You sign this note agreement that your bank'll finance the place and sign the deed over to me now. I already got the right amount on there for what the land's worth. After you through, I'll get the medicine for you and your boy. Y'all both be fine in a few days."

Chess Gordon leaned in toward the massive desk. With a sneer he added, "I buried the Watsons yesterday. I started to read some words, but it didn't seem right for me to read over them white folks. Just dug six holes over to the cemetery in Lucy. They died of the fever, so the few white folks left in town either got it or was too scared to come out to the burying."

"The proceeds from the loan will go to support the Coleman children?" Alice Sawyer asked.

"Yes, ma'am, and I think we ought to send them away since them and Media ain't sick yet."

"Where do you think they should go?"

"What's the name of that town you from up North?"

"Morristown, Virginia?"

"Yessum, that'd be a good place. Media could take 'em. I can get her East to catch the Streamline train. You can give her enough money to set up house up there."

"Where did you bury Raford and Stella?"

"In the family plot up back of the house."

"If I do this, will you let Media and the boys come back to visit the graves of their parents and grandparents?"

"Yessum, I'll be glad to let 'em on the place, if they ask permission first. After all, that's only fair since it'd be my place, paid for free and clear."

"You must never tell anyone we did this. You hear?"

"Why, yes, ma'am. This'll just be our secret."

"Allie, I must tell you everything." Those unspoken words forever remained her last thoughts in this life.

14—A SMOKING PIT

"Papa, this deep enough?" Son Erby asked from the barbecue pit.

"That's fine," Papa Gill replied from above on level ground.

"I'm glad because my back hurts something awful!"

"Boy, you ain't old enough to have a back." Gill Erby's eyes twinkled. "Tomorrow, the visitors to Lucy gone enjoy the meat we cooking for the Fourth of July Frolic in this hole in the ground." He paused to inspect the work further. "Space these five bars equal distance apart across the ledges. Let me help you out of there and we'll put some fire in that pit. We can season the hogs while the pit and the grate heat up."

Gill reached down, they grabbed each other firmly by the forearms and he pulled Son out of the pit.

"Papa, this looks good. I used to wonder how you set that up."

"Now you know." The two admired their work. They had

dug a full four feet to form this barbecue pit. The top two feet were a full four feet wide and the bottom two feet narrowed from the two-foot mark down. The ledge from the narrowed walls would support the grates on both sides with the thick steel bars underneath.

"Grab that old wheelbarrow," Papa said.

The boy took hold of the two wheelbarrow handles and followed Mr. Erby some thirty feet away to a burning fire.

"Papa, this smells good. What type of wood you use to make this fire?"

"You think it smells good now. Just wait until we put it under that meat! There's a little hickory…you ought not to put so much hickory in a barbecue fire. It's too strong. There's a good bit of pecan in here, but the wild cherry's what you smell."

"Why you use so many?"

"Each wood brings flavor. You can change the way things taste by how you cook it or what you put in them. Some people cook meat and just put some sauce on it." Shaking his head from side to side, Mr. Erby continued, "They call that barbecue, but it ain't. Real barbecue takes seasonings and cooking the meat slow over a wood fire. That's how you get real flavor."

"What we do now?"

"Put on these gloves and take this shovel to half fill the wheelbarrow with hot coals. Put the coals in the wheelbarrow real fast so it won't get so hot you can't work the handles."

Son loaded the burning wood into the wheelbarrow. A few pieces sparked and water fizzed as the coals contacted damp spots in the bottom of the steel wheelbarrow. The boy loaded the amount Papa Gill had prescribed.

"Dump those hot coals in the middle of the pit."

The boy negotiated the wheelbarrow over to the pit edge. The coals fell to the bottom with a smoky sizzle as Son raised the wheelbarrow handles.

Gill inspected the work. "Now, make about three more trips. Put some big pieces in this time."

Son moved back to the fire to continue his work and Mr. Erby pulled his pocket watch to check the time.

"It's almost four-thirty now. By five-thirty, we'll be cooking."

The boy dumped another full shovel of burning wood and coals into the wheelbarrow. "How long does it take to cook two hogs?"

"Well, we cooking whole hogs in quarters. And we gone cook 'em slow, twelve to fifteen hours." He pushed his straw hat back and scratched his head. "So, I reckon early morning tomorrow it'll be done."

Son headed back to the pit with his next load of fiery coals and burning wood. "Papa, where should I dump these?"

Mr. Erby stood at the back of the truck. Over his shoulder, he shouted, "Put the next two loads on each side of the first pile. Then put that last load all the way on the end where it won't even be under the grates."

Son dumped the second load. The coals hissed and sputtered like the first as the boy turned back to the burning woodpile for the third trip.

Using a pitchfork, Gill Erby pulled limbs heavy with leaves from the back of his truck. He laid them on the ground to the side of the vehicle. After working at his task for a short while, he turned to face the object of his efforts. The quartered carcasses of two hogs lay side by side in the back of the truck on top of a large piece of cardboard. A block of ice, melting in the July heat, sat in the middle of the eight large quarters of the two hogs.

The colored man raised the rear truck gate for use as a workspace, grabbed the cardboard and yanked it toward him. He stacked the meat on the passenger side of the truck. The barbecue operation entered an important phase when Gill Erby's meat-hook hands pulled a quarter of a hog toward him.

"Papa, I'm through with the coals. What you doing?"

"Getting ready to season the meat. Let's spread the coals out and put the grates back on the fire."

The two walked to the pit and Gill Erby picked up a shovel with a long, narrow metal handle. He used the tool to spread the hot coals and burning logs in the pit evenly.

"Son, run and get me one more load of coals. This time bring some pieces of wood that ain't burned much." He removed his hat and leaned on the long-handled shovel while the boy completed his latest assignment.

"How's this?"

"That's fine, dump it right here in the middle."

The boy dumped this load from the wheelbarrow and his father spread them.

"Let's put the grates on the rods," Mr. Erby instructed and wiped the sweat from his brow. The smoke caused him to squint.

Each grabbed the looped end of a pair of metal rods. "Son, don't fall in that hole or we'll know what you smell like cooked." They laughed, lifted the ends of a grate with the hooked end of the metal rods and lowered the first grate before placing its twin next to it on the rods in the pit. With both grates in place over the hot fire, Mr. Erby stood back to admire the result of four hours of work.

"Let's season this meat. I feel like cooking some barbecue!" The boy followed Gill back to the truck. "Son, walk around to the cab of the truck and bring me that box."

The boy moved to the passenger side, opened the truck door and grabbed a good-size cardboard box. He shrugged his shoulders after he looked down to see that the full box contained a thick piece of reddish wood, two butcher's knives, cloth bags and paper sacks.

"Papa, what's in these bags and sacks?" he asked.

"Boy, that's the most important part of barbecuing. Them the seasonings. Set the box down here. Locate the garlic and onions first."

"Which ones is it?"

"You'll know when you open the right sack," Gill Erby said and then he laughed.

The boy searched through the paper bags. One filled the air with a strong odor. "Whew, this's it!"

"Son, we gone do us a little cuttin' on these hindquarters." He grabbed a big butcher's knife and buried the blade up to the halfway point into the thick ham on the side with no skin. "Son, when we cut it like this, you don't ever want to break the skin on the other side. Go deep, but not too deep. I'll show you why in a while." Gill Erby took whole garlic cloves from a paper sack. He sliced the garlic into thick slices and inserted several down into the meat. The man repeated the process several times. Next, he pulled an onion from a bag and sliced it in the same manner. He stuffed it into the meat the same way he'd placed the garlic inside.

Son smiled at his dad. "Flavor?"

Gill Erby laughed. Knife in hand, "Fla-vorrrrr!" came his

reply. "Son, take that other knife and cut the string on those two big cloth bags."

Son opened the first bag and looked inside as he handed it to his father. It contained salt. The boy watched his father generously put salt into an empty bag.

"Careful, don't cut yourself watching me."

The boy refocused his attention and opened the second sack. An unfamiliar, pungent aroma rose to greet him. "What's in here?"

"It's called cumin. Chess Gordon gets it from the Watkins man. You talk about something good for hog meat! That's a good spice!"

Son chuckled at his father's excitement. "Papa..." Pausing to look around, he whispered, "You happy now like when we do our other cooking."

"I know tomorrow folks gone try to walk by this stand, but the smell of this meat gone pull them over here." Gill Erby paused as he poured a generous amount of cumin in his mixed bag of seasonings. He straightened up, pushed his hat up on his forehead and wiped his brow. "But, Son, you know what else got me grinning? Tomorrow, the people really will enjoy this meat! And just like when we do our other cooking, we gone get paid for what they like! We probably gone clear a hundred dollars on this barbecue even after I give Chess his cut."

Like a surgeon on an important case, Gill Erby bent back over the bag. Son handed him the next sack. It contained freshly ground black pepper. Next, the boy gave his father the ground red chili pepper. The final two bags were smaller. The contents of each surprised Son completely.

"Papa, this smell like nutmeg and cinnamon."

"That good news," he said, laughing harder than ever. "Because that's what they s'posed to be."

"But nutmeg or cinnamon is for sweets."

"Sure, you put them in sweets, but you can also put them on meat. Remember last year when Chess and I took that whiskey to that Italian fellow down in Memphis?"

"Yessuh. That was the first time we cooked for Cousin Chess."

"Well, a few years ago, that fellow, Mr. Capezio, fed us in his café."

"Papa, you ate inside the café?"

"Just like the white folks! You know how Chess Gordon is. White folks don't treat him like a colored man. He eats with 'em. Chess even walks right into city hall in Lucy and votes."

Son smiled and just shook his head at Cousin Chess's exploits. "Papa, what did Mr. Capezio feed you?"

"He gave us spaghetti and something called ravioli."

"Ravioli?"

"Son, it's a little Italian bread dumpling with meat inside. The ones he gave us had ground pork and ground beef. They were fried and then served in a tomato sauce. It was good eating! I told that white man that it was best thing I ever ate and I wanted to know what spices he used. He said his momma made it and the only thing different I heard in the spices was heavy nutmeg and a little cinnamon."

"Is that when you started to put it on barbecue?"

"Yeah, and boy, nutmeg with a little cinnamon just makes meat come alive in yo' mouth." Taking the paper sack, he continued, "You can go generous on the nutmeg like this." He used his left hand to add it to the bag. "Now, give me the cinnamon, we got to use it sparingly. It'll make the meat bitter if you use too much."

Son watched while his father added this last spice to the bag. He held the top closed and shook the big sack to mix the spices thoroughly. Mr. Erby turned the meat skin side up as he moved the block of ice aside. He completely covered the pork with the mixture before turning it over to season the other side.

"Son, you don't cut through the skin because you don't want any oil to drip out that side. When we start cooking the meat, we'll brown the skin side first. We'll turn it over after about five hours. The oil from the skin will help flavor the meat whilst it cooks the rest of the way. We only turn the meat that one time."

Gill Erby pulled the box of spices to the middle of the truck rear gate. "Son, hand me that next quarter and take one for you. Do like I did the first time and we'll be going to the fire with this meat in a few minutes."

Together, teacher and pupil worked to season the meat. Father and son moved in unison. Son reached for a clove of garlic. Like father, like son. As always, the boy mimicked his every move. He even tried to hold the knife and sprinkle the season mix just like Gill Erby did.

"Papa, what we gone do with that big piece of wood?"

Gill Erby grabbed the last quarter. He spoke as he quickly continued his work. "Pick it up and smell it."

The boy grabbed the reddish wood.

"You recognize the smell?"

"I know I smelled it before, but I can't remember."

"What does Mama Birdie make when you got a cold?"

"Sassafras tea."

"Yep, and this is sassafras root. You remember that sasferilla soda water you like?" The boy nodded in reply. "They make the syrup for it from this root. We'll put these leaves here next to the truck over the coals at the end of the pit. Then we'll put some of this root on top of the leaves. All that adds up to…"

"Fla-vor!" the boy interrupted.

"Now you know what I'm talking about."

Both Erby the older and the younger smiled wide and laughed deep. Gill Erby pushed the cardboard with the seasoned hog quarters back into the truck bed.

"Son, get the pitchfork and load the tree limbs back on the truck. You think you can back the truck over there without running it into the pit?"

The boy smiled the grin of all youth with structured responsibility. "Yessuh!"

"You get cracking and I'll check our pit."

An interested party watched the proceedings from his dark office in the cotton gin across Quito Road. Every year Rafe Coleman anticipated the activities in the Picnic Woods. He witnessed the work of the colored vendors to set up their stands to sell their goods at the Frolic. The aging lawman leaned back in his chair and puffed on the big cigar that protruded from his clenched teeth. Heavy tobacco smoke filled the room and Rafe ran the fingers of both hands through his thick red hair.

"Niggers and their Pallbearers Society…what a good cause." He laughed aloud and put his feet on the desk with a bang. "Tomorrow, I'm gone eat their food, drink their liquor and get some of their money. If I decide to, I'll have me one of their women. And, if anybody gives me any trouble, it'll be hell to pay!"

15—A CHILD'S REQUEST

At the same time on July 3, 1934, in the backyard at the Erby sharecropper shack, Sarah Erby's near-adult daughter asked a question important to her and her sisters. "Ma, you gone let us go?"

"We'll see."

"But, Ma, we been asking and asking. All you say is 'we'll see.' Everybody's going to be there. Why can't we ever go?"

"Girl, I didn't say you couldn't go. I said 'we'll see.' Quit worrying me and get them kids ready for supper. And when you come back, don't bring it up to me again in front of them."

"Yes, ma'am," the girl whispered. She bounded up the two back steps and let the screen door bang behind her.

Mama Birdie Mae didn't say a word. She leaned over the big black pot, stirring the ingredients of the sauce she'd made for Gill Erby's barbecue enterprise. The old lady paused from the circular motions in the pot to wipe the sweat from her face with her apron and noticed Sarah cast a sullen stare at her. "Girl, who you looking at with that ugly scowl? If I didn't know it was you, I'd 'a thought you was a wood bitch."

"Old woman—" Sarah smiled "—what on God's green earth is a wood bitch?" Miss Birdie always knew how to make Sarah laugh.

"Remember that wooden Indian in front of the store on Main Street in Memphis?"

Sarah nodded.

"You looked as stern and stupid as that Indian."

"Wooo, Mama, what kind of mother call her child a wooden bitch?"

Both broke into a hearty laugh.

Mama Birdie Mae resumed stirring the sauce makings. "Daughter, them dealings happened over a half a lifetime ago for you."

Smoke rose from the fire. They were silent.

"Mama, what all you put in this sauce?"

"Girl, my sauce is one of the few secrets an old woman like me can keep in a little place like Lucy. Y'all know every time I fart. I ain't telling."

Sarah laughed and shook her head. "You gone take your recipe to your grave?"

"We'll see. Like you told that child. We'll see. If I tell you what's in my sauce."

"I know you start with lard and melt it down. You added fresh chopped garlic, onions, celery, sage, and lemon juice. You put in fresh ground red and black pepper and you added a lot of salt. And after that cooked a while, you put in some brown vinegar."

Miss Birdie just ignored her.

"Mama?"

"Mama what?" Miss Birdie flashed a toothless grin.

"Huh! Now you going to add some more brown sugar, molasses, honey and tomato paste at some point. You got all that right there next to the fire."

"You heard the story about the bumblebee and the honeybee? Well, this bumblebee wanted to know how to make honey. So he followed a honeybee back and forth all day from flower to flower. The honeybee crawled around on some trees and even stopped by the hog pen. He left there and flew to the barnyard. Everything the honeybee picked up, the bumblebee picked up too. Both of 'em loaded theyself down until they could hardly fly."

Sarah waited. "Mama?"

No answer.

"Mama!"

No reply.

"Well, what on earth happened?"

"Oh, you want to know what happened. The honeybee flew back to his hive and made golden-brown honey. That old bumblebee flew home. He had all the ingredients but he didn't know squat about what to do with 'em. The bumblebee mixed his stuff around and he came up with something that—" Birdie Mae Lilliard squealed "—smelled like and looked like, and rhymes with sit!"

They both laughed and then returned to the dreaded silence that always accompanied Frolic time.

"Come here, child. Stir this pot for me a while." The old woman handed her the wooden paddle and Sarah stirred.

"Just keep it moving. Don't let that pepper burn. In a little while, we'll add the molasses, the sugar and the honey." She whispered, "Put the tomato paste in now."

Only the popping fire and an odd sound from a chicken in the coop broke the silence. Mama Birdie Mae thought Sarah still looked like the girl she was when it happened almost twenty years ago. Mama Birdie Mae stood behind her daughter and put her hand on Sarah's shoulder for a rare touch between the two.

"Daughter, Frolic time is hard for you every year."

Sarah looked over her shoulder, then back into the steaming pot to hide tears.

Mama Birdie Mae's eyes also filled with tears. "I know it hard for you because it a hard time for me. When it happened to you, it happened to me. I felt I shoulda stopped it some kind 'a way."

"Mama, wasn't nothing could be done, he just evil."

"Yeah, but he'll pay someday."

"Yeah, but he ain't paid yet!"

"I know." She stroked her shoulders. "I just shoulda kept you safe. If I had just taught you not to walk by yourself. I know that's why you don't ever let these girls go to the Frolic. But you just need to teach them to stay together. They'll be all right if they stay together in a crowd." Miss Birdie paused and bent over to pick up the metal gallon tin of molasses. "You gone let them girls go to the Frolic?"

A rooster crowed. Brownie the cow mooed from the barn. The two mules hee-hawed in chorus and Shebie barked as the kids poured out the back door. The rare, private interlude between mother and adult child ended.

In a soft, almost inaudible voice, Sarah replied, "I just don't know, Mama. We'll see."

They both wiped the tears from their eyes when a child approached.

"Mama, Grandmama, why y'all crying?"

Sarah and Mama Birdie Mae lied simultaneously, "Onions!"

The two women hugged. They laughed as Mama Birdie Mae poured the molasses slowly into the steaming black pot. Sarah led the children into the house to serve their evening meal.

After the last walked up the steps into the kitchen, Mama Birdie Mae pulled two spice packets from the recesses of her big apron pockets. Looking over her shoulder to ensure her secret remained intact, the old woman laughed as she generously added the contents to the simmering sauce.

16—SLIPPING INTO DARKNESS

Later in the July third evening Son and his father had just completed turning the last of the eight hog quarters. The meat rested on the metal grates at the boy's feet, skin side up. "They so pretty!" he said. In the lantern light, they admired the golden-brown pork skins with the X shapes of the grill burned into the quarters. The pork looked more like sculpture than barbecue.

"Let's take this piece off here…it ought to be more than done enough to eat." Gill Erby pulled a long piece of meat from one of the grills and held the golden-brown delicacy up by the cord wrapped around its length.

"Is that the tenderloin?"

"Yeah, you hungry?"

"I'm so hungry my stomach hurts."

"Well, you won't be hungry after you put some of this in your belly."

Son watched while Mr. Erby lowered a metal bucket filled with water and sassafras roots into the end of the pit with no coals.

"Son, put some more green pecan and sassafras limbs on the coals on that end."

He broke the long limbs and added the smaller pieces to the fire pit.

"Now, stir the coals and leaves just a bit." The sweet, aroma-filled smoke billowed from the pit as soon as the boy touched the pile of leaves and coals. Mr. Erby handed Son a piece of metal barn roofing. The two used it to cover the pit except for a small crack on the end near Mr. Erby.

"Papa, what's the water gone do?"

"The water adds moisture to the fire pit. It keeps the meat from drying out. You remember how we didn't cut through the skin?"

The boy nodded in the lantern light.

"Well, the oil from the fat caught in the skins when the hogs lay skin side down. Now that same oil gone baste our meat while it finish cooking. You know what that adds?"

"Flavor?"

"Righhhht! Now, let's try some of that tenderloin."

Mr. Erby walked to the front of the truck. Gill Erby paused momentarily as he looked across the road at the gin. He made a mental note of what caught his eye.

"Look what I brought back when I drove to the house a while ago." He held up a bag of store-bought bread and a quart jar of liquid. The man sliced the tenderloin while Son opened the bread. Mr. Erby grabbed two pieces of bread and placed a generous helping of meat on top. He poured the barbecue sauce on top and quickly raised the sandwich to his mouth for a big bite. "Hmm, hmm, hmm!" He looked up at his son. "You talk about good eating."

The boy nodded emphatically while his mouth wrestled with a huge bite of his sandwich.

17—ASSOCIATION BREEDS FAMILIARITY

"Can I get some money from you?" Bustie asked.

Rafe offered no reply. She waited, slowly pulling her dress over her slender shoulders. She glanced back at him; he sat in the chair in his office at the cotton gin, looking out at the picnic woods. After she stepped into the first of her shoes and struggled with the buttons of her old dress, she picked up her right shoe and adjusted a piece of cardboard over the hole in the instep.

No answer. Rafe Coleman gazed out the window at the activity across the street.

Bustie hoped sufficient time had passed to repeat her request.

"Rafe, can you let me have a little money?"

"Now you one of them let-me-give-me-can-I-have-some bitches. If you play with a puppy, he'll sure lick your face!"

Bustie recoiled. With Rafe, she never quite knew where she

stood, but this time his words cut. She continued to dress. "Nosuh. I just thought you might want to give me some."

"Gal!" Rafe shouted and swiveled the chair to face her. "I run this, not you. I'll give you something if and when I want. Don't you slide up to me asking without I first offer. You hear?"

Bustie pressed her back to the office door. She eased it open. "Yessuh," the crushed woman whispered, closed the door, moved through the darkness of the cotton gin and ran past the tall machinery used to separate the cotton fiber and seeds. Bustie emerged from the open bay doors on the west end of the building, hoping to leave her humiliation behind.

Bustie moved through the gin yard and watched the vendors setting up across the street. She wanted to get out of sight before someone saw her leaving Rafe's place of business at this time of night. A car sped by headed west from town. She wrapped her head in the shawl she held around her shoulders and followed in the automobile's dusty wake. For Thelma Louise Gibson Smith, the four miles to her house on Quito Road seemed longer than usual.

18—TRAINING A CHILD

Gill Erby leaned back against the side rail of the truck. "Bet your belly feel better now."

"Papa—" Son nodded with a smile while pointing toward the fire "—why don't you worry about the meat cooking overnight. Won't the new coals we put in before we turned the meat blaze up?"

"Where there's smoke, there's fire, but you got to remember one thing. If you got a lot of smoke, the blaze ain't just gone raise up and consume anything." Gill Erby paused. "You see, that fire's just like life. Things blaze up, but they can't take hold if you don't give them air. Smoke signals go up in your life…sure, you got a problem. But, guess what? Smoke can't consume nothing. It don't burn nothing. Smoke makes a mess and chokes you, but ask yourself this one thing. From the work with the barbecue, you know more about what else smoke can do?"

The boy thought about what his father could be asking. Finally, the message came through. "Preserve and add flavor."

A full and tired, but proud, old man looked at his only son in the moonlight. "You get that just perfect, baby boy. You gone have problems, but smoke don't consume nothing. It just shows you the heat and that something's going on in your life. Our fire ain't gone blaze up tonight, too much smoke."

19—CHANCE MEETING

Rafe sat at his desk for a while. His emotions churned about Thelma Louise. He cared about her, liked being with her. He sure liked what they did together. But he despised the smirks and laughs. Everyone knew about Rafe Coleman and his colored woman.

Folks also knew she'd birthed a boy with red hair all over his big head. Rafe smiled because that child was the only child who carried his blood. He looked at the half pint on the desk in front of him. But he no longer needed or wanted a drink. He stood to his feet and knew what he needed to do. Coleman headed for his truck. When its engine roared to life, Rafe Coleman headed west to find Thelma Louise and give her what she needed.

Gee Gibson wanted to make sure he didn't get into trouble in Lucy, so he drove his old car through town slowly. A cool breeze blew through the four open automobile windows. He felt the five one-dollar bills and the five dimes in his britches pocket, money he'd made singing at a club on Beale Street in Memphis.

Gee drove past the Picnic Woods. The smell of barbecue floated into the Ford windows and he looked at vendors putting the final touches on their stands. In perfect pitch and melody, Gee sang aloud in the dark car. "Gonna make me some cash tomorrow night singing at the Frolic." He sped up after the car left the city limits and he headed west toward Hope on the Bluff Missionary Baptist Church. Gee planned to show up late for the gospel singing that always accompanied the Frolic. About a mile out of town, Gee saw someone walking up ahead. He smiled. "I'd know them legs and that walk anywhere."

He slowed to a stop beside her. "Bustie, it's Gee. Get in this car. You know it's too late for you to be out here walking."

She hesitated. "Thank you, Gee, but I can make it."

"Baby girl, you could always do just about anything you had a mind to. I just want to help you make it. Where you trying to get to?"

"Headed home to see about my children."

"Come on in here out of all this dust. Gee can get you there in just a few minutes and your feet won't hurt nearly as much."

Bustie laughed. Unlike the two men in her life, Gee always made her laugh. "Now, Gee—" she melted as she flashed her wide, full-tooth smile "—I don't want no funny business on the way to the house."

"Now, Miss Gibson—" calling her by her maiden name "—you act like we still over at Miss Vick's room at Woodstock

School." Gee turned serious. "Thelma Louise, if I can't help you, I ain't gone hurt you." Gee looked into the rearview mirror at the headlights showing over the hill behind him. "Now, c'mon, baby, here come another car."

Thelma Louise grabbed the door handle. The car interior light came on when she opened the door. Her dress rode high on her thighs as she slid across the car seat. Gee had often wished for an opportunity like this with Thelma Louise. He looked at her pretty legs and flashed his gold-toothed grin just before she closed the door and pulled her dress back down.

Gee used to pull at her brassiere strap when he sat behind her at school. He always teased her, but he also treated her so very nice. Back then, Gee's older cousin Jude seemed like a better catch when she married Jude at fifteen. That was before Thelma Louise experienced his mean streak and unwillingness to work regularly or bring his meager pay home.

A vehicle came over the hill behind them just before Bustie stepped into the car. The woman closed the door and settled into the comfort of the seat. Gee gunned the engine, shifted gears and drove west on Quito Road away from Lucy.

Orphaned Bennie Gorlan often slept at the gin during the warm months. That was his plan for this July third night before the Frolic. Later, he planned to walk across the street to the Picnic Woods. Perhaps someone there would need some help and he could exchange his efforts for a meal.

He lay frozen on his little pallet on the loft floor of the cotton gin after Bustie left. He dared not move because it would be hell to pay if Mr. Rafe knew he'd been there the whole time. The lovers thought they were alone in the old metal building full of idle equipment. From his perch in the loft of the cotton gin, Bennie first laughed at their passionate exchange. But the young man's laughter turned to tears as he remembered his father, Chess Gordon, speaking to his mother, Ma'Dear, the same way.

20—SWEET TEMPTATION

"Where you going out this way?" Bustie asked after Gee continued driving west on Quito Road, out of Lucy.

"Baby, I'm headed over to Hope on the Bluff for the Frolic gospel singing."

"It's been so long since I been to a singing. I stay so busy working and taking care of children until I don't have the time."

"Life can't be all working. Sometimes you just got to let your hair down."

The old car kicked up a dust trail that almost hid a pair of distant headlights.

Finally, Thelma Louise replied, "I need to get home." Then, fishing him to see if he had heard the gossip, asked, "You know I got another baby since I seen you last year?"

"Yeah, everybody 'round here heard you got the cutest little redheaded baby boy." He paused to grin in the moonlight.

"That don't bother me none, this is Gee and you Thelma Louise. I still say let's go over to the singing!"

"Gee, you just know how to make a woman feel good."

"Girl, you ain't see'd the half of it. Who got your babies?"

"My girl Sue Nell got 'em and Jude might be there."

Gee laughed. "We're getting close to your house. I'd stop to let you check on 'em if we knew Cousin Jude ain't there. But I don't want no trouble, don't want a cause you none, too. So, if you going with me, we need to ride on by the house."

Thelma Louise argued with herself about going home to her responsibilities or having some fun for the first time since she was fifteen and her first baby came. They been without me all day and it's almost nine-thirty right now, she debated. The two little ones probably asleep, so a little while ain't gone make no difference for them. She remembered the unpleasantness with Jude. He doesn't want to see me no way. She remembered the words Rafe spat at her earlier, "I run this, not you," and intent formed in her mind as the old engine droned its tune.

Gee started to hum, then sang:

"Precious Lord, take my hand;
Lead me on, let me stand;
I am tired, I am weak, and I am worn.
Through the storm and through the night, lead me on to that light.
Take my hand, precious Lord, lead me on!"

"You just could always sing. I remember when you used to sing to us girls in school."

The old car roared over the next hill. Both Thelma and Gee saw her house in the distance cross the next low bottom.

"I'm so hungry and I ain't even got money for the collection plate."

He knew his money would come back from his cut in the singing, so Gee ran his hand into his pocket and gave her his five shiny dimes. "Here, baby, you put some of this in the plate. Miss Samella selling fish plates and cold drinks tonight. We'll get you a fish plate before I go on in the singing." Gee slowed down as the car approached her house.

Headlights came over the hill behind them in the distance. Their eyes met in the partially illuminated cab as he looked across the car at her.

"What's it going to be, sugar?"

"Keep going!"

Gee reached for the gearshift mounted on the steering wheel. He pushed the lever upward to place the car into second gear and gunned the engine. "Baby girl, we gone have a good time tonight!"

"So where you going this time 'a night and who's driving you?" Rafe muttered aloud.

He drove at a distance behind Thelma Louise and whoever picked her up. He wanted to ensure the ride ended at the shack she and Jude rented from him. Rafe smiled in relief when the car slowed near the two-room dwelling. His smile quickly turned upside down when the car sped up and moved past the house without stopping.

"Father, are you thinking about Grandmother?" Amanda asked. "Father, did you hear me?"

She reached out. Her touch on his arm startled Allen Sawyer Jr.

"Father, what deep thoughts hold you prisoner?"

"Young lady, it is just us now, just you and me. This will be my first July Fourth without Mother."

They sat silently in their parlor, off the grand entrance hall.

Sawyer broke the silence. "Your grandmother lived an interesting life. I can still hear her say to me, 'Allie, you must ensure you do the right things. Otherwise, people talk and your deeds come back to haunt you.'"

"Why did she always call you Allie?"

"She always thought me to be her little Allie." He put his face in his hands and took a deep breath.

"What is the most interesting thing that I don't know about Grandmother?"

He spoke through the fingers of his hands. "You wouldn't believe me. Alice Sneed Sawyer made things happen. She was quite the lady but did what it took to protect her own…" His voice trailed off. "I can tell you one interesting thing. My parents' union was the first for her and the second for him. He was a good bit older than she." He stopped and then continued, "Did you know my father won the Picnic Woods from Raford Coleman Jr., Conrad and Rafe's father, in a card game? That last straw between them got Father killed. You think Rafe's crazy? Rafe's not crazy, but his father…crazy should have been his middle name."

Abruptly, he stood and kissed her on the forehead. "Good night, daughter."

"Good night, Allie," she said.

His grin hid his sadness.

21—HOPE ON THE BLUFF

They called Hope Missionary Baptist Church, Hope on the Bluff. The church stood on a hill overlooking the Mississippi River. Music of the gospel singing and the crowd noise greeted them. Gee squeezed his car into a small space on the grass near the road. A car on the passenger side blocked Bustie's exit.

"Come out on this side, Thelma." Gee reached out his hand to Bustie. He looked handsome. His straightened hair was slicked down. Gee's starched white shirt closed at the collar to a perfectly tied square necktie knot. His coat opened to reveal red suspenders. He helped Bustie from the car with his right hand while holding the door open with his left and they stood uncomfortably close, face-to-face in the tight space between the cars. The awkwardness lasted only a moment because they shared a sweet kiss neither saw coming, the culmination of many years of Gee Gurley sitting behind Thelma Louise Gibson at Woodstock Training School.

"I waited a long time for that kiss," he said.

She smiled and dropped her head with newfound school-girl shyness. Automobile lights engulfed them and she recognized the truck that sped past. Without a word, Bustie stepped past Gee and walked toward the church.

"What's wrong, baby?" he whispered.

She batted back the tears.

Gee handed her a handkerchief. She wiped her eyes and noticed the blue in the hankie matched Gee's suit. She almost smiled, but with a troubled look, watched the truck turn the corner up the road.

"You want to go home?"

"Naw, we here now. Besides, you promised me a fish plate and a Co-cola."

"Come on back here with me, baby girl. I bet Mama Sam can fix you up." Gee took her by the hand and led her through the crowd of people who milled around outside the church, to a wooden vendor's stand whose horizontal rails were attached to a giant sycamore tree.

"Mama Sam," Gee said with enthusiasm, "you got any fish ready?"

Mama Sam was perpetually bent over. She turned her head to locate the source of the voice. She pushed her hair aside and wiped the beads of sweat from her face. She smiled wide when she recognized Gee. "Cousin Gee, that you, boy? When you get here?"

"Mama, just pulled up. My friend here's hungry."

Mama Sam squinted up at Bustie. "Who's that with you?" Before Gee replied, the old woman answered her own question. "Oh, you got Jude's Bustie with you. Gee, I'm getting

ready to take some fish out the grease soon as I finish season-
ing and breading the next batch."

She bent over her worktable. With large salt and pepper
shakers in both hands, the old woman generously applied the
seasonings to the fish.

Gee and Bustie watched while she flew from piece to piece.

"Miss Samella, is that big-bone buffalo?"

"Yeah, buffalo and carp," she grunted in an abrupt reply.

Gee sensed the tension. "Mama, you got any cold drinks?"

"That number three tub is full of them. Help yourself."

Gee took off his coat and rolled up his shirtsleeve. He pulled
bottle after bottle from the water. Finally, he straightened up as
he shook the icy water from his forearm and hand. "Mama,
there ain't nothing in here but Double Colas and Royal Crown
colas!"

"What the difference? Soda pop's soda pop."

"Oh no it ain't! A Double Cola and a RC cola ain't no Co-
cola. If it wasn't any difference, then why white folks used to
not let colored folks have Co-colas?"

Mama Sam laughed, "Boy, gone way from here."

"Now, you know it's true. Remember it yourself. It wasn't
too long ago that the white folks would cuss you and threaten
to whip you for asking for a Coca-Cola."

An older colored woman interrupted from her perch on the
opposite rail. "When I lived down in Alabama, they used to call
Co-colas dopes. They say that's why they wouldn't let niggers
have no Co-colas. They say them dopes made niggers act too
crazy to let 'em drink one!"

Bustie, Gee and Mama Sam laughed heartily. Bustie couldn't
remember having so much fun. She looked at the old woman.
"What kind of dope was in them?"

"I don't know. This old white woman I used to keep around 1901 was hooked on 'em. Her son used to send a boy from the drugstore to bring her one every day. That lady cut up something awful when that boy didn't come!"

Gee handed one of the distinctively swirl-shaped bottles to Bustie and they both took a long swallow. For a time, she forgot her troubles.

Bustie turned back to Mama Sam. "Miss Samella, you putting seasonings on the fish instead of in the meal. I didn't know you could do it that way."

Mama Sam stood straight up. "I'm cooking fish, not meal! You need to put the seasonings directly on the fish if you want it to taste the best all the way through."

"Mama," Gee interrupted, holding up his half-empty cola. "You got anything back there? We need a few quarter shots to top these drinks off."

"My name Samella, ain't it?"

The old woman bootlegger rubbed the breading from her hands and looked around with a twinkle in her eye, then pulled a half-pint bottle from her apron pocket. Gee handed her his cold drink; she held the bottle low and spiked the Double Cola with white lightning. A dumbfounded Bustie handed over her bottle and Mama Sam repeated the process.

"Over the lips, past the gums, lookout stomach because here it comes." Gee held a thumb over the drink and shook it before hoisting it for a gulp.

Bustie giggled; she mimicked Gee with a shake and an even bigger swallow of her own. The whiskey hit bottom in her empty stomach.

"Oh, Gee, it's been so long since I took a drink. I feel it going all the way to my fingertips and toes!"

Popping and hissing interrupted their conversation. Mama Sam scooped cooked fish from the black pot and into an awaiting pan.

"Hot fish! Hot Fish!"

People rushed to the stand. The seasoned vendor lifted the last few pieces from the boiling grease with her homemade utensil—wire screen attached to a long stick. She started fixing plates. Each contained two pieces of steaming fish on white bread wrapped in an empty wax paper potato-chip sack. She handed the first one to Bustie.

"How much I owe you?" Gee said.

"Let me see, a nickel each for the colas, a dollar for the four shots and fifteen cents for the fish. A dollar and a quarter'll wipe your slate clean."

"Thank you, Mama." He handed her two crisp dollar bills. She fished inside her apron for his seventy-five cents change. Mama Sam turned to serve her next customer.

"Told you I'd make you feel better." He looked at Thelma through schoolboy eyes. "Now, didn't I?"

She smiled pretty and nodded.

He reached out and held her hand. "You stay right here, baby. I'm going in the church to earn some money. Come in after you finish."

"Thank you, Gee." She squeezed his hand and he walked away.

She faced challenge after challenge. But on this night, Bustie Gibson Smith stood sipping her white-lightning-spiked Double Cola. She opened the potato-chip bag to get at the steaming fish sandwich, whose heat dissipated in the night air.

For the first time in her adult life, she slowed down to reflect. "It feels good to be out," she said and picked at the golden-crusted fish. She put a piece into her mouth. The seasonings were perfect. *It feels good to eat something I didn't cook.* She pulled the white rib bones from the buffalo and washed her feast down with her mixed drink.

She imagined herself curled up in the big white-barked sycamore limbs, looking down on the crowd, listening to the music. "I ain't worried with no babies. Ain't nobody ordering me 'round or pulling at me. Gee know he made me feel mighty good."

Inside the church, the master of ceremonies announced, "Give him a hand while he walking up here." Heavy applause exploded from the crowd in anticipation of a treat. In a few moments, a melodious sound floated from the open church windows. A familiar voice began to sing. Bustie turned, rose onto her tiptoes and saw Gee Gurley in front of the crowd.

22—EYE ON YOU

"Couldn't hear nobody pray. Couldn't hear nobody pray. Way down yonder near the River Jordan, couldn't hear nobody pray." The Colored Methodist Episcopal preacher sang inside his old Model T Ford. Elder Cephas, as Reverend Simon Peter Gordon was called by all who knew him well, drove southward from the Camp Town community. He slowed as he rounded the last left-hand curve in Bluff Road before he would see Hope on the Bluff. A truck sat on the left up ahead. His vehicle's lights engulfed the truck and his eyes caught sight of the Confederate flag in the driver's rear window.

"Lord have mercy. I wonder what he is doing out here."

The preacher slowed to a near stop as he approached. The vehicle's driver stepped into the headlights just in front of the parked truck. The elder noticed Hope on the Bluff in plain view just past the tree-lined curve when he stopped to speak to the man.

"Evening, Constable. How you?"

"Elder, I'm fine."

"Ain't no trouble tonight, is it?"

Rafe walked over to the preacher's automobile and put his foot on the sideboard. "Naw, Reverend, no trouble. I's just out riding and stopped. Decided to listen to the music from a distance. What brings you out?"

The elder pointed toward Hope on the Bluff. "They held the Frolic singing at Pleasant Grove last year and their Reverend Rollins came to visit us. So I figured I would return the favor."

"Now that's neighborly of you." Rafe laughed. "Surprised to know a good Methodist like you would go to a Baptist church."

Both men chuckled. Elder Cephas smelled the whiskey on Rafe's breath.

"Constable Coleman, church folks in the same business. We sow seeds. Denominations are just farming techniques. Showing folks God loves them is our crop."

Rafe pushed his hat back to scratch his head. "The white Methodists split over Negroes when my Granddaddy was a boy. They ain't back together yet."

"That's unfortunate." The elder glanced at the church. "Anything I can do to help you tonight?"

"Naw, I 'preciate it, but ain't nothing I reckon you can do for me."

"Well, have a pleasant evening," Elder Cephas said.

Rafe staggered a bit as he walked away. Elder Cephas noticed what looked like an old telescope in Rafe's left hand. The men made eye contact and Rafe returned to the car's running board and leaned into the window. "Preacher." The elder felt

Rafe's pungent breath brush his left cheek. "Preacher, you really think God loves everybody?"

Elder Cephas looked away toward Hope on the Bluff. "Constable."

"You, you know some of the things I done," Rafe said. "You know, ah, ah, what I'm speaking 'bout. Don't you?"

Elder Cephas gathered himself. Both his mustache and the hair on his head were solid white and cotton-bole thick. He wore his hair long, combed backward, and parted to the left. He looked at Rafe and worked to show no anger. Rafe looked old and seemed tired. In the moonlight-brightened darkness, Elder Cephas seized the opportunity. "Raford," he whispered, "God loves you, even after what you done."

Rafe pulled back from the window and eased his foot from the car. His eyes stayed on Elder Cephas.

Elder Cephas put his car in gear and looked ahead at the church lights.

"But, I forced her, she wasn't nothing but a child."

"You did wrong, but that's been a long time ago, over twenty years. Work on being a better man. Ask God to forgive you and then forgive yourself."

Rafe Coleman shrugged his shoulders, like a boy would. He looked at the dusty roadbed and kicked at a rock. It hit the Ford.

"Rafe, why don't you just head on home? Get you some rest and start over tomorrow."

Rafe Coleman nodded and a tear fell. He started to speak, but Elder Cephas gently waved his hand. "Raford," the elder spoke louder, "go home. Get some rest. Speak to God about it, like you talked with me." He whispered, "It's all right. He loves you anyway." The colored preacher pulled away.

Rafe Coleman raised his right hand and wiped his face.

★ ★ ★

Gill Erby pulled his watch from his pocket. He squinted in the dim lantern light. "Son, I'll get me some sleep."

"Do we need to check the meat before we go to sleep?"

"Check it for what?"

"To see if it's cooking fine."

The old man chuckled. "We done what we supposed to do. Now it's time to just let that meat and the fire and seasonings take care of the rest."

"But don't we need to make sure?"

"Boy, you know what faith is?"

Son shrugged his shoulders and cast a bewildered look at his daddy.

"Faith's the substance of things hoped for, the evidence of things not seen."

Son looked puzzled.

"Listen, we did all we should do to that meat. If you go take the top off now, all you gone do is let all the smoke and moisture out. We already agreed that's part of what give the barbecue flavor. You understand now?"

Son looked up at his father then gazed at the smoldering pit. "We might mess it up if we do too much?"

"That's it. Sometimes you need to turn things over to the Lord. We done what we could, it's out of our hands. At points like that, leave it alone. My momma used to call it 'let go and let the Lord.'"

Gill Erby saw a solitary figure walk across Quito Road. Even in the dark, he recognized the short gait of Bennie Gorlan. He was over there the whole time, Gill Erby spoke in his mind. Hope for his sake Mr. Rafe don't know.

23—CAST THE FIRST STONE

Elder Gordon pulled his car right up to the stand. His head-lights shone through the wooden planks and illuminated the few patrons who stood around. Before the old man turned off his headlights, he recognized a shapely silhouette swaying to the music on the other side of the enclosure. She held her arms wrapped across her upper body.

"Now I know why Rafe Coleman sitting up there in the curve with a spyglass. He's checking on you." The preacher sat still a few moments to gather his thoughts. "I bet I can do some-thing for the constable and these colored folks, too. Thelma Louise, I need to get you away from here."

The preacher approached the backside of the stand. "Evening, sisters," he spoke to Mama Sam and Bustie.

"Evening," both chorused.

"Sister Walker, can I speak with you?"

Mama Sam walked over and leaned on the rail, wiping her hands on her apron. "What can I do for you Reverend?"

"Samella," Elder Cephas nodded toward Bustie, "how long she been here?"

"Near about an hour now. Gee brought her."

"Gurley? She rode here with Gee?"

"Yessuh. I don't know what Gee doing with that wench! He paid for her a cold drink and a fish sandwich like they on a date or something."

"Now, Sister Samella, don't be harsh." He continued with his gentle whispers. "She's just a young woman in a tough place."

"She chose it!"

The elder used palm-down hands to instruct her to speak softer. "Samella," he continued in his smooth, baritone shepherd's voice, "you remember the story in the Bible about the people who brought a woman to Jesus caught in the very act of adultery?"

"Can't say I do," the old bootlegger lied.

"I preached it a few months back and thought you were there that Sunday. Let me remind you of my message. Some brought a woman to Jesus caught in the very act of having relations outside marriage. Per the Law of Moses, death was the prescribed punishment for that sin. You remember any of this?"

Mama Sam wiped her hands some more and looked over at Bustie. "Maybe, a bit coming to me now."

"Well, sister, they told Jesus the woman ought to be stoned to death. He just wrote in the sand. After a while, the Lord said, 'Let them among you without sin cast the first stone.' Well," Cephas chuckled, "they stood around for a while. Then, from the eldest to the youngest, they walked away one by one.

Finally, only the woman and Jesus remained. What you think of that?"

Mama Sam shrugged.

"Samella, just imagine how a woman caught in the act of adultery appeared. She may not have even been clothed."

"Well, ah, I, ah, never thought about it like that." She peeked up at him.

"We must remember how we might feel if we were caught."

Elder Cephas looked down at Mama Sam's neatly hand-embroidered apron pocket. The top of a half-pint whiskey bottle peeked above the opening.

She pushed the bottle lower into her pocket and dropped her head.

"Samella, now don't dare look, but Constable Rafe Coleman is sitting back up there in the curve of Bluff Road. You can't see him, but he got a spyglass on you."

"Thank you, suh, thank you for telling me."

"Now, I'll take Thelma Louise home. When you see Gee, you tell him I said to stay away from that girl."

"Yessuh, I'll tell Gee."

"I think you know how to handle Rafe if he shows up."

Mama Sam nodded; she knew a few dollars would sufficiently pad his pockets.

Bennie Gorlan moved through the crowd. Gill Erby watched him go from stand to stand, approaching the vendors. Each person sent the young man on his way.

"Gorlan!" Mr. Erby called. "Come on over here."

Gill Erby surveyed the young man as he walked to the truck. His clothes appeared not to have been washed in quite a while. He needed a shave. The matted mop on his head showed no comb had tackled his hair in quite a spell. He wore decent shoes, but the laces were broken and untied. The young man's appearance shamed Gill Erby; Bennie was Chess's son and he had done nothing to help him. At least he should have encouraged Chess to do something.

"Evening, y'all." Bennie looked at the ground.

"Good evening," said Erby the younger.

"Bennie, why don't you go over to that bucket of water and wash your face and hands. There's barbecue tenderloin here if you like some."

"Thank you, Mr. Gill! Thank you!" Bennie grinned. "'Um powerful hungry!"

"Son, fix two big sandwiches for Bennie and get him some water to drink."

The orphan rolled up his sleeves and washed his face and hands. As he returned, Son poured the sauce on the first sandwich.

"Y'all got that meat smelling good over here."

"I hope everybody at the Frolic tomorrow agrees. Help yourself to those sandwiches."

Bennie moaned between bites. "Mr. Gill, thank you for my supper. I ain't knowed what I'd eat today, but the Lawd always, always so good."

Gill Erby looked at Son. "It's called faith." The two watched him wrestle with the second pork sandwich. "Gorlan, what you doing every day?"

Bennie stopped chewing and mumbled over his food. "Nothing most days. Did a few odds and ends for Mr. Rafe today. Didn't amount to much."

"I'm probably speaking out of turn since I ain't even spoken with my wife. But how'd you like to stay with us a while and help finish the cotton chopping? You could sleep in our tack room in the barn. I ain't got much money, but we would share our food with you. And you'd have a roof over your head."

Bennie held his head erect, his partially chewed food showed as he spoke, "Mr. Gill, you ain't funning me, is you?"

"Naw, boy. I wouldn't tease about a thing like this. What you say?"

"That'd be the best thing happened to me since Ma'Dear died! Thank you," he whispered. "I'll do a good job for you. Thank you, thank you, thank you!"

Gill Erby shook the young man's hand. Son slapped Bennie on his back as the lad smiled and struggled to chew.

"Young fellows, y'all share the cover in that box over there. Son, I'm going into the truck cab and get me some sleep." He turned to look at the smoke rise from the barbecue pit. "Don't bother the meat none. By five-thirty in the morning, that pork's gone be falling off the bones on the grate. Night, y'all."

"Night, Papa."

"Night, Mr. Gill."

Simple as that, the Erby family adopted Bennie Gorlan.

24—GO AND SIN NO MORE

The preacher drove around the back-side of the stand and pulled slowly through the people who milled about the churchyard. He stopped where Thelma stood listening intently to the singing.

"Howdy, sister. You all right tonight?"

"Hey, Elder Gordon. When you come?"

"Little while ago." He turned his thick midsection and listened to Gee belt out another gospel standard. He looked back at the young mother of four, the woman of two men. "Step over here into my office, and let's talk."

Bustie leaned on the old Ford touring car.

"Now, Thelma—" he looked into her big pretty eyes "—I known you all your life. Blessed and baptized you after your birth." He paused before continuing softly. "I need you to hear me on something. Is that all right?"

She nodded her head.

"This's just between you and me. Is that all right?"

Thelma nodded again and stepped a little closer.

"How you get here tonight?"

Thelma nodded toward the window. "Gee brought me."

"Do you know Rafe Coleman's sitting up there just around the curve?"

"I thought I saw him drive by, but I wasn't sure."

"Well, be sure. I spoke with him. He's been drinking. You and I know how he can be after he's taken a touch or two. Don't we?"

She nodded; he couldn't find her eyes.

"Child, if you care anything about Gee, let me take you home."

She started to walk around the back of the car but stopped. "Elder, you sure you want to be seen with me. My reputation ain't so good."

"Come on, get in and I'll explain on the way to your house. Walk through the headlights so Mr. Rafe can see you leaving with me."

Elder Cephas pulled through the crowd toward Bluff Road, and the kindness in his next comments reached untouched places in her heart. "Sister, in the Bible, Jesus tells the story of some folks that caught a woman who was the wife of one man with another man."

When he finished the story, tears flowed down her dimpled cheeks. "Reverend Gordon, it ain't that simple. It just ain't that simple."

Elder Cephas turned south on the bumpy road. As they approached the fork to turn eastward on Quito Road, he remembered how his mother told him what she'd suffered at the hands of Raford Coleman Jr. and spoke from his heart. "I know what you living through. It took a long, long time for my momma, but everything turned out all right."

25—FROLICKING!

The Colored Pallbearers Society started the Lucy Frolic to raise money to bury the poor. Over time, it became an opportunity for the folks in Lucy and parts nearby to just have a good time on the Fourth of July with friends and family.

The oak-filled picnic woods across the street from the Coleman cotton gin hosted the annual Homecoming Frolic. Ownership of that land had passed to Allen Sawyer Jr. with the recent death of Miss Alice. Someday, those acres and all that Miss Alice owned would pass to Amanda Sawyer.

By the afternoon of Frolic day, more than two thousand people descended on little Lucy. The folks rode special trains from Memphis that the Illinois-Central line provided. They arrived by bus from Fayette, Tipton and Lauderdale Counties. Many Frolickers completed the trip on horseback or wagon from as far away as Mississippi and Arkansas.

Wonderful aromas met the noses of the young and old.

Wood smoke mixed with the aroma of barbecue, fried fish and hush puppies. The smells of cakes and pies mingled with the syrupy aroma of candied apples and cotton candy. The joyful sound of hot grease popping inside the big black pots mingled with blues music and crowd noise.

Children shouted as they rushed through the crowd. Women laughed and men boasted in groups about their latest or next conquest. Fireworks always made their way to the Frolic. Yeah, on any Fourth of July, the Pallbearers' Frolic was the place to be.

By late afternoon, bands played music, the hand-cranked Flying Jenny merry-go-round flew and vendors sold everything from toys to quilts to the most delicious food imaginable.

Someone occasionally offered barbecued goat. The vendors always cooked plenty of barbecue chicken and barbecue "Steak de la Nègre," better known as bologna. If it tasted good and one could eat or drink it, they sold it at the Frolic. Every year someone even cooked and sold barbecued raccoon. And the bootleggers never, ever ran out of whiskey, not even during Prohibition!

"Son, it's your responsibility to handle the cold drinks. Tie this money apron around your waist." Chess Gordon turned to his wife who worked pulling apart the roasted pork meat in a big pan. "Zoar, where's that money I gave you?"

Zoar walked over to the old man. "It's in one of the pockets."

Chess Gordon intentionally groped the middle of the apron in the wrong pocket. "Woman," he teased, "I think it's a whole bank in this pocket."

Miss Zoar protested, "Quit, you dirty old man." She smiled up at him. "That's my bank and don't you forget it."

Chess retrieved the paper sack of coins from a side pocket. "Girl, it's your bank, but nobody better cash any checks in that bank but me!" Zoar turned to walk away. Old Chess Gordon patted her rear. She walked back to her spot at the end of the table with a disapproving pout and a roll of her eyes.

The meat cleaver in Gill Erby's left hand fell hard on the thick chopping block and roasted pork. He laughed from his spot across the table. "Sounds like this lesson you teaching my boy includes more than just money." The heavy blade sounded as he chopped the meat into manageable chunks.

"How old you, Son?" Chess asked.

Smiling wide, Son answered, "Fifteen."

"Now, Gill, in a few years, this boy gone spend more on what I just showed him than anything else. So just count that as part of his fiscal education."

Son formed a puzzled look while the three adults laughed. Chess Gordon stopped laughing when Bennie Gorlan joined in from the tailgate of Gill Erby's truck. He sat just behind the stand.

Chess rose and stared at Bennie. Next, he peered over the top of his glasses with his one good eye at Gill Erby. Cousin Chess placed the money apron on the table in front of Son.

"Son, put the nickels and the pennies in stacks of five."

The boy's eyes widened after he looked into the bag. Cousin Chess read Son's mind.

"I know that more money than you ever touched at one time. But your papa and I spoke about this. You ready to handle it."

The boy nodded and slowly poured the money onto the table. He fumbled with the coins.

"Hell, boy, don't ever be afraid of cash. Money's just a tool.

Ain't any different than the shovel you used yesterday to dig that pit. Make cash do what you want and don't let it make you do what you ought not."

Chess Gordon sorted a few nickels and pennies into stacks of five. He motioned for Son to continue. "The Lawd gave you two hands. You used two on that shovel yesterday. Didn't you?"

Son grinned. "Yessuh," he answered.

Finally, Son completed the task.

"Boy, how many stacks of each you got?"

"Eight stacks of nickels and five stacks of pennies."

"Good, now let me help you understand what we got. How many is eight times five dollars?"

"Forty."

"Um, you get smarter by the day. There's twenty nickels in a dollar. So, how many dollars in nickels you got?"

"Two dollars."

"How many stacks of pennies you got and how much do they come to?"

"There are five stacks of pennies." He paused to calculate the next answer. "So, that'll be fifty cents."

"I'm starting you off with two dollars in nickels and fifty cents in pennies. Now, each soda pop is a nickel. If they take the bottle, that's another penny. So, how much you gone charge for a cold drink when they take the bottle?"

Son bit his lip. "Six cents?"

"You asking or telling me?"

"Six cents!"

The three adults and Son laughed. This time, Cousin Chess did not stop when Bennie joined in from afar.

"I bought a new watering trough so I could use it to cool the drinks today. How many soda pops you and Bennie put in there?"

"Six cases."

"'Um gone run some numbers you ain't gone get just yet. Six cases, now that's one hundred and forty-four cold drinks since there's twenty-four to a case." He looked up while pushing his brown straw hat back on his head. "Another six cases under this table, so that's two hundred and eighty-eight soda pops to sell today. At a nickel a piece, you gone take in fourteen dollars and forty cents. You agree?"

Son looked at Gill Erby, confused. Mr. Erby nodded his approval, smirking.

"Yessuh," Son answered.

"So, at the end of the day, 'um looking to you for fourteen dollars and forty cents plus two hundred and eighty-eight empty soda-pop bottles stacked back in these wooden cases under here. If the cases ain't full, I'll need a penny for every missing bottle." Chess turned to Gill Erby. "What word did that Italian use for understand the last time we saw him?"

"Capisce!"

"Oh, yeah. *Capisce.* Son, you capisce?"

All smiles, the boy answered. *"Capisce!* What we gone use to open the drinks?"

"Hot dog! I knew I forgot something! Zoar, you remember to bring that drink opener?"

"Naw, Chess. You said you was gone get it."

In the distance, a train horn sounded and the twelve o'clock whistle blew from the marble yard in town.

Chess Gordon pulled out his pocket watch. "Ain't got time to go get an opener now. The noon special right on time and it's full of frolickers." The old man scratched his head and looked down at his watch again. "Son, use this watch fob. It doubles as a bottle opener."

"Cousin Chess, what is this thing?"

"That Watkins man sold it to me a long time ago. He called it a swastika. Said it's a symbol used in both Hindu and Christian religion."

Son held it to eye level for all to see. "Sho' is pretty."

"Son, use this here string and hang it around your neck. That way, you won't lose it."

Son took the string and looped it through the swastika. He tied a square knot and hung it around his neck. The brass ornament shone in the rays of sunshine that peeked through the oak-leaf canopy above.

Son smiled as he examined the new bottle opener. "I wonder what it means."

"The fellow said it's a sign of prosperity and good fortune. It stands for completeness."

"That means we gone sell out today!"

The team laughed. Gill Erby brought the meat cleaver down on another chunk of pork. Miss Zoar continued to ready the meat for the crowd. Chess Gordon struck a match, raised it to his pipe and puffed until cherry-flavored smoke poured out. Bennie Gorlan soaked up everything Chess Gordon showed Son that day.

26—RECONCILIATION

Bustie's husband, Jude, listened to the tin roof popping under the noontime July sun. The screen-door spring produced its funny twanging sound and his daughter Sue Nell pushed the door open wide. Her eyes met her father's. Both looked down at a fair-skinned toddler waddling over to where the big man sat on the front porch.

"Lil' Red," as the Smith family called Thelma Louise's youngest son, "stay out there with Daddy while I finish getting ready. Daddy, you going to the Frolic?"

A preoccupied Jude Smith stared at the bright-skinned nine-month-old. The child tried to grab the big toe of the man's huge feet. Jude and the child joined in an impromptu game of cat and mouse; he maneuvered his foot to elude the child's reach.

"Daddy, you going to the Frolic or not?"

Jude frowned. "Naw, y'all go with your momma. I, I better

just sit here at the house." The girl stepped back in the house. The screen door slammed.

"I done told y'all to stop letting that door slam. That's what tears them up."

Sue Nell came back to the door and smiled at him. "Yessuh." She closed the door slowly.

Jude felt better. He thought, that's how your momma used to smile at me when she was your age.

Inside the two-room shack, the doting Negro mother helped Pal finish buttoning his shirt she had washed by hand earlier in the day. She rubbed some cooking lard between her palms and generously smeared the oil onto Pal's dark brown skin. She waved Joe over and repeated the process. "Pal, give me that hairbrush over there," and when he handed the brush to Bustie, she brushed Joe's hair and then started in on Pal.

"Aw, Momma that hurts!"

"Pal, shut up or something else gone hurt. I'm trying to get you ready so y'all can catch a ride to town."

Pal, the second oldest of the Smith children, said, "Momma, you ain't going with us?"

"Naw, baby, momma gone stay at the house today. Me and Lil' Red gone sit the Frolic out this year."

Sue Nell walked into the kitchen. "Momma, Daddy says he ain't going to the Frolic either."

Bustie looked very surprised. Jude never missed a chance at a drink and he always went to the Frolic. The woman reached into her pocket. "Now, Sue Nell, here's three dimes for you, Pal and Joe. You buy yourself a sandwich and let Joe and Pal split another sandwich. That'll be one dime. Then you use the other two dimes to get y'all on the Flying Jenny or to buy treats like some candy or a cold drank." She waved her right index finger at the three stair-stepped children standing in front of her. "Just remember, y'all stay together and share the money. When it's gone, it's gone! You understand?"

All three nodded.

"Now, go out there on the porch. Sue Nell, if you see somebody you know coming, flag them down so you can catch a ride to Lucy." The children walked to the front of the house. Bustie followed and stepped onto the porch behind them to witness the surprise of her life: Lil' Red lay on Jude's massive chest and both were fast asleep. The woman held her finger to her lips to keep the children quiet. She gently closed the screen, walked over to Jude and carefully removed the child from his arms.

Jude looked up when Bustie leaned over him to pick up the child. Inside her loose blouse, Jude saw two former close friends who were now strangers. She smelled good from the bath she drew that morning for herself and the kids. A rose perfume fragrance entranced him. Bustie smiled at him like only she could. Jude returned the favor like he had when he'd witnessed her blossom into early womanhood.

She nestled Lil' Red into her neck and turned to take the child into the house. In the distance, she saw a wagon drawn by two mules headed toward the house from the west on Quito Road.

Bustie placed Lil' Red on the cot where he slept. "Lil' Red, you ain't so little no more." The toddler smiled in his sleep. She hoped he stayed asleep for a while. Since he started walking early, the boy had really been quite a handful.

"Momma, it's Miss Birdie Mae and Miss Sarah," Sue Nell said from the roadside. "You think we can ride with them?"

Bustie held her finger to her mouth as she walked out in the yard. "Don't wake Lil' Red," she whispered. "If they got room, I bet you can."

The wagon bounced along. Sarah Erby pulled the mules to a stop in front of the Smith house. "Howdy, y'all doing all right?"

The Smith children waved. They followed Bustie to the roadside before she spoke aloud. "We do mighty fine today."

Sarah struggled with the reins to hold Ole Dan still. Attempting a man's low voice tone she said, "Hooo, there, Dan!" The mule settled down just a bit. She laughed. "You know this mule act an even bigger fool now since Mr. Erby bought the truck and don't use him much on the wagon. This rascal here needs a man's hand to keep him straight."

"Miss Birdie Mae, how you doing today?" Bustie asked.

Bustie's midwife spit a mouthful of tobacco juice over the back wagon gate from where she sat in the rear. "Girl, doing fine for an old woman." She looked at the porch to where Jude sat. "Howdy, Jude."

Jude waved. "How do, ladies and young ladies?" he called.

The Erby girls, delighted to be on their way to the Frolic for the first time, answered in chorus.

"Y'all need a ride to town?" Sarah asked.

"I'm gone send these three on. Me and Jude gone stay to the house. Can they ride over and back with you?"

"Sure they can," Sarah answered. "Girls, y'all make room for them back there. Thelma Louise, I'll see to it that they get back safe, too!"

The kids walked to the rear of the wagon and Bustie helped them climb on.

"Where is my Lil' Red?" Mama Birdie Mae asked.

Bustie said, "He's in there sleep with his bad self."

"Now, don't you talk about my baby. Don't you forget I told you the week he was born that one's mine."

"No, ma'am, I ain't gone forget."

"Thelma," Sarah called from the driver's seat, "we gone head into town. Me and Momma gone help Mr. Erby and Cousin Chess sell barbecue."

"All right, Sarah. Thank you for seeing to my bunch. Y'all mind Miss Birdie Mae and Miss Sarah."

"Get up," Sarah called to the mule team, and the wagon bounced away.

Mama Birdie Mae looked back after the wagon pulled up the road. Unusual, but it's probably good them two staying home together, she thought. She looked over at Sue Nell and thought how much she looked just like Bustie at that age. She surveyed the wagonful of children. Looking into each of their faces, Birdie Mae prophesied, "Bright future, that's all I see," she said softly.

"What you say, Grandma?" Sarah's youngest said.

Mama Birdie Mae started to laugh. "I said it's time to tell the story about when the snake took the Dootie Bug to the Frolic."

Pal said, "Uh-uh! Ain't no such a thing as a Dootie Bug."

"Yes it is. You want me to tell you the story?"

"Yeah, yeah, yeah," said the kids.

Sarah laughed and wondered how many times she'd heard this one.

Mama Birdie Mae pulled her juice-harp instrument from her dress pocket. She placed it between her lips and out come a rhythmic tune as she plucked the metal device. "You see, the snake took the Dootie Bug to the Frolic." She sang and strummed the Juice-harp again. "But the snake got to looking at the Dootie Bug and the Dootie Bug looked so good that he bit him. The Dootie Bug started to cry and the snake got scared. He say, 'Don't cry. I'll give you a half a dollar. You can go downtown, buy a drum.'" Miss Birdie clapped her hands and the youngsters joined in. "So, he gave him a half a dollar and the Dootie Bug went downtown and bought that drum. He beat that drum 'til the police come. When the police come, the Dootie Bug said, 'Don't get me.' He pointed at the snake and said, 'Get that man behind that tree-e-e-e!'" All in the wagon laughed because they were headed for the Lucy Fourth of July Frolic and the time of their life.

Bustie listened to their laughter from a distance. She turned toward the house. Jude watched her walk back. Then she did an unusual thing. Bustie kissed him on the cheek. Before she could move away, he swept her onto his lap with his massive arms; she did not resist.

"It's been a long time since you sat up there, girl."

"You spend so much time at your cousin's place on Joy Street 'til you acted like you ain't wanted me to sit up there."

She sat there on his lap and he looked down her blouse at his two lost friends. Neither said a word.

"I always wanted you. We just in such a mess."

"Jude, if you would just help some, it'd be better."

"My lazy ass should 'a nev'r let you work for him."

She put a finger to his lips and moved closer in his arms. She whispered, "Today's the first time you ever touched Lil' Red."

Jude paused to think about what she'd said. His eyes teared up. "He tried to catch my toes and I started playing with him…" His voice trailed off. "It wasn't his fault, it's mine." They sat in silence and finally, Jude whispered, "He just so cute and it ain't his fault." A tear trailed down his dark brown cheek.

Bustie looked into her husband's eyes for the first time in a long, long time. "Jude, this may sound funny, but it ain't your fault. It ain't mine's neither." She leaned in to kiss along the tear trail before pulling away.

Jude's nod confirmed he agreed and Thelma Louise Smith wrapped her arms around her husband's neck. For the first time in almost two years, she kissed him full on the mouth.

Jude rose from his seat, carrying his wife like a baby doll in his arms. When he reached the front door, she opened the screen. He stepped through the door and let it gently rest on his back while he stepped across the threshold. The screen made no sound when the two moved inside.

"Don't want to wake Lil' Red," he whispered.

27—NO JUSTICE

"Boy, gone get another drink!" Rafe commanded.

"No, thank you," Deputy Billy Tuggle replied. "That's enough for me. Don't you think it's about time we take care of this business?"

Rafe looked at his watch. "Naw, now, Billy, this is yo' first time out here to the Nigger Frolic. It's just three-thirty. Now, the folks at the county sheriff office done let you have this territory, but you got to listen to me if you want to get the most out of it. You hear?"

Shelby County Sheriff Deputy Billy Tuggle nodded his head.

"Pour yourself another drink. We need to sit here until the crowd gets just a little thicker. What did they tell you to do?"

"Do whatever you said and everything would be fine."

"Well, let me tell you something, hoss!" Rafe paused to put his feet up on the cotton gin office desk. "We gone sit here a little while longer. Then we'll get in my old truck and roll right across the road into the middle of them and park. In another hour, it'll be thicker over there with niggers than flies on a dead cow."

"Rafe," Billy started in the middle of his laughter, "they told me you was crazy."

Rafe's brow furrowed and he exploded. "Who the hell you be to call me crazy? Huh, just who the hell you be to do that?"

"Rafe, we meant in a funny kinda way." Billy's voice trembled. "Them boys didn't mean nothing bad."

Rafe put his feet on the floor and sat erect in the chair. "Hell, funny means funny and, well, hell, crazy mean crazy!"

"Rafe, I didn't mean nothing."

Rafe gazed out the small office window. "Hell, Billy, get another drink. There's another busload of niggers pulling up. Yep, we'll make some money today!"

Billy trembled a little when he reached for the fifth of whiskey. No wonder Charlie gave me this territory, he thought. This peckerwood's crazier than hell. He poured three fingers of white whiskey into the Mason jar and raised it to his lips for an attitude adjustment.

"Gill, this year gone be the biggest crowd ever at the Frolic."

Gill Erby looked up from his work and at the mass of people walking through the picnic woods. The grassy ground had already turned to dust. Seventy-five feet from their stand, a blues band belted out another song. "Chess, I think you right. We already sold nearly a whole hog."

"Yeah, I been sitting here watching it. Son, how many cold drinks you done sold?"

Son surveyed the empties under the table. He also estimated

the bottles others took away after paying a deposit. "Six, maybe seven cases been sold."

"Gill, can you stop what you doing and help Son count his nickels out."

"Sure, but you sure you want to do that in this crowd."

Chess Gordon stood and walked over to Gill. "You and the boy just put your back to the crowd." He opened the pocket of his khaki britches to show Gill a small, five-shot .32-caliber revolver. "Ain't gone be no trouble."

Bennie walked to the back of the stand.

Chess turned to address him. "Boy, you been somewhere goofing off?"

"No, sir. You said you'd give us a penny for every empty we brought back. There's twenty bottles in this case here." He set the wooden case on the back rail of the stand.

"Interesting, interesting," Chess commented. "Come on back here, Bennie, and sell these drinks while Gill and Son counts these nickels."

Son handed Bennie two dimes.

Bennie grinned and Son handed Chess Gordon's illegitimate child the bottle opener.

Sue Nell Smith and her brothers approached the front of the stand. The budding girl had spent her mother's dimes wisely. She and the boys rode the Flying Jenny. That cost fifteen cents. She bought a bag of candy the three of them shared with another nickel. With the last ten cents, she planned to buy two barbecue sandwiches for herself and the two boys.

"Miss Sarah, can we get two barbecue sandwiches?"

"Sure, baby. Let me fix them for you." Sarah turned to the table to open one of the large pans of pulled pork.

Sue Nell looked at the money on the table. It was more

money than she'd ever seen. She looked up to find Son Erby looking into her eyes.

"What's that?" Sue Nell said above the noise, pointing to a piece of white cloth that hung just above the pans of meat from a string. The cloth's dimensions were about two feet by two feet and its bottom half was cut into strips.

"That's a shoofly!" Son said. He welcomed the chance to speak to Sue Nell.

"A shoofly? What's that?"

"We moved it back and forth above the tables to shoo the flies away from the meat. That's why it's called a shoofly."

Sue Nell flashed Son her perfect smile. The dimples she'd inherited from her mother showed in each smooth brown cheek. Her curls had wilted in the West Tennessee July heat and humidity, but she threw her hair from her face and laughed. "Son, that's smart," she flirted.

Son Erby heard music when she spoke.

From his perch at the rear of the stand, Chess Gordon noticed the attraction between Son and Sue Nell. He moved to the front of the stand. "Little girl, when I was a little slave boy, my momma cooked for the white folks. She used to string a shoofly above the table. She'd tie a string to it. I sat on the floor and kept quiet while I pulled the string to move the shoofly and keep the flies off the white folks' food." He puffed on his pipe and blew up a big puff of smoke.

Sarah turned around with the sandwiches. "Here, baby. That'll be a dime."

Chess Gordon interrupted. "Keep your money, little girl. Hell, Sarah, fix another one for this other boy. Them Jude

Smith's boys. You know they need a sandwich to theyself!" He laughed and nursed his pipe again.

"Thank you, Mr. Chess. I'll tell my momma and daddy what you did for us."

"You welcome, baby! Son, get this girl and her brothers a soda pop apiece. On the house! Y'all take your food and walk around to the back to tell him what you want."

"I want a Nehi Peach!" Pal said.

"Me, too!" Joe shouted.

Son reached into the cold waters of the trough for the two soft drinks. Bennie handed Son the swastika bottle opener. Son opened each and handed them to the two boys.

He stood up tall and looked straight into her dark brown eyes. "Baby, what type drink you want?" He hoped she would notice for the first time that his eyes matched the color of their cat at the house.

"Son, I'd like a Co-cola," she cooed like a mourning dove. Perhaps she did notice, he thought. Every adult in the stand smiled.

"Bennie, you ought to be hungry. You ain't ate nothing since I been here. Would you like me to make you a couple of sandwiches?"

"Yes, ma'am, Miss Sarah. Thank you."

Chess Gordon chomped harder on his pipe; the smoke he puffed between gritted teeth poured from his mouth. "Gill, step up here, please, sir."

Gill Erby handed Chess a thick cloth satchel. "There's sixty-nine dollars in here."

"Thank you, Gill. Now, let me show you something. You see who's pulling into the picnic woods?"

"I saw him before you called me. This about the time they always come?"

"Yeah, it's always just before dusk when the crowd is the thickest. That way Rafe gets to show more niggers he's in charge 'round Lucy."

Gill Erby pushed the hat back on his head and wiped the sweat with his left hand. "What's the going rate?"

"Three dollars apiece ought to do it."

"Six dollars!" Gill Erby said loudly.

"Hush, fool." Chess quieted Gill with his hands. "If we were selling whiskey like I wanted to, it'd be five dollars apiece. Zoar, come here, baby doll. Here comes Rafe Coleman and the sheriff's deputy. Remember what I told you to do earlier."

Zoar nodded and pulled out four pieces of wax paper. She separated the papers into two stacks with two pieces in each, then reached into her brassiere and pulled out a roll of money. She counted off six one-dollar bills. She put three ones between the papers in each stack. Zoar made a sandwich for each piece of paper. She folded the wax paper around the meat, bread and sauce and pierced each with a toothpick to hold the sandwich closed.

Sarah could tell Zoar knew the routine well and turned back to Chess just in time to see Rafe Coleman drive through the crowd in his pickup truck.

"Howdy, Uncle Chess!" Rafe shouted almost at the top of his lungs. He stopped in the middle of the crowd. The Negroes scattered when they saw the law and Rafe enjoyed every second. The constable and the deputy got out and Miss Zoar walked up to the rear rail. "Here you are, Mr. Rafe, a sandwich for you and one for the deputy."

"Thank you kindly, Zoar." He handed one to the deputy. The young man's nervousness paralleled Rafe's confidence.

Sarah knocked a pan top to the ground and it landed with a bang at the feet of Birdie Mae Lilliard. The old woman grabbed the lid and glared at Raford Smith Coleman III.

Rafe stepped back from the stand, surprised. "Y'all got the whole family back there. Didn't see you, Birdie Mae. How you?"

Birdie Mae Lilliard glared at Rafe then spat over the top rail of the stand. "Evening, Constable."

"Me and the deputy," Rafe stammered, "we gone walk around and check things out." He left in a hurry, followed by a puzzled Deputy Billy Tuggle.

Son looked from adult to adult for an explanation. Why had Rafe Coleman got so nervous when he saw Grandma Birdie?

Chess Gordon laughed. "Boy, you don't know your grandma caused Rafe Coleman to get the only two ass whippings he ever took in his whole life?"

Son looked confused.

"Get Cousin Birdie to tell you about it sometime. She whipped his ass right in the middle of downtown Lucy. And when he decided to shoot her over it, I took this pistol and whipped his ass with his own gun. Chess pulled the .32 from his pocket. It happened right in front of the bank. It's the only time a colored person whipped a white man's ass in these parts and lived to tell about it!"

Silence fell among all at the stand.

"A low-down, broke-down son of a bitch! That's what he is!" Miss Birdie Mae said aloud.

A wide-eyed Sue Nell Smith giggled. Her little brother Pal laughed next. Bennie gave up his cackle. Soon most of the folks at the little barbecue stand laughed at how old lady Birdie Mae

Lilliard and Chess Gordon both whipped Rafe Coleman's tail on the same day. Mama Birdie Mae, Gill and Sarah kept straight faces.

I guess Rafe Coleman ain't as tough as he says he is after all, Son noted mentally.

28—ANOTHER CHANCE MEETING

Gee Gurley looked over at the girl sitting on the seat of his car. Was her name Mary or was it Martha? He couldn't remember so he decided to just call her baby for the rest of the evening. The pair left the Lucy city limits and sped south on Millington Road toward Memphis.

"I got one more place to sing, baby. It'll be just you and me after that." Gee hated how Thelma Louise got away last night. "Um taking you in the club with me."

The woman giggled at the prospect. She couldn't wait until the next day to tell the folks at her bus stop about her night with Gee Gurley at the Frolic and on Beale Street.

Gee drove right by the speed trap Rafe Coleman and Deputy Tuggle set up just outside of Lucy. He never saw the Shelby County patrol car until Rafe pushed the siren button. Gee Gurley shook his head. "Shit, this all I need tonight! Be cool, baby, just be cool. I got some money and I'll handle it."

★ ★ ★

Deputy Billy pulled the patrol car in behind the speeding car. He noted the license plates. The car slowed, pulled off the road and rolled to a stop.

"Give me your flashlight, I'll handle this one," Rafe said. He grabbed the heavy flashlight and stumbled from the car.

Deputy Tuggle shook his head.

Rafe shone the light into Gee's face. Next, he looked across the seat and illuminated the colored woman's entire frame.

"Boy, where you going!"

"I'm taking her home down to Memphis," Gee said softly.

"John-daddit! Speak up, boy! What you say?"

"I'm taking her home to Memphis."

"Seem like I smell whiskey. You been drinking?"

That question unnerved Gee. "Naw, I ain't been drinking," he lied. Gee cringed as soon as he realized he forgot to say "Nawsuh."

Rafe flung the driver's door open. "Nigger, get out of the car. Who you saying 'naw' to?" Rafe reached inside and grabbed Gee by the collar and yanked the small Negro from the car.

Rafe shoved Gee into the side of the car next to the rear door. He shone the big flashlight into his face. The blue suit caught his drunken eyes. He stepped back just a bit and shone the light on the automobile. Rafe's drunken mind tumbled for recognition of this nigger, and when he found his memory, struck Gee on the side of the face with his flashlight.

Gee flailed back. "Don't kill me! Don't kill me!"

Rafe hit Gee's forehead over and over, until he collapsed. The constable drew back for what he knew would be the final blow needed to kill Gee.

The colored woman screamed from inside the car.

Rafe shone the flashlight into her face and froze. What would Thelma Louise think if he landed that next lick? He let the now-unconscious colored man drop slowly to the ground.

"Shit!" Deputy Tuggle exclaimed as Gee Gurley hit the ground. "What a crazy son of a bitch!"

29—ROD LESSONS

"Son, hitch that damn mule up!" Chess Gordon said.

"I'm trying, Cousin Chess, but he won't cooperate." Seemingly on cue, Dan kicked and turned circles while pulling away from the sorghum-mill harness.

Chess Gordon stopped setting up the three molasses-cooking tables. En route to where Son and Ole Dan struggled, Cousin Chess picked up a thick stalk of sorghum, then grabbed the mule by the bridle and, without a word, swung his heavy weapon like an ax against a tree.

Son froze while Chess Gordon hit Ole Dan until both the old man and the mule panted heavily.

"I ain't got no time for this." Still gripping the bridle, he said, "Son, when you last fed him?"

"I gave him some sorghum seed heads and leaves this morning."

"How 'bout water?"

"Just, just before we left for here."

"Get that muzzle from over there."

Son moved fast; he didn't want what Ole Dan got.

The area molasses expert shook the mule's head hard. "Mule, I don't spare a rod on men, women, children or beasts." He showed the sorghum stick to Ole Dan. "Told Gill Erby years ago to kill you. Act up one more time today and I'll buy you to do the job my damn self!"

Son returned with the muzzle and handed it to the old man. He hit the mule three more times for good measure. Each blow landed against the animal's head with a deep thud. The final one broke the thick stalk. Chess stuffed the muzzle onto Dan's face and head. With the mule's mouth and the bottom half of his face completely covered, Cousin Chess fastened the ends over the top of the mule's head.

"Today, mule, no work, no feed, no water! Now, Mr. Son, I bet you a bucket of warm spit he ready now." He slapped Son on the back and checked the sorghum mill. "What you think?"

The boy shrugged and hooked the remarkably peaceful Ole Dan to the harness. Ole Dick waited, eating stripped sorghum fodder under a nearby tree before his own turn at the mill.

"Come here, Son."

The mill sat a few feet above the ground atop a heavy wooden platform made of twelve-inch-thick wooden beams. The squeezed juice ran from the mill, through a wire screen, and into the tub below.

"Let me show you how this works. Your job involves sitting on this bucket and feeding the sorghum through these two rollers. This wheel on top turns the rollers and the T-shaped metal top holds this pole that connects to the mule."

Chess Gordon peered over his glasses for affirmation from the boy. Son nodded his understanding.

"Remember one main thing—don't ever put a hand near these rollers unless you put this metal spike through this hole in the top. Walk over here so you see what I mean. I've seen this very mill take a man's arm off. It wasn't pretty. Be careful today. You hear me, boy?"

"Yessuh."

"Stop the mule and put this spike through the hole in the wheel down into the casing if the mill needs cleaning out. That way, the mules can't turn it and you can do what you need to about clearing the jam. Understand?"

"Yessuh."

"I'll whip you like I done that mule if I see you fooling with the mill without the spike in place." Cousin Chess lifted his glasses and winked his right eye at Son.

The boy recoiled from the sight.

"Son, let's put the wood under the cooking tables." He led the boy to the cooking shed.

Three identical tables sat side by side and measured about four feet wide and ten feet long.

"Cousin Chess, how long before Papa gets back?"

"Kind 'a surprised he ain't here already. He just needed to make two stops."

"How you want this wood placed?"

"Make two big piles under each end. Get the five-gallon jug of coal oil from my truck after you finish. Then we'll get that mule started and make some juice."

As the old man finished speaking, Son threw the first bundle of wood under one end of the nearest table.

"Why you use these thin willow limbs instead of thick wood like we use in a stove?"

"That's a good question and here's the answer. I collected that willow over two years ago and dried it in my barn. We need it dry to make quick heat and it's got to be thin so we can control it real easy. Controlling the heat from thick wood's too hard once the flames start to roll. Get moving. We got to squeeze and cook a lot today before sundown."

Allen Sawyer Sr. started the mill to make whiskey barrels for his distillery that was never built. When he died, Alice Sawyer inherited the mill and continued to manufacture wooden barrels from area hardwood trees.

The mill workers loaded the five white oak barrels without incident.

Gill drove back onto Quito Road and noticed Johnlee Gordon lying in the street. Gill Erby pulled the truck next to him just underneath the large shiny metal pipes that carried the sawdust waste into an open field across Quito Road. The huge piles of sawdust formed small mountains.

"Hey there, fellow!" the drunk man shouted.

"Hey yourself, Cousin Johnlee. Look like you started early today." Gill tried to help Johnlee stand, but liquor stole his balance.

"I'm going back round to Mama Sam's to get me another slab," Johnlee said, referring to a flat pint-size whiskey bottle.

"Johnlee, let me take you home. Don't you think you had enough?"

Several men working in the stave mill yard laughed and pointed. This inflamed him and he shoved Gill Erby so hard that Gill fell to the ground.

"Get your damn hands off me! You think you know so much 'cause you gone buy some of my no good daddy's land!"

"Now, Johnlee, I just stopped to help you."

"I don't need your John-daddit help. You ain't no better man than me. Get on back to the house to take some more orders from that straw-boss nigger daddy of mine."

"Don't you ever talk to me like that again! You hear me, nigger!" He shoved Johnlee so hard that he fell against the stone street post and ended up on his back.

Someone inside the stave mill threw the start switch. The sawmill blades roared to life and the exhaust shoot poured sawdust out like it did every day the mill operated.

Gill Erby's truck moved away down Quito and Johnlee shouted, "I'm gone kill you, John-daddit, for putting your hands on me. Nigger, I'll kill you dead for sure!"

Gill Erby drove across the railroad tracks on the west side of Lucy, and never looked back. He did not hear Johnlee's rantings.

But, everyone on that end of town heard what Johnlee Gordon said. Rafe Coleman stood on the front stoop of the store. His broad grin showed how entertaining he found the episode. Allen Sawyer Jr. shook his head over the ruckus, but when he entered the bank, a wide smile covered his face. Jim Falls showed his few teeth and doubled over in laughter at the show.

30—A WHIPPING THAT STUCK

Papa Gill brought Bennie back to Cousin Chess's farm. At first, Chess Gordon complained, but he shut up when the young man relieved Son at the sorghum mill while Gill Erby and Cousin Chess manned the molasses-cooking tables.

The old man stirred in the brew with a thick spoon. He tested the completeness of the sweet mixture by pulling the spoon upward to twelve inches above the cooking tray. Chess Gordon put his finger into the stream of molasses and touched the tip to his lips.

"Now, them's molasses! Gill, these here just sweeter than the other we cooked. Where'd you harvest the sorghum for this batch?"

"That juice came from the bottomland right down near that big Jabbok tree."

"I shoulda known these came from down there. That bottomland always produces the best molasses. Son, come over here and let me show you how real molasses taste."

The heat and steam from the three tables stifled the boy's breath. Cousin Chess handed him the spoon with just a little of the syrup on it.

"That sure is good!"

"Son, get me another barrel to drain this table. I don't want to let these burn 'cause they sure enough ready."

Son brought the old man a barrel. He laid it on its side and placed wood blocks on each side to keep it in place. Chess put a big funnel lined with the domestic material into the hole in the side of the barrel where it had been positioned underneath the spout. The molasses chef opened the spout to fill the barrel. The hot molasses ran through the coarse cloth and into the barrel. More steam rose as the hot sweetening hit bottom in the cool oak barrel.

Chess Gordon took his paddle and moved more and more of the thick fluid through the chain of trays until the fifty-five-gallon barrel was filled. He turned the spout off and pushed a round wooden plug into the hole. Chess hit the plug softly with his hand. That's when Tom Coleman rode up on his horse.

"How's everybody today?"

"Mighty fine, mighty fine."

"Son, get that two-wheeler. Tom boy, we'd be even better if you'd get off that horse and help Son take this barrel of molasses to my back porch."

"Sure, I'll be glad to help Son out anytime."

Tom got down, led the animal to a nearby tree and tied him there.

"Those fires throw off so much heat. How do y'all stand it?"

Son returned with the two-wheel wooden dolly in time to

hear Cousin Chess's reply, "Well, young Mr. Coleman, some of us work for a living. That's how we stand it."

The two boys wrestled the keg of molasses onto the two-wheeler and headed for the house.

"Gill, what's on your mind? You been quiet all day."

"I spoke with your banker today when I dropped Sarah off."

Chess frowned. "What did you talk with him about?"

"I tried to bring up getting a loan to farm this ground better next year."

Chess asked, "How'd that go?"

"Nowhere," Gill groaned. "Nowhere at all."

"What did he say?"

"It wasn't so much what he said, but it was how he said it. He acted like I'd cussed him because I was interested in making a loan."

They looked at each other. A worried expression came to Gill's face.

"What did you do?" Chess asked.

"Said something I wish I'd kept to myself."

"What?"

"Allen Sawyer Jr. now knows I know his secret."

"What secret?"

"Don't pretend you don't know," Gill said. He looked to ensure the boys were not near; they were not in sight. "I know what y'all did over to the Sawyer place years ago."

Chess said, "That damn Birdie Mae."

Gill frowned. "Mama Birdie Mae ain't told me that."

"Then, how you know?" Chess scowled as he leaned forward.

"My wife and I don't keep nothing from each other."

Chess stared at Gill. "I figured Sarah didn't know 'bout it."

"You figured wrong, she always knew."

Chess paused. "Birdie Mae think she don't know."

"That's one time Mama Birdie Mae's wrong. Sarah knows. She told me just before I married her."

"Hell, well, ain't that something. I thought your wife couldn't keep nothing."

"She sure kept that!"

"What did Mr. Al say?"

"Not much, but he got madder than hell, turned so red 'til I thought he'd explode."

"How did you say it? I sure wish you hadn't told him."

"I wasn't bold with it, but, Chess, you just don't understand. I didn't tell him. Allen Sawyer Jr. already knew. It was no surprise to him."

"Then, I wonder how he found out."

"Musta been his wife. It wasn't you and it wasn't Sarah. Mama Birdie Mae ain't spoke to him in over twenty years, so she didn't tell him." Gill paused, looked away and then directly at Chess. "It had to be his wife. She told him."

"She told him! How could she tell him? I didn't think she knew." Chess shook his head. "I wonder if his mother knew."

Gill shrugged and picked at a sorghum stalk. The two men sat there for a few moments. Neither made eye contact with the other.

Chess sought a safer subject. "How did things go when you picked up the supplies this morning?"

"It was worse than at the Sawyer place."

Chess twisted his face. He opened his mouth but Gill interrupted.

"Me and Rafe Coleman got crossways this morning. He

wants me to cook whiskey for him. He acted real crazy when I said this week was bad for me because of the molasses and cotton. I wish Papa Gillam never taught me to cook whiskey!"

"Gill, don't say that. Think of how many times you fed your family with that gift."

"Was it a gift or a curse?" Gill asked.

Chess shrugged in reply.

Chess said, "Rafe acts crazier than ever since he beat the hell out 'a Gee Gurley."

"Yeah, I know," Gill replied.

"Gee ain't his problem. His problem's that Bustie gal stopped going to his house. He crazier because he ain't getting no more of her sweet-potato pie."

That drew a smile to even Gill Erby's sour face. He looked at Chess Gordon and just shook his head. "There's more."

"What else?" Chess asked.

"I got into it with your fool son Johnlee after I left the stave mill."

"Last time I saw your momma-in-law, she said I ought to been sleep the night I got that fool." Chess paused; he chewed on the sorghum some more. "Hell, you know she right!" He howled with laughter, but Gill Erby remained serious.

"That fool fell down drunk out of his mind at 8:30 a.m. and went crazy on me when I tried to help him up."

Chess Gordon burst out laughing. "I'm sorry, Gill, but the look on your face. You looked like you mad enough to kill the both of them."

"Where Johnlee get something about me buying some land from you?"

"I told him," the old man said.

"You told him what?"

"I told him I was going to sell you this farm, the whole three hundred and fifty acres."

"Why you tell him something like that?"

"'Cause I am."

"And just how you think I'm gone pay for it?"

"Same way I did. Get you some niggers to farm it. That's one thing you got to learn, Gill Erby. You got to learn to think like a white man."

"Chess, what you talking 'bout?"

"I'm talking about you getting work done through other folks and working less yourself."

"What?"

"I got this farm and I kept it because I learned how to out-white-man a white man."

"When you decide all this and when was you gone ask me?"

"Hell, Gill, I ain't got to ask, you interested."

"Chess, I'm too old to get in that type of debt. Besides, Mr. Sawyer ain't gone loan me that type of money. I already had words with him over a loan to farm this place early in the season."

"Mr. Al would loan it to you if I told him to loan it to you. You shoulda said something to me. But he ain't got to loan you a dime to buy this place."

"How you think I can buy it then."

"Gill, open yo' mind. I can hold the note. This land's mine, free and clear."

"But where you gone live?"

"You know, I been wanting running water and an inside toilet for years. I got my eye on that Shea house down in town."

"Naw, Chess! You know the white folks ain't gone let you live there."

Chess Gordon laughed. "Don't tell me what white folks won't let you do. You just got to show them what's in it for them. The deed is in my safe, I already bought the place."

"Stop pulling my leg!" Gill Erby stared at Chess Gordon. "The white folks gone let you live in it?"

"Yeah, yeah, Allen Sawyer Jr. done cleared it with the Lucy muckety-mucks. That house is on the white side of the tracks, but it's the last house before you get to Nigger Hill. So, them good white folks gone let old part-Nigger Chess live there to enjoy his last few days."

"How do you do it?"

"Real simple, I think like white folks do."

Gill Erby stared in disbelief.

"Now, Gill, this place got four tenant houses on it. Half of the land in pasture and timber and the other half can be row cropped. Two of the tenants ain't cutting the mustard. I'm putting them out next week."

Gill continued to stare.

"Hell, Gill, this business. I ain't running no charity home. If you gone buy this place and cash flow it, you gone have to think the same way!"

Gill Erby stood there in disbelief. "Let me talk to my wife about it."

"I ain't talking to Sarah and I sure ain't asking mean-tail Birdie Mae. I'm speaking with Gillam Hale's boy about if he interested. Now, quit hemming and hawing around 'bout this."

The first real smile Gill Erby showed all day crept to his face. "Sure, I'm interested."

Chess laughed and shook Gill's hand.

"Chess, why you selling it to me instead of one of your offspring?"

Chess paused to think. "Lot of reasons, but the main one is this. I didn't raise my children right." He looked real old as he peered at Gill with true remorse. "Treated their mommas like dirt. They all got sick of me and left soon as they could. Zoar, my fourth wife, and she the first one I treated decent. She told me when I met her she wouldn't even keep company with me if I didn't treat her right." He paused. "But the main reason is your daddy made me promise this land wouldn't get back into white hands. I was watching you with that boy of yours. If you buy this farm and it gets to him, a white man will never get this place."

"Any specific white man you don't want to own it?"

"Hell, yeah!" Chess said. "And you know who that is!"

Chess and Gill heard Son and Tom shouting and rushed toward the house. As they approached, the two men saw the shocking source of the excitement. New molasses poured from the side of the wooden barrel into a rusty metal trough next to the porch. The two boys tried to put the stopper back into the molasses barrel. They could not because the hot, freshly cooked batch burned their hands.

"Son, put the barrel on its side! John-daddit! Lay it on its side! Damn, Damn, John-daddit to hell!"

Son finally followed Chess Gordon's instructions with the hole pointing upward. This stopped the spilling. When the two old men approached, Chess Gordon flew white-hot mad.

"Son, what in the hell is wrong with you? You spilled twenty gallons of the best molasses we cooked today!"

"Tom wanted to taste the molasses and I took the stopper out to give him some. I couldn't get it back in because they so hot."

Gill Erby looked down at the molasses mixed with dirt and chopped corn in the old metal trough. "Those molasses got so much grit in 'em now that they ain't fit for nothing but to make livestock sweet feed."

"Gill, take it for your livestock. Mine's gone be sold soon and I ain't making up no sweet feed for them." Cousin Chess looked up at Son and became even more agitated. "If you was my boy, I'd whip your tail. That's what I'd do. I'd just-whip-your-rear-end-good! Tom Coleman, you carry your narrow white ass home before I get some of it, too!"

Gill Erby's laugh boomed deep and loud and Chess Gordon did something he rarely did in public. He pulled off his hat and glasses. You could see his blind right eye. A vein popped up on the side of the old man's head. His face turned beet red. He threw his hat down and started to swear even more when it hit some molasses on the ground. Chess grabbed a handful of his solid white straight hair.

"Well, Chess, you always call him your boy." Gill Erby laughed even harder. "I always tells you to treat him like he was yours. So, you got my permission to whip him, like you always could."

Chess Gordon snatched his thick belt from his britches in one motion. He doubled the belt and grabbed Son by a sticky arm covered with hot molasses.

Tom Coleman jumped from the porch and ran toward his horse. Son hollered out loud. Bennie looked up from his work at the sorghum mill. Ole Dick stopped eating sorghum fodder and raised his head to witness this commotion. Despite all the noise, Ole Dan turned that sorghum mill; he knew what was happening.

Chess Gordon raised hell. He and the boy moved in a circular dance while the old man put the doubled leather belt on the boy's behind over and over and over.

Son Erby ended that day like Ole Dan started it, with a whipping that stuck.

31—EARLY HARVEST

Earlier in 1934, sparse April rains and dry days provided an opportunity for West Tennessee farmers to plant cotton and other crops early. Early planting translated to an early cotton harvest. Area farmers mixed cotton-picking time with their sorghum harvest and molasses cooking. The lack of even the slightest break meant they did not get that small rest they usually received between these two important events. Cotton prices sunk to an all-time low and folks felt the pressure of bad times. These circumstances added up to one thing. The 1934 harvest started in October with a bunch of tired and irritable people.

Jude Smith poured molasses over a big stack of yellow cornmeal pancakes. Bustie opened the back door and stepped into the small kitchen. She held a chamber pot in her hands.

"Bustie, you feel all right?"

"Naw, my stomach kind of queasy this morning." Testily, she added, "Jude, why don't you call me by my name? I hate Momma ever started calling me that."

Jude looked up at her and picked up a piece of thick bacon. Their eyes met when he bit down on the crispy meat. Neither he nor his wife spoke. They just looked at each other.

Lil' Red toddled into the room. Red curls covered his head. He walked over to Bustie. "Pot, pot," the young child said.

Bustie smiled. "Let me see if you in time." She reached under his nightshirt to find a dry diaper. She showed the baby her delight, "You're such a big, big boy." She loosened the diaper pin and sat the baby down next to her on the chamber pot.

"Jude, Sue Nell gone stay with the boys while I go over to Gill Erby's field on the Gordon farm to pick cotton. You ever speak with Mr. Chess about that house?"

Jude looked up after he forked more pancakes into his mouth. He started to chew. "Spoke to him the other day when I stopped to buy these new molasses," he mouthed between swallows.

She raised a full glass of water to her lips and swallowed most of the liquid in a series of gulps, but Jude said nothing else. Her husband continued his work on the pancakes. She looked down at Lil' Red. The look on his face showed he was taking care of his business.

"Good boy, that's just a big boy," she reassured the child.

"You got that boy going on the pot already?"

"Yeah, I saw him watching the other children, so I told him what to do." She made a funny face at the toddler. "We been working on it ever since. Right, big boy?"

Lil' Red smiled and jabbered. He held his hands straight up

and reached for his mother. She lifted him to his feet and attended to him. Thelma Louise laid the boy across her lap and arranged the cloth diaper around his waist. She looked over to check the pot and another wave of nausea engulfed her as she closed the diaper with a big safety pin.

Thelma Louise put the baby down on the wooden floor and covered the pot. She walked over to the old pie-safe cabinet and removed a box of baking soda. The woman shook a small amount of the white powder from the box into the water left in the glass. Bustie swirled the mixture and swallowed it down.

Jude stopped eating and looked over at his wife. "You all right?"

She nodded. "I ain't see'd anything since before the Frolic."

Jude crunched on another piece of the thick side meat, his only comment. He eyed his wife.

Lil' Red walked over to Jude. He reached his arms upward for the man to pick him up. "Da, da, da, da," the boy jabbered. Jude reluctantly scooped the thick toddler into his arms.

Thelma Louise sat back down in the chair next to the pie safe. "You hear me, Jude? I ain't see'd anything since before the Frolic."

Jude put a small fork of pancakes into Lil' Red's mouth. The toddler worked on the pancakes with his four baby teeth and gums. Jude smiled and ran his hands through the child's red locks. "When you gone cut this boy's hair?"

"You ain't supposed to cut a baby's hair too young."

Jude looked over at her. "This boy different than the children that was spoken about. It ain't gone hurt to cut his hair." He looked down at his now-empty plate and then his gaze returned to her face. He paused and added, "He's sure different." Jude ran his hand over the boy's hair again. "I better start my walk to the marble yard or old low-down Ely gone be mighty mad about me being late." Jude stood and lifted the baby high in the air over his head before handing the grinning child to his mother.

She looked up at him expectantly; her unmet need for reassurance showed all over her face.

"For some reason, Mr. Chess wants me to speak with Gill Erby about the house. I started to ask Mr. Chess what Gill got to do with it but thought better of it. I'll catch Gill sometime this week." Jude turned to pick up his old jacket from the back of the chair he'd sat in earlier. He slipped it on one arm at a time.

"Jude, I'm gone again."

"I heard what you said. When the baby due?"

"End of March, maybe the first of April."

"Da, da, da, da," Lil' Red drooled while he made sputtered lips.

Jude walked to the back door. He stopped to look at his wife and stood motionless at the screen for a moment. He snapped, "You know what the baby gone look like?"

She shook her head and looked at him. "I ain't been over there since before the Frolic, but I just ain't sure."

He stepped through the back door and slammed the screen door.

Jude walked through the backyard to the side of the house. He headed toward the front yard and Quito Road. The huge colored man whistled and turned east toward Lucy. He had no intention of another hard Monday at the marble yard; thoughts of Joy Street and the numbing allure of moonshine caressed his mind.

A frown came to his face, "Looks like we gone have an April Fool's baby next year."

★ ★ ★

In the front room, Sue Nell lay on the little cot she shared with Lil' Red. The girl heard the entire conversation between her parents. She thought of what she would face at school if the baby her mother carried looked like Lil' Red. She cried in silence.

"Y'all going to the field today?" After no verbal replies came from the crowd, the driver shouted again. "We'll give a free cold drink to anyone that works for us every day this week."

The members of the crowd mumbled among themselves but no one moved.

"They need another push," the man on the passenger side said. He shouted, "If y'all ain't got nothing to eat, we'll stand for your lunch until you get your day's wages."

After a considerable amount of murmurs and shrugs, a woman in the crowd asked the important question. "You say a free Co-cola?"

"Yes, ma'am!" the man behind the steering wheel replied. "Y'all get it Friday if you work for us for five days in a row." He paused to let it sink in. "And, like Chess here just said, I'm gone drive to town to get lunches from the store out of your daily pay if you ain't got nothing to eat. How's that sound?"

An elderly woman in the crowd shouted, "Mr. Rafe gets the pickers over here in Woodstock. He coming today?"

Chess Gordon opened the passenger door. He stood to his full height on the sideboard and looked over the top of the truck at the crowd. "Gill and I ain't talking to you about Rafe Coleman. Will Rafe Coleman buy you lunch in advance or give you a cold drink Friday?"

The mumbling ended. Three walked over to the vehicle and

climbed aboard. They moved to the front of the truck bed, climbed upon the tall side planks and grinned at their comrades. Slowly, others followed. Twenty workers packed the truck in less than two minutes.

Chess Gordon looked over at Gill Erby. "Told you! Soda pop and food always pushes the right button for folks around here." He laughed while Gill Erby smiled and just shook his head.

"Cousin Chess," Son Erby interrupted from his place on the truck seat between the men, "why we got to have so many folks?"

Chess Gordon banged his pipe on the passenger-side door. He squinted his only sighted eye to peep into the pipe and banged it again to complete the cleaning. "I been doing this for years, but this the first time your daddy went into commercial farming. That's why he needs more workers."

"Commercial farming, what's that?"

"Son, most folks farm just enough to make a living. They live on somebody's place and sharecrop or rent ten to fifteen acres of land. That's about all most families can handle alone."

"Papa, is that what we been doing?"

"Yeah, that's the size of it. We were living on the Coleman farm since way before I married your momma. Those fifteen acres over there was all we could handle."

"Gill, why don't you go back there to close the tailgate so we don't lose none between here and the field."

"All right," Gill Erby replied and he swung from the driver's-side door.

Chess Gordon struck a match on the truck dashboard. He nursed his pipe for a second. "Son," the old man began between puffs, "don't you forget this. The worst thing you can do is to only do what you can handle. All you need to do is to hire some other people." He puffed harder now. "Then you benefit from the money they make for you."

"Cousin Chess, why you smoke so much?"

Chess Gordon laughed. "Mostly habit. I started about your age."

"Why you do it?"

Cousin Chess answered the question with one of his own. "You ever tried tobacco?"

"Nosuh."

Chess Gordon looked to the left and then to the right. Gill Erby stood at the back of the truck squeezing one last worker onto the vehicle. "Here——" he handed the short black-and-brown pipe to the boy "——try you a puff."

Son quickly raised it to his lips. He puffed hard like he'd seen Cousin Chess do many times. The hot smoke filled his mouth and lungs and Son coughed hard. He handed the pipe back to a laughing Chess Gordon just seconds before Gill Erby put his hand on the driver's door handle.

"Y'all in the back stand clear of that tailgate. I don't want y'all to fall out."

Pride showed on Mr. Erby's face as he started the old truck. Cousin Chess nursed his pipe and blew the smoke out the window. Remnants of tobacco smoke lingered on Son's lips. He subconsciously added the love of tobacco to the many vices Chess Gordon taught.

Gill Erby turned the truck around and drove south through the Woodstock community down Hamlet Road to where it intersected with Woodstock Road. Professor Harris, the new young school principal at Woodstock Training

School, passed them headed west toward the school in his old car.

"Gill, Professor Harris might as well slow down. You got most of his class on the back of the truck."

The three laughed and Gill turned north for the short drive to Quito Road and Chess Gordon's farm.

"Chess, how much you think we can pick today?"

"Um, lemme see. You got some good hands back there. I know a few can pick three or four hundred pounds of cotton in a day. The children might pick just enough to pay for lunch and have some left over." He paused to run the numbers in his head. "We ought to get two thousand five hundred pounds out of this bunch today."

"That much in a day!"

"Yeah." Chess Gordon smiled.

"That means we'll do five acres today."

"No, that means this crew will do a little more than three acres."

Chess looked across at a puzzled Gill Erby. Son paid attention while the old man exhaled the last of the tobacco smoke and banged the pipe on the outside of the truck door.

"That's bottomland you farming and I rotate the crops on it. You ought to get a bale and a half per acre."

"A bale and a half!"

"Yes, sir! A bale and a half! That means seven hundred fifty pounds of grade A, half-and-half cotton."

"Chess," Gill Erby interrupted. "If we can keep these hands, that means we gone be through picking this fifty acres in about four weeks."

"Naw, we gone finish in about three. We're getting us some more hands. This just the first load! Me and Son here gone stay at the field and be the straw bosses while you drive over to Lucy to pick up another crew. I already had my brother Cephas talk it up for us at church yesterday. He got a whole truckload waiting for you."

"You got enough sacks for that many hands?"

Chess laughed. "I got more cotton sacks than you got hair on that bald head of yours." The truck filled with laughter. "Where were you and Son yesterday?"

Gill Erby looked around as if someone other than the three in the cab might hear. "Me and Son had a little business out at the Coleman farm. You understand?"

"Yeah, I understand. You know you ain't gone have time for that soon?"

"What you mean?"

"Don't forget your wife, Bennie and your other children picking over to where you stay. And somebody's got to drive this cotton to the gin." He pointed at Gill Erby with his pipe's mouthpiece. "My friend, this year that's you and not me."

"Hadn't thought of that," said Gill Erby.

The three grew quiet and Gill reviewed his many recent blessings. Chess Gordon filled his pipe for another nursing session. Son Erby daydreamed about his new habits and skills, some good and others bad.

His young mind raced. Two crews at two thousand pounds each. That's four thousand pounds in one day. The boy smiled and he looked up at the two most important men in his life. Son's wandering mind produced another thought when Gill Erby turned the truck west onto Quito Road to head for the field. Straw boss, he liked the sound of that.

32—EARLY BIRD

He patted the roll of crisp ten-dollar bills in his front right pocket. "That's another good piece of cash that nigger Gill Erby made for me and Conrad," he said aloud. "That boat captain acted so nervous this morning. I kept telling him that it wouldn't be no trouble 'cause I got everything fixed all the way to city hall, the county and even the feds!"

Rafe drove east on Cuba Road toward the Woodstock community. He passed the school when the tall Professor Harris got out of his automobile. The educator cordially waved, but Rafe exhibited his only recognition via his cold stare.

"I don't know what that nigger thinks he gone do today. Most of his pupils gone be picking my cotton." Rafe Coleman turned left onto Hamlet Road and drove north to the community where his steady cotton pickers lived. Less than ten workers stood together in a group about a half mile down the dirt road.

The white man swung the truck close to the workers on the left side of the road. Abruptly, he skidded to a stop too near them for comfort. A big cloud of red dust engulfed the group. "Omega," he said to the lady standing with the group, "go round the rest up. We got to get on to the field."

She made no eye contact; the woman replied slowly and carefully. "Mr. Rafe, ain't no mo' to round up."

"Omega, what the hell you talking about? I usually pick up near to thirty niggers over here in Woodstock."

"Another cotton truck came through here already. The others got on that truck and we the only ones left here."

Rafe Coleman flung the door to his truck open wide. He stepped down to the ground and pushed his hat back on his head. "Who picked them up and how long they been gone?"

She shifted her weight from foot to foot and replied, "Mr. Rafe, Gill Erby got 'em 'bout fifteen minutes ago."

Rafe's mind raced back to the fourteen dollars he'd handed Gill Erby last night for making the one hundred twenty gallons of whiskey that was now headed downriver to Memphis. He knew that wasn't enough to cash flow a truckload of cotton-picking hands all day at half a cent per pound plus sacks and incidentals.

"Hell, Omega," he pronounced it "Omiga" like the Negroes did, "anybody else with Gill Erby?"

"Yessuh, Mr. Chess was wit' him."

"Shhhittt! John-daddit to hell!" Rafe shouted and pulled his hat off simultaneously. He mumbled under his breath.

The ten workers fidgeted while Rafe reviewed his plight.

The crew included members of the two families that lived in the houses Rafe and Conrad owned on Hamlet Road. "Y'all get on back of the truck!" he fumed.

He mentally reviewed the faces of the missing workers in this area. Several bought groceries from him and Conrad on credit.

"Come Saturday, they gone wish they'd waited for me today," he vowed aloud. "I'll get these niggers started and then I'm driving to Lucy to pick up some more hands." He turned east on Cuba Road to head for his farm by way of Millington Road.

With a steely resolve in his voice, Rafe Coleman continued his solitary conversation. "Gill Erby and Chess Gordon getting too big for their britches. I'm gone bring them down a notch or two."

33—POLITICAL LESSONS

"Son, put that newspaper down and set this tripod and cotton pee up. I'd like to be ready for weighing before your daddy gets back with the next load of hands."

The boy placed the several-days-old copy of the *Memphis Press Scimitar* evening paper on the ground and carried the three-pole tripod back to where Chess Gordon sat.

"Where you want it, Cousin Chess?"

"You the straw boss out here, what you think?"

The boy squinted at the old man through the morning sunshine and shrugged.

"Ignorance ain't bliss. Hell, Son, it's a thinking world!"

Son surveyed his surroundings; he looked at the wagon placement and the field. Next, he noticed the position of the sun in the autumn morning sky.

"I think we ought to put it over there." He pointed to the other side of the wagon.

"And why over there, my young friend?"

Son looked straight at the old man. "It's near the wagon, so that'll make it easy to empty the cotton. And by noon, it'll give you and me a place in the shade between weighing sacks and writing the weights in the book."

"Huh," Chess Gordon snorted. He surveyed Son from head to toe. "You just might make something of yourself, you just might." The old man laughed and pulled on his pipe. "Get your book out and write the names of everybody in the field after you set everything up."

The boy started his tasks.

"Son," Cousin Chess interrupted, "what kind of world is it?"

The boy grinned wide, "It's a thinking world."

"Don't you ever forget it. You can figure out just about anything. Luck is a simple man's success. Chance ain't good enough!"

"Father, is this the one you want?"

Allen Sawyer Jr. looked up from his big desk. Amanda stood in the bank-office door with a large gray-and-red book in her hands.

"Yes, that's it. Bring it here and pull up a chair." He smiled and waited while Amanda complied with his directions.

"Father, what's in this ledger?"

"An accounting of the farm-operating loans the bank made the past several years."

He opened the book to a marked page halfway through the binder.

"We didn't make many loans this year. There are only a few people around these parts who do commercial farming. Most of them sharecrop and their landlords stand for the capital they need to operate."

Amanda leaned in toward the big desk. Her father watched her with interest while she studied the list of loans that filled about two-thirds of the thirteen-column page. Mr. Sawyer smiled while his daughter reviewed the details of each loan. He knew the girl understood to check the terms, including the amount, collateral values and interest rates.

"Father, why are these six columns marked stock prices?"

"That, my dear, is a smart thing your grandmother started years ago. You remember when we spoke last year about the Coca-Cola stock?"

"Yes, sir."

"Well, Grandmother convinced our farm customers to borrow an amount equal to the farm-operating loans to buy Coca Cola stock."

"How did she convince them of that?"

"Easy, she would not make the loan unless they agreed." Both father and daughter laughed in kind; each remembered the toughness of Alice Sawyer.

"Well, here's the real surprise. Our customers usually made more on the stock than they did farming."

Amanda's eyes widened. "Really!" she exclaimed.

"Yes, really. Let me show you the results so far this year." He put his hand on the column marked April. "We originated these loans in April. This is the price of the Coca-Cola stock on the day the Memphis Stock Brokerage purchased the shares on behalf of our customers. I tracked the prices for the end of each of the five months since we made these loans in early April. You remember how I explained to you before about that stock going up in value. What do you think of how the shares performed?"

Amanda put her finger on one line. Her eyes widened as she

understood the significant increase in the price over the six months. "Father, these increased by almost half!"

Allen Sawyer Jr. laughed. "People simply can't get enough of the great taste of Coca-Cola." He leaned back with a twinkle in his eyes. "And the bank makes more money because the amount borrowed doubles in size to purchase the stock. That means more interest income. But here's more good news— Lucy Savings Bank earns a commission of twenty percent on their profit."

"That's really smart!"

"God rest her soul. Mother deserves all the credit and not me."

"I recognize all the names but this one."

He looked to ensure his office door was closed. "Over the years, Lucy Savings Bank only loaned money to one colored man."

"Chess Gordon?"

"Yes, that's Chess Gordon and that's a special situation. The bank never extended credit to Nigras."

Amanda's blank stare made her father uncomfortable.

"I don't have to explain why we did it like that."

"Father, I understand. Grandmother first and now you didn't want to change."

"It's more complicated than that. Our customers would have a fit if we extended credit to colored people."

Amanda simply nodded and offered no reply.

"Amanda, we simply had no choice."

"Father, you and Grandmother are the bank! When you loaned money to Mr. Chess, you just did it because he was a good business risk."

"That was the main reason why," he replied, unnerved and

annoyed at his daughter's challenge. "But Chess Gordon also saved many of the white folks who survived the yellow fever epidemic."

"Yes, sir. But other colored people saved many of the people in Lucy in their own way." She paused before continuing. "They cooked the meals, raised the children, cleaned the houses, plowed the fields, chopped and picked the cotton, and some of them even nursed the children on their own breasts. If they were a good credit risk, we could have made loans to them as well."

They sat in a strained silence for a long time. Finally, Mr. Sawyer blew out the deep breath he had held inside since she spoke. "Daughter, you are right, but you're also wrong. Amanda, it's-just-not-that-simple! Would you like to come home one day and find ashes?"

Her eyes widened when his meaning struck like a ton of bricks.

"That is what's at stake, young lady. Do you understand now?"

She stammered, "Yes, sir."

"Over a year ago at Christmastime, you asked me to give some extra money to Sarah? Well, I gave her a little extra money. But that next spring, Gill Erby requested a loan to farm some land on Chess Gordon's place. I record every loan request, whether I approve it or not. This name is a code name for Gill Erby since I didn't even want to put a real request from him in our books."

Amanda looked expectantly at her father. "Did you secure Gill Erby's loans with Coca-Cola stock?"

"I declined that loan, never seriously considered it."

Amanda's eyes narrowed to small slits.

Allen Sawyer Jr. reared back in his chair, put his hands into his graying blond hair and crossed his fingers behind his head. "I never saw Gill Erby angry before that day. You would not believe the things he said to me. I'm still upset about it."

Amanda blew out a long sigh, crossed her arms and leaned back in her chair, too.

"You better scoot. The Coleman brothers are supposed to come by this afternoon. I need to review their existing loans so I'll be ready for their next scheme."

"Did you and Grandmother buy stock as collateral for their loans?"

"Of course not and I will not be loaning them any more money today either!"

"Morning, Ely," Rafe said to the marble yard superintendent.

"How do, Constable," the small, rotund white man replied as he walked toward the lawman's truck. "Surprised you ain't in the fields."

"Been once already, but I ain't got enough pickers," Rafe said to the superintendent.

Ely looked puzzled. "A truck passed headed west out of town a little while ago full of hands. I thought they was yours."

"Naw, wasn't mine." Rafe pushed the hat up on his forehead. "I believe I already know, but who was driving the truck?"

"That boy that live on yo' place, Gill Erby. Constable, you got nigger trouble?"

Rafe laughed. "Naw, no trouble, I just got to remind a few of 'em that I'm still the boss. I need a favor this morning."

He leaned into the window. "Speak to me, lawman." A wide grin showed half his front teeth missing and the remaining brown from tobacco stains.

"Ely, I need some help out to my farm. You keeping Jim Falls busy?"

"Try to, but you and I both know Jim ain't no count. I got half a mind to let him go."

"Well, I got a proposition for you. Let him work for me."

Ely shrugged his shoulders. "Constable, he wouldn't half pick his own cotton when he sharecropped with you." He scratched his head under his old felt hat. "Me and somebody laughed a week or two ago about all that cotton him and his wife left in the field a couple of years ago."

"Well, I don't need him to pick. I need somebody to help me keep the few niggers I got on the move."

"I see." He stood back and scratched his round belly through the place missing a button on his shirt. "That's mostly what I use him for here because he ain't gone do no work. What's it worth for him to come to work for you?"

"I'll give you ten dollars."

"Sweeten that pot."

"Tell you what, finish your big orders first. I'll get the money by here next week and I'll do something else." Rafe grinned. "I'll see to it you get a gallon of whiskey every month for the next three months."

"Rafe, I don't know."

"I'll make it a whole gallon of whiskey a month for six months. You in or not?"

"Ten dollars and six gallons of whiskey, just to let you have Jim Falls. Huh, I'd get rid of the whole crew I got here for that. I'm in!"

"What Jim Falls getting per day from you?"

"A dollar a day."

"That trash ain't worth that."

"I pay the colored boys seventy-five cents and I got to pay him more."

Rafe Coleman shook his head. "Well, you really get the best of this whole deal 'cause he ain't worth fifty cents. When can I take him?"

"He's around back writing some letters on a stone one of the other boys got to cut later today. You can get him right now." He took ahold of Rafe's arm. "Constable, when you gone get the money and them goods by here?"

"By next Wednesday, you'll be sipping free whiskey and counting cash."

"Raford, you might want to hire Jude Smith, too," Ely goaded. "I let him go last week. He came late, when he came at all. Now, how's Jude and his wife gone feed that redheaded toddler I see in the yard over their house?"

Rafe gunned the truck engine and abruptly drove behind the marble yard building to strike a deal with Jim Falls.

34—UNPLANTED HARVEST

The Erbys finished their cotton harvest at the bottomland they rented from Chess Gordon and at the sharecroppers homestead on the Coleman place. That autumn in 1934, Gill Erby experienced his best harvest ever.

"Son, where'd you put them gritty molasses you and Tom messed up over to Chess's house a few weeks ago?"

"They're in that steel barrel next to the barn."

"After breakfast, get about six buckets of chopped corn and a bale of hay out of the crib to make some sweet feed for the cows and mules out it."

"Papa, I'll do it right now," the boy said before he rose from the table. He put his empty plate into the dishpan on the countertop. With just a little direction, the robust fifteen-year-old could already do more work than most full-grown men.

A cool autumn breeze greeted the boy. The season change

had started in earnest and the tree colors had turned multiple shades of orange, brown, red and yellow. The muscular lad moved toward the barn and headed straight for the barrel. He immediately noticed the top to the steel drum was slightly off center. The boy touched the lid and felt the heat of the sun already beginning to warm the barrel and its contents, even on a cool late-October morning.

Son removed the steel lid and a familiar aroma rose to greet him. This smell at this place and time surprised the boy. He put the lid back in place. The boy turned toward the house just when Papa Gill came out of the kitchen door. The old man pulled at his overall shoulder straps and stretched his thick arms skyward.

Son waved his arms to draw his father's attention.

"What is it now?" he shouted and walked over to Son.

"Papa," the boy said in a hushed voice, "this lid was partway off the barrel. I put it on the barrel and I don't know how it got moved off. The barrel is almost full from the rain we been getting."

"That ain't a problem. The sweet is still in there, so we can still make feed from it."

"Well, remember there was also corn in that trough when me and Tom spilled those molasses."

Gill Erby shrugged his shoulders.

The boy took the top off the barrel. "Smell this."

The sticky, sweet fumes of corn whiskey mash greeted Gill Erby's nose.

"Lordy mercy!" He walked over to the barrel and placed both hands on the rim of the steel drum. "Lordy mercy," he repeated and shook his head. Mr. Erby put the middle and index fingers of his left hand into the barrel. He raised them to his mouth for a taste. The old man laughed.

"Son, you so good at making whiskey you even makes it by accident." That declaration brought a laugh from both father and son. "Boy," Gill Erby continued, "I guess we need to figure out what we gone do with fifty gallons of corn mash."

"But, Papa, how'd it make by itself?"

Gill Erby laughed. "Simple, molasses for sugar and corn for plant material. The good Lord supplied the water through his rain and—" he pointed toward the early-morning sun "—the heat!" Deep roaring laughter erupted from him after the prospect of selling this large quantity of whiskey settled on Gill Erby. Once again Son joined in the merriment.

Sarah Erby approached and asked, "Mr. Erby, what's so funny?"

Gill Erby placed the top on the steel drum tightly and said, "Now, Baby, sometimes a lady ought not to ask two men why they laughing."

"That doesn't count for old men and boys."

Mr. Erby tenderly ushered her toward the house. "Who you calling old?" Before she could reply, he called to his boy. "Son, clamp that barrel closed." He winked at him. "We'll handle that directly. Why don't you and Bennie just clean the stalls out and then load the last of the cotton in the wagon. We'll take it to the Coleman gin when I get back. I need to go talk to Chess Gordon about what you and me just discussed."

35—NATURE STUDY

The cloudless night sky showcased every star. He loved to look at them and wonder how God made each. He arrived at his usual conclusion. God made everything out of nothing and everything made was good.

A hoot owl broke the silence with a distant call and brought him back from his meditation. There was much to do, and unlike the Lord, Gill Erby and his boys had traveled here to make something out of something. Two days earlier when Chess Gordon heard about the accidental whiskey, the two men developed a plan to cook and sell the moonshine.

Gill listened to the drone of a tugboat on the river in the distance. The Mississippi lay a mile due west as the crow flies. The three Negroes worked way back in the woods near Saint Paul and Ray Bluff Road.

Many memories, both good and bad, filled his mind. He flashed a broad grin in the darkness while he thought about what he and the two boys needed to get done this cool October evening.

A screen made from the old tarp he always kept on the truck was draped over three small bushes. This barricade blocked any view of the fire from the west. Their position and the natural shape of the hill to their backs would not reveal the location to anyone approaching from the east, north or south.

Fresh clear water flowed from the old spring. It was amazing that the trio sat just thirty minutes north of downtown Memphis, but there they stood with the hill to their backs and sides and an open meadow below. The farmers who rented this land from Chess were through with their corn crop. So their enterprise would receive no interruptions.

Gill had added just a little yeast to the sweet mixture the day before. By nightfall, it had churned like a boiling pot and the brew worked off the remaining sugar into alcohol. But now the whiskey mash had a peaceful look to it and its top appeared like the crust on an egg meringue-covered pie.

"Boys, cooking overnight will finish this."

"Papa, the mash already produced alcohol. So why did you need to put more yeast in the mash?"

"Some alcohol was made, but the mash still tasted sweet. That means there's still sugar in it, so there's more alcohol to be made. I put the yeast in to work off the rest of the sugar. That way we'll get more whiskey out."

"Where'd you get that cooker?"

"Chess helped me fix this contraption up. It ain't pretty, but it'll work."

Bennie Gorlan scratched his head in bewilderment.

"What's the matter there, Bennie?" Gill Erby asked. "You ain't seen a whiskey still?"

The young man shook his head.

"Step over here and let me make you familiar with one. Son and I done plenty of this type work." He added with pride, "But this the first we cooked of our own. Right, Son?"

The boy smiled and nodded while he poured the first bucket of cool water into a big half-wooden barrel. He thought of clearing more crop land in the bottom for molasses next year and how this would not be the last whiskey he cooked without sugar from a white man.

Bennie stepped closer and Mr. Gill's tutelage began.

"Now, this is known as a *number 2 cooker*. It ain't the biggest, but it ain't the smallest neither. Son, don't you think it's a good time to kick it off?"

The boy smiled in the dark as he stepped up closer to the hillside where the base of the whiskey cooker sat. He retrieved a match from his pocket and struck it against a stone. The boy expertly protected the flame with his right hand. He laid it on the pile of wood scraps underneath the copper kettle. The fire they laid in earlier roared greedily to life.

"My favorite time is when the fire first starts. Bennie, notice this kettle," Mr. Erby said, pointing at the old copper instrument shaped like a potbellied stove with a narrow smokestack on top. Earlier, the three placed half of the fifty gallons of mash inside the kettle.

"When this kettle gets hot, the liquid in the mash turns into steam." He pointed to a long, straight copper tube that came from the very top of the kettle. "You call this the worm. It moves the steam across to the cooling station." His hand waved down the path of the curved piping from the kettle to the top of a ten-gallon wooden barrel. That barrel was connected to an open fifty-five-gallon wooden barrel with another iron pipe.

"You and Son need to keep this open barrel full of cool water. When the whiskey starts to cook, the worm pipe takes the steam through the top of the small wooden keg and into the water. That cools off the steam and changes it to liquid. It runs out this end and we catch it in a bucket. The last step is to pour it into those five-gallon jugs."

Obviously bewildered, Bennie scratched his head. "What is it when it turns to liquid?"

Gill Erby chuckled. "Some call it mule kick, ole john, or God's wine. Other folks name it white lightning or back-alley John. I met a man one time that said it was panther piss." He chuckled. "To me, it's just another cash crop folks buy."

Bennie still looked confused.

"It's white-lightning whiskey, Bennie," Son interrupted.

The flames crackled and sputtered; their intensity grew. It would not be long now before the heat rose in the barrel above the fire pit dug into the bank.

"Seems like I done this a thousand times, but each time's different. Y'all better fetch the jugs." Gill laughed. "This'll be your last empty-handed trip." He knew their next ones would be to carry full five-gallon jugs of whiskey to the truck.

Gill Erby used this spot in the old days when he first started to cook whiskey for Mr. Rafe. Back then, Jude helped him a few times. That was way before Son was old enough. This time, the contents in the whiskey cooker in front of him belonged to him. A smile showed on his face; he thought of what he would do with the money as he dozed off.

It was a quiet night, very quiet. A distant owl flew closer and eventually stopped in the huge white oak overhead. He called out for some twenty minutes. A snort nearby sounded like a male deer. Gill Erby dozed while the youngsters tended the cooker.

The work progressed smoothly and forty gallons of whiskey sat in the truck when Mr. Erby woke up to take a shift. The three ate snacks of eggs and fresh sweet potatoes Son cooked in wet newspaper in the whiskey-fire ashes.

"Fellows, this just like we done when I was a boy," Mr. Erby said. He pulled out his pocket watch to check the time. "Two-thirty in the morning. Keep going because I want that fire out at daybreak."

To the east, a loud squeaking, but almost barking sound rang out from just over the hill. Another animal made the same rousing sound again and again to the west. A third creature of the same species answered with an equally ferocious little cry of its own.

"Papa, what's that?" an alarmed Son asked.

Gill Erby smiled in the firelight. He opened his mouth to answer the boy, but Bennie beat him to it.

"Son Erby, don't be so scary. That ain't nothing but squirrels barking!" Proud of his expertise, Bennie stood more erect and he poured another bucket of cool springwater into the half barrel.

The three broke into laughter at the thought of Son being scared of a squirrel.

Mr. Erby thought of a trick worth playing. "Y'all want squirrel and gravy for breakfast?"

"Yessuh! It ain't nothing better than squirrel and gravy," Bennie answered.

"Take this empty pan and a bucket of that spent mash to that grove of trees where you hear those squirrels. If you put this mash out, the squirrels will taste out of it. By daybreak, they'll be so drunk you boys can walk through and hit squirrels in the head with a stick."

"Papa, you funning us?"

"Naw, I done it myself," Gill Erby lied with a straight face. "Squirrels smell the corn and come to it. There's still enough alcohol in here to get anything that eats it drunk. Go on and I'll watch the still."

The always hungry Bennie took the bait first. "It's worth a try for some squirrel and gravy."

"Papa, you up to something," Son said.

The squirrel barking continued in the background.

"Son, just keep thinking about that tender meat with brown gravy Mama Birdie Mae gone put with it." Papa's eyes twinkled in the firelight.

Bennie picked up the bucket of mash and Son grabbed a wide pan. Without further debate, they walked over the hill toward the squirrel barks. A snipe hunt, of sorts, began.

Gill Erby leaned back and looked up at the stars. He gazed at the whiskey-still spout. A steady stream of liquid cash poured into the wooden bucket. Mr. Erby smiled wide about the hopeless wild-goose chase the two scared boys just started. But his grin really began with visions of his crop.

"All this fun and 'um getting paid for having it."

36—PLOTS AMONG KIN

"Everybody gone?"

"Jim Falls was the last one. I ain't seen or heard from him in over an hour."

Rafe pulled a pint of sealed Canadian whiskey from his desk drawer. "Well, Cousin Johnlee, sit down and have you a drink."

"Rafe, don't you start that cousin shit."

"Now, Johnlee, you know my daddy and your daddy two brothers. That makes me and you first cousins."

Johnlee eyed the whiskey. "Whole lot of good that's doing me. I'm just a seasonal hand who works in your gin."

Rafe pulled two Mason jars from another drawer and kicked the cane-bottomed chair next to the desk toward Johnlee. "Rest a spell and take a drink." Rafe broke the seal on the bottle and poured the brown whiskey into a jar.

Johnlee's eyes widened when the liquor level passed the middle of the jar.

"Hell, sit down," he added and he poured a second drink in the other glass. Johnlee took a seat. Rafe nodded toward the first and bigger drink as he picked up the second jar.

"Past the teeth and over the gums, look out gullet 'cause here it comes." Rafe drank the jar's contents in a series of gulps.

Johnlee followed suit but never took his eyes off Rafe.

Rafe poured himself another and Johnlee returned his jar to the desktop. Rafe put a small amount in his glass and loaded Johnlee's jar up again.

They raised the jelly jars a second time. Johnlee gulped like a man not used to things. Rafe calculated his next move and sipped slowly this time.

"Know something, Johnlee? I've intended to speak with you." Rafe paused to sip his whiskey.

"What's that?" Johnlee returned his empty glass to the desk.

Rafe filled the glass even higher and spoke. "I just wondered what you and your siblings would do with Chess's farm if something was to happen to him. You know, your daddy's on up there and y'all need to think about things like that."

"Don't even bring that bastard up." Johnlee's nostrils flared; he smelled the whiskey in the jar and took another sip. "One thing's for sure—my brothers and sisters hate the country. They moved to Memphis or up North and said they was never coming back here!" He frowned and took another big swallow. "Hell, Daddy used to work us like we was slaves."

"I know what Ole Chess did."

"You know, he divorced Momma the other week. Didn't give her nothing after all the work we did."

"Naw!" Rafe feigned.

"Yeah, Momma called for me over to Mama Sam's. You know I'm renting a room from her in the back of her place right now." He paused to take another gulp. The effects of the whiskey hit Johnlee's weary body and empty stomach; he slurred his next comments. "Momma cried something terrible. She got eight children by that nigger." He looked down and paused, shook his head before he lifted his eyes to meet Rafe's. "And all he did was beat her and call her a black hag!"

"Johnlee, that's just awful." Rafe had witnessed his daddy beating his mother, too, and Johnlee's comments surfaced suppressed memories. "One thing everybody got in common— all of us got to die. That includes Chess Gordon." He finished his drink, remembering the black eyes his mother stayed home to hide.

"I'll drink to that!" Johnlee crowed.

The whiskey concealed and numbed their pain.

"If something was to happen to Chess, you and me could sign a legal agreement for me to loan you the money to buy out your brothers and sisters. We could agree for me to buy that place from you at a nice profit. What you think of that?"

Johnlee presented the Mason jar a fourth time. His eyes looked like drowsy slits. "John-daddit, I never thought of that, but it sounds good to me." He cocked his head to the right side and mulled over the idea in his clouded mind. "How much of a profit?"

Rafe poured Johnlee another drink and then paused as if he had not already thought this out entirely. "Um, five hundred dollars would be a good amount. Don't you think?" He pushed the half-filled jar toward Johnlee.

Johnlee grasped the glass and raised it to his lips. He paused. "Don't know," he slurred. "You got me in a world a trouble the last time I helped you trick some kinfolk."

"You still remember that?" Rafe frowned. "That been twenty

years ago. Besides, that was different. That involved a gal. This ain't nothing but business!"

"Yeah, but Cousin Birdie Mae still hate me over that."

"Hell, Johnlee, ain't anybody got to know 'bout this but me and you."

37—ONCE A MAN, TWICE A CHILD

The bathtub stood on big claw-type feet. Curved lines and deep sides formed its deep bathing chamber. The end where you sat sloped gently back into a comfortable reclining position. She helped him step into the tub and he moved his hands backward and forward. His silly motions produced little-boy splashes that escaped the tub's steep white-enameled sides.

"Boy, quit splashing that water," Zoar reprimanded him, and kneeled to help with his bath. "You got water all over my new yellow blouse."

Chess looked at her through merry eyes. "No, ma'am. I ain't gone quit. That is, unless you gets in this tub to make me."

"Now, Chess Gordon, I ain't getting in a tub with you!"

"And why not?" He grabbed the sides of the big bathtub and moved side to side. "There's plenty of room."

"Stop, boy! You getting me wet! Be still so I can wash your back."

"I'll sit still for that."

"Huh," she replied, "you grinning like the cat that ate the canary."

"Me? Girl, the only canary here is one in a pretty, yellow blouse. Besides, a canary always safe with me."

Zoar ignored his suggestions and lathered his back with the P&G soap and a soft brush. "Chess, when we gone move in here?"

"Sunday night."

"Why Sunday night?"

"I got four reasons, but the most important one is that Rafe Coleman will be out of town."

"Why is that important?"

"Well, possession nine-tenths of anything. When he finds out I own this place, you and me already will be in here. About that same time, he bound to find out I sold my farm, his old family-home house, to Gill Erby."

She completed washing his back and rinsed it with warm water. "That's just three reasons. What's the fourth?"

"Gill Erby and Jude Smith gone do all the moves. The last move they do will be to move Bustie and Jude into the empty tenant house on the west end of the farm."

Zoar continued his bath by soaping his shoulders and chest. "You and Mr. Gill sure y'all want in the middle of that?"

"Zoar, I'm tired of standing by and watching white men take colored women. Rafe Coleman's granddaddy did it with my momma and didn't give us a damn thing! That's why I took what I got! Then, Allen Sawyer did the same thing with Birdie Mae's momma."

"What Miss Birdie Mae got to do with Allen Sawyer Jr.?"

"I ain't speaking about junior. His daddy, Allen Sr., was her daddy."

"You never told me that. Mr. Allen Sawyer over to the bank is Miss Birdie Mae's half brother?"

"Yep, sure is. Her mother had two sons and Birdie Mae by that old man. The boys died in the first fever epidemic along with his first wife. He married a younger woman after that. That was Mr. Al's momma, Miss Alice. Soon as old man Sawyer got killed, Miss Alice put Birdie Mae and her momma off the place without a penny."

"Oh, my! So Sarah is the niece of Allen Sawyer Jr.?"

"Yeah, she's his niece, but she's his maid just about every day of the week, too. She keep house for him and ought to own part of the house."

Chess Gordon reclined in the spacious tub as Zoar washed his hairy chest.

"That's why I'm trying to do a little something for Jude and Bustie. Rafe got that baby over there by Bustie, but he doesn't do for her."

"I hear she gone again."

"Huh," Chess grunted and shook his head.

"Yeah, and I bet only time can tell if it's Rafe's baby or if it's Jude's."

"Well, Jude came to see me about moving on my place. I told him to speak to Gill and he did. Jude can be a good worker."

"When he works," Zoar added.

"Well, Gill's willing to take him on."

"That's a lot a bitter pills for crazy Rafe to swallow all at once."

"Yeah, but it's time for him to swallow some of what he

makes other folks take. He moved back here as a young man just so he could take the farm back from me. That's why that paddy hit me and put my eye out!"

"Now, Gordon, don't get your head all steamed up. You know how it goes when you start talking about that. That was twenty years ago when y'all got to fighting."

"Huh, only got one regret over that. I shoulda killed him when I had the chance."

Zoar hit him on the shoulder. "Quit talking like that."

"Well, it's true. He needs killing. I'm old now, but he knows I still would kill him if I have to."

"Gordon, you ain't that old."

"Get in this tub and I'll prove you right."

"Go away from here, Chess Gordon."

"You know. Rafe's kind of crazy in a way about that piece of land. I just don't know why. But that bastard ain't gone get it back. Never!"

"I just hope you know what you doing."

"Rafe's bark worst than his bite."

"Tell Gee Gurley that," she said. "He doing 11-29." Zoar referred to 11 months and 29 days, a standard southern prison sentence for the downtrodden who committed no real crime but show up at the wrong place and wrong time.

"I ain't Gee Gurley. Rafe know not to mess with me."

"Yeah, but what about Gill Erby and Jude Smith?"

Chess pursed his mouth and shook his head with an ease and rhythm. He scooted under the deep water in his bath. Surfacing to wash soap from his eyes with his hands, he replied, "Only so much I can do, only so much."

The bathroom grew silent and he turned to look at her. "There's another thing I need to tell you. You know I went down to Memphis to the lawyer to get the papers put together for Gill Erby to buy the farm. Well, I also did some other things. I got my final divorce from my last wife so you and I can get legally married now."

Zoar smiled wide. She grew up poor and security was a concern for her.

"That ain't all. Me and Gill Erby went to Memphis last week. We paid up the money for the new government social security pension. So, if anything happen to me or to Gill, you and Sarah can draw our pensions." He paused to look at the younger woman. His affection and concern showed on his face. "I put this house in your name, paid for free and clear. And I put those three hundred acres I own in Tunica County, Mississippi, in your name."

"Chess, you know I didn't marry you for money," she protested. "I just told you to treat me right."

"Girl, this is part of treating you right. Now, there's one other thing. When Gill buys the farm, he gets everything except the cemetery plot. I put that in your name and you own an easement across the farm to have access to it. You bury me out there when I die. After I'm gone, I want you to deed it to Son Erby. But don't you do it before Rafe Coleman's dead. You hear?"

"Chess, quit all this talk about dying. You'll probably outlive me."

He became even more serious and turned to put his wet hands on both of her arms. "Zoar, this real important to me. Do what I ask you on this."

She kissed him on the mouth. "Gordon, don't I always do what you ask me."

He smiled and began to laugh. A puzzled look formed on her dark brown, round face. His laughter turned into a howl.

"What's so funny?"

He stopped grinning and faked a pout. "You didn't get in the bathtub when I asked you."

A happy Zoar Gordon reached for the top button of her yellow blouse. "One canary coming in!"

38—OTHER FOLKS' BUSINESS

An eavesdropper waited a sufficient amount of time after Rafe and Johnlee left before he crawled from the same hiding spot in the cotton gin loft where Bennie Gorlan listened to the July third interlude between Bustie and Rafe. He stretched his body before coming down the narrow ladder.

His eyes found the door to the gin office. He tested the door and marveled at his good fortune when he found it unlocked. Moonlight from the office window greeted him inside the small space. He saw the near-empty fifth of whiskey on the desk, raised the open bottle to his lips and took a long drink.

She lay in bed listening to the night sounds. The low fire in her old cookstove made gentle pops and hisses. In the distance, a lone whip-poor-will issued occasional midnight calls. She heard Ole Dan acting up in the barnyard. A cow mooed softly, as if she called her calf for a nighttime feeding.

Birdie Mae Lilliard lay awake. She was not sure of the time but knew it to be some time well after midnight. The old lady slept fewer hours than usual, even for her. The little room off the kitchen seemed lonely to the old woman. Soon, she thought, we'll be where the whole family can sleep under one roof.

Miss Birdie reviewed the previous evening when Sarah came home from the Sawyer residence...

"Momma, you got another one of them letters. Who always writes you every few months from Virginia? You ain't never been up there. Who you know in Virginia anyway, Momma?"

"Sarah Erby, take care of your business and quit trying to take care of mine."

"But, Momma, it's just peculiar, never a return address on the envelope and always the same neat and pretty handwriting."

Mama Birdie Mae glared over her shoulder and she stirred the stew.

"The postmark always said Morristown, Virginia until today. This one came from right here in Lucy. You reckon your secret friend done come to Lucy?"

"Girl, give me my letter!"

Sarah paraded over to where her mother stood at the stove. With a grin, she handed the brown envelope to her, and Mama Birdie Mae turned back to her cooking.

The old woman made a big production when she snatched the letter from Sarah's hand and put it in her middle apron pocket.

Sarah walked back to the long kitchen table. She sat down and smiled at her mother. "You ain't gone open it?"

Mama Birdie Mae tasted the stew but made no reply.

"Momma, ain't you at least going to open the letter?"

Her mother ignored her once again.

"Momma!"

"I should a beat you mo' when you was a child."

They laughed and Mama Birdie Mae picked up a folded cloth and turned back to the stove. She spoke while bending over to pull a large pan of corn bread from the oven. "Go tell the children dinner ready."

"Yessum. I guess I better go before you beat me."

"Heifer," Miss Birdie said. She smiled while lying in bed that night. She got out of bed and struck a match. The single flame illuminated the little bedroom and she used it to light the wick of a kerosene lamp. Mama Birdie Mae squinted at the postmark. It read, Lucy, Tennessee. "Somebody mailed this letter right here in town." She tore open the end of the envelope and pulled out its contents. Like always, the brown parcel held three twenty-dollar bills inside beautiful stationery. Except, this time, something was different. The agreement was for the stationery to be blank, but this time the paper contained a note.

I am home in Lucy for the first time in over fifty years. I cannot wait to see you. Sincerely, Baby Sister. P.S. I met Allen Sawyer's daughter yesterday. She is tall and beautiful just like her grandmother at that age. I am going to make it a point to cultivate a relationship with her.

Birdie Mae stood there for quite a while rereading the brief note in disbelief. Finally, she pocketed the money. The old fair-skinned colored woman didn't quite know what to make of this note. Her eyes landed on her beautiful cook stove. She chronicled its ornate floral markings, the hot-water heater built into the side of the wood box, six oversize cook isles and the big oven.

"Girl, I paid for this stove with your twenties. You know you done helped me a lot over the years with all the money you sent me. But, Baby Sister, you playing with fire right now. You playing with fire. Why on earth would you come back here? And why you tell me about getting close to that girl?"

Birdie Mae did what she always did when a letter came from Media Coleman Sneed. She removed the isle top, leaned over the stove and placed the envelope and note directly onto the hot coals. The old woman watched the flames totally consume both. That's when the meaning of the note came to her. "Damn, Chess Gordon told her!"

"Why're you up, young lady?"

Amanda Sawyer turned to see her father looking at her from the kitchen door. "Hello, Father. I couldn't sleep so I came downstairs for a glass of milk."

"That sure is an odd glass of milk." He pointed to the piece of chocolate cake on a saucer in the girl's hands.

"The milk needed something with it. Since Sarah baked this for me today, I thought I should eat a piece."

"A convenient excuse."

"Father, did you know a lady named Media when you were a boy?"

"Did I know Media? Sure I did. I was too young to really get to know her, but my mother told me all about her. Mother said her hair reached her ankles and every boy around here thought she was the prettiest girl in these parts. What makes you bring her up?"

"I stopped in to visit the high school today and she came with Miss Ruth to pick up Tom Coleman. They checked him out early to drive to Memphis."

"You met Media Coleman Sneed. Do you realize who she is?"

Amanda buried a big piece of cake in her mouth. She shook her head no.

"She left here near the end of the second yellow fever epidemic. Have I told you that story?"

"The one of how Mr. Chess saved your life with this concoction from the slave days. Oh, no, Father, you have never told me that one," she mocked with exaggerated excitement and a falsetto voice.

"Children, what is coming of them these days? The important thing is you met Media Coleman Sneed. She grew up right here in Lucy. Mother arranged for her to take the Coleman brothers to Virginia to raise them after both their parents died in the epidemic. Media was about eighteen when they left. She met a rich young man just after they arrived. He fell madly in love and married her so fast that Mother said it made your head swim. Your grandmother and I took the train north to attend the grand affair."

"You remember it after all the years?"

"Daughter, you don't forget weddings like that. It was like royalty marrying. Her husband went on to become a congressman and later a senator from the state of Virginia. Besides, that's when I first met your mother."

"Oh, so that's the real reason you remember."

Mr. Sawyer smiled and nodded his head in short quick motions. "How was Mrs. Sneed?"

"She seemed fine. She is a very pretty lady, even at her age now."

"Describe her to me."

"What do you mean?"

"How did she look?"

"Describing a woman for my father seems odd."

"No, eating chocolate cake at 1:00 a.m. is odd. Now, tell me about Media Sneed."

The girl struggled to swallow another big bite. "Petite with beautiful light brown eyes. Her complexion is very fair and her lips were small and kind of cute. She has evenly grayed hair, like salt and pepper mixed half and half in a single shaker. She wore it pulled back into a neat arrangement on the back of her head. It was kind of plaited with a ball at the end. Her hair must still be very long because the ball was so big it looked almost like a small hat." Amanda paused to drink her milk.

"Speaking of hair, what are you going to do with that thick mop you got back there? It's gotten mighty long."

Amanda blushed and reached back to fluff her thick mane of dark brown hair. "I don't know. It's so thick and it's hard to manage at times. But I just don't want to cut it short."

"Well, you're old enough to decide that. And next year, on April first, you'll be twenty-one and you'll get to decide many more things."

"You mean my trust fund."

"That is exactly what I mean. What else did you notice about Media Sneed?"

"What do you mean?"

"I don't know. I'm just curious."

"That's about all I remember about her looks. She's a pretty lady, nice dresser also." She put another piece of cake past her lips. "One thing seemed odd. After the school office monitor left to get Tom, Miss Ruth introduced us. She told Mrs. Sneed I was your daughter." Amanda paused. "Father, she just stared at me. It made me a little uncomfortable."

He looked alarmed and for a time made no reply. "Well," he started, "I don't know why she did that, but," he lied, "I know this. If Media is anything like my mother described, she is one of the sweetest persons you could ever meet. She and Mother became quite close before she moved away. She helped Mother adjust to the Southern ways and always admired Mother's beauty."

"So, she is nothing like Rafe Coleman, I presume."

Walking toward the girl, Allen Sawyer, Jr., replied, "No, she's definitely not like her brother Rafe. I will see you in the morning, young lady." He kissed her on the forehead.

"Good night, Father. Tell me in the morning about your dreams of Media Coleman Sneed."

39—BIRTHING A BABY

Spending time in a home alive with laughter and the footsteps of even one child was a treat this woman had not known in years. She enjoyed time with Tom again. Her first day with the family confirmed what she learned from his behavior during his six-week stay at her home—he was a sweetheart of a child. She laughed when she told him she would take him to see the mayor of Memphis. Tom piped up, "You mean Mayor Jones?"

"No," Aunt Media replied, "I mean, Boss Crump, the real mayor."

Even young Tom understood.

Media Coleman Sneed lay awake in the guest bedroom at the home of Conrad and Ruth Coleman. She offered to take a suite at the Peabody in Memphis but gladly accepted Ruth's invitation.

Tomorrow, she would visit Brother. After that, Media had to see Birdie Mae Lilliard, who'd changed her life years ago.

She had not been prepared for the bold scheme her friend had suggested when Rafe and Conrad's mother mistook her for her daughter, Media.

She still vividly remembered the horrible stench of death that day during the summer of 1878. She was one of three young Negroes who entered the parlor of Miss Mary Coleman, wife of Raford Coleman Jr. "Media, come help me wake your daddy up."

Brother, Birdie Mae and Baby Sister just looked at each other.

"I told you," Brother whispered. He turned his head away from the white woman whose unstable mental state was apparent.

Birdie Mae whispered, "Brother, where Media?"

A young Chess Gordon whispered a reply, "She in her room god-awful sick with the fever. If she don't get better soon, she gone die, too."

"I'm gone to see about her," Birdie Mae said.

The slender young mulatto walked across the porch area while Baby Sister and Chess stood at the edge of the parlor. Baby Sister cried. She even felt sorry for the nasty, hateful young Rafe, who sat in a daze on the parlor sofa next to his mother as she held baby Conrad in her arms.

During the wagon ride to the farm on Quito Road, Brother told them Raford Jr. died over four weeks earlier, but Miss Mary wouldn't let him bury the man. The stench from the decaying body met you in the yard. The body of Raford Coleman Jr. still lay just a few feet away in his open coffin.

Baby Sister wondered about the thoughts in Rafe III's already twisted mind. He stared at his father's dead body while the flies continued their work on the grotesque corpse.

"Media," Miss Coleman said, "wake your daddy up so he can go to town on an errand. Would you shake him for me?"

Baby Sister cried aloud and buried her face in Brother's shoulder.

"Don't cry, Baby Sister. That Paddy ain't never gone hurt another colored person again." His reference to the paddy rollers slave patrols escaped the demented Miss Coleman.

"Shush!" Birdie Mae sternly said. "Pretend you Media and tell Miss Mary we gone to the bedroom and you'll help wake your daddy up when you come back."

Baby Sister sobbed.

Birdie Mae pinched her. She pinched her hard! The pain snapped Baby Sister out of her near hysteria. She heard Birdie Mae whisper sternly, "Do what I'm telling you now. Gone now. Say it."

"Momma, I'll wake Daddy up when I come back from the bedroom," Baby Sister shakily said, from the porch. Neither Miss Coleman nor Rafe III turned from the rotting body to acknowledge her words.

Birdie Mae motioned for them to follow her. They passed the parlor and entered the hallway where they peered into Media's room. Birdie Mae said dryly to Chess and his little sister, "That white gal already dead."

Chess and Baby Sister recoiled from the shock of yet another death.

"Eula," Birdie Mae barked, calling Baby Sister by her given name, "This is time to think. Quit sniveling. Us got to do something. It gone sound crazy, but we got to do this. You hear me?"

Both nodded. "Y'all just saw how Miss Mary thought Eula Mae was Media."

"Most folks around here can hardly tell y'all apart. The both of you got the same daddy. Her hair's even the same as yours, but hers just a bit longer. Eula, change places with Media."

"Do what?" Chess Gordon exclaimed.

Birdie Mae paced back and forth and the energy within her flowed.

"All three of us got more white blood than we got colored, but they consider us black and them white! We dirt poor and they got money to burn. Most all the white folks around here dead or done left town and Miss Coleman look like she gone be dead befo' long." Birdie Mae paused and looked down the hall to make sure no one else heard her speak the unspeakable.

"Brother, you heard me. She needs to be Media and then let's bury Media like she's Eula Mae."

Eula's eyes widened at the horror of the suggestion. "Birdie Mae, you gone crazy!"

"Huh, I got mo' sense than I ever had befo'. Y'all come here and help me." She led them into Media's bedroom.

The white girl's body lay on the bed; her long hair was strewn all over the bedside and onto the floor.

A high-pitched whine escaped Baby Sister.

"Shush!" Birdie Mae commanded.

Birdie Mae picked up a pair of scissors and some string from the dresser. She cut the string into two pieces, and Chess and Baby Sister watched as the young colored woman gathered the dead girl's hair and tied a piece of the string tightly around the hair just below the shoulder line. Her three thick middle fingers measured a distance below the string knot. She tied the second piece of string there. Birdie Mae cut the hair between the two strings. With the long mop of the dead girl's hair in her hands, she faced the wide-eyed brother and sister.

"Baby Sister, you reborn. Chile, you white now. From now until the day you die, your name is Media Coleman."

Chess and Baby Sister just looked at each other blankly.

"We might need this hair to pull it off. I'll wash it out and dry it later. Until I get a hairpiece put together, you keep your hair up like you got it now. Now, Brother, you go out there and pull the parlor door shut. Then, come right back." Chess stood there and Birdie Mae sternly said, "Move out, Chess! Move out!"

Chess left as ordered.

Birdie Mae grabbed the bedclothes and wrapped the girl's body in them in one motion. She folded the feather-tick mattress over the body and cut one of the bedding-support ropes with the scissors. "Help me, Media," she instructed Baby Sister. When Chess returned, Birdie Mae pulled the bed away from the wall and cut the same two ropes on the other side of the bed with the sharp scissors.

"Y'all help me tie the mattress up." She looked up from her work. "C'mon!"

Chess and Baby Sister complied and the three soon completed bundling the body.

"Now, Chess, you go get Aunt Liza and Momma. You tell them what I done. I know they ain't gone like it, but it'll sink in on them during the ride back here." Birdie Mae looked at the bundle on the bed defiantly. "This girl here the one that convinced my white daddy's new wife to put me and Momma off the Sawyer place. We taking back some of what is ours. You hear me?"

"You right, Birdie Mae," Chess replied.

Baby Sister stood in a daze.

Birdie Mae barked out orders. "Let's get this body out of

here to the wagon. After that, we'll convince Miss Mary to take the boys out of the parlor." Suddenly, Birdie Mae slowed down, and in a very quiet farewell, continued, "Media, when you get Miss Mary back on this side of the house, me and Chess gone get the lid on that coffin and get Mr. Raford's body out of here. We can't leave him in the house stinking like that."

"Birdie Mae," Chess began, "if we all live through this fever, we gone be a whole lot better off."

The three nodded in agreement.

The lady in the Coleman guest room in November 1935 had never allowed herself to review the details of that afternoon. She could only outdistance that day's memory by pretending it had never happened. She had tried not to remember. But, even after fifty years, she did. "We really did it. I just still can't grasp it."

40—YOUNG AND OLD BUCKS

Just before the break of day, Gill Erby checked his double-barrel shotgun. It held the usual two heavy-pellet shells. "You young bucks forgot something."

Son knew everything about how to run a whiskey operation. His knowledge included the full routine of breaking camp.

"Papa, the whiskey and the cooker loaded. Bennie buried the mash and I made sure the fire is completely out. It won't put out no smoke after we gone."

Mr. Erby patiently listened. "What about them squirrels?"

"Papa, we forgot all about that. You think we got any?"

"Who knows, but you better look for a good stick. You don't want a squirrel to bite you over there."

Son located an old burlap sack and two strong branches. He handed one to Bennie. "Let's go see what's over there."

Mr. Erby peered at his watch. "Five a.m. Just enough time

to enjoy this and still meet the transport boat at the rendezvous point on the river." He decided to let Son and Bennie get into the tree grove before he walked over to enjoy the humor from their squirrel hunt.

Son led the way through the early-morning twilight. Bennie followed dutifully. Mr. Erby stood at the top of the hill and watched until they walked into the forest line. He slung the shotgun over his left shoulder and traced their steps toward the big trees.

Son went along with the proceedings, but he still believed Papa intended to play a joke on him and Bennie. The two reached the pan and, to Son's complete surprise, something had licked the container clean. The youths looked at each other and began to scour the woods for signs of squirrels.

Mr. Erby stood at the edge of the oak grove. He could hardly contain himself while the two boys walked from tree to tree looking for the little rodents. The old man didn't know something had eaten the mash when he crept up on the two boys.

Bennie stopped moving. He grabbed Son by the arm and nodded directly ahead of them. Sitting less than forty feet away was a small white-tail deer. Both boys froze. Son wished he had Papa's shotgun.

The young buck deer sat on his haunches. He looked at the two boys and shook his head from side to side. The immature, four-pointer struggled to his feet. He had obviously discovered the mash during the night.

This scene became more complicated when a much larger

buck and a large doe staggered from some underbrush to the right of the boys. Company dined on the whiskey mash with the young buck.

The big buck stamped the ground and arched his back. He never noticed the frozen boys, but he glared at his younger rival. He charged the smaller buck, which quickly ran a short distance away. The much larger male stopped in the spot where the young male had bedded down. He whirled around with his back to the boys before urinating in the shallow indentation. In full mating ritual, the big deer dropped down and rolled in the spot. He abruptly stood up and violently beat a nearby bush with his massive antlers. The doe drunkenly trotted over to the spot. She curled her upper lip and smelled the ground and the buck's body.

An anxious Son Erby counted the massive antler rack. The points numbered twelve on the heavy male. Son moved to his right to touch Bennie's arm. His single step found a dry twig that snapped beneath the pressure from his foot. The doe looked straight at Son and Bennie. She turned and disappeared into a nearby thicket, but the enraged old buck faced the two boys. The agitated animal rotated his head from side to side and rotated his ears slowly in different directions but could not decide what sort of enemy the boys were. Then he lowered his head and charged!

Gill Erby cocked both barrels when he stepped between Bennie and Son. He calmly pulled the shotgun from his left shoulder. When the deer was less than ten yards away, Gill Erby unleashed the fury of both barrels. The heavy blast mowed the buck down, but his momentum carried him to less than a yard of the trio's feet.

Mr. Erby broke open the heavy weapon. The two spent

shells jumped out and he reloaded the gun. He shot the writhing animal one more time to put him out of his misery. The dust cleared and the three looked to their left as the young buck staggered into the thicket.

"John-daddit! He coulda killed us!" Bennie exclaimed.

Mr. Erby removed his hat and hit the boy upside the head. "Don't talk like that with the way the Lord just blessed us. That's just another way to take the Lord's name in vain."

The always shy Bennie lowered his head, a sullen look etched into his face.

"Where you get that anyway?"

Bennie provided no answer.

Son spoke up. "I got it from Tom. Mr. Rafe says it all the time."

"Don't forget, you ain't Tom Coleman."

The three stood in silence until the tense moment passed. Gill Erby looked at the big animal and pulled his watch from his pocket. "It's almost 5:30 a.m. I got to get gone to meet that boat. Bennie, take this pocketknife and field dress the deer. Son, you follow me back to the truck for the ax and some rope. Cut down a sapling and tie the deer to it. If y'all walk straight through there—" pointing toward the southeast "—you'll come out of the woods near Hope on the Bluff Church. Leave the deer in the bushes and flag me down. I'll be over there in an hour to get you after I make the delivery and drop off the still."

They made eye contact in the twilight before Gill Erby left. "Remember—" he pointed at the dead animal "—what happens when you drink the stuff we make. Come along, young buck," he called over his shoulder. "I can't be late."

Gill Erby's economic interests blinded him to his own sound advice, just as it had Gillam Hale and everyone who ever fired up a whiskey still. Making and selling ole john produced the same results as its consumption.

41—SOMEONE'S OUTSIDE

Jude Smith lay awake in the front bedroom of the three-room house he now rented from Gill Erby. He still couldn't believe that bastard fired him from the marble yard.

He bitterly thought, Bustie ain't even working now; winter gone be tough with no money coming. No matter how he tried to sleep, he remembered being fired. Over and over, he also reviewed the words spoken to him during the afternoon by his former boss man.

"Jude, get on out of here! Ain't nothing I can or would do for you."

Just after midnight on this cool November day, Jude heard someone driving down Quito Road. The vehicle slowed when it reached their sharecroppers' shack. The growl of the engine preceded its arrival. That familiar noise made the big man swear under his breath. Jude Smith would know that sound anywhere. He'd heard it when that same truck slowed down to drop his Bustie off on many past nights when they lived on the Coleman place. Jude swung from bed to peek out the window. Glaring headlights blinded him.

From the other side of the bed, Bustie said, "Jude, what is it? Who's outside?"

The headlights illuminated the front room. Jude whispered, "A bold son of a bitch, that's who. If I owned a gun I'd use it right now. That's Rafe Coleman's truck."

The driver killed the truck engine and turned off the headlights. "Jude! Jude Smith, I need to speak with you!"

"Jude," Bustie said, "that ain't Mr. Rafe."

Jude stared blindly out the front window into the thick darkness.

"You hear me?" The voice shouted again. "Come on out here and let's talk a spell."

Jude lowered the top window. "Who that out there?"

"Johnlee! It's me, Jude, Johnlee Gordon! Can you talk with me a spell?"

"What we got to talk about this time of night?"

Sue Nell padded barefoot into the room from the side bedroom. "Momma, who is it?"

"Gone back to bed, child. Everything's all right."

Outside, Johnlee held his hand to his mouth. "I need some help with something I got to do tonight. It pays well!"

Jude's eyes had adjusted to the darkness. He looked over at a worried Bustie before he reached for his britches.

Son learned a great deal in the short time since he first went to the Coleman farm. Pint-size no longer described the young man. He grew to be big for fifteen. Sarah often fussed about how hard it was to keep him in clothes.

The boy never did mean things, kept his laughs lighthearted, and his sisters usually bore the brunt of his sense of humor. His charm overflowed like never before. Grandma Birdie accused him of being mannish. The boy never figured exactly what she meant, but for some odd reason, he felt a sense of pride whenever the old woman used that term for his new demeanor.

This day in late November 1934 came and went very much like most others. It was the Saturday just after Thanksgiving. Gill and Mr. Conrad settled up the week before the holiday. Sarah's joy overflowed when Mr. Erby came home with figures from their account. They actually cleared a profit, even after all their expenses and the treachery from the Coleman brothers. It was a happy time and you could feel the joy in the house as the holiday season unfolded.

Sarah Erby became even happier after the Erbys moved from the Coleman farm to the place Mr. Erby purchased from Cousin Chess. Jude Smith, Mr. Erby, Bennie and Son moved three families the Sunday night after the deer incident. In addition to the Erbys, they relocated Cousin Chess and Miss Zoar to their new house in town and Jude and Bustie Smith moved into one of the empty tenant houses.

That night, Son lay on his little cot by the stove in the front room. As Chess Gordon urged, Son had developed a habit of reviewing his plans and actions. He would sit and study yesterday, today and tomorrow. It helped him keep up with what needed to happen next. The boy believed he could plan anything out just like Chess Gordon said.

Earlier, he and Papa took the last several hundred pounds of cotton from their old tenant house on the Coleman farm to town. As Son lay in bed reviewing the day, his mind wandered to the unusual events from earlier in the week.

Mild-mannered Gill Erby usually would not argue with anyone, but Son witnessed him do so this week. In fact, Papa got into two arguments. Those heated debates raised questions that went unanswered for Son. At the right time, he'd speak with Papa about it, but so far that moment's arrival lay in future plans.

During their visit to the gin, Son tried to talk to Bennie, but he didn't seem interested. Bennie abruptly left the Erby home just after they moved to return to work for Rafe Coleman. Son took advantage of his rare free time to catch up with his friend Tom. The mixed pair sat outside while their fathers pored over farm accounts. All who passed them noticed, but the two simply acted like any boys together, having fun on a fall day.

Son and Tom joked and chatted for more than thirty minutes when an old Model T Ford truck pulled onto the gin lot.

"Howdy, Tom. How's my favorite nephew?" Rafe Coleman said. He ignored Son.

Both boys picked up the slight.

Tom answered his uncle with an unenthusiastic, "Hey, Uncle Rafe. I'm doing fine."

"John-daddit, is that the best hello I get today?"

Tom, with more energy said, "No, sir. It's good to see you."

Son read the shining badge on his left shirt pocket: Town Constable Lucy.

"Niggah, what you looking at?"

In humble submission, the boy dropped his head, shrugged his shoulders and softly mumbled the truth, "Nothing."

Rafe spat out the wad of tobacco from the corner of his mouth too close to Son's feet before he stomped toward the gin entrance.

"Son, don't mind Uncle Rafe. Aunt Media said he's just

wound too tight." The boys again threw rocks at the road sign across the street. The sign read, Welcome to Lucy, Tennessee, pop. 210.

Rafe Coleman entered the building and immediately started in on his younger brother. "Conrad, I done told you to keep Tom away from that little nigger! Why on earth you let him play with that buck I'll never understand."

Mr. Conrad turned toward his brother. The comments embarrassed the mild-mannered man. He looked back at Gill Erby apologetically and dropped his head to begin looking at the numbers in front of him once again.

Inflamed, he walked past Gill Erby to where Conrad sat at the desk. "You listening to me? Stop letting Tom play with that buck that belongs to this nigger here."

This time Gill Erby looked up at Rafe Coleman. There was already a frown on the black man's face from the news on the unfair grading of his cotton. "Mr. Rafe, we never done you no harm. Why you treat us so bad?"

Rafe Coleman turned toward Gill Erby. He popped his slapper out of his pocket and used it to strike the palm of his hand. He glowered at Gill and said, "Nigger, I'm talking to my brother."

Gill Erby stood to his feet so quickly that the narrow wooden chair fell to the concrete floor with a bang.

Conrad Coleman quickly stepped between the two men. "Gill, why don't I drop by your house this week after I review your account some more. It looks like you cleared a hundred twenty-five dollars this year."

"You gone learn to stay out of business that ain't yours. You hear me, boy!" Rafe trembled in anger as he spoke. "Don't forget I ain't never had enough of two things—that's the front end of a woman and the back end of a man!"

Gill Erby returned Rafe's determined stare.

"Nigger, I'll kill you for rearing up to me. Who you think you looking at? You act like you a big muckety-muck because you bought a little piece of land!"

"Gill, let me walk you out," Mr. Conrad continued. He put his arm around the colored man and moved him toward the door. He looked into Gill Erby's face and said, "I'll see you later this week when I bring your settlement check." With that, Conrad closed the office door.

Gill strode from the cotton gin. He looked down to see the two boys sitting on the ground near the office window. Their faces showed they'd heard every word of Rafe's tirade.

"Son, let's get to the house. Tom, see you next time."

As they drove to their new farm and home, Son noticed Jude Smith up ahead.

"Papa, that's Mr. Jude."

"Yeah," Papa Gill attempted to joke himself into a better mood, "I think I'll tell him you want him to be yo' daddy-in-law."

"Papa, now don't you start."

"I noticed you paying attention to that Sue Nell when we moved everybody."

Son laughed from the nervous tension.

"Ain't nothing wrong with a boy your age being sweet on a girl. She's a pretty little thing."

Gill Erby looked at his watch. "Wonder where he going this time of day?" He slowed the truck to a stop next to his new renter. "Howdy, Jude. You want a ride to the house?"

"Yessuh, that's the only good thing I heard today."

Son opened the door and shyly moved over.

Gill Erby smelled whiskey after Jude got into the truck. "Where you going this time of day?"

"That old bastard fired me. Wouldn't even tell me why."

"That's bad, Jude…sorry to hear it."

The three rode on in awkward silence. Gill Erby pondered his new landlord position. He needed the first month's rent that was past due.

The new landlord clumsily broke the silence. "I stopped over to the house yesterday. Looks like your wife showing good now. When's that baby due?"

Jude shouted his reply. "Why you gone around my house during the day when I ain't there?"

"Jude, I went to just see about the place and see if anything needed to be done."

"I don't want you out there 'less I'm home."

"Whoa, who you talking to like that?" The anger from his encounter with Rafe Coleman seeped to the surface.

"You think you better than me just 'cause you own the place. Well, you ain't shit!"

Gill Erby slowed the truck to a near stop.

Son looked from one man to the other.

"Jude, ain't nobody talking to me like that. Especially one that lives in a house I got to pay for and that ain't paid the first month's rent. If I need to go anywhere on my place, I'm going."

"You sitting there acting like some high-class nigger. But you ain't. Hell, look like you want to be like my last landlord. You want to collect rent and the pay ain't cash!"

Gill Erby stopped the truck. He held up his hands to calm the enraged drunk. "Now, Jude, that's a lie and you know it! It a dirty lie! I'm trying to help you."

"I don't need no John-daddit help. You ain't no better than me. Same man done bumped my wife's head off the headboard done bumped your wife, too!"

"Jude, get the hell on out of my vehicle!"

Jude burst out the door and slammed it. "Nigger, I'll kill you if I ever catch you around my house. You hear me? I'll kill you!"

"I expect the rent at the end of the week or you find somewhere else to stay!" The truck tires spun in the sandy red mud of Quito Road, and the vehicle pulled away.

42—TOMORROW NEVER CAME

It was the first time Son saw Gill Erby truly angry. His father's movements and even the way he handled the truck during the drive back to their new home showed his agitation. As Son reflected on the day, he didn't understand the things said about his mother. He wanted to ask Papa about it, but the time didn't seem right. Maybe they could talk about it tomorrow.

From his solitary cot, Son listened to the girls' rhythmical breathing. One yawned, sighed and turned over. The stove next to him made gentle popping noises; it held a bellyful of wood that Papa had him put into it just before bedtime. Son smiled about how his father always checked the stove before bedtime. Papa would get the poker iron and move the log stack around every night before retiring. He did this no matter how well prepared the fire seemed.

"Papa, the fire's already stoked," Son often said. Usually, Gill Erby made no reply and only opened the stove to do it again.

Son remembered deciding to teach Papa a lesson when the boy was thirteen. He filled the stove as usual and decided to turn the hot end of the stove poker iron out for his dad to pick up. When Gill Erby picked it up, he calmly yelled in pain and dropped the metal rod to the floor.

He turned to the boy and softly said, "Son, ain't nobody done that but you. Get on up and let's head out to the barn to handle a little business. Don't bother to get dressed. Come on in your bedclothes."

Son got out of bed and dutifully followed his father out the back door to the barn.

Mr. Gill said over his shoulder when he walked from the front room at the old house, "Don't forget my strap, we gone need it to take care of what's on my mind."

Son thought to himself about that night. After that incident, he made sure his humor paid the proper respect to the recipient of the joke.

The boy heard his pooch, Shebie, whine from beneath the floor. It was just a soft little signal that Shebie let out at night to tell Son that he was there. At the old house, Son would drop him a biscuit fragment through the knothole in the floor. But this night, the boy whispered very softly, "Shh, shh." In the distance, he heard an owl hoot just before he dropped off to sleep.

Sometime later, a slow growl from Shebie awakened Son. The cadence of the growl meant one thing; someone was outside. Son listened for a few more seconds. He got down on his knees and put his mouth to the floor. Quietly, the boy told the animal, "Hush, boy." He only said it once.

Son stood up and dressed quickly in the darkness. The only noise he heard was the old clock on the mantel ticking the seconds away. Son made his way across the big hallway parlor into the side room where his parents slept. He heard the heavy, even breathing of Gill Erby when he entered the room.

Sarah sat up in bed. The lightest sound usually awakened her. From the back-side of the bed she said, "Son, why you up? What's wrong?"

"Someone's outside."

"Boy, how you know that? I ain't heard a sound."

"Shebie's growling and I can tell by the way he's growling."

With that last sentence, the dog let out a stern growl and broke into even stiffer barks. Son and Sarah started to rouse Mr. Erby at the same time.

"Wake Up! Someone's outside!" they said, shaking the exhausted farmer from his deep sleep.

"What, what?" came from Gill Erby, still in a stupor. When he gained his senses, he swung his feet onto the floor and told his son, "Son, hand me my overalls and get the gun."

Son already had his father's overalls and handed them to him. Next, he partially closed the bedroom door and reached between the old wardrobe and the wall into the corner for the shotgun and the bag of shells hanging next to it. Son opened the heavy weapon and put a shell into each chamber. He handed the gun to Papa and Gill Erby strode to the front door, clicked the big gun closed and removed the door latch. "Son, hush that dog!"

"Shebie, hush!" The command to the animal brought instant calm. Once again the mantel clock issued the only audible sound.

Gill Erby wondered what time it was. His youngest girl issued a squeaky cry from the bedroom. Sarah comforted her and the girl's whimpers subsided as quickly as they began. He opened the door, the shotgun in his dominant left hand when he crossed the threshold. It was pitch-black, the moon had set earlier in the night. Beautiful stars lined every inch of the sky. He took one step away from the door and heard his son follow him through the portal.

"Son, get back in the house."

They heard a crisp *click, click.*

Papa Gill shouted, "Inside!" and shoved his only boy inside as a single boom sounded.

The strong push threw the boy to the floor. It happened fast, but to Son it seemed like slow motion. Papa took the brunt of the shotgun blast in his lower right side. The force of the gunshot knocked Mr. Erby to the other side of the door where he landed on his knees.

A stunned Son Erby landed flat on his back in the darkness. He looked into his father's eyes as Erby reached for the doorknob.

"No, Papa!" Son shouted, but Gill Erby pulled the front door closed.

In the darkness, the man with the shotgun readied himself for a second shot. He made out Gill Erby's form on his knees on the porch. The coward raised the gun for one more blast to complete his work. He never got the shot off.

Shebie sank his teeth into the man's right calf. Shebie owned a strong bite and the man felt every inch of the front canines sink deep into his flesh. Like Son trained him, Shebie bit. He bit hard and he bit deep. He shook the man's leg from side to side.

"Ow! Ow! Ow! John-daddit! You son of a bitch!"

Inside the house, Son heard it all. The stunned boy felt something hot on the right side of his neck and shoulder. Blood covered him. He'd been shot, too!

A gun went off. The man struggled to get away from Shebie. He turned his back on the porch and hit the dog with one mighty blow after another. Finally, he got free.

Gill Erby took that time to locate his gun with his left hand, raise it unsteadily in the dark and fire both barrels at his unknown enemy in the yard.

The two barrels released their fury and Gill Erby fell back against the front door. Blood now poured from the serious wound he'd suffered. He did not know if he'd hit the man or not, so he was determined not to go into the house. Instead, he gathered himself and ran around the west side of the house to the barn.

"Baby, latch the door! Baby! Baby! Latch the door! Use the telephone to call the law!" he shouted while he ran. Gill Erby stepped inside the barn and closed the door behind him. He placed the bar over the double doors, put his back to the wooden barrier and sank to the floor. He loaded his gun one more time before he passed out.

Gill Erby finally received his rest.

43—JOURNEY ENDED

Elder Simon Peter Gordon approached the lectern and looked at the crowd in the small building that overflowed into the yard. It was the first Saturday in December 1934 and people stood in every free spot from the front to the very back wall of the church. Sightseers even peeked through the closed windows down each side of the church to get a glimpse.

The preacher had never seen a group this large at Pleasant Grove. He looked down on Sarah Erby. Tears streamed down her face. A daughter under each arm flanked her.

"Today and many of those ahead are difficult ones," Cephas declared, looking behind Sarah. The pastor turned his gaze to young Son Erby, partially named for him. "But I know God can heal all wounds. Today, we are gathered here for the home-going celebration of our dear brother Gill Erby. I ask that some of you seated in the crowd move to provide room for the family. Ushers, would you come to assist us."

The most unusual thing happened. The throng of Negroes parted in the rear of the church. Allen Sawyer Jr. led several whites into the packed sanctuary. Behind him walked his daughter, Amanda. Tom, Conrad and Ruth Coleman followed the young lady. But the final person in their party made Reverend Gordon's mouth drop open. Media Coleman Sneed was the last person to squeeze through the crowd toward the front of the church. Cephas was pleased that Baby Sister had come.

The courage of these new members of the funeral crowd inspired the preacher. He watched Sarah and her daughters walk away from the open coffin. His gaze fell on the only son of Steward Gill Erby. Son approached the coffin with old lady Birdie Mae.

Son looked at Papa's body. Mama Birdie put her arm around him. The old lady stood more erect than she had in years. She waited a sufficient time before ushering Son to a seat on the front-row pew nearby. "Mama Birdie Mae, why he shining so much?" the boy asked when they sat down next to Sarah.

"That's just the sweet oil the undertakers put on him to prepare his body for burial."

Elder Cephas spoke again, "Ushers, could you place six chairs here to my left just in front of the stove for our guests. Seat them near the family." He waited and watched the mourners view the remains. Elder Cephas thought about Steward Erby. He always reminded him of his own father. It was going to be a tough eulogy to bring. More so, because it was a first. In forty-five years of ministry, he'd never led a worship service attended by whites.

Conrad and Ruth Coleman and Baby Sister sat in the back row. Banker Sawyer, Amanda and Tom Coleman sat in the first row of folding chairs.

Chess Gordon acknowledged Banker Sawyer and Conrad Coleman with a nod. He sat directly across the church on a back row of what was considered the men's section of the small church. His thoughts raced. Gill Erby signed the mortgage just days before his murder. How could Sarah pay that mortgage now? He also thought of that dumb-ass boy of his at the Shelby County Penal Farm. Why the hell would Johnlee kill Gill Erby?

Chess bent over and reviewed his every failing as a man, a husband and a father. Chess couldn't look at Sarah Erby or Son. He felt like what he was, an old, tired colored man. Miss Zoar broke the traditional seating code. She reached over to hold his hand. Her thoughtfulness brought the first smile to Chess's face since he got the news four days ago.

Amanda and Sarah made eye contact when the young lady took her seat. Sarah knew the determination required for the whites to come to this funeral. The love Amanda's presence showed reached through the young widow's thick wall of grief. She returned a smile to the child she'd reared. The white boy picked a chair next to the spot where Son sat on the front pew. Tom touched the colored boy on the knee when he sat down.

"Son, I'm here," Tom whispered. "I'm here."

Finally, Elder Cephas motioned for the funeral directors to replace the coffin top and forever close the remains from human view.

"Papa, no, Papa! Papa!" one of the Erby girls screamed. Her outburst signaled a new release of cries from the family and murmurs from the crowd.

Elder Cephas took charge again. "We'll proceed with our program now. Reverend Clethas Morrow of Hope on the Bluff Missionary Baptist Church will lead our devotion." On his way to the lectern, the Baptist preacher whispered, "Preacher Gordon, this program got the prayer before the scripture. You know us Baptists read the scripture *before* we pray. What you want to do about that?"

Elder Cephas saw the anger in the Baptist preacher's eyes, but he also discerned the man's hurt. The Methodist preacher remembered a time when he would have responded along denominational lines, without the wisdom his years walking with God had provided.

"Reverend Morrow," he whispered, "this family has a Baptist and a Methodist tradition. I'm most concerned with their comfort in this tragedy. You handle it the way you feel led." The elder gathered his preacher's robe, walked to his seat and silently prayed.

When Reverend Morrow got to the podium, the Baptist preacher said, "Friends, let us bow our heads and go to the Lord in prayer."

44—COLD TIMES

"Mr. Rafe, you think you gone get that ground back now. That Sarah gal can't make the first note this year by herself."

A preoccupied Rafe Coleman replied, "I don't know."

"But you know I'm right. How she gone farm a place like that with no man? What you think, Mr. Rafe?"

"John-daddit, Jim! I think you worry the hell out of me. I'm trying to see what them niggers down there in the colored cemetery is doing. Jim, gone in there in my truck glove box and bring me my spyglass."

Jim Falls shrugged before he walked to the truck and opened the passenger door. He reached inside the glove box and retrieved the single-shaft telescope. Jim walked back to where Mr. Rafe stood and handed him the instrument.

Rafe extended the glass before he raised it to his eye. He started to laugh. "John-daddit!" he exclaimed. Just enough leaves had fallen from the trees between the white cemetery, where Rafe and Jim stood on the hill, and the colored cemetery for Rafe to make out what the colored men were doing.

"What is it, Mr. Rafe? What they doing?"

Rafe continued to laugh, but made no reply to Jim's questions. After he looked a while longer, he handed the glass to Jim. "You got to see this. This gone be just too good to miss."

Jim Falls took the spyglass. He squinted when he raised it to his face. Finally, he found the spot Rafe had viewed. He laughed too. "Huh, huh, huh! If that boy ain't cold, he gone be when they put him down in there." He rubbed his whiskered chin and jaw before he turned to look up to Rafe with a toothless grin. "How you think all that water got in that grave?"

"Simple, these woods all around Lucy are so full of gravel rock that water moves through underground. That's why they're finding so many gravel pits all over the place. They probably hit an underground stream of water when they dug that grave."

"Mr. Rafe, gravel worth much?"

"Jim boy, those new roads ole FDR building makes finding gravel almost like finding gold."

"Speaking of money, Mr. Rafe, I need to get started with that next batch of whiskey you want me to make. You ready to take this sugar out to the farm?"

"Naw, let's wait a spell. I want to see it when they lower that nigger into that grave full of cold water. This I just got to see."

The two white men laughed so loud that the two-man grave detail actually heard them in the colored cemetery below. The workers stopped bailing water with their metal buckets to look through the trees. Sweat poured from them and steam rose from their uncovered heads on the cold and clear early-December day.

"Who that laughing out loud?" the first digger asked.

"It's two white men. I can't see their faces but I see a truck with an old Confederate flag and the crossed bars in the back window."

"Hell, it's that crazy ass Lucy town constable, Rafe Coleman."

"I hope they stop that racket before they get here with the body."

"Me too! Because it ain't gone be funny to the family when they get here and all this water's in the grave. Look! It seeps back in the grave as fast as we bail it out. How we gone bury that man in all this water?"

"We just gone let the coffin fill up with water and sink him in the grave. Then we'll add dirt and let the water just run out as the mud settles to the bottom."

"Them women gone holler something awful when they see that!"

"Yeah, but that's the best we can do."

"It makes my flesh crawl to just think on it."

"Mr. Rafe, you ready to go yet? It's cold out here. Besides, staying around a cemetery this long gives me the creeps."

Rafe Coleman looked at Jim Falls. "Quit worrying me about leaving. We'll stay until they put him in that water. Look, they all gathered now, so it won't be long."

"Sarah, why don't you let us commit the body after y'all leave?"

The widow looked blankly at Elder Gordon. "No, sir. Do it now. I need to be here."

"But, Sarah, the water might upset you more."

"I want to be here. Do it now."

Reverend Gordon looked toward the funeral director. "Brother Jenkins, please proceed."

"Men," Funeral Director Jenkins said, "each of you take a strap and we'll pull the posts out after you lift the coffin."

The pallbearers on each side of the grave grasped the end of a long thick cloth strap. The straps ran under the coffin to the pallbearer on the other side.

"Lift him now," Mr. Jenkins said. The six men lifted together. After the coffin rose, Mr. Jenkins and another man pulled away the two four-by-four posts where Gill Erby's coffin had rested. "Now lower him slowly. Watch out because the water is gone come out when he starts down into the grave."

Son Erby watched while they lowered Papa Gill's coffin into the water-filled grave. The wooden box floated at first, but the hushed crowd heard bubbling sounds and the coffin slowly filled with water. It seemed to take forever for the first end to sink.

"Hold that lower end up until more water rises inside. Let him down slow and even," Mr. Jenkins solemnly advised.

Son watched his daddy's floating coffin sink lower in the cold muddy water and Son silently swore, I'll kill the bastard that did this. I'll kill him dead.

The angry boy heard a woman relative shout, "Don't put him in that cold water. Please! Don't put him in there. It's just too cold in there!"

Rafe Coleman pulled his hat to the front of his head. He looked down on the throng of Negroes below through his spyglass. Jim Falls walked back to the front of the truck.

"They put him in yet?" Jim asked.

"Yeah, and he's sinking fast. Let's see how them women cash flow that place now," Rafe said. "Chess might want them to have it, but one thing's sure about that red-skinned nigger. He don't run no charity house." Rafe scanned the crowd through the spyglass. Rafe found Chess Gordon. Next, his gaze stopped on Ray Erby and he noticed for the first time how much the boy looked like Gill Erby. A shudder went up his spine; it seemed like the little nigger returned his gaze. Rafe abruptly broke away, walked toward the truck and started the engine without a word. The engine's roar startled Jim. "Mr. Rafe, what got into you?"

The annoyed driver offered no reply. He reached for the steering wheel-mounted gearshift. The now-shaken man pulled the handle to place the truck into first gear. Rafe gunned the engine and released the clutch as the old Ford lurched forward. He punched the lever forward into second gear just before he turned left to exit the cemetery.

"Mr. Rafe, why you driving like a bat out of hell?"

Again, Rafe offered no reply. He hit the clutch and pulled the gearshift down to third. Their speed increased. All Rafe Coleman could think about was the look on Ray Erby's face and those bloodcurdling screams of the colored women. They took him to a place he never intended to return.

The constable steered the truck into a right turn at the next street. He never slowed down. Jim Falls felt like the vehicle sped through the turn on two wheels. He reached for the dashboard. "Them Nigger women squealed like pigs at a slaughterhouse. Did you hear?"

"Jim, shut the hell up! Just this once, shut the hell up!" The screams rang in his ears, no longer screams from the colored cemetery; instead, sounds from the days after his daddy died echoed in his ears. He heard his mother and Media cry. Rafe Coleman's entire life was a race to outdistance those memories. He knew Ray Erby now began a similar contest. Rafe Coleman did not wish that on anyone, not even the uppity young colored boy who stood between him and his lifelong obsession of reclaiming his papa's farm.

Media surveyed the churchyard. For some reason, their small group lingered behind after most of the colored people moved on to the cemetery. Conrad, Ruth and Tom headed toward the car. Media glanced at Amanda who stood next to her father. They exchanged smiles.

"Amanda," Media began, "Ruth tells me you attend West Tennessee State Teachers College."

"Yes, ma'am. I graduate this spring with a teaching degree."

"Are you going to teach?"

"I can either teach or work at the bank with Father."

"I have some business in town and decided to take a suite at the Peabody Hotel for the next few days. Would you come to join me for supper day after tomorrow?"

"Mrs. Sneed, I'd love to join you."

"Shall I send a car for you?"

"Yes, ma'am. I live in a dormitory called Mynders Hall. What time should I plan for the taxi to arrive?"

"Six o'clock should be fine." With a smile, Media added, "I look forward to getting to know you better and sharing some old-fashioned Southern-belle wisdom."

45—ESAU'S ANGER

Anger clung to him all day and chased him, tossing and turning, in his bed at night. Images forced shouts and screams from his lips throughout the spring nights. In his recurring nightmares, he saw his father sitting open-eyed against the barn door. The old man's stare was not warm or loving. Gill Erby's light brown eyes no longer existed; instead, Son looked into eyes of coal.

On this March 1935 evening, the old mantel clock's tick, tick, tick counted the morning seconds and his life away. The boy slid out of bed and put his clothes on in an instant. The clock showed a quarter to five when he headed outside. Papa used to get him up to feed Dick and Dan at about this time, he thought. After that, they milked the two cows before breakfast. Son remembered, Gill Erby laughing his deep hearty laugh and saying, "Put something in his belly if you want it to work."

A bird sang as he pulled the door closed. For the birds,

spring meant happiness. Son Erby knew no joy; he only knew that last fall Johnlee killed his Papa Gill. Anger had gnawed at the boy's belly and anguish had clouded his mind since that day. A mockingbird flew up and down from its perch; the bird made call after call. The beautiful songs had no effect on the boy.

Since Mr. Erby died, Sarah didn't know what to do with Son. From her bed, she heard her boy toss and turn most nights. Sometimes she tried to talk him out of his moods, but similar emotions consumed her, too.

Most grown folks whipped children for the looks Son sent her way, but Sarah just let him alone.

Instead of reaching for Mr. Erby's razor strap that still hung from a big nail next to the back door, she spoke softly to the boy and just waited. She waited for the mood to leave him and for her sweet Son to return. She also wished for that frame of mind to depart from her.

After the boy left the house, Sarah sat up on the side of the bed. She looked straight at the old wardrobe Mr. Erby treasured because it came from Gillam Hale. Gill Erby's widow stood and walked up to the big piece of furniture. Even in the morning twilight, she saw herself in its double-mirrored doors. Her face showed that sleep had eluded her during the night, as she knew it had Son.

Sarah Erby opened one of the large wardrobe doors; she pulled at a sleeve on one of Mr. Erby's shirts. She never washed it. She thought it still smelled of him.

"I know now what it meant to have you," she murmured.

One of the girls moaned in her sleep and Sarah released the garment. She closed the wardrobe to begin dressing. The young woman examined her body's gentle curves after she pulled her old gown over her head. She didn't appear to have had any kids. Sarah Erby felt the needs of any young woman, which included physical desire.

When she stepped into her dress, her anger dogged her like Son's chased him. Today, like every day, she knew madness would shadow their every step. Gill Erby's absence denied all the things he used to be, just for her, for Son, and for all that knew him.

Son Erby descended the steep porch steps one at a time. The boy stretched and then lowered his arms while looking up at the waning morning stars. He pulled his braces over his shoulders, picked up a rock and angrily threw it at the mockingbird. The singing sentinel flew into the rage of its alert call.

"Skeek, skeek, skeek, skeek!" called the gray bird. It flew overhead as if to jeer at its attacker.

Son grabbed at the sleek form flying just out of reach. The mocker flashed the white strips underneath its wings when it sped past. His eyes tracked the bird and it swooped to a safe barn-top perch. The bird immediately stopped his alarms and resumed joyous call after call.

The resentful boy posed in mock hunting position. "Boom, boom!" Son said aloud. Son Erby also imagined locking the gun sights on Johnlee Gordon.

"Morning, Son." Mama Birdie Mae invaded his private war. "You gone shoot my mockingbird?"

"I didn't see you there."

"I been out here a good while, enjoyed the show that bird puts on every morning until you run him off."

A rare and sheepish grin crossed the youngster's face. But he remembered to be mad and his scowl returned.

"Come here and sit down. We need to talk a spell." Lord, she prayed silently, answer his questions so he can go on.

The old woman embraced him. He resisted her hug at first. Slowly, his reluctance waned and, in an almost pleading fashion, the boy fell against Miss Birdie's bosom. The torrent flooded from the boy's eyes and he sobbed uncontrollably from the grief only the son of a dead man could know. Mama Birdie Mae joined him.

"Son, it's hard, I know, but it's gone be all right." Over and over, she said, "It's gone be all right." She pulled his head down to her lap. He lay there with his arms around her hips, like he did as a young child. Son's sobs subsided and his grandmother rocked him into a much-needed peace only sleep could provide.

Mama Birdie Mae touched the man-child sprawled across her lap. He'd only fuss and frown if she tried this while he was awake, but she leaned over and kissed him on the cheek.

The old woman whispered prayers. "Lawd, he ain't a man, but he ain't a boy neither. This boy was his papa's shadow all his life. What happens to a shadow when the one that cast it goes way? God, for him to still exist, you got to help."

Back and forth she rocked her boy. She remembered moving in with the family to preserve the only male seed of her daughter and son-in-law.

"Take the madness from him. You know what to do. He acts like a full pot on a hot stove. The least little push and he's over the lid. Keep him from boiling over. Take his anger. Let him shadow you, Lawd. Take that whiskey making—it ain't gone amount to no good. Take it out of his life before it takes the life out of him like it did his papa and grandpapa."

46—APRIL'S FOOL

Nothing Bustie did quieted her newborn son. He screamed bloody murder from around midnight when he woke up to 4:00 a.m. This mother of five ached from exhaustion and lack of sleep. Her baby was hungry and she possessed nothing for him.

The women in her family called their bust size the Gibson curse. Normally, this included the ability to produce large amounts of milk from their full bosoms. She knew now it had been a blessing and not a curse at all. For some reason, her milk had not come. She could not produce enough milk to satisfy the child, and Bustie shed tears of her own in the front room of her shack.

Maybe, it all my worrying, she thought. Bustie also couldn't do anything for her other four children. She needed some help and she needed it soon if her young ones were to survive.

Lil' Red peacefully lay on the cot next to Sue Nell. Bustie

looked at them both. Sue Nell's dark brown contrasted with the skin of the toddler. She was such a good girl and so full of life. Bustie smiled and thought about how playful she herself had been at thirteen when she first fell for Jude Smith. He was four years older than Bustie and his powerful body and good looks attracted her. He'd possessed a gentle spirit back then. Bustie liked that about him the most. Jude had liked Bustie for other reasons. She wondered when or if his gentle spirit would ever surface again.

The girl's lithe upper body flowed out of the simple cotton gown; she already looked like a Gibson woman. Bustie shook her head at the task of keeping her out of trouble as she gently roused her oldest child.

Jude rolled over toward the wall in the iron double bed Bustie no longer shared. Instead, she slept in the big chair across the room next to the rectangular stove, the house's main source of heat. The big man snored like a bull as soon as he settled down.

Sue Nell awakened and opened her mouth. Bustie put a single finger to her lips and mouthed behind pearly white teeth, "Don't wake the babies." She motioned for the girl to follow her into the kitchen.

Sue Nell moved away from Lil' Red. The chubby boy sighed just a bit when his big sister slid out of bed. His rosy cheeks and small pouted mouth belied the fuss the eighteen-month-old would raise if he awakened. The girl started to touch his hair like she always did when she made him laugh. Instead, his caretaker pretended to rake through his tangled locks. Sue Nell smiled before following her mother into the kitchen.

The girl whispered, "Momma, what time is it?" Before Bustie answered, Sue Nell already had another question. "Momma, what happened to your eye?"

Bustie raised her hand to touch the tender left side of her face. She looked away from the girl and walked over to check the wood fire in the tiny cookstove. The woman turned to face Sue Nell. Bustie spoke in even tones filled with defiance to the girl's pointed question. "It's time for you to get up. I got to cook for Mr. Rafe this morning and do his washing and ironing. I'll be back after midday."

"But, Momma, I wanted to go to school today."

"Shoosh, shoosh," said the woman with her finger to her lips. She shook her head, and her thick curls moved in unison. "Don't wake up Jude and them babies." She continued in a quiet tone, "We ain't got a scrap to eat. There's a little oil and meal. Now, you get dressed and go out to the henhouse. I hope the hens laid last night. Pull an onion out of the garden and chop it up. Scramble the eggs, if you get some, and mix the meal and onion in before you cook them. If it's more than three, save some for Jude. If it ain't but three, split it between you and the kids. Let Jude, Lil' Red and the baby sleep, but hide what you got for Lil' Red to make sure he eats something. The baby will wake up hungry soon so you better give him this."

Sue Nell looked a little confused and she raised the bottle to eye level.

"It's breast milk I squeezed," her mother explained. Bustie hugged the girl. Into Sue Nell's ear, she whispered, "I'm sorry about school, but Momma got to get some food in this house today. Understand?"

Sue Nell nodded her head.

A determined Thelma Louise Gibson Smith walked past Sue Nell and out the back door to start the bitter journey back to Raford Coleman III.

★ ★ ★

Sue Nell pulled on her old dress as her mother walked by the side window and crossed the dusty front yard to walk east down Quito Road. Tears flowed down the girl's cheeks. She cried not because she would miss school. Not getting to see her friends did not upset her. Hopes of seeing Son Erby today did not cause her to cry. She didn't even mind keeping the baby and Lil' Red. Sue Nell's sadness started and ended because her mother left for Rafe Coleman's house. She knew exactly what that meant.

Anger fueled her brisk stride. Her sturdy legs would easily carry her the distance to Mr. Rafe's house. She'd let herself in with the key Mr. Rafe said would be under the back step. In a short time after her arrival, he would awaken to the smell of his breakfast. Bustie knew she would take care of his washing, his ironing and his other wishes. She didn't want to, but today, Bustie vowed to feed her five children.

"This time it'll be different!" she spat out. "I'm going to get something just for myself if he wants me." A worldlier Thelma Louise returned to Rafe Coleman that spring morning on April 1, 1935.

Next to the wall in the front room, Jude Gibson stopped snoring. Through the paper-thin walls, he listened carefully to his wife and daughter's conversation. He waited for his daughter to finish dressing. His helplessness froze him in place and a streak of madness ebbed through his powerful body. Tears filled his large brown eyes.

What do you do when you only make fifty cents for a twelve-hour workday? Jude questioned himself. How can you erase the memory of seeing a midwife pull a second fair-skinned child from your wife just six weeks ago? What can a man in my place do about his wife leaving to cook, clean and whatever else for the same man that fathered her last two children?

He listened intently when Sue Nell padded from the room, put on her shoes and exited the back door. Through the hangover from the bad whiskey he drank at Mama Sam's last night, Jude decided to wait for the right time. He remembered the events of the night Gill Erby was shot. I'm still surprised I ain't in jail like Johnlee, can't figure why he ain't told nobody I was with him.

He visualized Bustie in her walk to Rafe Coleman's and turned over to look directly at the newborn lying on the sofa. It cut like a knife to even look at the boy and remember how the mingled blood got in his veins.

Jude thought, that bastard is gone pay; he sure is gone pay. Jude Smith sat up in the middle of his bed.

"Amanda, happy birthday!"

Amanda held the telephone earpiece in her hand and stoically replied, "Thanks, Father."

Mr. Sawyer laughed deeply like he only did when speaking with his Amanda. "Yes, young lady. It is I. 'Is this really you?' would be the better question. I'd think you were avoiding me lately if I didn't know better."

"Why would you think that?" she asked.

"You haven't been home in six weeks. That's a record for you. And you wouldn't even let me see you for your birthday today. Is everything all right down there at West Tennessee State Teachers College?"

"Yes sir. Everything's fine."

"You sure?"

"I'm just trying to finish my last term."

"Well, don't get huffy. I just didn't want to have to come down there and get some young man straight."

"Don't start that again."

"What's a father to think? I just called this bright Monday morning to make sure you were fine."

"Really, I am. You know what else?"

"No, what?"

"I am so glad you're my father," she said unsteadily.

"You were such a nice April's Fool surprise twenty-one years ago. Speaking of that, how did you celebrate your birthday?"

"I didn't have time."

"All work and no play make a girl dull, dull and duller."

"Like Sarah would say, 'Talk about the pot calling the kettle black.' Speaking of Sarah, how is she?"

"She's fair, quieter than usual. She asks me about you more frequently than ever."

She changed the subject to one more to her liking. "Your question about celebrating my birthday made me think of something. Tell about the night I was born."

"Sure," he answered. "I'll give you my secondhand details again. Dr. Turnipseed told your mother and me that you weren't due for eight weeks." Mr. Sawyer laughed and hit his knee loudly with his open right palm. "Add that to the long list of things Dr. Turnipseed bungled. I'd traveled with your grandmother and Dr. Turnipseed to Little Rock, Arkansas, on business."

"So, you were away when I was born."

"Young lady, you know that. Your mother and I used to tell you this story at bedtime."

"I know, but there's one thing I don't remember. Who delivered me if Dr. Turnipseed was with you?"

"We never spoke about it much because of how your grandmother felt about it."

"Well, who delivered me?"

"Dr. Turnipseed nor I never would have left if we had known you were coming early."

"Who, Father?"

"Chess Gordon got the resident Lucy midwife, Birdie Mae Lilliard, to bring you into the world."

"So, that was just another great service from Mr. Chess."

"Yes, little lady, it sure was."

Silently, Amanda Sawyer thought, you just don't know how great of a service Chess Gordon did for me.

"Why is this so important now?" Allen Sawyer Jr. asked.

Before she answered, Amanda thought, my meal with Mrs. Media Sneed made it important. Aloud she lied, "No reason. I just asked after you brought up my birth."

"Amanda, there is something else we need to discuss. I spoke with the superintendent of Shelby County Schools this weekend. He asked if you were coming to work for him or for me." Allen Sawyer Jr. held the phone and his daughter made no initial reply. "You still haven't decided?"

"Yes, sir. I'm coming to work for you at the bank."

"Hooray, hooray! You just can't know how happy I am to hear that!"

"Someone else wants to use the telephone. I need to get off," Amanda said.

"Do you need anything before I go?"

She paused.

"Amanda, are you there?"

"Yes, sir, I'm here. I just need to hear you say you love me."

"You're all I have left in this world. I love you with every fiber of my very soul."

"I love you, too," she said softly. "And, Mr. Sawyer, could I trouble you to pick me up Friday night after you close up the bank?"

"I certainly can and I surely will."

"I want to see Lucy this weekend."

"Just Lucy?"

"You too, Father."

Smiling wide, he said, "I will come for you as soon as possible Friday evening after closing time. See you then. Goodbye, daughter."

Allen Sawyer Jr. laid the telephone handset back on the cradle. "I just cannot imagine what has gotten into Amanda. She seemed so distant and preoccupied. I guess it's just school. She'll snap out of it after graduation in a few weeks and she sees her new Ford Coupe."

She hung up, but her head remained on the wall in the lobby of the women's dorm, Mynders Hall, at West Tennessee State Teachers College. No one wanted the telephone. Amanda just needed to get off the line. She had trouble calling him *father* now. Talking with him made her feel better. But, right now, Amanda needed to know the entire truth.

47—TALK WITH A LAMB

The weather warmed enough in April for Bennie Gorlan to sleep in the tack room in Mr. Rafe's barn. The young man looked around the cold barn room and loneliness engulfed him. Since Ma'Dear died ten years ago, he'd moved from place to place and odd job to odd job.

His existence on the fringes of society around Lucy filled many conversations, but no one did anything about it before Gill Erby took him in last year. After things got a little complicated at the Erby home, it just didn't seem right to stay. So, voluntarily this time, Bennie survived alone again. As usual, the man Ma'Dear said was his daddy lifted not one finger.

Bennie quickly fed the livestock before he partook of his own meal. He ate cold leftover biscuits and a small piece of cheese from his meager previous evening meal.

After the big draft mule finished eating, he harnessed the animal and hooked him to the turning plow. Together they made their way around to the back lot.

Then he did an unusual thing for a young man. He stopped to pray. He was discouraged and, in fact, angry about his circumstances. Bennie prayed like Ma'Dear used to pray. He used her same words. She always called Jesus the Lamb.

"Ohhhhh, Lamb! Ohhhhh, Lord! Ohhhhh, Lamb! Ohhhhh, Lord! Thank you, God, for waking me this morning. Thank you for another day. Thank you, Lord, for my meal. Jesus, help me make another day. Help me come through, Lord! Jesus, give me the strength I needs right now, God! You knows I'm all alone, but Lawd, you can make me feel like you with me. Help me, God, to plow this here field today. Thank you, God, for waking me this morning. Thank you, Lord, for keeping me warm all through the night. Ohhhhh, Lamb! Ohhhhh, Lord! Ohhhhh, Lamb! Ohhhhh, Lord!"

By now, Bennie got into his prayer. It started out as his private time, but his happiness at the small victories that seemed to always come his way, no matter what, made him forget to be quiet. Right there, at the end of the field rows, behind Mr. Rafe Coleman's barn, Bennie shouted his prayer over and over. Unconscious to his surroundings, he lost track of time. He just prayed. He prayed like his very soul depended on it. The burdens he carried just made it happen, it was not routine or planned.

"Ohhhhh, Lamb! Ohhhhh, Lamb! Ohhhhh, Lamb! Ohhhhh, Lord!"

"Boom, Boom!" came the explosive sound that only a double-barreled shotgun brings.

He jerked around and fell onto his butt on the dusty ground. He ducked down to shield his face with his hands before checking to see if he was hit.

Mr. Rafe Coleman III stood a few feet away. He broke open the big double barrel. The gun ejected two empty shells from its chambers and the smell of gunpowder filled the previously sweet morning air. Rafe stuffed two new shells into the gun and slammed the weapon shut. The big man strode toward Bennie with the fury of hangover-interrupted sleep coupled with an already unstable personality.

Pointing the gun straight at the young field hand, Mr. Rafe vented his anger. *Click, click,* sounded as he pulled the hammer back on both chambers of the shotgun. "Don't you ever bring your black ass around my house again and make all that damn noise this early in the morning! Who the hell you talking to anyway? Either you or that damn Lamb you keep shouting at got to leave here right now or I'll blow your asses to kingdom come!"

From behind Mr. Rafe, a soft sweet voice, the answer to Bennie's distressed prayer, interrupted this desperate scene.

"Mr. Rafe, why don't you come on into the house so I can get your breakfast." She stepped backward and paused for him to see her before retreating toward the house.

Rafe Coleman looked over his shoulder to see Thelma Louise peering around the corner of the barn. He smiled slowly at the colored woman before he turned back to Bennie. With the barrel still pointed in the Negro's face, he released the hammers of the armed gun chambers. He smiled wide because his unholy prayers had been answered. Rafe deliberately broke the weapon open and pulled both shells from the 12-gauge shotgun.

The big white man turned slowly to enjoy his early-morning repast. "Thelma, girl, I'm glad the Lawd sent you to see about me. A nice, hot morning meal sounds like just the thing

I need to put me in a better mood." A rooster let loose a strained early-morning crow as Rafe moved from Bennie's sight.

Bennie Gorlan stood to his feet. He shook the dust from his knees and rear. Looking skyward, he said, "Thank you, Lawd! I'm glad you sent her, too! Even if it ain't gone be the meal that gets that peckerwood to feeling better."

"You gone get just eleven months and twenty-nine days," one deputy told Johnlee.

Another chimed in, "Boy, you need to gone and confess. Or, do you need a little more convincing." He slowly popped his palm with a worn police nightstick.

The first deputy added, "Hell, Johnlee, a year ain't so long. We'll offer you a good deal if you confess. You'll get more time if it goes to trial. They just might even fry you."

Johnlee Gordon reviewed what Rafe Coleman and all those sheriff's deputies had said over and over to him when they'd questioned him about the murder of Gill Erby. He looked at the bars of the cramped Shelby County Penal Farm jail cell. He thought, I shoulda never got mixed up with Rafe Coleman in the first damn place. When I get out of here, I'll fix it with him good! He said a quick prayer. That would be then; this was now.

"I confess, I killed Erby," he whispered back in December to his accusers.

48—BACON AND EGGS

Rafe watched her from the kitchen door as she poured his coffee.

"Craving your other breakfast?" the coy woman inquired.

"You just gave me what I ached to have."

Thelma Louise looked across the room at Mr. Rafe. He looked like a little boy that stole a cookie before his evening meal.

"That right?" She walked over and placed a cup of black coffee on the table in front of him. Bustie smiled and swayed back to the stove. She knew he liked watching her move around his kitchen.

The young woman looked back over her shoulder. Again, she flashed Rafe the perfect smile the years of brushing daily with sassafras twigs had produced. She thought while looking back at him, I like the way he watches me.

"Girl, don't go away no more."

She offered no reply. He may not want breakfast, but what they'd just shared came nowhere near to completing her needs. She placed a piece of bacon in the hot skillet.

"You hear me! I don't want you to stay gone again."

"When you get this electric cookstove?"

"Put it in just before Christmas. I hoped you'da been back before now to use it."

"It's nice. The folks I'm gone work for down in Memphis got one almost just like it."

He stood to his feet and stepped toward Thelma Louise from his safe spot at the table. "What's that about you working in Memphis?"

"My sister Doreen got me a job maiding for a family down there. Me and the young'uns will move next week." Bustie focused on the now-sizzling bacon. She dared not look into Rafe's face or he might detect her lies.

"Now, why you want to go down to Memphis when you can just stay here and work for me?"

The stove warmed the skillet and the bacon really began to sizzle. Thelma Louise looked over at Mr. Rafe, but he looked into her open blouse instead of her face. She closed the top buttons.

"We got another son," she spat at him.

"That fat bastard Ely enjoyed reporting that to me."

Bustie stared at Rafe. "You know they're starving along with my other three?"

Neither the man nor the woman blinked in this contest of wills.

"I ain't got food in the house to eat, can't feed yours and can't feed my others." A flood of tears rolled from her eyes.

Rafe stepped a little closer. "Now, now, don't worry."

"Don't worry!" She felt a new power over him. "I ain't seen you since the night somebody killed Gill Erby. I'da thought you killed him except you was wit' me after you sent Johnlee to trick Jude away." She looked up at him and wiped her eyes with the backs of both hands. Bustie recovered with a bright smile. "I didn't know who that second set of headlights was when you drove up after Johnlee and Jude left. You a bold white man!"

"At first you seemed like you wasn't glad to see me," a smiling Rafe retorted.

She pouted and wiped her big eyes. "I acted glad enough later, didn't I?"

"Yes, ma'am, you did!" He smiled again.

She glanced at him; he looked so different when he smiled. "It worries me that Sue Nell knows."

They stopped speaking and the skillet's sizzling sounds outlined their silence.

"I'm worried. Folks talking about you really killed Gill Erby and I can't say a word. It bothers me so 'til my milk ain't even come in. The women in my family usually make so much milk that we have to squeeze it out to keep from getting the milk leg because our babies can't drink it all."

"Let them niggers talk."

"Rafe, I wish you wouldn't use that word!" she shot back and then retreated to her work.

Neither spoke for a while.

The hunger in her stomach and the ache in her heart gave her new courage. "Rafe, me and my children starving almost every day and you don't do nothing about it! I can understand you not feeding the first three, but the other two is yours!"

Rafe Coleman felt shame and bowed his head.

"You ought to see them, they look like you spit them out." Her voice trembled, her pain showed when she continued, "I'm tired of watching my babies starve and go without, tired, just so tired." She turned the bacon, the grease popped and her tears flowed down her cheeks again.

He picked up a writing tablet and pencil from the kitchen table. Rafe Coleman sat down and methodically wrote on the pad of paper.

Bustie dared not look around. She'd spoken more of her mind to Rafe in those brief moments than ever before. With Rafe, you just never knew how he would receive something. Bustie cracked two eggs on the side of the cast-iron skillet with her left hand while using her right to move the almost done slab bacon. The hot oil sizzled after she dropped the double-yoked eggs into the pan. They danced in the hot oil.

Rafe walked back to the stove and stood closer to her than he normally did. He spoke in a soft trembling voice even Rafe did not know he owned. "Thelma Louise, take this down to the store. You ain't gone have no trouble with hunger again."

She turned her eggs carefully in the hot oil; this was no time to burst the yokes. Thelma removed the meat from the skillet. Her hands trembled and her eyes produced more tears after she looked at the note.

It read,

Conrad, Thelma Louise is gone come to the store every week. You give her *ANYTHING* she wants and put it on my account. We'll settle up every month like always. Raford Coleman III.

Bustie folded her priceless financial passport and quickly tucked it from view into her brassiere. Rafe placed his large hands on her shoulders; he turned the small woman to face him.

"Did that ni—" He paused to correct himself. "Did he do that to your eye?"

She nodded pitifully.

He gently kissed her lips then her forehead before wiping away her tears with the thumbs of both hands. But he stepped away from her as fast as he had approached. The brief tender moment passed and, for now, Rafe Coleman needed a safe distance between them again.

He walked to the doorway and posed a startling question without turning to face her. "If I buy a little house, would you move there?"

Surprise caused her to pause before she answered a question she rehearsed continually. She'd known her answer since Christmas Day 1932, the first time he'd touched her.

"Me and all my kids?"

"Uh-huh," he said slowly. "All five."

"What the folks gone say?"

"Same things they say now."

"Rafe, you sure you want this?"

"Yeah," he drawled. "Thelma, I done thought about this a whole lot. I want it." He stammered the next sentence. "I, I, I want you," he proposed.

"What if you change your mind later and put me down?"

"Folks say a lot about me, but I don't go back on my word." He never turned around. "You know that. I'll never change my mind."

She just stared at his back. Disbelief framed her face. Finally she located her memorized words. "I'll move to the place you get," she stammered on, "if-you-p-p-put it in my name."

He looked over his shoulder at her. Rafe Coleman winked and he smiled. "The house gone be in your name."

They both stood there while she removed the over-easy eggs from the skillet and placed them on the plate next to the crispy slab bacon.

"Now, what else you worried 'bout?"

"Why you doing this and what gone happen to Jude?"

Rafe turned around. With a lowered head, he said, "I can't tell you exactly why…" He shrugged like a lost boy. "Sometimes, I just feel old and alone."

The young woman smiled at him. "You coulda fooled me."

He smiled back. "Them two boys the only offspring I got in the world. I know even now, this wrong. You the wife of another man and I'm taking you. Really," he added with a smile, "I done took you." He gazed into those clear eyes of hers. "Thelma Louise, ain't nothing gone happen to Jude unless Jude causes it."

Thelma Louise Gibson Smith turned off the electric stove and pushed the skillet aside. Her stomach hunger subsided. Rafe walked toward his bedroom in the back of the house. When Thelma Louise followed, she noticed milk flowed freely from her breasts and wet her blouse through the brassiere.

The Ford purred when Chess Gordon pulled into the place that used to be home for him. Son and he were overdue for a good long visit.

"Damn it! Those fields ought to be plowed already!"

The automobile slowly moved past the house and into the

backyard. Chess smiled when he saw Son sprawled across Birdie Mae's lap. The boy sat up abruptly when he heard the engine noise. Chess's smile turned to a frown when it sunk in on him that Son lay across his grandmother's lap like a child.

"Morning, Birdie. That's a mighty big baby."

Mama Birdie Mae laughed at first, but her expression changed when she remembered what Chess Gordon probably told Baby Sister. Her stern reply surprised him. "Remember, he mine no matter what you thinking."

"Birdie, what's got you riled this morning?"

"Huh, a nigger like you don't come around unless he wants something."

"Birdie Mae, I know my ice don't get as cold as a white man's ice, but me and your boy gone talk!"

Sarah Erby stepped through the back door at that moment. "Morning, Cousin Chess."

"Sarah, how do today?"

"Mighty fine. Why you need to speak with Son?"

Chess Gordon stepped from the car door. He could see he needed to stand to say this speech to these ole girls. And Birdie Mae's lip riled him. "I was holding back because of the circumstances. Y'all been dealt a bad hand, but you ain't the only one holding ugly cards. It's time to face some facts. A nigger like me holds your mortgage, and the first note comes due this winter. It ain't gone get paid if you let this boy, naw, this young man lay 'round like a lap baby!"

He paused for a rebuttal but neither woman spoke.

"It ain't gone get paid from fields that ought to be plowed and they sitting there full of weeds. Now, me and Son got business to take care of that can pay the mortgage. I'll help him but y'all got to pay the debt service if you want to keep the place. After all, where else you gone stay?"

The mockingbird began to sing from his perch high in the tree above the backyard. Birdie Mae Lilliard opened her mouth, but she thought better of her planned words.

"Son, get in the house there. Put on your Sunday go-to-meeting clothes, but leave off the necktie."

"Where we going Cousin Chess?"

"You need to see a few things to clear your head and get you on the move. But mostly I need you to meet two good friends of mine down in Memphis, Mr. Tony Capezio and Judge Francis Monahan Jr."

Birdie Mae folded her arms across her breast and glanced at an equally silent Sarah.

49—TAMING THE BEAST

The katydids sang their songs and Jim Falls looked up at the sun in the April-morning sky. Across the field another of the big green grasshoppers answered the first's call. "Even grasshoppers ain't alone." He looked around the yard of the old farmhouse. "How did Gill Erby scratch a living out of this place all those years?" Jim Falls thought about his wife and their Sunday-afternoon telephone conversation…

"I ain't coming back," she'd said. "Busting my backside and what for? I tell you why. Just so some white trash with a little more money and land than me can get rich. It ain't no way!"

"But, Sue Lynn, I thought we could work things out."

"Jim, I done moved on. You do the same. I went to see a lawyer last week about filing for divorce when I figure out how to pay for it."

The young mule Mr. Rafe had supplied Jim interrupted his thoughts. Like his current master at the reins, this beast did not want to be here this morning either. The animal hesitated under the plow's burden and slowed to a near stop.

"Get up there! Get up! Get up, mule, get up!" Over and over, the always frustrated and equally inept Jim Falls popped the reins hard across the creature's back.

A family of blue jays chorused their disapproval of Jim's treatment of the mule. The birds screamed their alarm calls and Jim struggled with the untrained animal. Halfway through the field, he made the mistake of looking back at his work, and the row in progress curved recklessly.

"Whoa! Whoa, mule!" The mule quickly obeyed the command to stop. He looked back at Jim Falls as if to say, Can you make up your mind?

Another katydid's call echoed across the open field. Jim stood there and listened for the answer from another insect neighbor. In the distance, a family of crows issued call after call.

Jim Falls felt alone and he got mad. "How in the hell did that nigger scratch out a living here?"

"Now, Son, ain't no telling where you going with Chess or what you gone see. I know him, so you might go to all types of joints. Mama Birdie wants you to remember who you are today. You hear me, boy?"

His curiosity already on the rise, the young boy answered with a nod.

Outside, a solitary Chess Gordon gazed across the fields in back of his old place. He knew this land like the back of his hand; his entire life played out up and down these fencerows.

"A lot of my life doesn't make me proud," he whispered.

"Cousin Chess," Sarah shouted, "Son ready!"

The old man looked back toward the house where he'd spent most of his eighty-plus years. He felt very old; the fight in his spirit was gone. He started the short distance back to the house. As he approached, he saw that Son stood on the porch in his Sunday white shirt and brown pants. Sarah and Birdie Mae flanked the boy on both sides.

Chess smiled. Under his breath, he declared, "We gone break that apron-string hold on him today." Louder, he continued, "Boy, you know something," Chess chorused aloud, "you looks just like your grandpappy, Gillam Hale. If I didn't know better, I'da thought it was him standing there instead of you. When did you grow so tall?"

Son smiled wide like he used to before Papa Gill died. At that moment, he forgot all about his circumstance.

"Momma says I grew some this winter."

"Your momma's right. Come on down here, we got places to go and people to see."

The boy jumped from the high porch to the ground. Chess felt more alive just watching him. As Son landed, the former slave made a mental note of the watch chain that hung from the boy's pocket.

"Ladies, we'll be late, but I promise he'll be fine."

Sarah smiled, but Birdie Mae Lilliard frowned.

Chess Gordon remembered something. "Son, open up the trunk of the car."

The boy walked around and turned the handle at the rear of the Ford. The sudden honking of geese and fowl filled the air. Son laughed aloud when he saw two crates full of birds.

Before he noticed, Chess Gordon stood next to him. Pointing at the crate to the left and then the right, the old man instructed, "Son, these guinea fowl and geese are the best watchdog a man can have…they'll keep you apprised anytime somebody come, day or night."

The boy and the old man made eye contact, nothing needed to be said. Both understood. Momentarily, Chess Gordon marveled at how close to his eye level the once-chubby child stood.

"Boy, how tall you stand now?"

Son laughed. "I don't rightly know."

"It's sure a lot more than it was this time last year." Chess Gordon looked down at his high-water dress pants.

"Cousin Chess," Sarah chirped loudly from the porch, "he growed more than four inches this past year. Son's almost as tall as Mr. Erby…" Her voice trailed off.

Chess saved the moment. "Boy, put them fowl in the chicken yard."

Son lifted the wooden crates by the handles. He strode off toward the same chicken-yard location where runaway slave Gillam Hale had grabbed a young Chess Gordon more than seventy-five years ago.

The former Chess Boy pulled his pipe and tobacco from his pants pocket. "That boy even walk like Mr. Gillam."

From the porch, Birdie Mae spat into the yard. "That what worrying me."

The old man turned to look up at her. The first cousins eyed each other.

"Son," Chess shouted after the boy. "Keep 'em in that pen until they get used to calling this home. After you feed 'em a few weeks, they ain't going nowhere else. Get your old granny to show you how to set them so you can get a new brood this summer." He struck a match to light his now-filled pipe. Smoke filled the air and drifted off to meet Son when he returned.

"You want the crates?"

"Naw, I don't farm, I'm a city slicker. Remember?"

Both the old and the near-man laughed.

"Put the crates on the porch, they might come in handy to carry something for you on occasion." Son and Chess knew the old man meant whiskey. "You going with me or not?"

"Yessuh!"

"Then, us go!" He walked to the driver's door before raising his hand. "Birdie Mae, remember that big old American chestnut tree down there you always begged me to not cut down?"

She nodded her head slowly.

"Well, y'all better get a sawmill man on it this year. That's some expensive lumber that shouldn't get wasted. That tree got the blight that's killing all the chestnut trees. It'll be dead in a year or two."

Cousin Chess climbed into the Ford and slid behind the wheel. He surveyed Son from head to toe. He brought the car's engine to life and shifted into reverse. "Son, that your daddy's watch in your pocket?"

"Yessuh."

Chess shifted the car into first gear. "Pull it out and let me see it."

Son pulled the shiny gold watch from his britches watch pocket. The Coca-Cola swastika watch fob shone in the morning sun while Chess turned left onto Quito Road.

"Boy, I meant to speak to you about that watch fob I gave your daddy."

"You want it back?" the boy began defensively.

"No, I ain't no Indian giver, but I want you to stop wearing that ornament."

A puzzled Son looked up at Cousin Chess.

"Pick up that *Press Scimitar* newspaper from yesterday on the floorboard down there. Read the headlines aloud and look at the picture beneath it. You'll know why you need to stop after you read it and see that picture."

The boy picked up the paper and straightened it out. Chess smiled when Son's eyes widened.

"'Storm clouds gathering over Europe.' Cousin Chess, look! That symbol's the same as this thing on Papa's watch. What's it all mean?"

"Well, Son, it pretty complicated. But, basically, a new group of folks is running the country of Germany now. They call themselves the Nazi party."

"What's the Nazi party?"

"It's kind of like being Democratic or Republican. So far, these Nazi folks ain't nice people. Kinda like the klan. Only they work by day. They downright crazy and they got big plans, as far as I can see. They took the swastika from being a Hindu religious symbol to being their own thing. So, Son, you don't want to be connected with that."

Son laid the paper down and removed the brass watch fob. "I guess it don't mean what it used to mean."

"Naw, it don't. You'll find as you get older that many things that used to mean one thing mean something different later on." He paused and looked at the boy. "I like that." He repeated it. "'Many things that used to mean one thing mean something different later on.'"

"Cousin Chess, the Nazis did that with the swastika. The cross is a religious symbol. What's the difference in the Klan burning a cross and folks still using the cross for a good thing?"

"I don't rightly know," he said, recognizing the depth of the boy's question and feeling discomfort with the comparison. "How about driving an old man the rest of the way to Memphis? You think you can do that?"

"I sure will try!"

"A try is usually all it takes to get something done." Cousin Chess pulled to the side of the road.

"Son, put this on your mind. Gill used to tell me how good you made whiskey. Any truth to that?"

The boy smiled. "I do all right."

"Well, think back on the things you got in the barn at your place. What you need to make whiskey that you ain't got?"

Son provided the answer he'd mulled over for weeks in his head. "Sweetening and a still to cook it off, I got a barrel for a setup container. And, of course, I need a place to cook."

"I'm holding two fifty-five-gallon barrels of molasses on hand since last fall. How much whiskey can you make with that much molasses?"

"More than I ever made at once before. I figure over two hundred and fifty gallons!"

"What you think about going into business together?"

"How much you gone get for me?"

"Boy, I ain't gone get you nothing. Get it yourself."

Son returned Chess's stare.

"Let's split everything fifty-fifty. I got the sweetening and the cooker. You got the know-how and the time. You need to make some cash. What you think?"

"Mighty fine! That sounds mighty fine to me. But who'll buy it and what about the law?"

Chess Gordon pointed toward his head. "It ain't never a problem finding somebody to buy whiskey. That's the other way I'll earn my share. That's why we going to see Mr. Capezio on Beale Street and Judge Monahan at the Shelby County Courthouse. Always remember this. That stuff between your ears ain't just gray matter. Them is brains up there. Make sure to use them. Now, drive an old man to town."

"You sure I'm old enough to handle it?"

"Boy, a whole lot a folks gone ask if you old enough for what you fixing to do. You got to answer that yourself."

Son Erby guided the V-8 Coupe down Quito Road.

An elderly man teaching a sixteen-year-old boy to move forward from a terrible tragedy is a good thing. But many of the things that used to mean one thing mean something different later on.

50—ODD BEDFELLOWS

"Judge Monahan, someone's here to see you."

The judge looked over his glasses at the clock on the wall. "You know I don't like to be disturbed."

"Yes, sir, but it's Chess Gordon."

The judge's stern face morphed into a smile. "Show Chess in here!"

The law clerk left and in a few moments returned with the tall light-skinned Negro.

Judge Francis Monahan Jr. used his hands to grasp the wheels of his chair. He rolled around his large desk to meet Chess Gordon halfway. "An old Republican like you isn't ashamed to be seen in my chambers?"

"Now, Judge, since y'all Democrats running everything, we Republicans got to have friends on our side too. Especially with all the changes y'all new president making."

The two men exchanged hearty laughter. Chess approached with his hat in his hands and the two shook hands firmly.

"How are you, my dear friend?"

"Judge, I'm fine for an old man."

"Chess—" the judge waved toward a sofa to the side of his desk "—have a seat. What can I do for you?"

"Well, Your Honor, I need to speak with you 'bout a couple of things. You know about my son being up at the Shelby County Penal Farm."

"Yes, Chess, I was not involved directly, but I followed that case last year with much interest. Who was it he was convicted of killing?"

"Gill Erby."

"Gill Erby? Why does that name ring a bell?"

"Gillam Hale."

"That's it. Gill Erby was Uncle Gillam's boy. Where would I be if it wasn't for Gillam Hale?"

"How long did Gillam Hale stay with y'all?"

"He was there before I was born and he stayed there until he left here in 1883." The judge paused in thought. "So, Gill Erby was Uncle Gillam's boy. I never made the connection. I only knew it was your son in trouble. It surprised me when I did not hear from you last year."

"Judge, that boy of mine ain't no good, but he didn't kill Gill. I promise you that."

"You sure?"

"He told me he didn't."

"Every inmate at the penal farm says that."

"Yes sir, but I know Johnlee. I know when he lying and when he's telling the truth."

"Well, who did it?"

"Johnlee wouldn't say. He's scared. But I think my redheaded nephew did it."

The judge laughed. "Rafe Coleman? What a waste of humanity!"

The two men laughed. The judge winced in pain and grabbed his left thigh. He rubbed the leg vigorously with both hands.

"Judge, how's your physical condition?"

"The polio is as it always is. I move forward and it reaches up and grabs me back. But I continue to move forward."

"I know you're proud of your president."

"Yes, I am. I do wish more people knew he had polio. His handlers always make it look as if FDR was a physical perfection. I want folks to know the struggle it takes for him to just get out of bed."

"Judge, my son got eleven months and twenty-nine days. Any possibility he could get out early for good behavior?"

"There is always a possibility. Didn't he confess?"

"Lots of colored men confess."

"But did he confess?"

"Yes, sir, he did." Chess lowered his head and rotated his hat in his hand.

Monahan thought of all the years he had known Chess. Chess Gordon looked old. "Chess, you know what strikes me as odd?"

"No, sir."

"I'm the son of the judge that tried a murder case so many years ago. It involved a Rafe Coleman, a colored man named Gillam and a rich banker named Allen Sawyer. All we need today is to get Allen Sawyer Jr. involved and this would truly be ironic."

"I hadn't thought of that, but you right. Mr. Al is all we need to get the current generation of players together."

"How is Allen?"

"I ain't seen much of him. He seems preoccupied. Especially since his daughter is old enough to come into her money this year."

"That matter comes before my court, so I cannot discuss that with you. But I can say we will see what happens with one Johnlee Gordon."

"Thank you, sir. Thank you."

"You said you needed to discuss two matters with me?"

"Yes, sir. Now, we just spoke about Gillam Hale. Can you picture what he looked like?"

Judge Francis Monahan Jr. leaned back in his wheelchair and closed his eyes briefly. "Sure," he said and he opened his eyes. "I see him as if it were yesterday when he left."

"Well, Judge, I got his sixteen-year-old grandson outside. I want him to meet you."

"Who are his folks?"

"Gill Erby was his daddy."

"Chess, you play it both ways. Don't you?"

"Always have, Judge, always will."

"Why do you want me to meet him?"

"Well, the most important thing is I need to get him to be able to cash flow the farm his daddy bought from me last year."

"Is it the old Coleman place?"

"Yes sir, the home house."

"How's Rafe taking all this?"

"Now you see why I think he killed Gill Erby."

"Hmm, I see. Well, that's good land, but a sixteen-year-old will have a hard time making that place pay on farming these days."

"Yes, sir, but that boy got the same skills Mr. Gillam had."

The judge leaned forward in his chair and laughed aloud. "No, Chess!" he laughed aloud.

"Yes, sir, he got the gift and I want him to use it."

"You are pulling my leg."

"It's almost like Jesus turning water into wine."

The judge giggled like a little gal at a birthday party. He shook his head and shuddered while he laughed.

"Guess what else? He the spitting image of Mr. Gillam."

"Get him in here! I want to see this."

Chess Gordon opened the chambers door. "Son, come in here." Chess stepped back and held the door wide. "Judge Francis Monahan Jr., this is Raymond Simon Erby. Ray Erby, allow me to present the Honorable Francis Monahan Jr."

Judge Monahan appeared spellbound. "Come here, young man. Let me get a good look at you. Close the door, Chess."

Chess closed the door; Son stepped forward and shook the judge's hand.

"Raymond, do you realize how much you look like your grandfather?"

Son looked at Chess. He spoke only after Chess nodded his approval.

"Papa used to say it all the time and Cousin Chess says it, too."

"Son, you look just like Uncle Gillam. Just like him! I understand you have some business problems. What is it you seek?"

The boy looked at Chess Gordon.

"Tell him what we talked about, Son."

"Well, sir. I, I, I got a farm I'm gone to inherit from my papa. He left it to me in his will. Cousin Chess showed me the will today. But the farm is mortgaged to Cousin Chess and it's got to be paid off."

"How much is the mortgage?"

Son looked at Cousin Chess. Cousin Chess nodded again.

"It, it's $9,500."

"Hmm, that's a lot of money. Don't you think?"

"Yessuh."

"What's the first payment and when is it due?"

"Nine hundred dollars is due at the end of the year."

"Well, now. You sound like quite the young businessman. You must have a good teacher."

Son and Chess grinned wide.

"Now, Raymond—" Judge Monahan smiled when he said this "—how do you think you can raise this money?"

"Well, I'm gone to put in a crop and there are a few other enterprises I can do."

"These other enterprises pay well?" The judge smiled.

"Yessuh."

"How can I help you?"

Son looked at Chess. He received another reassuring nod. "Well, I need to be able to run my business and there's probably a few folks 'round that won't like that."

"Anyone in particular?"

"Mr. Rafe Coleman would probably be the first."

The judge moved to the left in his wheelchair. He pushed his glasses up on his nose. "You got anything against Mr. Rafe Coleman?"

The boy's expression changed to a slight frown. He gave no verbal answer and shrugged his shoulders instead.

"You will need to put aside whatever you hold against him. Can you do that?"

No answer came.

"Raymond, I need your answer before we proceed. Can you put those things aside and go into business with Mr. Rafe despite how you feel?"

The boy looked to Chess with angry eyes.

His new mentor nodded. Facing the judge again, Son's barely audible reply came from clenched teeth. "Yessuh, I can put it aside."

Judge Monahan removed his spectacles. He waved for Son to come closer to him. Slowly the boy complied. "Young fellow, I tell you what. I'll give Constable Rafe Coleman a call. He and I know each other quite well. We do not always agree, but we work together to get things done. His attitude toward you will change after he and I speak. Wait a few days on your other enterprise and go see Mr. Rafe next week. Your farming will more than keep you busy until then. What do you think?"

"Thank you, Judge Monahan. Thank you, sir! But, but, ah, you want me to go see him?"

"Raymond, I know there are issues with your family and Rafe Coleman. Only you can decide if the farm is important enough for you to do business with Raford Coleman III. Is it?"

The routine repeated. He looked to Chess; the old man nodded. Son whispered, "Yessuh."

"Excellent. Now, come see me during crop lay-by time to let me know how you are doing with both your enterprises. Chess, where is this will the boy mentioned?"

Chess Gordon handed the judge a piece of paper. He started to look at the document.

"Chess, do you attest and swear Gill Erby wrote this by his own hand and the signature herein is that of one Gill Erby?"

The two men dared not look at each other because they both knew Chess's answer was a lie.

"Yes, sir. Gill Erby wrote it and he signed it, too!"

"Chess and Raymond, I shall see to it that this matter is brought before my court in this afternoon's session. Raymond, when you reach maturity at twenty-one years of age, you will own a three-hundred-fifty-acre farm. Of course, that means you need to cash flow a $9,500 mortgage. Are you prepared to do that?"

Son turned to Cousin Chess.

The judge very purposely interrupted. "Don't look at Chess. You will be the one making those payments. Chess might help you some, but you got to cut the mustard. Your momma will try to help you, but she can't do much." He looked over the top of those wire-framed spectacles at the end of his long, thick nose. "It's all on you."

Son gathered himself. "Yes sir," he answered firmly. "I'll do whatever it takes."

The judge looked at Chess. The two older men shared a slight twinkle in their eyes at Son's strength.

"Now, you two let me get back to judicial matters, or I might be late for dinner tonight. Mrs. Monahan wouldn't like that. Now, would she, Chess?"

"Not the Miss Margaret I know. How is Miss Margaret?"

"She's fine. I shall tell her you asked about her."

Chess and Son turned to go.

"Raymond, bring me a Mason jar of your enterprise results when you come to see me next time. Age it a bit so I can see if you truly are like Gillam Hale in that regard as well!"

Son's eyes widened and Chess laughed as they left. Chess turned back toward the judge. "Thank you, Your Honor."

"No, Chess, thank *you*. This made my week. You ought to drive this young man over to the café for a midday snack to celebrate his good fortune."

Judge Monahan rolled himself back behind his desk. "Gillam Hale's grandson." He just shook his head. "I wonder what ever happened to Uncle Gillam after he left here for Charleston, South Carolina. Walter!" the judge summoned his clerk.

The man stepped into the open chambers doorway. "Yes, sir."

"Call up to Lucy, Tennessee, to the Coleman Brothers Cotton Gin office. I wish to speak with Constable Raford Coleman III. Try his home and his brother's store if he's not in the office. I want to speak with him immediately."

"Yes, sir. Do you need anything else?"

"No, thank you. Just let me know when you get him."

Judge Monahan started a daydream and Walter returned to his outer office. My father would have put me in an asylum because of my polio if not for Gillam Hale. His grandson will have every chance to succeed. Judge Francis Monahan Jr. placed his hands behind his head. Raymond, I think you will do whatever it takes, just like Gillam Hale did.

Jude Smith came home to find a near-empty house. He sank to the floor next to where the wood heater used to sit. Most of what little he had was gone. No note told him where Bustie took the children. His few clothes lay tied in two meager balls. Only the cookstove remained from their other personal items in the cold, empty sharecropper's shack.

The fury welled up in Jude Smith. "That white trash behind this." Jude sprang to his feet with the agility a man his size should not possess. "This time, he's gone pay for it. He's gone pay." He stomped across the room, snatched open the front door, and, in the early spring morning, walked back to Lucy, forgetting what he'd contributed to his circumstance that day.

51—FOUND AMONG THE REEDS

She drove her new Ford east along Quito Road toward the farm where Sarah Erby and her family now lived. A determined young woman turned the car into the driveway and pulled up the hill. Thunder sounded from the dark clouds gathering in the spring sky.

"It sure looks like rain," Sarah said from the rear seat. "You get straight back to the house after you drop me off."

Amanda offered no reply. She drove past the house and pulled in around back. Three geese in the chicken yard trumpeted their arrival. Amanda stopped a safe distance from the back porch.

"Miss Amanda—" Sarah touched the young woman's right shoulder "—child, what's your trouble?"

"No troubles, finishing my schoolwork and starting at the bank were on my mind."

"Well, you've frowned all morning and that ain't like you!"

She offered a smile to Sarah.

"Now, that better. I told Son when he dropped me off that I hoped you was in a better mood than the last time you came home."

"Where is Son?"

She pointed through the trees, "He better be down in that bottom getting the fields plowed. Bennie's working with him."

"I knew about Jude and Thelma Louise living on your place. When did Bennie join you?"

"We needed another tenant for that little place on Johnson Road. Son and I spoke about it. I suggested we put Bennie in it. He gone raise a crop and work for Son."

"How is Son?"

"Ever since Chess Gordon took him to Memphis this past Monday that boy has smiled almost like he used to before Mr. Erby got shot."

"I'm glad." She reached out her right hand. Sarah grasped it with her left and squeezed it tight. The older woman opened the rear passenger door. Reluctantly, she released Amanda's hand, wiggled her fingertips into a wave and walked around the rear of the auto toward the back porch. "Miss Amanda, see you next time."

"Sarah. I promise it won't be so long until I see you again." She paused and shared the smile she knew that news would bring to Sarah's face. A boom from the thunder of the approaching storm interrupted their joy. Amanda shouted over the natural obstacle, "I need to speak with Birdie Mae about a dress I want her to sew for me."

Sarah nodded and, with a little wave, ascended the steps and disappeared through the rear screened doorway.

Amanda wondered how this conversation might go. She needed answers that only Birdie Mae could provide.

★ ★ ★

He looked over his shoulder. The pride of the operation he now ran moved up his backbone. He thought it over carefully. More could be done in a day with organization and specialization. Everything started with the big middle-buster plow he ran. Ole Dan slowed slightly under the strain. Son alertly swung the small whipping stick he kept just for this purpose. The thick willow switch produced a whipping sound as he swung it again quickly.

"Get up, Dan. You want me on you?" That simple swish sound from a thick switch, coupled with Son's stern command, steadied the beast. The mule knew his new young master to be very different than the older gentler hand he used to ignore. Dan understood Son Erby would beat him mercilessly at the least sign of noncompliance. He pulled his share of the load step for step beside his gentler counterpart, Dick.

Behind Son and a few rows over to the right, Bennie Gorlan easily guided the harrow through the rich, bottomland soil. He followed the middle buster after Son made a pass up and back to form a single row. The middle buster opened the area between what would become two rows after an initial plowing with a turning plow. The duo had completed the turning plow work a day earlier, on Friday.

"Son, that mule act like a different animal since you work him."

Son heard Bennie's comments when he passed farther to the right in the field.

Bennie added a coded message to show his respect for his new boss while he headed the opposite direction. "That mule knows what to do and who's the boss out here! It Mr. Son

Erby! Ole Dan doesn't want you to beat him. Get up there, hoss! Get up!"

The acknowledgment from Bennie brought smiles to Son's face. Bennie walked to the left side of the harrow the borrowed horse pulled through the twice-plowed soil. The harrow topped the rows and prepared the soil for planting with the small spikes on the rectangular-shaped implement.

The eyes of the hired hand and his boss met whenever Bennie and the horse passed Son plowing with Dick and Dan. Working for Son Erby made him feel good. He felt comfortable on this place again.

He thought of the small house he now lived in on the farm. For the first time in a long time, Bennie had a place he could call home. His thoughts drifted to Miss Sarah. Bennie knew she would be there, looking as good as ever, when they got back to the house. He smiled. "Get up, hoss! Get up!"

A growl of thunder sounded after a lightning shaft pierced the sky. "Bennie, we gone need to quit soon. Some weather coming in from the west."

The first sprinkles of rain hit the windshield when Birdie Mae Lilliard pushed the screen door open to peer at Amanda over the top of her glasses. Slowly, she stepped through the doorway and the screen door closed behind her. The old woman walked over to the porch's edge. She grabbed one of the porch posts.

"Evening," the old woman began.

"Good evening, Birdie Mae. Can you come out to sit in the car? I need to speak with you."

"Miss Amanda, don't you know a storm coming up? You need to get on back to town."

"I really need to speak with you."

"But the dress can wait. We can do it another time."

"Birdie Mae, it is important I speak with you today!" A flash of lightning crossed the distant sky. The thunder boomed loudly and added a slow growling rumble. Both waited patiently for the noise to subside.

Birdie Mae pulled her shawl over her shoulders and obediently walked toward the porch steps. She moved down, one step at a time. The old woman paused to look at Amanda after she reached the last step. She knew Amanda had lied about needing advice on a dress. Birdie Mae started toward the driver's-side rear door.

"Come sit up front with me," Amanda directed.

The experienced colored matriarch ignored the comment and opened the rear driver's-side door. She groaned while she struggled to step up and into the back of the automobile.

"These old knees told me all day it would rain." The old woman settled into the seat directly behind Amanda. As if a switch were thrown, the bottom fell from the sky and big drops of rain began to pour.

"Birdie Mae," Amanda's young voice trembled, "tell me about the day I was born."

Birdie Mae took the shawl from her head. She refused to even look at the young lady in the front seat. Instead, she peered through the raindrops as they fell on the passenger-side rear door. Her demeanor appeared stern even by standards for her. No answer crossed the old woman's lips.

"Birdie Mae, my father," the girl stumbled as she realized what she was saying, "he, he told me you delivered me." She paused and turned to look directly into Birdie Mae Lilliard's silent face. "Birdie Mae, is Sarah my mother?"

Birdie Mae worked her lips and mulled over a reply while she looked into Amanda's eyes. For a time, this odd pair stared into each other's faces. The all-knowing midwife offered no answer.

"How can you just sit there after I asked you about something like this?" Her pent-up anguish and emotion from keeping this secret for the past three months spilled out.

Birdie Mae Lilliard finally broke her silence. She looked into Amanda's face. Very softly she spoke the secret she'd planned to never reveal. "Chile, Sarah is your momma. It's the truth."

Amanda noticed fog on the windows from their body heat. The filmed windows formed a safe cocoon, making her father's Packard the perfect place to share their secret.

"But, Birdie Mae, how? How could she be my mother?"

"Baby Sister must have told you this. It ain't serving no purpose! No purpose at all!"

Amanda leaned her head against the window glass. She remembered that cold January day when Miss Media Sneed sent the car for her. "She said they used to call her Baby Sister when she was a girl." Tears ran down her cheeks and she added, "That is what she said her name was until you made her pass for white."

"Baby," Birdie Mae began tenderly, "this ain't something you supposed to know."

"Who else knows? Does Sarah know?"

Birdie Mae shook her head. "I made sure of that. And she don't never need to know!" Birdie Mae added sternly. "Ain't nobody know but Baby Sister and that no-good brother of hers."

"Which brother? Rafe Coleman?"

Birdie Mae actually laughed. "No. Rafe Coleman is Baby Sister's half brother. But he doesn't know it. He thinks she's his whole sister who was named Media. The real Media is dead. If he did know, that bastard woulda told everybody by now. The no-good brother I'm talking about is Chess Gordon. He knows!"

The rain's patter on the car was the only audible sound. Softly, in a tone of regret, she added, "Chess came up with the idea."

"But how could he plan such a thing?"

Birdie Mae shrugged her shoulders. "We ain't had no plan. It just happened."

"But how?" Amanda turned around to look Birdie Mae fully in the face. Tears filled her eyes. Birdie Mae was her real grandmother. The weight of it all settled on her. She dropped her head and sobbed.

"You know Alice Sawyer hated me."

Amanda nodded.

"That ole witch hated me because she knew she done me and Sarah wrong. Me and Allen Sawyer Jr. got the same pappy? Bet you ain't never heard that."

"Yes, ma'am, I have. A couple of years ago I read Grandfather's will in some old records in the bank's vault. That's when I found it out. I saw your name on a slave listing on some old property tax records as the offspring of Allen Sawyer Sr."

"What did you say?" Birdie Mae asked curtly.

Amanda wiped her eyes and looked up to see an angry scowl on Birdie Mae's face.

"I just said I saw your name."

"No, ma'am, that ain't what I mean. You said, 'Yes, ma'am' to me!" Birdie Mae pointed an index finger bent from years of hard labor at Amanda. "Listen here, Lil' missy, you listen well! Don't you ever say 'yessum' to me again! You wasn't supposed to know this. But just because you do, don't change a thing. Far as I'm concerned, you still Allen Sawyer Jr.'s daughter."

Amanda cried harder.

"You might as well to stop that sniffling. Ain't going to change nothing. Besides, look at you. Think what it'd 'a been like for a girl look like you to grow up colored! Every dirty black buck and filthy-minded white man woulda been in line after you!" She added, "And, me or Sarah couldn'ta stopped the peckerwoods and it woulda been hell holding back the niggers."

Amanda wiped her face with both hands. Birdie Mae unfolded her handkerchief. She touched Amanda on the shoulder and handed the dainty piece of cloth to the startled young woman.

"Thank you, Birdie Mae," she stammered.

"Chile, you gone be all right." Birdie Mae patted her shoulder and smiled. "It just ain't every day a pretty young white woman like you finds out you got just a touch of colored blood."

Amanda looked up from the handkerchief where her face was buried. Somehow that seemed funny. She laughed heartily for the first time since she ate supper with Mrs. Sneed in the Peabody Hotel.

Birdie Mae joined her with a brief chuckle of her own. "All you got is a touch. My momma was half-white. My daddy and Sarah's daddy was white. Your daddy's white too. You more white than colored so it fitting for you to be white!"

Amanda struggled to absorb it all.

"It's just gone take a while for you to get used to it."

"But you still have not told me how!"

"Well, the will you saw ain't the first one. Alice Sawyer did away with the real one. Papa Allen left me some land and some money. He left a fund to set up a school for the whites and the coloreds."

"How do you know?"

"I was a young girl, but I remember it like it was yesterday. The old man showed it to me before he got shot."

"I saw the newspaper clippings on that too," Amanda blurted out. "Rafe and Conrad Coleman's father shot Grandfather." Her face contorted when she realized her last statement was not true. "He really was my great-grandfather. Wasn't he?"

Birdie Mae nodded at her granddaughter, separated from her by more than the seat. Lies, secrecy and a separate system based on blood and color lines established their division.

Amanda and Birdie Mae looked up when a car sloshed down Quito Road. Neither could see who it was.

"Missy, you need to get 'way from here! You can't stay here this long."

"Before I go, I need to know more. How? How did it happen?"

"You were switched by accident. It was Chess," Birdie Mae whispered. "Allen Jr.'s wife and his blood just didn't mix. Some folks call it having blue babies. Sarah got pregnant the same time that year. But Sarah was further 'long than Miss Sawyer. You were due to come any day, but Miss Sawyer shouldn'ta gone into labor for almost another three months." Birdie Mae paused and sternly added, "But she went into labor anyway."

Birdie Mae made eye contact with the young woman. Amanda nodded to show she followed the story.

"Chess Gordon's second wife, Maedell, was staying over to

the Sawyer place to help Miss Abigail out. Allen Jr., Miss Alice and Dr. Turnipseed left town on business. Maedell called Chess and he come to me when Miss Sawyer took sick."

"So you came to deliver her baby?"

"Yessum, I did."

Amanda Sawyer's startled look was obvious at her real grandmother saying yessum to her.

"I've said yessum since you turned twelve. I ain't gone change now and you better not either!"

Amanda nodded and wiped the moistness from her eyes. She steeled her resolve and nodded again, more firmly this time.

"Chess Gordon begged me to go. I didn't want to because of the fact Miss Alice and I hated each other so. But I went so Miss Abigail and her baby wouldn't suffer."

"You took Sarah with you?" Amanda interrupted.

"I did. At that point, I didn't let her out of my sight. She wasn't but sixteen years old." She paused, feeling the anguish of reliving the details. "But carrying you ain't bothered her none. Even with her first, having babies just like having a cold for Sarah."

Amanda looked up when the old woman said it. "Somehow, I just always knew she was my mother."

Birdie Mae ignored the sentiment and plowed ahead with her tale. "Chess came to town to get us. Me and Sarah were living in them shanties Mr. Rafe and Mr. Conrad got down in the bottom in back of the cotton gin in Lucy. Sarah went into labor on the wagon ride to the Sawyer place." Birdie Mae paused and looked at Amanda again before she continued, "When we got to the house, Miss Abigail was far along so I birthed the Sawyer child first. It was a boy. Miss Abby passed out. I tried to save the baby but he was already gone when he come out. He was blue and way too early…he was a blue baby for sure. I worked on him and even blew in his mouth, but he wouldn't come around. So I laid him aside and saw to Miss Abigail."

Birdie Mae continued in a monotone voice. "I took the boy back into the other room when I went to see about Sarah. Your head was crowning when I got into the room." She laughed. "You came out just as quick as could be. And, did you holler…sounded like somebody was trying to kill you!"

Amanda Sawyer could see the pain on the old woman's face from reliving it. "After I cleaned you up, Sarah held you and you got just as quiet as could be. While she held you, I did some work on Sarah. When I got through with her, she fell asleep with you in her arms. So I picked you up and you hollered again. No matter what I did, you wouldn't stop. So I put you in a reed basket and walked out in the hallway. I set you down on the old buffet that sets upstairs in the Sawyer place."

Birdie Mae blew out a sigh. "First, I peeked in on Miss Abigail. She was still sleeping, so I walked to the stairs to call that chicken, Maedell Gordon. She was so scared she wouldn't even come upstairs." Birdie Mae drew almost sullen when she continued, "Chess walked up. You were hollering so Chess whispered, 'You done good, Birdie. Is it a boy or girl?' 'It's a girl,' I told him. I carried you into the bedroom across the hallway, tried to quiet you down, but you hollered like I ain't seen a new baby holler before or since. I set the basket on the bed and took you out of it to try to quiet you down. Nothing worked."

She stared at Amanda. "That's when the mix-up happened. Chess said, 'Miss Abigail gone be pleased about it being a girl.' I said, 'Chess! This Sarah's baby! Miss Abigail had a boy and he's dead in the room with Sarah. He came here dead!' Chess said, 'You got to be lying.' 'Naw, I ain't. This Sarah's girl.' We was whispering so Miss Abby wouldn't wake up, but I don't know why because your hollering shoulda woke up the dead." She offered a prideful but comforting smile to her secret grandchild. "Chess said," she continued, "'This baby's so red you can't tell she got no colored blood.' I told him, 'Brother, remember, she ain't got much.' I looked at the back of your ears. The true color a Negro baby gone be is on the back of the ears. Yours was totally white. I told him, 'She ain't gone darken up neither. Look at her ears.' You hollered like I was killing you. I put you back in your basket and set you down on the buffet again. We walked back down the hall so we could hear ourselves think. Me and Chess was still talking when Miss Abby come out of her room. Real pitiful like, she said, 'My baby!' I fixed my mouth to tell her the truth, but Chess jumped in. 'Miss Abby, it's a girl. Ain't she pretty?' Miss Abby picked you up, little reed basket and all. She walked to me real slow, cradled you to her breast like she would die if she didn't have you. That white woman said out loud, 'Thank you, Lawd. I just knew my fourth one would be all right.' I got ready to tell her the truth again, but Chess grabbed me by the arm and shook his head. So I didn't say nothing." A thick silence fell and Mama Birdie Mae paused for a few seconds. "And I ain't said a word 'bout it since but one time…" Her voice trailed off. "I just act like it never happened."

The details calmed Amanda. Her awkwardness with it passed away with this second detailed telling. "Birdie Mae—" she paused and the two made eye contact again "—who is my father?"

"You sure you want to know?"

Amanda paused to think. "Yes, I need it all."

"Well, this is the worst of it." She dropped her head. "The year before you was born..." She paused and the pain of it hit her like the very thought of it always did. "The year before you were born, Rafe Coleman raped Sarah at the Fourth of July Frolic. He messed her up. He yo' daddy."

Amanda Sawyer held still in the front seat of her graduation present. A long time passed and neither of the car's occupants spoke a word.

Birdie Mae decided this was enough for her in one session even if the young woman wanted more. "Miss Amanda, you need to get away from here."

Amanda looked at her watch. "Birdie Mae, I need to talk with you some more, but I better get back or Father will be worried."

"I know. We'll talk some other time if you want. Young white women can't stay at the house of colored folks too long. It just don't look good."

The irony of this forced involuntary giggles to burst from their lips. For a few brief moments, they allowed their true identity to show—a grandmother and granddaughter sharing a secret, special time.

They stopped laughing and Amanda asked the obvious. "Who did you say knows about me?"

"Chess does and he told Reverend Cephas. They buried the Sawyer boy baby at Pleasant Grove Cemetery. I just found out last fall that Baby Sister knows. I guess Chess told her."

"And Sarah doesn't know?"

"No'm. But, it's the funniest thing. It's almost like she always did know. She took just as good care of you as she did the others she and Gill Erby had at the house. And, chile, you cried so much after Chess and Maedell took Sarah back to his house that night. You stayed sick with the colic until Sarah came to wet-nurse you a few weeks later."

"Sarah nursed me?"

Birdie Mae nodded. "Miss Abigail's baby came so early 'til her milk didn't come in."

"How did that happen with the relations between you and the Sawyers like they were?" Amanda knew the answer before Birdie Mae could reply.

In unison, they said, "Chess Gordon!"

It was a quiet evening. The storm passed to the northeast. The rain stopped and the sun peeked through a break in the clouds of the western sky. Amanda reached forward to wipe the fog from the passenger window. She pointed to the northeast across the bottom to the clouds above Big Jabbok. "Look, Birdie Mae, there's a rainbow in the sky," she said to her secret grandmother. "There must be a pot of gold in that direction."

"That's a good sign, a mighty good sign."

"I've never seen a vertical one like that."

"Me neither," the old woman replied.

"Birdie Mae, does Rafe Coleman know?"

"Hell no!" Birdie Mae replied. She pulled a pearl-handled two-shot derringer pistol from her dress pocket. The sunshine glistened on the nickel-plated barrel. "And I done told Chess Gordon, I'll kill him dead if Rafe ever find out!"

A knock came on the window of the car. "Miss Amanda, why you and Momma out here so long and what y'all talking about?" Sarah stood there with her hands on her hips.

Birdie Mae pushed the derringer into her apron pocket and opened the rear door. "Sarah Erby, this is an A and B conversation…C your way out." The old woman cackled and she struggled to step from the back seat. "Y'all been watching my pots since I been out here?"

"Yes, ma'am."

"Well, let's get in here and have supper." She clasped Sarah's arm and guided her toward the porch. "Miss Amanda, you just bring the material and the dress pattern by here when you home next week. I can get it made for you in time for graduation."

Bennie unhitched the mule. "We plowed some ground today."

"That's right and we gone plow just as much tomorrow."

"Tomorrow? What you talking about, Son? Tomorrow Sunday!"

Son Erby flashed his pretty smile. "Bennie Gorlan, I know tomorrow's Sunday. But the rain may dry up enough to get some work in. A man needs to do what he can whilst he can. We working tomorrow."

"But, hell."

"Nigger, don't 'but hell' me!'" Son interrupted. "We got to get this field planted with corn this week. If Rafe Coleman was cussing you like a dog, you'da just showed up Sunday and hitched up them mules!"

"You ain't Mr. Rafe Coleman!"

The two young men eyed each other, both with a bad set of nerves after a long physical day.

Son broke the tension. "Well, one of these days, you just might look up and find me just like Mr. Rafe." He struck a pose with his hands on his hips and stood erect and tall like Mr. Rafe always did. He twisted his face, harked, and spit a big wad of saliva down onto the sandy roadbed. The mockery did the trick. Both chuckled. "Besides, as warm as it is, that setup gone be ready by tomorrow night."

"We gone work in the day and then cook whiskey Sunday night?"

"Yeah, Bennie, how else am I gone get to be like Mr. Rafe Coleman?"

Even the dog-tired Bennie couldn't resist this joke.

"Hold Dan's reins for me." He handed the reins to Bennie. Son jumped over the small ditch that paralleled Quito Road. He clambered up a small hillside and disappeared into a thicket of reeds.

Bennie assumed that Son had entered the bushes to relieve himself, but in a few moments his young boss man stepped from the bushes holding a pillowcase. Bennie looked up at him. "Son, what you got there?"

Son Erby grinned. "Clothes, I got a date tonight so I need you to take the animals to the house. See they get feed and check 'em over."

"What kind of woman gone see you this dirty?"

"The finest woman you ever see'd."

"Huh, you ain't old enough to know what to do with no woman!"

"Well, I'll tell you the same thing I told her when she asked me how old I was. I said, 'I'm old enough to reach all the buttons and pull all the levers on any piece of equipment I handles.'"

"Boy, Son Erby, you just a mess. But she can't be good-looking, fooling with a boy."

"Huh! She's something special. You'll see."

Bennie grinned. "Where y'all going?"

"First, she gone pick me up and take me to her house so I

can take a bath. After I get me some trim, we'll probably go 'round to Beale Street."

"Boy, you ain't see'd a piece of trim since Miss Sarah birthed you into the world."

A car sped over the hill just ahead. Bennie and Son looked up in time to see the driver flash the headlights twice.

"That's my Sweet Thing," he said aloud with glee.

"Who?"

"She like folks to call her Sweet Thing."

"Heh, heh, heh, Son, boy, you something else." Bennie looked at his young boss with true admiration. "You just something else!" The headlights of the approaching auto fell on Son, muscular, confident and hungry looking. A wisp of a mustache Bennie had never noticed before hung under the young man's nose. He held his head high as the car approached. Dan tried to pull away when the automobile drew near. Son Erby hung the bundle of clothes over his left shoulder. "Dan!" he called.

The mule froze at the young master's single word.

A shiny, dark blue automobile slid to a stop right next to them. The three animals pulled away, but Bennie held them firm.

"Hey, baby," Son Erby said over the purring engine. He grinned from ear to ear; he looked at Bennie and then back to Sweet Thing.

"I see I got a lot more to teach you about how to treat a lady." Her sassy voice filled the air after she killed the engine. "Is this any way to greet a woman who drove all the way out here to pick a man up?"

"Baby, I'm sorry." The young man responded. He swung the bundle from his shoulder and quickly stepped up to the driver's window. Son leaned in and kissed Sweet Thing full on the mouth. Bennie swallowed hard.

Son pulled back just a few inches. "Thinking about that carried me all day."

She reached up and placed her right hand on his left cheek. "Raymond, I love it when you talks sweet."

Bennie noticed the red fingernail polish on each dainty finger. He froze in his tracks. Sweet Thing's golden-brown skin glowed in the waning evening sunlight. Her soft jet-black hair framed a peach-shaped face. The hairstyle she wore included bangs that fell to just above her arched eyebrows. She smiled even wider and showed perfect teeth like Bennie had never seen. To the left, just below sculpted lips, stood the cutest, single dimple imaginable. She looked at least twenty-five.

"Who's your friend?" Sweet Thing's melodious voice added to the scene's serenity.

"Baby, this is Bennie Gorlan. He works for me."

"Hello, Mr. Bennie. You all right today?" Sweet Thing chirped. When she flashed Bennie the smile where many men had gotten lost, her dimple reappeared like icing on a fresh cake.

Bennie was so entranced, he forgot to answer.

"The cat's got your friend's tongue."

Bennie put the reins of the animals in one hand and removed his hat. "Howdy."

"He just ain't used to a fine and good-looking woman," Son interjected.

"What about you, Raymond? Any fine, good-looking women been talking to you lately?" she hissed with a touch of true jealousy.

"I'm speaking to the only fine woman I know." He leaned in for another passionate kiss.

Bennie's lips puckered and a stirring occurred deep inside

him. "Uhhh," involuntarily escaped his throat when Son pulled away a second time.

"Bennie, see to that stock after you get home and tell Momma I'll be late."

Sweet Thing pushed the door of the full sedan open. She slid toward the middle of the seat. Her move revealed a tight-fitting red dress with shimmering bangles on the bodice and hemline. The garment rode up across shapely thighs when she glided over the seat.

"Get in here and drive a lady to town so you can tend to your business."

Son tossed his bundle into the back seat. "Bennie, see you tomorrow morning at the usual time." Son Erby gunned the engine and sped away. The tires spat out red sand and the three animals tried to pull away from their solitary caretaker.

"Whoa, whoa," Bennie said calmly. He looked after the car while it sped west on Quito Road. "That boy sure growed up fast. And that gal, that Sweet Thing's as fine as the hair on a frog!" He turned eastward toward the farmhouse and pulled the reluctant beasts behind him. Ole Dan pulled away, but Bennie ignored him. His mind locked on the beautiful older woman.

Ahead in the road, Bennie made out a form. In an instant, he recognized her walk. For the first time, Bennie knew just how to approach her. He understood just what to say to get her to flash him the smile he craved. This time, he would not allow the fact that she was older hold him back. Bennie Gorlan determined to seduce a lonely, widowed mother.

52—CAST YOUR BREAD

"Come in, Constable. Thank you for taking the time from your busy schedule to come to see me." The man at the desk greeted Rafe but did not look up from the neat piles of papers in front of him.

Rafe Coleman held his hat in his huge hands. They trembled and his usually squared shoulders sagged like old pillows. He licked his lips to form a carefully worded reply. "Your Honor, it ain't frequent when someone like you calls for me. So, so, when your clerk telephoned to say you wanted to see me, I took the first free time on your schedule." Rafe cleared his throat. "What you want to speak with me about, Judge?"

Judge Monahan peered over his spectacles at the small-town lawman. He'd never liked Rafe Coleman. This meeting would certainly produce no change in that. "How's business in your part of the county?"

"Business is good. Me and my brother, Conrad, doing a good trade at the store and our cotton gin."

"That's always good to hear. It is good to hear the Colemans continue to prosper. But—" the man in charge paused and looked up from his papers "—how about your other endeavors? How are those businesses performing?" At Judge Monahan's direct question about his illicit activities and the cold stare from his sky-blue eyes, true fear fell on this man so used to evoking terror in others.

"Uh, uh, Judge, sir, uh, uh…" He paused to smile wide and opened his arms in a begging posture. "What you mean?"

"Constable, your summons here is not social. You know exactly what I mean. For years, it has been known that you make substantial income by producing illegal whiskey in the Lucy area." He peered over his wire-framed spectacles. "Now, proof of your blatant disregard for the law has recently come to my attention. Raford, I am very concerned about this. Do you understand now what I mean?"

"Yessuh."

In a daggerlike tone, the judge added, "Then, let me hear you say, 'I understand what you mean'!"

Rafe swallowed hard, "I understand what you mean."

The judge looked up at him.

"Suh," Rafe added.

Judge Monahan paused. "Well, that was not so difficult. I hope the rest of this conversation and any future interactions we have on these issues go as easy." He paused to look at Rafe and awaited the normal reply to a person totally in charge.

"Yessuh."

"Now, I want you to know I have spoken with the Boss about your activities and my concerns. He told me that I have his blessing to handle this situation in any manner I see fit. Do you understand?"

"I understand." Rafe knew Boss Crump could easily turn control of his situation over to the man he stood before now.

The judge gave up trying not to show his enjoyment. A smile crossed his face and he leaned back in his wheelchair. "Well, that is a good start to us reaching an understanding to my satisfaction today. Do you think we can reach an understanding, Raford?"

"Why, yessuh!" He scratched his head. "Yessuh, we sure can!" Rafe mentally calculated the cost of paying off a judge.

"Wonderful," he replied. "Listen to my terms."

Francis Monahan wanted no part of money from this small-time villain. He exacted a price far more expensive than any Rafe estimated. "Constable, I recently met a fine, industrious young fellow. His name is Raymond Erby. I understand you know of this young man?"

"Yessuh."

"Well, you do know that Raymond is the grandson of Gillam Hale? Did you know that, Constable?"

Rafe nodded.

"Gillam Hale meant a great deal to me in my formative years. He performed a service for me I never had the opportunity to repay directly to him. But any help I give his grandson will go a long way toward making things right. What do you think of that?"

Rafe felt his eyes dance from the stress. He remembered the half-full pint of white whiskey in the glove box of his truck. He licked his lips in anticipation. Would he ever get out of here?

"Constable, what do you think of that?"

"Judge, that makes fine sense to me." His voice reached a high pitch he never knew he possessed.

"Good, then you will understand my terms fully. You are to cease and desist from any harassment, threats or endangerment to Ray Erby and anyone related to him. You are to ensure that he has the same protection in his business ventures, legal or otherwise, that you have in both your legal and your more illicit work. You are to make contact with Raymond within one week to ensure he knows you fully support his efforts. Is that understood?"

Soberly, Rafe whispered, "Yessuh, I understand."

"Good, I thank you for taking time from your busy schedule to come see me today. I know it will be difficult for you, but I appreciate your willingness to come to terms with this."

"You're welcome, suh."

The judge leaned back over his papers. Without looking up, he said, "You may go."

Rafe exhaled as he turned to exit the torture chamber and get to the half-empty pint.

"Constable!" Judge Monahan interrupted his escape. "A deed recently crossed my desk for a piece of property being recorded in the name of a Negro woman." Judge Monahan looked into Rafe's eyes. "I believe Thelma Louise Smith was the name. You know anything about that, Constable?"

Rafe's eyes found the floor. He rotated his hat in his hand and lied via a shake of the head.

"You see I have eyes and ears all over this county. The young man has full access to me, so remember I will know how well you comply with my terms. I remind you that I am the type of man you want to appreciate your actions and not otherwise. Do we understand each other, Constable Coleman?"

"Yessuh."

Judge Monahan waved Rafe Coleman from his presence.

The shaken constable closed the barrier behind him. "Whew," he sighed. He opened and started to close the door behind him when a tug by an angry Conrad Coleman pulled it back open. Rafe forgot that Conrad waited in the outer office.

"Told you not to buy that house for that woman and your mixed brood!" he said with a quiet force Conrad had never before used with Rafe.

Rafe Coleman offered no argument. He walked toward the medicine he needed in the safety of his truck parked near Forrest Park in downtown Memphis. As he walked, Rafe thought of what Nathan Bedford Forrest, an avowed racist, original wizard of the Ku Klux Klan and his father's Confederate general, would have to say about his agreement to help a colored boy make money.

Chess Gordon leaned over and placed the empty Coca-Cola bottle on the counter. He struck a match on the countertop and puffed his lit pipe intently. Smoke billowed from his mouth and he began to speak. "Yeah, I put that boy right. If it hadn't been for me, he wouldn't have the beginnings of a crop right now. Son gone be ready to pay the first note on that farm because of what I done!"

"I'm glad to see Son's doing better. Good thing he has you to help him, Chess." Young Tom Coleman swallowed the last drop of his soda.

"Miss Ruth, any truth to the rumor I hear about this young man going North to live?"

"Yes, Chess, it's true. Who told you?"

Not wanting Miss Ruth to know he got his info from Baby Sister, Chess lied, "Son musta mentioned it to me after he spoke with Tom about it." Chess recognized his own slip and decided to leave on that note. "Well, Miss Ruth, I better get on further. See y'all next time."

When the old man moved toward the store exit, Mother and son chorused, "See you, Chess."

When the Ford's engine roared to life Tom, who still hoped to convince his mother against his move to Virginia to live with Aunt Media and attend a fancy school, said, "Momma, I never said anything to Son about moving to Virginia to live with Aunt Media. I wonder how Chess knew."

Miss Ruth ignored her son's question, but she did not miss the thought. "Tom, you'd better go to the back and get finished with the chores your father left you before he and your uncle Rafe get back from Memphis."

"Stop by the gin office. I want to pick up another pint I got in the desk over there."

"Hell, I won't stop. I am going straight to the store. After I get out, you can go back to the gin and get all the whiskey you want."

For the first time in their lives, Rafe Coleman did not dominate Conrad.

"I told you not to keep fooling around with that bitch. Your mess is all over the county! Even decent folks like Judge Monahan know about it."

"Conrad," Rafe said with unusual softness from the passenger seat of his truck, "never let me hear you call her that again."

Conrad drove past the gin without slowing. In fact, he increased speed in direct defiance of Rafe's request to stop and his defense of Thelma Louise. Rafe threw the empty pint bottle in the ditch in front of the picnic woods when the truck sped by the gin site.

"That's why Ruth and I are getting Tom the hell out of here. We're sending him to Virginia to finish his schooling. We don't want him spawning with these colored women. You did it, Daddy did it. Hell, his daddy before him did it. That's why we got Chess to deal with now!"

Conrad gunned the engine and the truck jumped the rough railroad crossing going into Lucy.

"And, and, hell, we'll never get that land now that the judge is protecting young Erby. You better not touch him for nothing! You got to help him! We'll never get that gravel from Papa's place and it's all your doing!"

Rafe showed a restraint not previously part of his character. "Conrad, I hear you."

Conrad slowed down when the truck flew past the stave mill into town. "Plus, if there really is some money buried out there, we'll never get it."

"Ain't that Chess Gordon up ahead?" Rafe asked.

They both noticed Chess's blue car coming their way. Chess waved his left arm to extend an invitation for the Coleman brothers to stop.

"Now, just what does he want?" Conrad's rage continued.

"He probably wants to rub salt in our wounds."

"Yeah, I'm sure he does since he for sure knew about your meeting with the judge." Conrad added, "Hell, I don't think I'll stop."

"I got an idea! Conrad, go ahead and stop."

Conrad cast a puzzled look in Rafe's direction.

"Trust me on this one, brother!"

The younger Coleman brother slowed the vehicle and stopped just past the noise of the stave mill sawdust-exhaust shoot. Rafe placed his left hand on Conrad's leg.

Chess Gordon pulled up next to them. He lifted his freshly lit pipe from his mouth to expose a victory smirk. His thin lips expanded into a facewide grin, showing his store-bought teeth.

"Howdy, Conrad. Howdy, Rafe. Y'all all right today?"

Conrad refused to look at him. He fumed while Rafe did the talking. "We doing jes' fine, Chess. I met with Judge Monahan today. He made it clear how he felt about certain matters regarding Ray Erby."

Rafe's direct manner in this major defeat surprised Chess. "That a fact," Chess drawled.

"Yeah, he sure did. I'm gone make it a point to speak to young Erby about his farming and his other enterprises to see how Conrad and I can be of service to him."

"Fine! That's mighty fine! You know, that Son's going to be all right. Did you know he already got his crop planted?"

"Naw," Rafe continued with mock enthusiasm.

"Yeah, his cotton, his corn and his sorghum already up. He got to start chopping any day now. Why, I bet that boy gone have such a good crop it won't be no trouble paying that first note to me on his mortgage this year."

"Good, good. I see the judge spoke with you about helping young Erby, too!"

"Naw, I'm doing this on my own. I put his daddy on that farm and I'll see to it that the boy keeps that place. The fact the judge wants it done's just icing on the cake." Chess returned the pipe to his mouth and sent thick smoke across his lips and out the car window.

"Well, Chess, tell me one thing." Rafe patted Conrad on the

leg. "How long before you tell him to stop farming that place and mine the gravel out of that bottom?"

Chess Gordon squinted at Rafe and Conrad. "Rafe, what the hell you speaking about?"

"That gravel's too valuable with all these roads being built to keep making crops on that ground."

Conrad grinned wide at Chess and Rafe leaned across the seat toward the driver's side of the truck.

"You didn't know there was gravel in the bottomland over there?" Conrad quizzed.

"There ain't no damn gravel on that place!"

"Now, Chess—" Rafe smiled coyly "—I don't know it to be a fact myself. But when I was a boy, Papa told me over and over there was gravel on that place. He said he found it when he was digging a hole in the bottom to look for the missing Sawyer money."

"That's just a lie. It's just a damn lie!"

"Now, Chess, don't be upset with us. Surely a good businessman like you didn't sell that place without factoring in the mineral rights for something as valuable as gravel into the price."

Chess's one eye glared at the Coleman brothers. He sat speechless.

"And, Uncle Chess, don't forget. That Sawyer money is buried out there on that place somewhere. Daddy always swore it was there. He just never could locate it. I always thought you knew it, too, and found it sometime over the years. You did find it before you sold it to the Erbys, didn't you?"

A snickering laugh escaped Conrad's lips and Chess Gordon sat speechless in his pretty, blue automobile. Rafe pinched Conrad to shut him up. Next, he copied the same motion Judge

Monahan used to dismiss him from his inner chambers; Rafe waved his hand forward for Conrad to drive on.

"Chess, see you sometime," Conrad added. He gunned the engine and drove away.

Both brothers laughed and Conrad checked the rearview mirror. "Rafe, his car hasn't moved yet."

Conrad pulled in front of the store and parked the truck. "Brother," he said to Rafe, "what made you think of that?"

"You remember when Media made us read *Tom Sawyer* when we were boys?"

"Yeah, I remember. I mostly remember how much you hated it."

"Well, I designed my expressed dislike to make Media mad. I really liked the story."

"You are lying."

"Naw, I ain't, I really did like it. And, my favorite part was when ole Tom tricked his so-called friends into doing the dirty work of painting that fence for him."

"Big brother, sometimes you make me want to kill you for your stupidity. But your intelligence amazes me today."

"Thank you, Conrad."

"You're welcome. Guess what I got hidden in my desk drawer in the store office."

"A pint of sealed bourbon whiskey."

"Now how did you know that?"

Rafe snickered like a young boy. "I found it last week but I had the forethought to leave it for a special occasion."

"Two weeks, two brilliant decisions. There just may be hope for you. Let's get in here and see how much we can drink before Ruth catches us."

The Coleman boys swung from the pickup.

"Look, Rafe—" Conrad pointed toward the west end of Lucy "—your uncle Chess's still sitting there."

"Baby brother, he's sorting through that pile of bricks we just dumped on him. I believe he'll do the dirty work to take the land back, or he'll run himself crazy thinking about all that money he just let go to spite us. Either outcome's fine with me."

Ruth Coleman stepped from inside the store and handed each man an opened Coca-Cola.

"That's mighty nice of you. Thank you, Ruth," Rafe said.

Miss Ruth pursed her lips. She felt herself blushing from Rafe's sudden manners.

They were shocked when their first big swig revealed the soda was laced with bourbon whiskey.

"I found a pint in Conrad's desk last week and started to hide it from him. But I figured you two deserved something special after your meeting with Judge Monahan. It appears to have gone very well based on your expressions."

"Sister-in-law—" Rafe turned to Conrad and they chinked the two bottles "—let's drink to that."

"You coming to the meeting tonight?" Ely said to Jim Falls.

"Hell, that tonight?"

Ely gulped a big swallow of back-alley-bourbon. "Uh huh. You know the constable's situation gone be talked about tonight. Klan don't approve of him no more. Bought a house up in Millington for that wench who birthed them two griffs by him. Bought her that car, too!"

"I know she living up there. He had me and another colored fellow move her one day when Jude was gone and the big chillum was at school."

"You helped move her?"

"Yeah, but I didn't know it was her house. He got the colored fellow that helped me move her teach her to drive it. He said she was paying him back for the car."

"Did you ask what she used for currency?"

"What you think them ole boys gone do?" Jim queried unsteadily, unsure which side to take—the Klan's or Mr. Rafe's.

"Hard to say. You know, Mr. Rafe's still pretty connected. So, this matter's kind a delicate."

"Plus, Rafe Coleman'll kill you! That peckerwood's crazy!"

"Yeah, I know that! But I know he ain't got no damn business keeping house with that nigger woman! Hell, he takes care of her like she white! Next, thing you know, he'll be arranging to leave her and them half-breeds his money or even his businesses."

"Ain't no danger of that. He crazy about Mr. Conrad's boy Tom. Mr. Rafe told me over and over that boy gone get his money when he die."

"Well, that's good news. At least, he ain't gone totally crazy. Since you told me how he is about young Tom, maybe we'll just burn the house down and leave it at that."

Jim Falls reached for the comfort of the whiskey. "What if the woman and the children get hurt?"

"Since when you start worrying about niggers and their brood? You been working for Rafe Coleman too long."

Jim Falls liked the Klan meetings and the camaraderie, but killing a woman and five offspring, even if she was colored... Jim couldn't handle that.

"This whiskey and all this talk about nigger women got me hungry." Jim needed to change this subject.

"Let's go to the café for some breakfast," Ely suggested.

"Ely, man, that's the best idea you had today."

"You go on over. Tell them to start me some sausage and eggs. I'll be there directly."

Jim Falls exited the small office by the front door and headed across the street to the Lucy cafe. Their day started like Ely believed it would end at the Klan meeting that night at Peckerwood Point in Tipton County. Action prompted by shallow talk and rot-gut whiskey.

Allen Sawyer Jr.'s straw boss shuffled through the papers on his desk for a few moments. He decided to have one more drink before going to get those eggs.

Jude Smith lay still a few minutes. He certainly got an earful from his sleeping place under the Marble Yard office back porch. He lay just beneath the office window. "So, Rafe Coleman's gone leave his money to Tom Coleman after having two boys by my Bustie." Jude Smith's twisted and hung-over mind knew exactly how to pay Mr. Rafe back. "He can't leave a dead boy nothing."

His outside sleep chilled him to his very core. His latest drinking binge left him achy and dull-witted, but rage churned him to action. He decided to deal with Ely first. Jude's blood flowed through the veins of three of the children that bastard joked about killing.

Jude just lay there a while trying to decide what to do and when to do it. As he pondered Ely's fate, the phone in the office rang. Jude listened in again.

"Hello."

"Mr. Ely, this Sally over to the café. Your sausage and eggs almost ready. I know you like them hot so you better come on."

"Thank you, hon'. I'm coming right now."

★ ★ ★

Jude crawled out the back side of the porch, stood to his full height, stretched really hard, and walked to the rear door of the Marble Yard office to do something no colored man ever had the nerve to do in Lucy before. A man filled with vengeance snatched the door open while Ely took his last swig of the white whiskey, the last swallow Ely took of anything.

Action prompted by shallow talk and rot-gut whiskey followed.

53—MAY AND SEPTEMBER

"Papa! No, Papa! No! No! I got to help Papa! Papaaaaa!"

"Son, wake up," Mama Birdie Mae said.

Son Erby swung violently at his adversary.

"Wake up, Son?"

Mama Birdie Mae's earlier urgings never reached him, but this stern call of his mother brought Son Erby back to the conscious world. He looked around in a sleepy but frightened stupor to see his grandmother at the foot of the bed. Sarah stood across the room.

Son Erby felt afraid and ashamed. Bad dreams haunted him constantly. He put his face in his hands and cried.

Sarah sat down beside him and hugged him close. He grabbed her waist with his two strong arms. Mama Birdie Mae held out a Mason jar half filled with water. "Drink this," the old woman commanded.

The sniffling boy rose from his momma's lap, took the

glass and drank a few swallows. He frowned from the bitter taste.

"Drink it all!" she instructed.

He gulped down the remaining few swallows and laid his
face back in Sarah's lap.

"He sleep?" the old woman soon asked.

Sarah nodded. "Momma, what you give him?"

"Two ounces of paregoric in that water."

"No wonder he went to sleep like that. That ain't too much,
is it?" She worried about the opium extract.

"Be too much for a baby, but he ain't exactly no baby. He'll
sleep until his kidneys wake him up in three or four hours."

Sarah chuckled. "He my baby."

"He farms in the day and cooks whiskey at night. He's a
man."

"Don't talk like that, Momma."

"You and me both know that's what he doing. Where else
you think he gets the type money he brings in here?"

"He's running around with some older woman on Saturday
nights."

"How you know who he with and when?"

"Bennie told me," Sarah said. "He told me he and I needed
to get together, just like Son and his older woman."

"And what did you say?" Miss Birdie grunted.

"I was nice when I told him no. It took all I could to wait
'til later to laugh—it was the best laugh I had in a while."

Rafe missed her when she was away. Their time together
occurred early in the morning or if he drove back to the house
during the day. She arrived on schedule, at 7:00 a.m. sharp. He
listened for the familiar sound of her General Motors V-8

engine. He waited to hear her car roll along the gravel of his driveway at the start of each day. The old Buick ran quietly but he heard it. Rafe listened as her key opened the door to the kitchen. He heard her place her bags on the table, and his ears waited for the sound of her steady steps toward his bedroom.

"Morning, Thelma Louise." Even though he knew every inch of her, he surveyed his woman from head to toe when she approached the chair next to his bed.

"Morning yourself," she shot back, flashing him a sly smile she knew he loved. "You ready for breakfast?"

She kissed him on the cheek when she handed him the morning paper.

"Yeah, breakfast sounds good." He watched and she swayed away toward the kitchen. Rafe hesitated a few moments before rising from his seat to follow her. As he walked, he surveyed the paper and noticed an article he wanted to read: Joe Louis Urged To Fight Germany's Schmelling.

"I can't wait to see the Bronze Bomber whip that Nazi."

"What if Joe Louis can't whip him?" said Thelma Louise.

"Oh, he's going to win," Rafe said. He shook the paper loudly and spread its pages wide. "He's gone to beat that German like he stole something and got caught. Can't nobody beat Louis."

"I never thought I'd hear you root for a colored man."

After he ducked behind his newspaper, he said, "I'm doing a lot of things we never thought I'd do."

"Sho' 'nough."

"Louis's real name is Joe Louis Barrow." He moved the conversation to safer waters. "His next fight's gone be on the radio. You think you might come over here that night and listen to it with me?"

She put the skillet on the electric stove. She replied as she cut thick patties from the stick of pork sausage, "I can do that."

The sausage began to sizzle and its aroma oozed throughout the room.

"Father, how on earth did you get those ugly scars on your leg?"

Allen Sawyer snatched his long socks up and pushed his pant leg down. "It, it, it," he stammered, "it's just a few scratches I got last fall."

"Those are mighty ugly. They look more like bites to me. How'd you get them?"

"I went hunting last fall and fell down the side of a ditch."

"You better be more careful," Amanda lectured, pointing her left index finger at the old banker. "That must have been quite a ditch to hurt you that bad."

He changed the subject. "Where's Sarah?"

"She called to say she'd be late. Son's sick today and can't drive to bring her. I'll go get her after I dress."

Amanda's hair was undone and she was still in her robe. "Since you keep banker's hours, would you like me to go pick her up?"

"Sure, I'll call Sarah and tell her you are coming."

Birdie Mae put the earpiece to her ear and leaned in to the mouthpiece on the wall to say, "Hello."

"Birdie Mae, is that you?"

"Yes, this is Birdie Mae."

"Good morning. This is Amanda Sawyer."

"How do, miss?"

"I'm fine, thank you. I called to tell Sarah Father's on his way to get her."

"That fine, Miss Amanda."

"What's wrong with Son?"

"Well, to tell the truth, he working himself to death to pay for this farm. You know Chess Gordon's gone take the place back from us?"

"No, I did not know that. Why would he do something like that?"

"Because he just ain't never been for nobody but Chess Gordon. That's all I can see. He done called the note on us. We got forty-five days to pay the loan off in full or get out."

"Birdie Mae, I want to arrange a loan for you."

Birdie Mae put her hand to her mouth before she replied. "Miss Amanda, you know your daddy won't let you do that."

"Birdie Mae, we have to try."

"Well, I just was going over the different places in my mind for where we can move. We ain't going back to the Coleman place."

"Birdie Mae, Allen Sawyer Jr. will have to say *no* to me because I will ask him later today."

"Mark my words, he ain't never gone say yes. His momma would turn over in her grave and it'd kill him to help us have a place of our own."

"I just don't understand this. He's your brother!"

"Miss Amanda, don't speak about that on the telephone. Don't hurt yourself."

After a few seconds, Amanda asked, "Did you know anything about Father hurting his leg?"

"No'm, what you mean?"

"Scars run all over his right leg. He said he fell down hunting this past season."

"I ain't heard Sarah say nothing," Birdie Mae said.

"They look more like bites to me."

Birdie Mae Lilliard thought for a moment and said, "Miss Amanda, did you know that our dog bit the legs of the man that shot Gill?"

Neither spoke. Amanda finally broke the silence and said with disgust, "I will make that loan."

"You sure?" Birdie Mae asked.

"Yes, more sure than I've ever been about anything in my whole life."

Birdie Mae whispered, "Miss Amanda, I'm gone speak my mind to him."

"Yes, you grind him into little pieces."

As Allen Sawyer drove into the yard, the car startled Sarah. "Why's Mr. Al here?"

"Miss Amanda sent him to get you so you won't need to walk. You go get ready."

Sarah went in the back door and Birdie Mae Lilliard gingerly took the steps one at a time. Her glare met Allen Sawyer Jr.'s eyes when she reached the foot of the stairs.

54—BLOOD UNTIL THE END

"Morning, Birdie Mae. How're you today?"

"I'm all right for an old lady."

"I'm pleased to hear that."

"Well, you ain't gone be so pleased to hear what I got to say."

Allen Sawyer Jr. opened his mouth to reply, but Birdie Mae silenced him with a slow wave of her right hand. She placed her left foot on the sideboard of his Packard and leaned into the automobile window.

"Tomorrow, on Wednesday, me, Raymond and Sarah coming around to Lucy Savings Bank. We coming to see Miss Amanda because we ain't gone deal with you. Later today, Miss Amanda's gone tell you about the money your bank is lending us. You do know Chess Gordon decided to call his note on us?"

Allen nodded his head.

"You also know he doing it to get the gravel?"

"How'd you know about the gravel?"

"Mr. Gillam told me when I was a young woman."

"Gillam Hale?"

She stared into his face and he looked away after a moment. "Now, Miss Media Sneed done arranged for money to back our note with your bank. I know y'all ain't never loaned this type of money to a Negro, other than Chess. But let me tell you why you gone do it this time."

Allen Sawyer Jr. looked blankly at Birdie Mae.

"First, your wife told me about your daughter. Did you know we spoke about that?"

Allen shook his head. His gaze fixed on the steering wheel; his mouth opened in horror.

"She knew all along where Amanda came from. She said she told you after she knew she was fixing to die." Birdie Mae paused. "And did you know I told Miss Alice the truth about Miss Amanda? Did you know that, Mr. Al?"

He shook his head, refusing to venture a look at her.

"Yeah, I told her. Miss Alice had the nerve to brag to me one time about the scholarship Miss Amanda got from Lucy High. She said Nigras couldn't get the scholarship. Well, I gave her an earful about colored children and scholarships. We had a big blowup right over in your kitchen at Sawyer Manor. She was shouting at me about it and how you needed to know. I told her that you already knew and that we might as well tell everybody in the whole county. That's when she had her big stroke."

A tear dropped on his left cheek. She handed him one of her floral handkerchiefs. He surprised her—he took it.

"There's two more things you need to know. I wrote all this down, twice, and sent one to Miss Media Sneed. I told her to publish it if anything else strange happen to me, Sarah or Raymond. A lawyer in Memphis got the second copy. It's sealed in his safe and can't nobody get it but me or my grandboy."

Allen tried to speak, but, again, she waved him off.

"There's one more thing you need to hear. I can't prove it, but I know Johnlee Gordon didn't kill Gill Erby. And I know whoever did it was bit up all over his legs by our dog." Nastily, she spat out, "Mr. Al, Miss Amanda and I both know you done it."

He dropped his head; huge tears fell from his eyes.

"You don't want nobody to know this, neither do I."

A look of total surprise flashed on Allen Sawyer Jr.'s face.

"The fact Amanda knows punishes you enough." Birdie Mae drew closer to him. "She ain't never, never gone forgive you. Why would you do that to Gill Erby? He never did nothing to nobody!"

In a pitiful voice, the murderer replied, "Gill got angry over a bank loan I denied him. The second time I said no he told me he knew about Amanda and hinted he might tell. I couldn't let him do that."

The back door's spring twanged, and Sarah approached from the rear of the house.

"Now," Birdie Mae added with amazing calm, "do we have an understanding?"

He nodded and struggled to compose himself.

"We even." Birdie Mae whispered. "My words killed Miss Alice and you took Gill."

Sarah moved down the steps. She walked past her mother. "Howdy, Mr. Al," she said and got in the rear seat.

Rafe Coleman picked up the ringing telephone. He looked across the table at Thelma Louise. Her smile gave him joy and the feeling this provided him spread to his cheery greeting. "Hello."

"Mr. Rafe! That you, Mr. Rafe?"

"Yes, what's wrong, Jim?"

"Mr. Rafe, I'm here in the Marble Yard office. Get down here quick. Somebody done beat Ely to death."

"What you say?"

"I said somebody done killed Ely. I was in here talking to him earlier. And, and, he was gonna come over to the café and eat breakfast with me. He told me to have the girls cook him some sausage and eggs. Well, well, Mr. Rafe, I come back after he didn't show up and his food was ready. And, he's a laying here in his own blood."

"You sure he dead?"

"Yes, sir. I'm sure. His eyes wide open and he ain't breathing. He already turned cold."

"Did you see anybody when you came back?"

"Yessuh. I saw Jude Smith cross the railroad tracks and head toward the woods when I came back here."

"Did Jude know you seen him?"

Thelma abruptly dropped her coffee cup to the table. A frown appeared above Thelma Louise's brow.

"Yessuh. He saw me looking at him and then he ran on into the woods going back to the north out of town."

Rafe Coleman sat there for a few seconds. "Did you call the sheriff yet?"

"No sir, not yet."

"Well, when you hang up from me, call them. I'll beat them there. Don't you touch nothing else. After you call, just step outside and keep anybody else out until I get there."

"Yessuh, I'll do it, Mr. Rafe."

"Jim, there's one more thing." He rubbed his unshaved chin as he paused. "Don't say nothing about Jude. Keep that between me and you; I'll make it well worth your trouble."

Jim Falls hesitated. "Yessuh," he whispered.

Rafe placed the telephone back on the cradle.

"Rafe, what happened with Jude?"

"That was Jim Falls. Somebody done killed Ely Gunn up at the Marble Yard office. He saw Jude running away just before he found the body."

"You think Jude did it."

"Probably. But, it ain't important what I think. What's more important is what the white folks around here think and do." He stood up and had to catch the chair behind him to keep it from falling. "Go home and pack a few things. Take the children to Memphis to your momma's place."

"But…"

He raised both hands with open palms. "Woman, do what I tell you. It's a bunch of folks around here mad since the newspaper published the deed to your house. Stay in Memphis 'til this blows over."

She looked down at her coffee cup. "All right."

"I need to go."

"Rafe, remember," she paused before adding, "he's still my children's daddy."

"I know."

Rafe walked back to his bedroom and picked up his badge, pistol, and hat. He had turned away from his night stand when he remembered he might need his slapper, and stuffed it in his rear pocket.

55—HABITS DIE HARD

"Boy, you need to stop running around at night cooking whiskey and carrying on. You hear me?"

Son made no reply. He drove the truck along Quito Road toward Lucy. He hoped his mother would drop the subject if he ignored her.

"Boy, don't ignore me. You ain't got to cook whiskey no mo'. Miss Amanda said the bank gone give us a loan to pay Chess Gordon off. Didn't you hear me say that?"

He nodded and worked hard not to show his anger.

Mama Birdie Mae cleared her throat. "Son, tell Sarah what you told me this morning."

Son drove along for a few seconds before he once again broke his promise to Gill Erby that he not to speak of making whiskey. He started as they entered Lucy. "Momma, it's not that simple. I agreed to deliver fifty gallons of whiskey by Friday.

That's the deal every week. If I don't show up, they'll get mighty mad."

"Let 'em be mad."

"Sarah, you don't want these type folks mad with you. They might hurt Son." She paused, then said, "Son, stop over there. That looks like Elder Cephas. I need to speak with him."

Son slowed the truck and pulled into a space a short distance from the elder's automobile. He put on the brake and killed the engine of the old vehicle.

"You and Sarah go do a little shopping whilst I speak with the elder. Howdy, Elder," she said while the preacher descended the steps.

"Hey, Cousin Birdie Mae. How y'all today?"

Son and Sarah exited the truck on the driver's side as the preacher approached the passenger door.

"Do we need to be introduced to each other?" he said to Son when the young man turned toward the store.

Son understood Elder Cephas's reference to his long absence from church. He shook his head for no.

"Morning, Elder. How's my pastor?"

"Sister, I'm fine, but I been without you, too." The elder pointed the index finger of his right hand at Sarah and Son as both walked up the steps. "Come on back. It's not good to stay away too long."

Neither mother nor son replied. Son moved down the walk and away from the preacher. His mother dutifully followed him and they headed toward the Coleman store. Son held the screen open wide for his mother.

"Howdy, Sarah. Howdy, Ray," Miss Ruth greeted them. "Y'all doing all right?"

"Yessum, we fine today."

"Son!" Tom Coleman shouted from the back, "I've not laid eyes on you in a month of Sundays."

"Hey, Tom." Son smiled, genuinely happy to see his friend. "I been working to get my crop planted."

"Speaking of work, Tom, you'd better get out to the ice-house and move those things around like your father told you. The grocery delivery truck should be here with those supplies soon," said Miss Ruth.

"Son, can you help me for just a few minutes?"

"Yeah, but not for long. We got some business."

"Let's go out through the back."

"Momma, I'm going out to help Tom. I'll be right back."

Tom pushed his key into the rusted padlock. The young man struggled with the lock before a click sounded. He swung the heavy storage-room door open wide. "Son, you remember three years ago when we got to fighting right over there by the cattle pen?"

"Yeah, I remember how I was whipping your tail until Bennie pulled me off you."

Tom Coleman mocked his friend with a feigned punch into Son's stomach.

Son stopped smiling. The punch did not change his mood, but rather, something he saw over Tom's shoulder. "What's the possibility of me getting three sacks of sugar off that truck?"

"Why on earth do you need one hundred and fifty pounds of sugar? You cooking again?"

"The sun shines every day? 'Course I'm cooking!"

"If I get you the sugar, I want in on the proceeds."

Son stopped laughing. "How you know about such things?"

"You think you the only boy whose pappy taught him this old enterprise? How much you cooking?"

"We," he said to his new partner, "need fifty gallons by Friday night."

"Elder, that brother of yours ain't shit—excuse me, Preacher," said Birdie Mae to Reverend Simon Peter Gordon.

The elder shook his head.

"You know he didn't need to do us like that."

"It is unfortunate," the clergyman replied.

"Unfortunate, hell! Excuse me, Preacher. You know Chess don't need no mo' money."

"Well, Sister Birdie, what are y'all going to do?"

"Reverend, what you mean?"

Moving his hands as if he were in the pulpit preaching, Reverend Cephas said, "I mean, where are you going to stay?"

"You tell that no-good brother of yours we gone stay right where we at. When Sarah and Son get back here, we going down to Lucy Savings Bank. Allen Sawyer Jr. gone approve us a loan to pay Chess off. We keeping the farm."

"Is that a fact?"

"Fact it is."

"Now, why is Banker Sawyer inclined to approve a loan for you?"

"Preacher," Birdie Mae replied with her own toothless grin, "he got his reasons."

56—REVELATIONS

"I'm going over to Chess Gordon's house to deliver the proceeds check from the loan we made today." Her words dripped with a flavor new to her lips, pure venom.

"Daughter, Chess won't be pleased. You sure you don't want me to deliver it?" He wanted to protect her still. He truly loved her. Her condemnation was more painful than the losses of his wife and mother.

"Thank you, but this is something I will do."

Amanda Sawyer and Allen Sawyer measured each other. Each understood how much the other knew. Each knew the other's secret. Neither must ever acknowledge it to the other.

Allen Sawyer Jr. rose from his father's large desk and as he tried to place his hands on her shoulders, she moved away and stared at him. A deep disgust showed on her face. He knew he would never touch her again. Tears formed in her eyes and hung there for a moment, before they cascaded down her flushed cheeks. She left his office and exited the bank.

"God forgive me," he prayed silently. Forgiveness was available, but not release from the consequences. A miserable, lonely house awaited him. A daughter he loved deeply hated him. He died spiritually that day. His burial in Lucy Cemetery would not occur for over a decade.

"Brother, you just don't get it! Do you understand how good God's been to you?"

Chess Gordon pouted like a child. He made no reply to Reverend Cephas's challenges.

"Think, man, born a slave and now you have more blessings than you have room to receive."

"I don't give a shit. I'm taking my place back. That gravel and the lost money was not figured in the price."

"Chess. Think about it—"

"I been thinking, ever since Rafe told me. I bet I even know where it is. The money got to be near the chestnut tree back there in the bottom. That damn Birdie Mae used to come over there every year in the spring and fall. She'd sashay back there and pretend she was looking for polk salad in the spring. In the fall, it'd be persimmons and chestnuts. She'd always say, 'Chess, don't you cut Old Jabbok down. That tree stands so pretty.'"

"Chess, what if God asked for your soul tonight?"

A reminder like this usually frightened the wits out of anyone as old as Chess Gordon and with his sordid past the elder's question worried Chess's heart. As usual, Simon Peter Gordon accomplished his task.

★ ★ ★

They mixed their two barrels of mash. Tom listened to the sound of the river coming to them on the wind. "You cooked back here before?"

"Yeah, many times," Son answered, and he poured a clear liquid in the brew of both containers.

"Son, why you putting rubbing alcohol in the mash?"

"This batch got to be done by Friday night for us to come back and cook it off. I put in a little extra yeast and this alcohol to kick the mix off faster."

"Son, that might make someone sick."

"It ain't gone hurt nobody none."

"Son, I told you there isn't no such word as *ain't*."

Son stirred the alcohol into the mash and pulled limbs over the sunken containers.

Tom noticed the change in his friend. He didn't care if it hurt people or not.

The young partners finished the camouflage in sullen silence. Without admiring their work, the two headed for the truck, a few hundred yards away.

Tom declared, "This business ain't for me."

Son Erby decided to drive to Millington after he dropped Tom off near town. Sweet Thing had taught her eager pupil well and he wanted to continue the education of a young and willing Sue Nell on how a man talked to and acted with a woman.

To his surprise, there was no answer in the dark little house Mr. Rafe purchased for his adopted family. Rain fell as he turned back onto Millington Road to head for Lucy and home. Lightning joined the storm's elements as he drove. Son saw a lone person walking through the downpour one mile south of town. He decided to pick up the unfortunate soul.

When Son approached, the walker didn't turn, so the truck's headlights did not reveal his identity. The young man slowed to a stop just past the person. He reached over and cracked the door. He shouted, "You want a ride?"

"Thank you, buddy," came the excited reply. He ran forward and opened the truck door wide.

Something was familiar about the man who climbed in. Son shifted to first gear. "Where you trying to get tonight?"

Son shifted to second gear and the stranger answered, "I'm headed to Lucy." It was a familiar voice.

Son shifted the truck to third gear and it picked up speed. A bright bolt of lightning shot across the sky from west to east. The light from the flash lasted a few seconds and the new comrades looked at each. Johnlee Gordon sat in the truck with Son Erby. Son checked his .32 revolver. He gripped the wheel of the vehicle and floored the gas pedal. They flew along in tense silence; only the old truck's groaning engine made a sound.

"Conrad, Miss Gunn burying old Ely mighty quick."

Conrad looked down at the wooden box in the freshly dug grave. "She told Ruth she wanted to get it over."

"I hear she's putting him in an expensive casket."

"Yeah, Ruth and I took her to pick it out."

"In a few years, the box and the coffin gone rot anyway. I don't see why folks put that type of money in the ground. Hey, why she putting that old boy over here so close to these thick woods?" Rafe asked as he tried to look into the thick bushes.

He shrugged. "Normally, Ely handled all these arrangements

for cemetery matters. But, since he's not around, I had the boys dig it where the widow asked."

"Ironic ain't it. Old Gunn just hated colored folks and we burying him this close to the colored cemetery."

"Why you let them boys dig it so deep? This grave almost deep enough for two people."

"I don't know. I got old Bob and Bennie to dig it. Bob was drunk and Bennie, well, he was Bennie." He eyed Rafe directly. "The law got any idea who done it?"

Rafe already knew, but wanted to confirm, the brothers were alone. "Conrad, I'm gone tell you something you need to keep to yourself. Nobody knows but me and Jim Falls. Even Ruth can't know because of what'll happen around here if it gets out. You want to know?"

Conrad nodded.

"Will you keep it a secret?"

He hesitated before answering, "Uh huh."

"Jude Smith killed Ely."

"Shit! These white folks would go crazy if they found that out. Is that why you asked me about selling that farm and house to Jim Falls at such a low price?"

"Yeah, that's his payoff. But, I still think he's a leaky bucket. The first time he's drunk, he'll blab it."

The wind began to blow and Conrad and Rafe remained silent.

"Going to storm this evening," said Rafe.

"Yeah, I think it is. Rafe, there's something I want to ask you. Did you kill Gill Erby?"

Rafe paused. "Allen Sawyer did it."

"Why in the hell would he do that?"

"I don't know. Me and the sheriff could never get it out of the old bastard. So, we just pinned it to Johnlee."

"Damn. So that's why Sawyer changed his mind and gave us the loan this year."

Rafe nodded and smiled. "Information is a valuable thing to have."

The wind picked up some more and the brothers noticed the coming darkness.

"Conrad, I want you and Ruth to send Tom up North to Media. There's just too much shit around here to overcome."

"Why you say that?"

"Well, you ain't gone like this, but I saw the grocery truck driver when I was up in Millington today. He sold Tom some extra sugar two days ago.

"Conrad, he's been out a lot this week. He told me he was going over by the river. I think him and that Erby boy somewhere off the west end of Quito cooking whiskey right now."

Conrad made no initial reply. "Hell!" crossed his lips momentarily. "Let's get out of here. We need to go find them boys."

The two men walked away from the fence row that separated the neatly trimmed white cemetery from the colored plot behind the dense woods. Conrad asked the million dollar question. "What you gone do about Jude?"

"I don't know. Thelma Louise asked me to not hurt him."

They exchanged glances. For the first time, Conrad realized how much Rafe cared about his colored woman.

"I been looking for Jude by myself for the past two days. I don't know what I'll do when I find him."

Rafe's search would have ended if he had just stepped through the fence and into the woods. Jude Gibson lay just thirty feet into the bushes from the grave site. He heard every word the brothers spoke and remained still until he heard Rafe's truck start up and drive away.

"Mr. Rafe," a hungry and nasty Jude said after he stood from the honeysuckle thicket where he lay, "information is a valuable thing. After I pay Jim Falls a visit, I'm gone find yo' boy over to the river. I know exactly where they probably at 'cause that Bennie Gorlan bragged about where they cooked when Gill killed that deer!"

"Son, why you so quiet today?"

Son blurted out, "Did your uncle Rafe kill my daddy?"

A speechless Tom Coleman stared at his friend in the flickering light from the fire beneath the cooker. He gathered his wits. "Son, you know Johnlee Gordon killed Gill."

Son toyed with his father's watch. "I thought I knew that until two nights ago. I drove over to Millington to see Sue Nell after we made the setup and I dropped you off." He raised his head to look at his friend. "I picked up a guy in the rainstorm. It was Johnlee Gordon."

"Why on earth would you pick up Johnlee Gordon?"

"Hell, I didn't know it was him! I still can't believe he out after just six months."

Both boys fell silent.

"Well, what happened?"

"I almost shot him," Son said as he pulled a silver pistol with pearl-white handles from his pocket.

"Where you get that gun?"

"Cousin Chess gave it to me before we fell out over our land."

"Put that thing away!"

Son looked at his friend. He saw how serious Tom was and put the pistol back into his left front pocket.

They sat at the cooker with only the woods sounds until Tom spoke. "Why didn't you shoot him?"

"He swore he didn't kill Papa. Johnlee said he was out working with Jude Smith the night somebody shot Papa. I'm gone get whoever done it!" Son turned toward his friend. "Johnlee said Mr. Rafe did it."

Neither boy spoke.

Finally, Son went to the still to check the runoff of condensed whiskey.

"The bucket'll be full soon. I'll just change it out now." Son picked up an empty one and swapped it with the near-full container from beneath the still's cooling coil spout.

"I noticed this afternoon that the fire you made produced almost no smoke."

The young entrepreneur laughed. He stirred the coals beneath the still. "That's an old bootlegger's trick. I used chestnut wood to make the daytime fire. It doesn't produce much smoke when it burns, so it's perfect for day cooking."

"Why's that important?"

Son laughed at him. "Dummy, that's so the Revenuers won't see a trace of your fire."

"Your daddy taught you that, too?"

Son nodded his head. Both boys wondered who'd killed Gill Erby.

"Tom, we'll be finished when this last batch cooks off." Son pulled his father's watch from his pocket. He held it toward the light of the fire under the still. "It's almost midnight."

"Momma and Daddy will kill me."

"Well, you wanted in."

Tom Coleman thought, yeah, but this will be the last time for me. Aloud he replied, "Hand me that box top with what's left of that spread."

Son picked up the piece of cardboard. He pulled back the wax paper to reveal a mix of bologna, hog's-head souse and liver cheese. Onions, pickles, mustard and crackers covered the meats. He grabbed a few morsels and stuffed them into his mouth as he handed the box to Tom. "Here, Tom," he mumbled.

Jude Gibson stumbled from the bushes as Tom took the meat tray. "White boy, your luck just run out!"

"Conrad, it's like looking for a needle in a haystack. I'm scared we won't find them."

"Rafe, I am, too. I wanted to say the same thing for the last three hours since we stopped by the farm and found Jim Falls dead. You think Jude killed him?"

"'Fraid so." He held up the piece of cloth Jim still clutched in his right hand when they found him. "We'll know if this matches Jude's shirt when we find him."

"That's if we find him. You think we need to bring the sheriff patrol in on this?"

"Not yet," Rafe said. He remembered Thelma Louise's request. They walked along in silence. The bushes crackled under their feet and the brothers tried to stay on the path.

"Rafe, we need to go back and get some help. We'll never find those boys alone."

A familiar smell floated to Rafe's expert nose. He froze and sniffed aloud into the wind. "You smell that?"

Conrad approached and stood next to his brother. He repeated Rafe's three short sniffs. The sweet, sticky smell of corn whiskey mash drifted to his nostrils. "I smell whiskey," Conrad said.

"Somebody sure cooking near here. The wind's out of the west, so it's got to be from over that bluff."

A single gunshot pierced the night air. Without speaking, the Coleman brothers ran toward the sound.

Jude walked over and snatched the box top with cold cuts from Tom Coleman. He gobbled down a few mouthfuls before speaking again. Mustard and onions spilled from his thick lips as he chewed. Tom cowered below him on the ground.

The angry man remembered his mission after his stolen snack began to satisfy his physical hunger. Without a word, he kicked Tom in the face with all the force his powerful body could bring to bear. Tom Coleman rolled away like a rag doll. The young man moaned and writhed on the ground in pain.

"Mr. Jude, what's wrong with you?" Son Erby shouted.

Jude turned on him. "Boy, this don't concern you. You don't want no parts of this." Jude filled his mouth with more meat and threw the box top to the ground. It landed next to a double bladed ax near where Tom originally sat. "This here just what I need." He picked up the ax and turned greedily toward the white boy.

Tom looked up just in time to see the giant raise the ax high.

"Ahhhhh! Ahhhh! Ahhhh!" Tom screamed.

"Where's your white trash uncle now?" Jude started to swing the ax.

A gunshot pierced the night air. Jude froze. Tom stopped screaming. Both looked at young Erby. Son held the pistol over his head from the shot he fired into the sky. He leveled the gun at the man.

"Put the ax down Mr. Jude! Put it down or I'll shoot you!" His left gun hand trembled as if he was freezing.

Jude turned toward the colored boy. He lowered the ax and held it half-way up the handle with his big right hand. Without another word, he charged Son Erby like the bull he was. He crossed the ten feet between he and the boy in an instant.

Son pulled the trigger. The bullet hit Jude in his right shoulder when he swung the ax. The tool flew toward the boy from Jude's hand after the bullet tore into him. The handle hit Son's bicep and the pistol flew from his grasp. The ax blade dug into Son's thigh just before Jude hit him with the force of a train.

Son fell over backwards. They landed among the large stone jugs of whiskey. Jude pummeled the boy with all his might as soon as he recovered from the fall to the ground. His fury hid the fact he had been shot. His goal now included getting rid of Son so he could finish his work on Tom. He jumped cat-like to his feet and picked up one of the five-gallon jugs. Son held up both hands in a feeble attempt to cover his face. Jude held the jug high as he prepared to crush the boy's skull.

Three shots rang out and Jude Smith dropped the jug. It shattered and the white whiskey poured onto Son Erby. Jude fell atop Son and his blood poured from the three bullet wounds in his back. The alcohol mixed with the blood from Son's and Jude's wounds. Tom kept pulling the trigger until Mr. Rafe stepped from the bushes and pulled the emptied revolver from his hand.

Son pushed Jude's dead weight from him. The man rolled over on his back and fell to the boy's left atop the broken whiskey jug fragments. Son Erby sat up. He looked down at Jude. Each of the Negro man's labored breaths appeared to be his last.

His mind cleared from the blows to his head and Son Erby recognized Mr. Rafe stood next to Tom with his .45 in his left hand. The gun pointed at Jude and Son. In his right hand, Rafe held the now empty .32 caliber pistol Son and Tom just used on Jude. Rafe and Son made eye contact and both surmised they knew another sordid notch was just added to this gun's history.

"You ain't sending me to jail for this like you done Johnlee! I shot him to save Tom and then Tom shot him to save me. You hear me, Mr. Rafe! I ain't going to jail!"

The scene fell silent and the whiskey still whined, signaling the completion of the last batch. The only other sounds included Jude's labored breathing and the whine of the fire beneath the cooker.

Jude Smith felt life slipping rapidly from him. For a change, he decided to do something good at his exit. He pawed in the approaching darkness of death for the boy's leg. "Boy, boy," he said and his own blood sputtered from his lips with the sounds. Jude gripped Son's thigh.

Son turned toward the man. He remembered his family's teasing about what Jude would think of his feelings for Sue Nell. In the darkness, Son somehow knew Jude looked at him but could not see him.

"Boy," Jude continued, "Allen Sawyer killed your daddy. Mr. Rafe didn't do it. Mr. Al did." With that revelation, Jude Smith breathed his last. He died with his eyes open wide, just like Gill Erby.

Son sprang to his feet when he realized the man was dead. At that moment, Son Erby did not feel like a man. He understood he was just a boy and that boys cried.

Mr. Conrad walked forward to put his arm around Tom. He seemed in a trance.

Rafe Coleman put his long lost .32 in his pocket and he returned his .45 to his holster. He remembered how he felt as a young boy in Lucy when he witnessed death for the first time. "Son," knowing only folks that cared about the boy called him that, Rafe continued, "Son, let's break whiskey camp and get out of here!"

Son looked at him in fear. He did not know what to expect.

"Everything's gone be all right. We need to get you two boys home." Mr. Rafe walked over and put his arm around the Negro youth.

"What we gone do about Mr. Jude?"

A bright idea sprang into Rafe's head. He suppressed and then allowed a smile. "Mr. Conrad and me gone take care of him. Now, you boys can't say a word about this to nobody. You hear!"

Tom escaped his trance long enough to nod.

"Yessuh," signaled the temporary return of Son's faculties.

"Momma, what you writing?"

"A letter to Son."

"Why you writing Son a letter?"

"There's some things I need him to know."

"What kind of things?"

"Sarah Erby, take care of your business and get out of mine."

"Momma, he my business, too!"

"Sarah, this letter is to be read by the boy after I'm gone." She held up a second letter. "I wrote this one for you. Neither of you ready to know this stuff yet."

Sarah and Birdie Mae eyed each other, neither spoke.

"Momma, Miss Zoar was just on the telephone when you were out in the bottom. Cousin Chess died in his sleep last night."

"Huh," was Miss Birdie's sole reply. Sarah moved away toward the house.

Sarah returned to the bedroom and sat next to her boy. She listened to him breathe. He was Gill Erby's seed. Before feelings of dread engulfed her, she reflected to earlier in the week when she, her mother and two of the children she bore transacted a bank loan. Sarah thought, Momma can write all the notes she want. I knew Amanda was mine the second I walked into the Sawyer house to nurse her after she was born.

Conrad Coleman said, "Bennie, y'all cover him up now. I'll come back to pay you directly."

Conrad and Rafe walked from Lucy Cemetery together. They stopped fifty yards from the grave to look back.

"Rafe," Conrad smirked, "how long you think it'll be before that fancy coffin and wood box rots and them two boys' bones mix together?"

"I don't know, but one thing's sure. The Coleman family plot ain't the only cemetery 'round here with white and colored in the same ground."

"Big brother, sure you right." The two laughed and they separated to walk toward their vehicles.

When Rafe Coleman reached his pickup truck, he climbed inside and removed the Stars and Bars tag from his window. Later that day, Thelma Louise was bringing two curly-red-headed children to their first meeting with their father. He loved that flag and the boys he'd never seen. He loved his southern heritage, those irrational feelings of hate mixed with natural love.

Birdie Mae Lilliard stood her sentinel's post on the back porch. "Mr. Gillam, looks like they paid you back for what they did to you and your family. Too bad we still dealing with what you done to it." She surveyed the bottomland and the neatly arranged rows of growing crops. Old Jabbok towered above it all. She knew there was treasure Gillam Hale had hidden safely in the gravel-rich ground at the dying giant's base, but it was too soon to tell Son Erby about it. The worst things wrong with most of us were planted by those who love us the best.

Despite Mama Birdie Mae's best efforts to convince him otherwise, Son Erby knew he would find a way to deliver the fifty gallons of old john Mr. Capezio expected next week and he would do the same many times in the years to come. He knew the risks and he knew the consequences. He made his choice. It was the wrong one. He knew it.

Son Erby also knew he would find a way to repay the treachery Allen Sawyer Jr. had dealt his family.

The seed sown by Gillam Hale waxed strong in the soul of his male offspring. Son reaped the crop Gillam had sown.

The Gillam Hale Family—Public

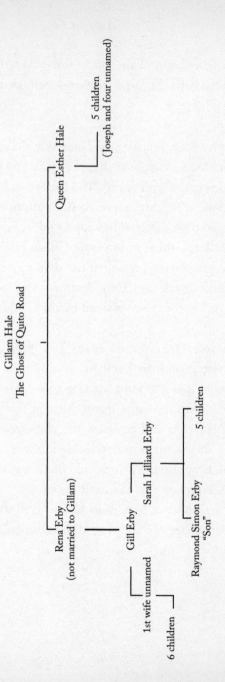

The Sawyer Family—Public

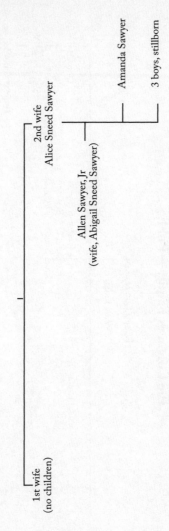

Allen Sawyer, Sr.

1st wife
(no children)

2nd wife
Alice Sneed Sawyer

Allen Sawyer, Jr
(wife, Abigail Sneed Sawyer)

Amanda Sawyer

3 boys, stillborn

The Coleman Family—Public

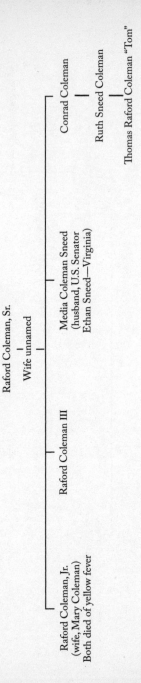

Raford Coleman, Sr.
|
Wife unnamed

Raford Coleman, Jr.
(wife, Mary Coleman)
Both died of yellow fever

Raford Coleman III

Media Coleman Sneed
(husband, U.S. Senator
Ethan Sneed—Virginia)

Conrad Coleman
|
Ruth Sneed Coleman

Thomas Raford Coleman "Tom"

The Gordon Family—Public

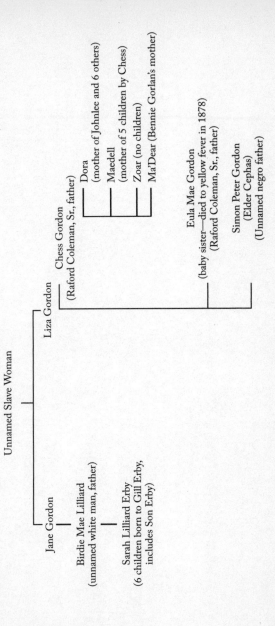

Unnamed Slave Woman

Jane Gordon

Liza Gordon

Birdie Mae Lilliard
(unnamed white man, father)

Sarah Lilliard Erby
(6 children born to Gill Erby,
includes Son Erby)

Chess Gordon
(Raford Coleman, Sr., father)

Dora
(mother of Johnlee and 6 others)

Maedell
(mother of 5 children by Chess)

Zoar (no children)

Ma'Dear (Bennie Gorlan's mother)

Eula Mae Gordon
(baby sister—died to yellow fever in 1878)
(Raford Coleman, Sr., father)

Simon Peter Gordon
(Elder Cephas)
(Unnamed negro father)